T0300803

PRAISE FOR
The Mechanics of Memory

"*One Flew Over the Cuckoo's Nest* meets *Inception* in Lee's stunning debut. A must read." —**James L'Etoile, award-winning author of *Dead Drop* and *Face of Greed***

"A technological thriller that keeps us perched on the edge of our seats as well as our disbelief, Lee pulls it together masterfully. Can't wait to see what's coming from her next." —**Linda L. Richards, author of *Dead West*, One of Amazon's Best Books of 2023**

"*The Mechanics of Memory* is a swift, twisty speculative novel that grabs you from page one. With engaging characters and intriguing science, the reader is absorbed throughout. For fans of Blake Crouch and other high-end speculative twist rides." —**Shannon Kirk, international bestselling author of *Method 15/33* and the gold medal-winning *The Extraordinary Journey of Vivienne Marshall***

THE MECHANICS OF MEMORY

THE
MECHANICS
OF
MEMORY

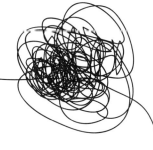

AUDREY LEE

CamCat
Books

CamCat Publishing, LLC
Fort Collins, Colorado 80524
camcatpublishing.com

Hardcover ISBN 9780744310399
Paperback ISBN 9780744310412
Large-Print Paperback ISBN 9780744310450
eBook ISBN 9780744310436
Audiobook ISBN 9780744310474

Library of Congress Control Number: 2024930027

Book and cover design by Maryann Appel
Interior artwork by Hordieiev Roman, Sarmdy, Anhelina Lisna, Olga Ubirailo

5 3 1 2 4

TO SAM AND REBECA

Who despite knowing all my stories
still manage to love me unconditionally.

I do believe you think what now you speak,
But what we do determine, oft we break.
Purpose is but the slave to memory.

—William Shakespeare, *Hamlet*

ONE YEAR AGO

NEVER FORGET

"COME WITH ME," Luke said. "Before it all disappears." He leaned across the kitchen counter and pushed at the lid of her laptop.

Hope swiveled in the turquoise kitchen stool, feet hooked in the rungs. Luke moved through the sliding glass door and onto the tiny patch of uneven concrete in the backyard, black Nikon hanging from a worn leather strap off his right shoulder. Hope watched as he pointed the camera at the sunset, then turned to aim the lens into the house.

"Don't." Hope covered her face with a laugh. "Yuck."

"Then get over here." He waved at her. "It's magnificent."

Hope slid off the stool, grabbing two lowballs and a bottle of single malt from the counter.

The desert sunset was spectacular. Shimmering sheets of fuchsia and amethyst were splashed across the scarlet sky, palm trees and rough mountain peaks silhouetted against it. And above their outline, a moon so luminous it may well have been dipped in gold, hung lower than seemed possible.

Without meaning to, Hope reached out to touch the moon.

"Didn't I tell you?" he said.

She smiled. "You did."

Luke snapped more photos, from every conceivable angle and with every possible lens attachment. He paced the length of the yard, barefoot, camera case knocking against his hip.

"So antsy," Hope said, depositing glasses on the end table and climbing onto the lounger.

"Stay just like that," he said. He pointed the Nikon at her, shutter clicking like gunfire.

"You could simply enjoy the sunset, you know," Hope said. "We could enjoy it together."

Luke set the camera on the table and reached for the bottle. The Macallan sounded a hollow pop of anticipation as it opened.

Hope swung her legs over his as he handed her a glass and settled in. Her toenails were painted dark blue this week, fresh from a pedicure with Charlotte this morning. Luke didn't care for her nail polish choices, especially when she went blue. Corpse toes, he called them.

"Tomorrow you'll be a big TV star. Are you nervous?"

Luke sipped his scotch. "Maybe."

"Is it because Natasha Chan is the host?" Hope asked. "And your thing for Asian ladies?"

"So now I have a thing?" Luke laughed, his hand trailing through her long hair. "You were supposed to be meek and submissive. I was grossly misled."

"At least I'm good at math," she said. "I'll try to work on the meek part."

"Good luck," Luke said. "And it's not because of Natasha Chan, it's because I don't want to make a fool of myself in front of all six viewers."

"I'm sure you'll have at least seven," Hope said, laughing. "Plus, you're brilliant and amazing. And a published author. It's very sexy."

"Nerdy science books don't count as sexy," he said. "And you forgot devilishly handsome."

"I'll never forget." She closed her eyes, focused on the feel of his fingers. "Don't ask her to say something in Chinese, though. Total turnoff."

"Damn, that was my opener," Luke said, tracing her earlobe with his thumb. "After the ribbon cutting at the new facility today, Jack hinted this could mean a big promotion."

Hope opened her eyes. "Are you sure that's what you want?"

Luke shrugged. "It's the next logical step."

"I know." Hope sipped slowly. "Just—be careful what you wish for."

Luke pulled her close and Hope breathed him in, fingernails tapping on the glass. They made a tinkling sound, like bells.

"Let's run away instead," she said, picking a leaf from his hair. "Scrap it all and establish a new land. Become rulers of our own destiny."

"Is this before or after we become dealers in Vegas?" Luke's mouth twitched. "Or start an ostrich farm? Or open a kabob restaurant called Shish for Brains?"

"It has to be mutually exclusive?" Hope laughed.

"Where should we start this new land?" Luke took her hand, pressing his lips against her palm. "Also, we're going to need something catchier than New Land."

Hope closed her eyes. "The Bahamas, of course."

"Of course. And how will we pay the bills?"

"We won't need money," Hope insisted, "because we'll be in charge of the New Land. To be renamed later. But if you must, we can open a waffle stand."

"I do make a damn fine waffle," Luke said.

"We'll call it the Waffle Brothel." Hope twined her legs together like a pretzel. She trailed a finger up his arm, just to the elbow, then back again.

"Horrendous," he murmured. "You're making it hard for me to concentrate."

"We could live in a lighthouse." Hope stilled her finger on his wrist. "And have kangaroos."

"You're like a kindergartener on an acid trip sometimes," Luke said. "Kangaroos aren't even native to the Bahamas."

"Kangaroos are evolutionarily perfect," Hope said. "They have built-in pockets. It's genius."

Luke smiled. "Then we'll import them. And build a kangaroo sanctuary on the beach. So we can see them from the lighthouse."

He lay back and Hope matched her gaze with his, to the endless universe spread above. The red had all but disappeared, and the moon glowed even brighter in the darkening sky. A scattering of stars emerged, blinking at them like jewels.

"Given your exhaustive attention to detail, it sounds like a solid Plan B." He placed a hand on her thigh, a lazy, casual gesture Hope felt far beneath the layers of her skin. "I'm in."

"Promise?" Her voice held the barest tremor, almost imperceptible. Imperceptible to anyone but Luke.

He held his face level with hers. Sometimes they shared these glances, moments of razor-edged intimacy. Moments when they were the only souls of consequence, raw and infinite, a singularity. Moments when Hope wanted nothing more than to be swallowed whole, by Luke and by whatever lay within.

Hope broke the connection, bottom lip in her teeth. Then a grin appeared, and she held her pinky in front of his face. "Promise?" she asked again.

Luke burst out laughing. "A pinky promise? You really are five." But he hooked his pinky into hers, and with his other hand, pulled her on top of him. "I'm sold," he said into her hair. "Waffles in the Bahamas it is."

Hope closed her eyes as she kissed him. Maybe they could.

❧❧❧

HOPE'S PHONE VIBRATED on the nightstand, rattling the jewelry she'd dropped there a few hours before. She typed a hurried response and activated her phone's flashlight, leaving the bed and padding quietly to the bedroom door. As her hand touched the doorknob, Luke's voice cut across the silence.

"Sucker." He was propped up on one elbow, face sleepy and amused. "You know she only calls because of the French fries."

Hope smiled, moving back to his side of the bed. "I don't mind," she said, placing her palm on his bare chest. "She'll have her license soon. And then college. There isn't much time left."

Luke's face softened. "You want me to go too?" He yawned, mouth open wide like a bear.

"No way." Hope touched his cheek. "You'll ruin girl time."

At the door, she paused to tap a small white picture frame mounted above the light switch, twice. For luck.

"She has you wrapped around her finger, you know," Luke called.

"I know." Hope blew him a kiss. "So does her dad."

❧❧❧

"SHE DOESN'T GET me *at all*," Charlotte said, popping a piece of gum in her mouth. "If I tell her anything, she uses it against me. I have *no* privacy." She let out a long, theatrical sigh, punctuated with maximum adolescent exasperation.

"It's a scary world out there." Hope glanced in the rearview mirror and changed lanes. "All parents want to protect their kids."

"You don't know my mom. And I don't need protection." Charlotte cranked the air-conditioning and tapped her blue fingernails on the dash. "Were your parents like that? Nosy?"

"We didn't exactly have open lines of communication." Hope turned down the air. "If it wasn't about getting into Harvard or becoming a lawyer, it wasn't discussed."

"So you were a big disappointment," Charlotte said.

"You have no idea," Hope said.

"Can you help me with my essay on *Hamlet*?" Charlotte asked. "It's due Tuesday."

"Of course," Hope said, pulling into the parking lot of the Burger Shack. It was the only place open all night, thus the de facto home to anyone within a twenty-mile radius who was hungry or high, or both. Charlotte called it the Stoner Shack, but even so, she couldn't deny their chili cheese fries were transcendental.

Years ago it had been a kitschy fifties diner, but today the only remnants of the former Shake, Rattle, and Roll were the defunct jukeboxes welded to the tables.

They stepped from the car, Hope locking it with a beep and a flash of headlights. Charlotte led the way across the pavement, walking in a wide circle to avoid a kid throwing up in the bushes.

"I wish she was more like you," Charlotte said, holding the Stoner Shack door open for Hope. "Relaxed."

"I'm far from relaxed," Hope said. "I have the luxury of not being your parent. I just get to be your friend."

"Aww." Charlotte held her right hand out, fingers and thumb curled into half a heart. Hope matched it with her left.

✦✦✦

THEIR PLASTIC CUPS were nearly empty, though the silver tumbler on the sticky laminate table held more Oreo shake. The plate between

Hope and Charlotte contained only a few soggy fries, a generous pile of chili and cheese, and a puddle of ketchup.

"Straight out of the fryer," Charlotte said, returning to the booth. She set a fresh basket of fries between them, spots of grease soaking through the paper lining.

"Perfect timing," Hope said. She ran a fry in a zigzag through the chili and ketchup.

"Oh no, now you're doing it too?" Charlotte said.

Hope tilted her head. "Doing what?"

"Making patterns with your food, like Dad." Charlotte made a face. "Is that a two?"

Hope studied the paper plate. "I never realized I did that."

"You guys already share one brain. And the looks . . ." Charlotte mimed gagging. "You act like you're my age. Cringe."

A gaggle of boys entered, calling loudly to each other and jockeying for position at the counter. One was the kid formerly puking by the entrance, but he looked recovered. Another peeled off from the clump, pausing by Hope and Charlotte on his walk to commandeer a booth.

"What's up, Charlie?" he said shyly.

Charlotte's cheeks reddened, and she tucked a lock of hair behind her ear. "Hey."

"I thought you'd be at Brody's tonight." He shoved his hands into his pockets. The kids around here usually had two distinct auras—money or no money—but Hope couldn't tell with this one. He didn't have an air of entitlement, but he didn't seem like a townie either.

Charlotte crumpled her napkin into a ball. "I had to study. We can't all be gifted like you."

"I can help you tomorrow." The boy glanced over his shoulder at the crowd filling their sodas. "I mean, if you want. If you're not busy."

Charlotte flipped her hair. "I'm not busy."

Hope pulled on her straw noisily.

"I'll hit you up tomorrow." The boy backed away with a wave.

"What happened to Adam?" Hope asked.

Charlotte tapped her nails on the table. "He turned out to be a dick."

Hope made a noncommittal noise.

"Don't be all, 'hmmm, that's interesting,'" Charlotte said. "I know you guys hated him."

Hope tried to keep a straight face. Luke wasn't even able to say his name most days, referring to Adam only as "that arrogant little prick."

"But you were both right." Charlotte put her chin in her hands. "Did you ever date an asshole?"

Hope nodded. "Almost married one."

Charlotte perked up, looking intrigued, but Hope tilted her head toward the boy. "So, is he a prospect?"

"He's smart. He's different than the boys at my school." She grinned. "But don't tell my dad. He'll get totally triggered."

"Look Charlie, you're the most important person in the world to him," Hope said. "Which means no one will ever be good enough for you. But it also makes you lucky to be so loved."

"I know." Charlotte rolled her eyes. Again. "I'm just tired of the Adams of the world."

"Me too," Hope said. "But there are good guys out there too. They just aren't as easy to spot. Trust me: the good ones are worth it."

"And that's my dad? One of the good ones?" Charlotte wrinkled her nose, still too cool for feelings, though her eyes looked wistful.

Hope smiled. "I'm certain of it."

TODAY

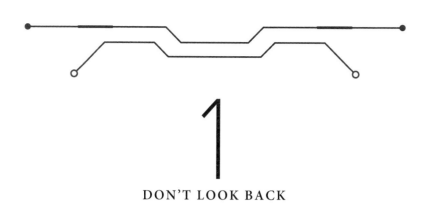

1

DON'T LOOK BACK

HOPE
The Wilder Sanctuary
Rancho Mirage, California

"AND HOW ARE the nightmares?"

"Fine." Hope shifted, pushing stringy hair from her face with her palms. "I haven't had any this week."

"None at all?"

Hope shook her head slowly, face impassive.

"That's important progress." Dr. Stark looked impressed with his own abilities, as if he'd performed a special magic trick to protect Hope from herself. Perhaps in a way he had.

Dr. Stark jotted notes on his tablet with a pointy gray stylus. "Are you sleeping any better?"

"A little. An hour or two at a time." It was a lie. She hadn't slept at all.

Hope focused on the San Jacinto Mountains outside the picture window, framed by the endless blue of the summer sky. Desert sky. It was hard to think about darkness right now, with so much light around her. "Does that mean I'm getting better?"

"As we've discussed, it's important you get concentrated stretches of sleep." Dr. Stark flipped his tablet to expose the keyboard, typing with a renewed purpose. "It will help you make progress in the Labyrinth."

The word *Labyrinth* filled Hope with a viscous dread. She knew she'd visited it dozens of times since arriving at Wilder, though never remembered what had happened there. "I told you I'm never going back."

"You did," Dr. Stark said. "But as *I* said, it's important to try and push through. It helps you confront what you're avoiding."

"I'm not avoiding anything," Hope said. Another lie.

"I'm increasing your temazepam to thirty milligrams," Dr. Stark said. "And tomorrow evening I'd like you to spend some time in ViCTR using the Erleben device. Say, forty-five minutes?"

Hope glanced at the ceiling. She wanted a cigarette in the worst way.

"Great," he said. "Check in with the pharmacy after our session."

Stark was doing the casual Friday thing that day, though Hope remained uncertain if it was, in fact, Friday. He resembled a prep school student, with his shiny polo shirt and immaculately pressed chinos. The polo looked brand new, still creased in the sleeves and too white, almost blinding. Hope couldn't picture Dr. Stark performing the tasks of mere mortals: changing the toilet paper, taking out the garbage, shopping for polo shirts. Maybe his wife did all that. Maybe she bought five polo shirts in different colors from Neiman Marcus, hanging them in an orderly row, next to his dry-cleaned Italian suits in clear plastic bags.

"Is there anything else you want to tell me?" Dr. Stark asked, still typing, fingers thin and bare.

"Are you married?"

"Divorced," he said. "More thoughts about last year, perhaps?"

"Nothing else," Hope said. She glanced outside again. "Have there been any messages for me?"

"I'm sorry." Stark shook his head. "But I promise to let you know if there ever are."

An artificial chime reverberated through the room's speakers, and Dr. Stark smiled. "We'll pick up again next week."

Hope wiped her hands on her pants and rose, heading for the shiny glass door.

"Hope," Dr. Stark said.

She paused, hand on the doorknob.

"Be well."

"Be well, Dr. Stark."

HOPE LURKED IN the corridor outside the pharmacy door. Everyone here called it the Roofie Room. Dr. Stark discouraged the nickname, though she'd heard him use it when he didn't think anyone was listening.

She leaned against a wall under a framed print. *I Choose to Make the Rest of My Life the Best of My Life,* the typeface commanded. Wilder was overrun with these platitude posters—inspirational phrases printed on backdrops of pink orchids, mountain scenes at sunrise, soft-focus tree branches with dappled green leaves. The one on Hope's bedroom wall depicted a wooden plank bridge disappearing into the horizon. *Don't Look Back. You're Not Going That Way.* Graphically speaking, it was a minor improvement over the poster she remembered from seventh-grade English class, the one of a ginger kitten with huge eyes, suspended in a tree by its claws. *Hang in There!* in bubblegum-pink balloon letters.

The hallway loomed empty and silent, like all of Wilder. Staff believed in maintaining a serene, nurturing environment at all times, right down to the soothing smells pumped through the ducts. That day, the scent was a pungent eucalyptus.

Like any pharmacy, the Roofie Room had a high white counter serving as a barricade to a wall of shelves, each one boasting orderly containers of unlabeled amber bottles and plastic baggies full of pills. Willy Wonka's Pharmaceutical Factory.

Dr. Emerson appeared from behind the shelves, smiling when she noticed Hope skulking under another poster: *Healing Begins with a Single Step.* "How can I help you?"

"Dr. Stark changed one of my prescriptions." Hope approached the doctor and craned her neck to see above the counter.

"He doubled your dosage." Dr. Emerson moved her mouse, perfectly arched eyebrows knitting together. "To the maximum recommended."

Hope shrugged. "I'm having trouble sleeping."

Dr. Emerson removed a nonexistent piece of lint from her white coat. She smoothed her already perfect blond hair, pulled back from her face into a tight, sleek ponytail. Then the doctor launched into her spiel about the side effects and the short-term nature of the meds, how Hope shouldn't do anything like operating heavy machinery or driving. How she should tell someone if she developed hyperaggressive tendencies or suicidal thoughts. Dr. Emerson sounded like the placid voice-over in a drug commercial. Erections may last more than twenty-four hours. Death may occur.

Hope smothered a snicker.

Dr. Emerson didn't appear to appreciate being interrupted during her enumeration of drug interactions and contraindications. She resumed typing with bright pink fingernails and pursed lips. "You'll have it tonight."

Another chime sounded.

"Will you please give this to Spencer?" From her coat pocket, Dr. Emerson produced a box of chalk and handed it to Hope. "Also, tell him to come see me. I have a delivery from his mother." Dr. Emerson tapped a manila envelope near her mouse.

"Do you want me to take that too?" Hope extended her hand.

"Absolutely not." Dr. Emerson pulled the envelope away, as if Hope's hand were a poisonous viper. Obviously chalk was the outer limit of what Hope could be trusted to courier.

"Have any messages come for me?" Hope asked.

Dr. Emerson made a show of clicking around her computer, though Hope already knew the answer. It was the same answer she'd received every week since she got to Wilder.

"I'm sorry, nothing today," Dr. Emerson said. "Enjoy your dinner, Hope. Be well."

As Hope turned to go, she heard Dr. Emerson repeat her name. Her tone was expectant, like a teacher whose class hadn't responded with the proper good morning: fake cheer tinged with annoyance, an undertone of challenge.

Hope paused. "Be well, Dr. Emerson."

THE FOOD WAS, as always, a gourmet affair. All meals at Wilder were perfectly prepared and stunningly plated, served on bone china at a table with a view. This place had a Michelin star under its belt, at least according to their website. Everything passing the residents' lips was clean: nothing processed, no GMOs, all fresh and organic and assembled expertly by in-house chefs. Farm to nuthouse.

When Hope first arrived, she would have gladly slit someone's throat for a corn dog and a Newcastle. After a month, the urge had mostly subsided. She now ate her whole grains and her sustainable wild salmon in balsamic reduction with little fuss. Unfortunately, there still wasn't enough diazepam in the world to make a bed of braised kale pass for a corn dog.

Quinn placed a plate of shrimp on the table, chimichurri sauce sloshing over the side and forming green puddles on the wood. He lowered himself into the seat next to Hope and ran his napkin along the rim of the dish. "What I wouldn't give for a good Malbec to wash this down," he said. "A 2004."

Hope raised an eyebrow. "Good luck."

Quinn speared his shrimp, cutting off the tails with deft fingers like a chef at Benihana. He carefully placed each tail, pointy side out, fanned along the edge of his plate. "Did you see the new recruit?"

A few tables away sat a man, much younger than they were, late twenties or early thirties maybe. He was tall and thin, with sandy-blond hair and a face that somehow seemed honest. He stared out the window with a vacant expression behind his tortoiseshell glasses, fork suspended in hand over his untouched salad.

"His name's Carter," Quinn said. There were no last names at Wilder unless you were a doctor. Then there were no first names. "Silicon Valley startup guy. High-functioning depression, anger and aggression issues, panic attacks." Quinn held thumb and forefinger close together. "And a touch of PTSD, of course."

"How do you know shit like that?" Hope asked, squeezing a lemon into her infused water and taking a drink. Cucumber. The worst.

"I know all kinds of shit," Quinn smirked.

Hope didn't usually pay much attention to the revolving door of Wilder Weirdos, and even less to Quinn's inventory of afflictions. But that night Hope couldn't help but stare at Carter. He seemed familiar somehow, though unlike the many celebrities surrounding them.

"I feel like I've seen him before," Hope said.

"Did you ever play that game Magic Words?" Quinn asked. "He invented it when he was a kid. It was all over the news for a few months."

"Maybe that's it." Hope continued to stare, trying to remember. But the more she focused, the harder it became.

"I think he's pretty too," Quinn said. "Let's go find out if he's single. Be, you know, a supportive network of healing." He cupped his hand over his mouth. "We should bring him into the fold before someone else does."

In a different life, in her life before Wilder, Hope never would have befriended Quinn. He would have run in an entirely different social strata, too beautiful and polished and wealthy for the likes of her. But here at Wilder, the serfs dined alongside the barons, and Quinn had sought her out and forced a friendship after mere hours, when she still wore the same expression Carter wore now.

"Jesus, we're not in a gang. He doesn't need to be jumped in." Hope turned from Carter and pushed zucchini around on her plate, a little yellow boat sailing through the quinoa sea. "Go over there and introduce yourself if you want to get in his pants."

"Has anyone ever told you that you're a giant buzzkill?" Quinn leaned back in his chair, tilting it at an alarming angle. He wore the standard Wilder Weirdo uniform: elastic cotton pants, a gray short-sleeved T-shirt, white sneakers without laces. Yet only Quinn could manage to make it look stylish. "In your old life, did you ever enjoy pushing the envelope a little?"

"Sorry," Hope said. "I've never been a risk-taker."

AFTER DINNER, HOPE knocked on Spencer's door. Thanks to Quinn, everyone called him Spooky Spencer, and these days mostly just Spooky. He was the youngest of the residents, thin and slight, a curtain of jet black hair usually hiding his pale face. He didn't speak when he first arrived two months ago, then only a few words, croaked out when spoken to. Spooky spent all his free time with his *D&D* magazines, hand-drawn maps, graph paper, and pencils spread out in front of him, murmuring about campaigns and hit points and initiatives.

Shortly after arriving, Spooky started drawing on the wall in his bedroom with a stub of a purple crayon he'd nicked from the Creative

Connections Room (surprisingly, a clever pejorative had yet to be assigned). Spooky drew a crescent moon in the top right corner of his wall, like that bald kid in the children's books. No one could figure out how he climbed so high to reach, knowing he'd also have some kind of hell to pay for defacing the property. He'd probably be sentenced to three days of mandatory restorative yoga, or a week writing lines in the Zen Garden. *Every day is a gift.*

Surprisingly, Dr. Stark was delighted when he discovered the purple moon. He thought giving Spooky an outlet for his expression might help him connect with people. So Stark submitted a work order and had one wall of Spooky's room painted with chalkboard paint. He even gave Spooky all the chalk he wanted. Now an elaborate white forest spread across half the ebony surface: bare, eight-foot aspen with sinister cuts in their bark, vines and thorns and brambles winding from floor to ceiling. A path began in the bottom left corner, splintering into several directions as creepy, nondescript animal eyes stared from hidden spots in the trees. Spooky called it the Shade.

Hope knocked again. She examined the box of chalk from Dr. Emerson, its bright green and yellow markings anachronistic against the muted tones of Wilder. The box reminded Hope of her father, who often returned from business trips with a box of crayons for her. It was always the big box of sixty-four, the one with the useless sharpener built in. Impractical purchases were rare in her family, and new crayons were a commodity. Hope would drop to the floor and dump the box onto the ground, smelling the wax and grouping the crayons by color, blunted tips lined up perfectly like a rainbow fence. They always seemed so full of promise.

After the third knock, Hope entered. Spooky was at his desk, watching the door.

"I didn't see you at dinner," Hope said, holding up the chalk. "But Dr. Emerson sent this for you. And she said to tell you there's a message from your mom."

His voice was too soft to hear. Maybe it was *thank you*. Or maybe it was *fuck you*. One could never tell with Spooky.

Hope set the chalk on his nightstand and looked at the Shade. Spooky's chair creaked as he rose to stand nearer.

"Where does that go?" she asked, kneeling. She placed a bitten-down fingernail on the fork in the path, smudging it a little.

"Mirror Gate," he said, inclining his head right. "And this goes to Hollow of the Moon." He licked his pinky finger and wiped away the smudge.

"What happens there?" She moved closer to the path.

Spooky retrieved a stub of chalk from his desk to touch up the part she'd smudged. "It's where the souls are collected and cleansed." He added more detail to a birch tree along the road to Mirror Gate.

She wasn't sure she had a soul anymore, but if she did, Hope wasn't certain she wanted it cleansed. So much for connecting with people.

BACK IN HER room, Hope reached far under her mattress for her notebook and pens. Her room was searched daily, including the spot under her bed and the corners of her closet. No expectation of privacy existed for anyone at Wilder, yet she still felt a compulsion to stash her few things away. It was also why she chose to write in code.

It wasn't an elaborate, beautiful mind kind of code. For Luke's last birthday, Hope bought secret decoder rings from a bookshop selling quirky trinkets. Two silver rings with the alphabet running around the bottom half, the top half spinning to reveal a number in a tiny window. Luke had laughed when he opened it, getting it instantly, slipping it on his finger and turning it around and around. For a time, they sent coded messages to each other, quickly discovering it took twice as long to write a note and ten times longer to decode it. Luke had even created a spreadsheet to make it faster. Eventually that exercise, along with so many rituals and routines and secret languages preceding it, was abandoned. Yet in that brief stint, Hope had memorized the twenty-six pairs, and still repeated them in her head when she couldn't sleep.

Now the coded numbers came quickly and fluidly, like a native tongue. Sometimes she caught herself thinking in the code too, rather than words: 1-26,18-4-23, 17-6-4-14.

It wouldn't take a cryptographer to crack; it was the simplest of substitution ciphers. A third grader could do it. But she also figured no one cared enough to invest the time.

That night, Hope opened to a new page and recounted her day in simple, unpoetic prose. When writing in numbers, it was much easier to do it this way. No commentary, no feelings or emotions, just a list of the day. *Dr. S. + 30 mg t. Yellow zucchini. The Labyrinth.* She never revisited her writing, knowing that if she did, it would be unsettling to have forgotten.

She checked the time and flipped to the end of the notebook, to a different section. It was here she tried to recount her life before Wilder, where she tried to parse out her last year, where she wrote about Luke.

Hope wrote what she could, a paltry few lines. There simply wasn't much to call forth from her lost year. Hope's old life had revolved around empirical facts, a habit that was still deeply ingrained. But she had little certainty these days, and even less stock in her memories. As a result, this journal section had seen little progress over time.

The chime rang, presenting her with a few minutes before her meds arrived, preceding a night which would soon become thick and foggy. This was her most lucid time of the day, and in thirty minutes it would all fade into the ether. She glanced at the door out of habit even though she knew at least ninety seconds remained, then closed the notebook and stowed it safely under the mattress.

A tech, Jonah, shuffled his bulky frame into the room. Hope accepted the fluted paper cup holding two pills—one oblong and white, one pale pink with a line through the middle, both small and both mighty. She knocked them back in one gulp, without water.

Hope opened her mouth and lifted her tongue, but Jonah never inspected. He didn't get paid enough to give a shit. He merely bobbed his dark head, wished her well, and extinguished her overhead light.

Soon the heaviness began to drag her into the abyss. Hope avoided sleep whenever possible but knew a fight against those fifteen additional milligrams would ultimately be futile. She felt her limbs go numb and braced for the inevitable nightmares.

But at least Luke would be there.

2

INTO THE VOID

LUKE

Palm Springs, California

L UKE WOKE IN a sweat, Hope's name in his mouth, heart racing. Reality came sluggishly as he registered his surroundings: living room sofa, a full moon outside the window, alone. His partially open laptop had fallen into the space between his hip and the back of the couch, muffled voices from Netflix jarring in the stillness. He retrieved the computer and set it on the coffee table.

He flopped against the cushions, attempting to hold on to details now slipping away with haste, water tumbling over pebbles. His mind was filled with a dense white forest and a dirt path, blurring the more he tried to focus. And Hope, of course. His mind was always filled with Hope. Luke retrieved his phone from the coffee table: 1:12 a.m. He lay in the darkness for a little longer before jabbing at the call button.

"Thank you for calling the Wilder Sanctuary. How may I support you?" The young female voice was buttery smooth, a radio DJ spinning late-night ballads. *And here's one for all you lovers out there . . .*

"I'd like to speak to Hope Nakano." Luke cleared his throat and added, "Please."

"It's after hours, sir." He could hear her typing. "May I ask your name?"

"Luke Salinger."

The tapping ceased, with a pause and a breath before the pleasant voice continued. "I'm sorry, Dr. Salinger. Ms. Nakano has requested no outside contact."

"Can you give her a message, then?"

"We prioritize our guests' privacy at Wilder. I apologize, but I'm obligated to honor Ms. Nakano's request."

"Christ," he muttered. How many times had she said that party line? To how many boyfriends and wives and agents and journalists? "Get me Elliot, then." His voice was weary, straining against frustration. "He's certainly not a guest."

The operator's tone remained serene. "One moment, please."

A click, followed by a pause, followed by Enya or Brian Eno, or some other trance-inducing, brain-cell-killing artist. After five minutes, it had lulled Luke into a dreamy paralysis. He held the phone away from his ear, watching the time elapse: 7:12. He pulled at a stray thread on one of the throw pillows: 8:27. 8:31.

At 11:48, the voice returned. "Thank you for your patience, Dr. Salinger. I'm connecting you to Dr. Stark."

"About damn time," he said, into the void.

"Luke," said a tired voice. "It's one in the freaking morning. And you know damn well you can't talk to her."

"How is she?"

Elliot Stark sighed. "No different from last month, or the month before. As my weekly emails describe, ad nauseum. Did you really wake me up in the middle of the night for that?"

Luke suddenly couldn't figure out why he so urgently needed to call Wilder. It felt critical, a few moments ago, when the talons of the nightmare were still sharp on his skin. "I had a bad feeling," he said, words trailing off at the end.

"I'm taking over her sessions," Elliot said. "And I upped her temazepam to thirty milligrams."

"Are you kidding?" Luke sat up. "That's going to turn her into a zombie, with all the other shit she's been taking."

"She hasn't been sleeping. She says she gets a few hours, but we know she's lying. It's critical she sleep. Sleep facilitates—"

"Reconsolidation," Luke finished, feeling his chest contract. "I know. I wrote the damn protocol."

"You also know these things take time," Elliot said. "I'm doing the best I can, I promise."

Luke swung his legs over the side of the sofa and rested his elbows on his knees.

"I want to see her."

"Impossible."

Of course Luke knew it was impossible. He'd made it that way. "Can you get a message to her, at least?"

"What's gotten into you?" Elliot asked. "You know the rules, and you know what's at stake."

Luke looked at his screen, at the picture of a two-year-old Charlotte on the carousel at Disneyland. "I know," he said.

"And even if I took your message, I wouldn't be allowed to give it to her."

"Allowed?" Luke said. "Doesn't it say Stark on the fucking letterhead?"

Stark laughed, his voice brittle as eggshells. "You know Jack can remove me from the org chart as quickly as he put me on."

"Jack doesn't have to know," Luke pressed. "Can you stop being his lapdog just once?"

"Careful." Stark sounded like a parent whose toddler was testing his patience. All Wilder staff trained to be unfailingly calm, but at this hour even Elliot could lose his cool. "We both know being on the wrong side of Jack Copeland is never a good idea."

"Elliot," Luke said. "One message. Please."

His exhale rattled in Luke's ear. "I can't make any promises."

Luke closed his eyes. "Do you have a pen?"

"A pen?" Stark's voice was a little less professional, and a little more like the Elliot he used to know. "*I* still have a reliable memory."

"Not for this," Luke said.

Muffled noises came through the phone. "Fine. I'm ready."

Luke rattled off a long series of numbers.

3

RESIGNED SURRENDER

✧✦✧✦✧

HOPE

The Wilder Sanctuary
Rancho Mirage, California

S HORTLY AFTER DAWN, Hope slid back into consciousness. She sat up in bed gingerly, unsure if the weight of her body would hold. A gauzy film filled her head, and her limbs felt alien. In her old life Hope had been an early riser, creeping out of bed hours before Luke opened his eyes. She'd sit outside on the porch, sipping coffee and watching the sky turn from indigo to gold to soft blue above the mountains.

But here at Wilder, mornings were a burden. They were too honest, too recalcitrant, too cold. Mornings here were difficult to face alone, with nothing but your own retreating dreams for companionship.

Hope switched on the monitor mounted to the wall. No actual television existed here, no Netflix or Hulu. There was no television anywhere at Wilder; Dr. Stark felt it impeded growth. Instead, the available channels were all meant to inspire calm. Sometimes movies ran on a loop, but never anything Hope could stomach for too long. They were limited to sappy, uplifting stories regaling the triumph of the human spirit, adult versions of the after-school special.

The home channel played instrumental music over a picture of the Zen Garden, like in a hotel room. *Welcome to the Wilder Sanctuary*, it said. *Supporting your Wellness Journey.* It was strange how Wilder advertised themselves to people who were already here, as if anyone watching this screen had a choice.

The next channel was a slideshow of the ubiquitous prints of motivation. Sometimes Hope watched this channel in the early-morning hours as she did now, playing a little game to try and match the posters with where they lived at Wilder. On this slide the slanted, loopy font was superimposed over a blurry window framing a blue sky, a ceramic pitcher of orange gerbera daisies on the windowsill. *Love yourself as you want to be loved.* The same poster also lived on the wall outside Dr. Emerson's office.

Hope passed the weather channel, yoga and deep breathing rituals, an offering of rain continuously falling into a brook. Not for the first time, Hope wished there were something to binge, something to pass the endless hours and let her escape into a world that wasn't her own for a while. In the early days, the languor was intrusive, almost suffocating. But months of the same had slipped Hope into a sort of muted inertia, a resigned surrender to her new life.

She longed for the ritual of watching television in bed with Luke from the laptop propped on his legs, head nestled in her spot just under his shoulder. The rhythm of his breathing, the safety. The feel of his hands, which would forever remain indescribable.

Hope knew she drove him crazy with her comments as they watched, though Luke always patiently paused to talk. Hope couldn't remember what they'd been watching before she came here, and wondered if Luke was still watching without her. Did she expect him to wait?

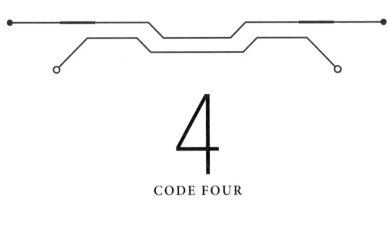

4

CODE FOUR

✦✦✦✦✦✦

HOPE

The Wilder Sanctuary
Rancho Mirage, California

T HERE WERE WHOLE-GRAIN waffles for breakfast. Everyone loved waffle day at Wilder, save Hope. Waffles and pancakes were never served with syrup or even butter here, but some organic, low sugar compote made with locally sourced berries. An additional insult was the turkey bacon, a culinary calamity like baked potato chips or cake pops. And finally, the greatest travesty of all: the complete absence of coffee. Wilder only offered flowery, spiced teas: hibiscus, passionflower, rose hips. It tasted like some old lady's potpourri in a cup.

Luke made the best waffles in the world. His recipe used yeast, requiring it to rise on the counter overnight. Hope loved waffles on Saturdays, primarily because she enjoyed watching him cook. She would sit in the kitchen on late Friday nights, legs wound around the turquoise stool, glass of wine in hand as he sprinkled yeast over the warm water and melted the butter. If the milk was too hot or the water too cold, the yeast wouldn't proof, and the waffles would be lost. Luke would give her this little scientific lecture each time as he stirred milk and butter, sticking his finger in it to test it, prattling on about metabolizing starches and sugars.

He never failed to get the temperature exactly right, but Hope was still unduly concerned on those Fridays, sneaking into the kitchen to peek under the dish towel. She would scrutinize the batter's distance from the top of the bowl, receiving a gentle scolding like a child out of bed too many times. But the batter never failed to rise, and the waffles and bacon were always perfect the following morning.

Hope customarily woke long before Luke, but never on Waffle Saturdays. On those mornings, Hope would open her eyes to the melody of plates and cutlery tinkling, the glorious smell of coffee and frying bacon floating into the bedroom. She would pad to the bathroom, run a toothbrush a few times over her teeth, wipe the sleep from her eyes, check herself out in the mirror. In those days, looking in the mirror wasn't nearly as disorienting. Then she would tiptoe back to the bed and get in, pretending to be asleep until he came in to wake her. *Wake up, Sleeping Beauty,* he would say. *Breakfast is served.*

A discordant chime rang, forcing Hope to abandon her reverie and focus on the dining room and Quinn, waving at her like an air traffic controller from a table with Spooky. Quinn frequently chose a different person to eat with, often strong-arming Hope into joining. He called it speed dating. The expansive dining area boasted twenty-five round tables of various sizes. On warm days, of which there were an abundance in the Coachella Valley, they also opened the patio.

While there were never more than thirty residents at Wilder at any given time, they needed all those tables. The vast majority were celebrities who chose to hide behind their Prada shades over any human interaction. At meals, most people ate alone or, when unavoidable, separated at large tables in mutually agreed upon cones of silence. Never Quinn, though.

Hope plunked her waffles and fake jam and fake bacon unceremoniously on the table. "Hey Spooky," she said. "How did you sleep?"

Spooky's black hair brushed against his waffle. "Fine."

"He was telling me about his life before Wilder," said Quinn. "Did you know Spooky used to work in a comic-book store?"

Hope found it surprising Spooky said anything to Quinn; he never said more than three words to her. Yet Quinn did have a gift for making people talk, if only to shut him up.

"What store?" Hope cut a tiny piece of waffle. It tasted like fried Play-Doh, or the little cakes she used to make in her pink plastic oven, baked with a hundred-watt bulb. She forced herself to chew, and to swallow, and to repeat the whole process again. If she didn't eat, an attendant would note it on their tablet. Then Hope would have to explain to Dr. Stark why she wasn't eating, and they'd watch her like a hawk and weigh her every day.

Spooky whispered into his glass of grapefruit juice.

"What?" Quinn said. "Forces?"

"Fortress," Spooky said, a bit louder this time.

"Why did you leave?" Quinn asked.

"I got a new job." Spooky swallowed a few times, eyes darting about. "But instead I came here."

"What kind of job?"

A clatter of metal and broken glass put an end to Quinn's interrogation. Hope swiveled in the direction of the noise.

It was Nina, one of Wilder's more permanent fixtures. Nina was forever claiming she was nearing the end of her thirty-day detox, though it was rumored she'd been at Wilder since it opened.

There was something a bit off about Nina: her makeup was too harsh, eyes a bit too wild. She had the appearance of someone who was likely attractive once but was now rapidly and purposefully going to seed. Quinn said she had made millions winning some reality television show five years ago. He also swore she used to be a porn star before that, under the stage name of Kitty Diamond. A hundred thousand views on Pornhub, Quinn insisted. Hope had no verification of this. And the last thing she needed was to be caught checking out porn during her thirty minutes of internet use a week.

Nina stood at the buffet line now, amid dozens of shattered juice glasses. The tech standing nearby was speckled with splashes of cranberry and pineapple. Chefs in their tall white hats observed, alert but unmoving.

"I'm a motherfucking super star," Nina shrieked, stabbing at the air with a finger. "Goddamn A-list, bitches!" Nina stomped along the row of steaming chafing dishes, throwing lids on the floor, seizing handfuls of tofu scramble and waffles and launching them at the techs.

A siren screeched through the speakers in the room, and from their track over the crown molding, red lights pulsed. Bars descended from the ceiling, their clangs reverberating as they locked into place. The techs circled closer to Nina. Hope noticed her nightly pill pusher, Jonah, with a finger on his ear like a G-man in a spy movie.

"Page twenty-two," Spooky recited, into his lap. "'Code Four. In the event a resident may cause harm to oneself or others, physical restraint will be used.'"

Hope gripped the arms of her chair, desperate for a cigarette. She hated Code Fours. She hated all the codes, though she'd only experienced Four through Seven. Five was a fight, Six was a nonemergency medical issue, Seven was someone crying hysterically or refusing to go to yoga. Seven was okay; more attendants would materialize and usher a resident to the Roofie Room. Eight was a security breach, and so far that hadn't happened. But Codes Four, Five, and Six meant the bars, the sirens, and the flashing red lights.

Her throat tightened with the smell of smoke and ashes and copper in her nose. She closed her eyes and counted to ten. In and out, as Dr. Stark taught her to do.

Hope felt Quinn's warm hand on top of hers.

"It's okay, *Mi'ja*," he said. "Nina's just having a moment." He slipped his fingers around her palm and squeezed.

Hope squeezed back.

Dr. Emerson hurried through the kitchen door, shiny heels clicking across the tile. Two massive men in white dress shirts, scarlet ties, and charcoal pants flanked her on either side.

"See?" Quinn said. "The Men in Gray are going to make everything better."

Dr. Emerson approached Nina and bent low to her ear, voice drowned out by the siren wail.

"Naughty girl, naughty girl," Spooky said. He rocked from side to side, chair legs lifting off the ground each time he moved. They made a rhythmic click-clack, adding to the din in the room.

"Get away from me, you fucking cunt!" Nina yelled, springing back against the buffet table and rattling the dishes on top. "You don't think I know what you're doing here?" She addressed the room now, flailing her arms about and spattering food onto Dr. Emerson's magenta suit. A blob of tofu and green onion hit her square in the face, but Dr. Emerson remained unruffled. She gave a poised nod to the Men in Gray. They grabbed Nina, each taking her underneath an arm.

Nina tried to shake them off, but her frail frame was no match. "Don't you get it?" she screamed to the room, digging in her heels. "We're not crazy. They're making us crazy. They *want* us crazy!"

The room stared back at her, still as a desert night, unimpressed. Most continued to eat, oblivious to the melee around them. But the new guy, Carter, was riveted, watching Nina's obstreperous performance as if she were a movie.

"Selfish whore!" Nina whipped her head around to address Dr. Emerson again. "You want my money! I earned that shit!" Her yelling faded as she neared the kitchen door, so Hope could only hear the occasional outburst of "motherfucker" or "cunt" or "star."

Jonah pulled out his phone as Dr. Emerson crossed the room. The sirens stopped, red lights ceased to pulse, bars lifted from windows. The kitchen staff returned with towels and mops and dustpans, efficiently disposing of the shattered glass and spilled remains of breakfast, the big cleaning machine following the mayhem left by Things One and Two.

"Please continue to enjoy your breakfast." Dr. Emerson smoothed her hair and wiped a piece of red pepper off her arm. "Nina will be given the care and attention she needs on her journey to wellness. Remember: 'Mistakes are our teachers.' Dr. Green will meet you for goal setting earlier than usual this morning, to process." She glanced at her wrist, where there was no watch. "And then later today, we will have yoga in the Zen Garden. Be well." She beamed, as if she'd announced a surprise trip to an amusement park for a class of sixth graders.

A mumbled chorus of "Be well, Dr. Emerson" followed from most of the residents in the room. Hope was not one of them.

LOCATED IN THE basement, the laundry facility was Hope's favorite room at Wilder. It bore no resemblance to the sleek and sterile environment above, divorced from the polished surfaces and sexy technology.

Perhaps that's why it felt normal, a solace from the ever-present serenity and stifling order of the institution. No one had bothered to tack up inspirational posters or paint the walls in a soothing palette. Best of all, the aromatherapy didn't reach the laundry room. Hope loved the white-noise hum of the machinery and the smell of the hot, freshly dried clothes.

As a small child, in order to escape the escalating fights between her parents, Hope would climb into the dryer. She'd take her stuffed elephant, Ella, and close the dryer door just enough to keep the inner light on, rocking back and forth, whispering reassuring phrases into Ella's blue ear.

At Wilder there were five huge stainless steel dryers lining one wall, soldiers at attention, exposed pipes and crinkly silver wormlike vents snaking out behind them and disappearing into the ceiling. They were far larger than her childhood dryer, maybe even large enough for Hope to get in, though she'd never tried.

What she loved less was laundry detail with Quinn. He followed her around like a little duckling, refolding the sweatpants and T-shirts she'd finished and stacked into a haphazard pile. It took twice as long to finish her chores when Quinn chose this job—longer if he felt particularly chatty, which was almost always.

Jonah was hunched on a white plastic stool facing the washer, dark muscular arms resting on his knees, eyes at half-mast. Jonah rarely spoke, and smiled even less. He usually conveyed his directives with a grunt or a pointed look. Quinn felt it was his own personal crusade to crack through Jonah's shell via flirtation bordering on harassment.

"One would think," Quinn mused, piling all the white napkins with their perfectly matched corners in neat groups of ten, "that since Tomás is dropping sixty Gs a month at this place, I wouldn't be forced to perform daily manual labor."

Quinn's boyfriend was a venture capitalist. He lived in Chile half the year and in the Hollywood Hills the other half. He also owned a ten-million-dollar house out in Indian Wells, so he could visit once a year and play golf at the Vintage Club.

"It's supposed to give us a sense of community," Hope said.

"Utter crap," Quinn said. "I bet they don't make you do chores at the one in Malibu or East Hampton."

"There's other places like Wilder?" Hope asked.

"Oh, nothing's like Wilder," Quinn said. "The Wilder Sanctuary is the Rolls Royce of luxury treatment centers. Wilder makes the Betty look like Walmart."

"Snob," Hope said.

"Guess what?" Quinn flashed his gossip grin. "I discovered our handsome friend Carter is single."

"Isn't he a little young for you?" she asked. "And what would Tomás think?"

Quinn chuckled. "I don't discriminate when it comes to matters of the heart. And Tomás keeps paying the bills, so I stay out of his hair. Truthfully, I wouldn't be surprised if he forgot I was in here." Quinn took the pile of T-shirts Hope finished folding, spreading each one on the metal table and creasing them expertly into little gray envelopes.

"And in an almost criminal twist of fate," he continued, "while single, Carter doesn't play for my team."

"Thoughts and prayers," Hope said.

"I guess it's just me and Jonah until some fresh meat comes along." Quinn made kissy noises at Jonah. "Right, Toots?"

Jonah gave an eye roll before returning to binge-watching the laundry.

"But that means he's fair game for you," Quinn said to Hope.

Hope made a face. "No thanks."

"Why not?" Quinn asked. "You don't have someone on the out-side, do you?"

Hope fixed her gaze on the hand towel she was folding. During her first months at Wilder, Hope checked her email weekly and arrived early to the dining room on Visiting Days to wait for Luke and Charlotte.

But her emails went unanswered, and no one ever visited. And while she continued to inquire about messages, Hope had long since abandoned the belief that any would come.

But she didn't say this to Quinn. Instead, Hope finished her pile of hand towels and pushed them across the metal table. She watched his fingers fly over the cloth. "Why would I hook up with someone who has admitted to the multiple ways in which they are unstable?"

"Those are the best kind," Quinn countered. "Way better than the ones who don't know how fucked up they are."

A loud buzz propelled Jonah to his feet. He opened the washer door, extracting a small portion of its contents and lumbering to the dryer to place his pile inside. Then he plodded back again to the washing machine to do it all over again. Jonah reminded Hope of an ant building an anthill, one tiny grain of sand at a time. Lather, rinse, repeat.

"It's like watching paint dry," Quinn whispered. "Or *Eat Pray Love*."

"Why rush?" Hope resumed her folding. All they had at Wilder was time. A mind-numbing stretch of minutes and hours and days fell into each other, piling up and blurring together. Every yesterday was the same as the one before; every tomorrow would be the same as today. Anything completed quickly only made the day last longer. "He probably gets paid by the hour."

"Speaking of money," Quinn said. "I've been meaning to ask about your financial status, Hopeless."

"Because you're unabashedly nosy?" Hope asked.

"Girrrrl, that's how I know you aren't from money." He tapped his temple a few times with his index finger. "Because where I come from, figuring out someone's net worth isn't being nosy. In fact I took a class in it at Exeter."

"I definitely didn't go to Exeter," Hope said. "I'm an orphan. Isn't that how all the epic adventures begin?"

"If you only read tween fantasy, or Dickens. Not in real life," Quinn said. "But I say embrace your poverty. Wear it like a crown. It's de rigueur to come from the streets. It's like high-waisted jeans."

"Thanks for the support." She held a bath towel to her nose, breathing in. Wilder used the same fabric softener Hope used to apply, before Charlotte made them switch to a more environmentally friendly option. Hope took another deep inhale, wishing she hadn't switched brands, wishing for something that would remind her of home.

Quinn leaned forward on his palms. "What I really want to know is, who pays your very considerable wellness bill? You've been here almost as long as I have. No one comes to visit, and I see no evidence of a sugar daddy, mama, or sugar parent of any kind. And we know there are no free rides at the Palace of Psychosis."

He creased a snowy white bath towel into thirds and folded it on top of itself. "Wait, are you one of those people who won the lottery and went bananas?"

"I'm here on scholarship," Hope said. "I killed it on the Beck Depression Inventory."

Quinn extended his bottom lip in a pout. "Fine, be that way. But you can't hide your demons forever."

5

THREE-CARD MONTE

CARTER

The Wilder Sanctuary
Rancho Mirage, California

C ARTER RESTED HIS ankle over his knee, tapping his foot to the rhythm of the song running through his head. "Creep," Radiohead.

"How are you adjusting to life at Wilder?" Dr. Emerson asked.

Carter pushed up his glasses and surveyed his surroundings. Dr. Emerson's office could have been lifted directly off the set of a television drama, from the aesthetically pleasing knickknacks to the books with their pristine spines, grouped in soothing colors of blue, gray, and green. Carter wondered why there weren't any red or yellow ones. Were they only allowed to read books with the right color? Or were all the good books published in those shades?

Dr. Emerson gave a polite little cough, drawing his attention. Shit. He drifted off like that all the time.

Carter placed his foot on the floor, struggling to remember the original question. "How am I adjusting?" He employed this trick often, when he hadn't been listening and needed time to catch up. "I guess I'm adjusting fine."

"Are you comfortable?" Dr. Emerson moved the cup of sharpened yellow pencils on her ordered glass desk. She used her tablet exclusively, so Carter couldn't figure out what all those pencils were about. She smoothed her hair before crossing the room to sit. "We care about creating the best possible experience for all our guests."

Carter thought it was funny how all the doctors spoke about Wilder as if it were the Ritz-Carlton. Maybe they'd had customer service training, like the consultant he'd brought in a few years ago when his help desk was belittling callers.

"I'm . . . I'm fine," he stammered, annoying himself. He was saying *fine* too damn much. He honestly didn't know what he was expected to say in these sessions and he hated disappointing people. Dr. Emerson had only been pleasant, but he had the feeling he wasn't telling her precisely what she wanted to hear.

It didn't help matters that she was beautiful, disarmingly so. She could have been a model: slim, leggy, blond. Really leggy, and really blond. She always wore red lipstick, making it hard to look away from her mouth. Maybe that's why he was consistently on edge during these things.

"I have to tell you," Dr. Emerson said. "I love Magic Words. I still play it as part of my morning ritual."

"That's nice to hear," Carter said.

"It's still shocking to me that you were so young when you created the game," Dr. Emerson said. "Just a teenager."

"I, well, I was nearly twenty," Carter fumbled. In truth, he was sixteen when he designed the app. But Carter didn't do well with praise.

Dr. Emerson stabbed at her tablet with her stylus, frowning, lifting it up and shaking her head with almost exaggerated annoyance. "Updating," she said, glancing at Carter from beneath her long eyelashes. "Again. I blame the Mad Hatters."

Carter smiled. "No offense, but I think your device is small potatoes for the Hatters."

"Well, you're the tech expert, not me," Dr. Emerson said. "All I know is they were behind the scandal at Kent Rousseau's company last year and revealing the fraud at Apex the year before."

"Supposedly," Carter said. "But it's gotten to the point where anytime corporate corruption is exposed, people automatically assume it's the Hatters. It all sounds like a made-up conspiracy theory to me."

"I also heard the head of the Mad Hatters is a woman," Dr. Emerson said.

"Rogue?" Carter chuckled. He felt more at ease now, talking shop. "I've heard Rogue's a woman, a teenage kid, and Steve Jobs in hiding. But most people don't think Rogue really exists."

"Oh?" Dr. Emerson said.

"They think he or she's a group of people, or total fiction," Carter said. "Just to have a figurehead to rally around."

"Finally, it's working." Dr. Emerson flashed Carter another smile and crossed her legs. She wore a tight dress and bright red stiletto heels, which stood out sharply against the rest of the room. Especially the books. "Let's pick up where we left off last week."

She scrolled through her screen. "I was quite impressed at how many details you were able to recall. Such an acute memory is unusual. You're making incredible progress quite quickly. Don't you agree?"

He realized his attention had been drifting again, and knocked his foot into the coffee table, rattling the items on top. She was now watching him staring at her legs.

"Could I have some water?" Carter asked, feeling his face warm.

Dr. Emerson poured him a glass from the crystal pitcher on the table. Carter held it in his hands, spinning it around, not drinking.

"Did you enjoy your time with ViCTR?" Dr. Emerson asked.

"Victor?" Carter repeated. "Oh, you mean the Erleben device." He tilted the glass, watching the water flow close to the rim and back again. "I don't know. I just focus on all the problems. Always working, I guess."

"Then we'll keep you away for a while. Create some distance," Dr. Emerson said. "Though let's explore that further. Work. Why you left your company."

Carter adjusted his pant leg. The gray sweatpants he wore now felt foreign. At Maelstrom, he wore a tie with a custom-tailored suit most days.

When you start your company at nineteen, and everyone you hire is at least ten years your senior, a power suit helps to close the gap a little. At least that's what Jordan had said, when she took him to Union Square and smiled as he paid more for a tie than he had for his first apartment.

"I'm still foggy about the last few months," Carter said, even though it was far longer than a few months.

Dr. Emerson didn't look up. "You left after an issue with some employees."

Carter leaned in, forearms resting on his knees. "I did?"

"You worked with a woman, Nadia, for a few years at your startup," Dr. Emerson continued. "Your company—what was it called?"

"Maelstrom?" Carter offered uncertainly. He had intended it to be a statement, but it came out like a question.

"Of course. Maelstrom." Dr. Emerson nodded her approval, and he felt a little better. "You were at an after-hours work function. You accused Nadia of engaging in inappropriate behavior with another employee. Rohan Kapoor?" She said it as a question, but it didn't seem like she was looking for an answer. "He became involved in the disagreement, and you attacked him."

"Rohan?" Carter's stomach sank. He rubbed his hands on his thighs. Rohan was a later hire, and he'd been lucky to scoop him up right out of Berkeley. He was a hard worker, enthusiastic, smart. "I attacked him?"

"You broke a beer bottle and struck him repeatedly with it," Dr. Emerson said.

"Is . . ." Carter swallowed, a metallic taste in his mouth. "Is Rohan okay? Did I hurt him?"

Dr. Emerson sighed. "Mr. Kapoor has been in a coma since the incident. He had extensive damage to his face, which will require reconstructive surgery. As of yesterday, there was no change in his condition."

Carter held up his hands, fingers splayed. He studied them, inspecting both sides as if they'd only now materialized at the ends of his wrists.

"Dr. Emerson, I don't remember any of that."

"None of it?" She inclined her head, and Carter knew he'd screwed up again. "Nothing about it sounds familiar?"

Carter rubbed at the pounding rising in his temples. He willed himself to remember something, anything. He took a sip of water. "I do remember the work party. I don't even remember Rohan being there. Maybe he was. We sang karaoke. I thought I left early." Carter opened his eyes, blinking away the spots. He angled himself away from the window. The sun seemed so much brighter here than at home. "I remember leaving early."

"You remember leaving early?" Dr. Emerson's voice was soft, and her right eyebrow lifted slightly.

Did he? A few seconds ago, Carter had been certain. Now it didn't feel authentic anymore. "I'm pretty sure," he mumbled.

"After any trauma, our brains do whatever they can to rewire themselves and return to stasis," Dr. Emerson said. "It's a survival mechanism. When the trauma is particularly damaging or significant, it's common for our brains to suppress all our memories, feelings, and associations to that epicenter event. I believe this is the case for you. The key to healing is to accept the existence of the epicenter, to realize you're fighting against yourself by denying it."

Carter met her gaze. "But how can I accept it if I don't remember it happening?"

"That's what we're here for. We have many established techniques to help your recall, to break through and exhume your lost memories." Dr. Emerson balanced the tablet on her knees, shiny nails tracing around its edge. "You simply need to be open to unlocking these memories."

Carter nodded, though he still didn't see how he could think about something that wasn't there in the first place.

"What many people don't know is our long-term memories aren't stable." Dr. Emerson crossed her legs again and leaned closer to Carter.

He pushed himself a little further into the chair back. Looking at stunning women was one thing. Getting close to them was an entirely different experience.

"Memories are fluid. Each time we think about an event, the memory reforms, stronger and more powerful with each iteration." Dr. Emerson continued her speech, seemingly unaware of Carter's apprehension. "This process is called reconsolidation. It explains why our memories change over time. Have you ever had an experience which at the time made you think you would die from the sheer embarrassment?"

Carter flushed a little. Pretty much the story of his life. "Sure."

"But months or years later, when you think about it, you laugh?"

Carter nodded again because he knew Dr. Emerson wanted him to, though it never happened like that to Carter. All his embarrassing moments were an endless montage of stupidity, as fresh and mortifying as the day they occurred.

"This can work negatively as well," Dr. Emerson said. "Imagine someone who experienced a frightening event while say, driving over a bridge. Even after they are safe, it is upsetting each time they remember it. That thought process becomes a cycle, reinforcing the connection between the memory and the fear. It can become so extreme that simply seeing a bridge on television can be terrifying."

"Makes sense," Carter said.

"We work to resurface your epicenter event and interrupt your memories during the reconsolidation process. So you can ultimately achieve closure." Dr. Emerson poured him more water. "I realize this is disconcerting, but I'm here to help. Wilder is here to help."

"Sounds good," Carter said, for it seemed he was supposed to feel good about help.

"'Purpose is but the slave to memory,'" quoted Dr. Emerson. "We can help you remember. If that, in fact, is what you want. The question really is, Do you truly want to remember?"

Carter had absolutely no idea what she was talking about. He thought about his first major adult purchase, a new car. He'd just started Maelstrom and couldn't keep driving his brother Cole's ancient Honda Civic. At least according to Jordan.

At the dealership, trying to purchase something respectable, he was upsold by the fast-talking dealer, sucked into a verbal three-card monte. When Carter attempted to haggle, the dealer winked and made a big show of checking with his manager before making an exception "just for him."

Dr. Emerson reminded him a little of that guy.

"Carter? Do you truly want to remember?"

"Yes," he finally said. "If I did something terrible, I need to know."

"Excellent." Dr. Emerson nodded. "It's a simple series of treatments, but it will likely take a little time to fully uncover your memory. It first involves a medication that blocks the norepinephrine in your brain. That's the chemical causing the flight-or-fight response in your body. It can hinder your recall because it can—to simplify—block access to your memories."

"Sounds fine." Carter had drifted off again, but it probably didn't matter.

"In our sessions I'll take you back to that night and talk through the details to support your recall. We'll do some mental exercises to help you focus and get rid of the block. In the meantime, you'll work on visualization to call up additional details. You must do this without discussion with anyone, to avoid clouding your recollection. Usually, we use the Erleben device to clear your mind and cement the memories, but in your case we won't. We have a space here, called the Labyrinth, for more intensive recall sessions."

"The Labyrinth?" Carter clenched his fists. He pictured some machine he'd have to sit in, electrodes sticking out of his head, laser beams and implants and injections all going at once.

Dr. Emerson laughed. "I know it sounds mysterious, but it's very effective."

This whole thing was nuts. A few weeks ago, Carter was running Maelstrom, a thriving company, taking meetings with investors, discussing budget numbers and retention rates. Forever trying to move the needle. After an eternity of startup struggle, they were finally in the black, thanks to landing a whale fifteen months prior. He remembered how happy he was, toasting with Jordan and feeling like he'd finally achieved something.

And now this. Trapped at Wilder, told he'd attacked a friend, and remembering none of it. The problem was, when Carter studied his hands again, he could almost feel the neck of the beer bottle in his fingers.

"Let's do it," he said. "As soon as possible."

Dr. Emerson smiled.

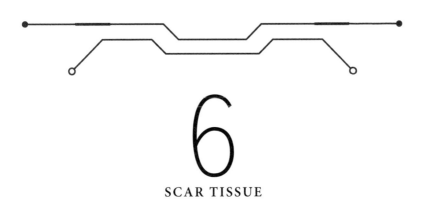

6

SCAR TISSUE

HOPE
The Wilder Sanctuary
Rancho Mirage, California

"ARE YOU SLEEPING any better?"

Hope shrugged. *Better* was a relative term.

"Do you think the temazepam is helping?" Dr. Stark asked.

"It seems to make the nightmares worse," Hope said.

That day his tablet lay closed on the coffee table. Stark sat in the uncomfortable armchair, ankle resting on his other knee, a yellow pad balanced on the space between. He wore very un-Stark socks with his black slacks and pinstriped dress shirt that day. They were bright purple, splashed with orange and red polka dots. He hadn't written anything during the last ten minutes, but now he picked up his pad and his pen.

"My daughter," Dr. Stark said.

"Sorry?"

He tapped the pen on his ankle. "The socks. My daughter Morgan got them for me. She thinks they make me less boring."

"And do they?"

"I think my boringness extends beyond my feet," Dr. Stark said, with a laugh. "But we all do silly things for the people we love, don't we?"

"Why are you using paper today?" Hope asked.

Dr. Stark glanced at the pad. "We had a network glitch, and everything needed to be reset. With all the Mad Hatter cyberattacks lately, security here has been tightened. Now the whole system runs through one central platform. But that means when something goes down, it all goes down."

Hope didn't particularly care. She preferred to eat up her time here with anything that wasn't about her. Though Dr. Stark wasn't as easily distracted as the other doctors had been.

"Let's just talk," he said, making a show of setting down his pad and pen. Stark poured a glass of water from a cut crystal decanter on the coffee table and slid it across to Hope. Then he poured his own and set it on a marble coaster.

She put the glass to her lips, watching Dr. Stark over the rim. It tasted like melon, sharp and unpleasantly tangy.

"According to Dr. Emerson, you've had nightmares since you were young?" he asked.

"Off and on, as long as I can remember," Hope said.

"Morgan suffered from night terrors when she was a toddler. It was quite distressing; despite being a clinician and knowing there wasn't cause for worry." Dr. Stark sighed. "But as a father, you want to protect your child over anything."

Hope liked how Dr. Stark often spoke about his daughter. It was a welcome contrast to Dr. Emerson, who probably just booted up from her charging station each morning.

"Your nightmares must have been worrisome for your parents as well," he suggested.

"I wouldn't know." Hope shrugged. "I never told them."

Dr. Stark looked surprised but quickly put his face back in order.

"Japanese father, Chinese mother," Hope said by way of an explanation, though Stark didn't appear further enlightened. He must not have many Asian patients. "My parents are old school. You solved your own problems. And kept quiet about it."

"I see," he said, though Hope knew he didn't. "Your family history is a bit . . . thin."

"We aren't close," Hope said. "We had a falling out, almost twenty years ago."

"Oh?" It was the same sound Dr. Emerson had made when they had this conversation months ago, same breath of anticipation, same lean forward. Only with her, Hope hadn't shared more.

"When I was in my twenties, I broke off an engagement," she said. "He checked all the boxes, so my parents were furious."

"What boxes?" Stark asked.

"Chinese, med student at Stanford, wealthy family," Hope said. "My cousins called him Tony the Trifecta. And on top of that, he was charming and romantic. Everyone loved Tony."

"But you didn't?"

Hope shifted on the sofa. It seemed like several lifetimes ago. She'd barely thought about Tony in the last decade and almost never spoke about him. Hope rubbed at her face. The room was unbearably hot; sweat was beginning to pool under her shirt. Dr. Stark poured more water.

"He fooled everyone, especially me," Hope said. "He was controlling. Manipulative. And emotionally abusive. I didn't see it for a long time."

"Can you give me an example?"

Hope almost laughed. She could give him a hundred. In the early days, Tony had been flattering, effusive in his compliments about everything: her appearance, her clothes, her wit, her cooking. It didn't take long for the compliments to stop and the manipulation to begin, but the change had been so subtle at first, the little digs skillfully masquerading as love, as concern, as protection. *I'll drive, you know how you are with directions. Let me take care of it. I don't want you to go alone.* Within eight months Tony was able to drop any pretense of love altogether, because by then they were far past pretending.

I believe you *believe it happened that way.*

There you go again, rewriting the narrative.

I'm not the villain here, you are.

Hope pulled her knees to her chest, wrapping her arms around her legs. Dr. Stark didn't even flinch when she put her sneakers on the couch, as Dr. Emerson would have. "He constantly corrected me. Everything I said was just a little wrong. I forgot important details of the story, told the incorrect date or place, exaggerated the circumstances or misrepresented something. It was worse when we'd be with friends—his friends; by then I didn't have any of my own friends. He made me question everything I did, said, thought. It got to the point where I would look at him for permission to make even the smallest decision. For three years."

"So you finally left," Dr. Stark said. She could tell the doctor was jonesing to pick up his pad again. His eyes kept darting toward it with the same clenched expression Hope used to have when she hadn't smoked a cigarette in two hours.

Hope nodded. "Then he punished me for leaving, made it his mission that I'd be nothing without him, that I'd have no one."

"Including your parents?"

Hope groaned inwardly. "It could only be my fault things disintegrated. I'd embarrassed them."

At last Stark couldn't stand it anymore and lunged for his pad and accessories, scrabbling like an alcoholic who discovered a fifth of gin stashed in a cabinet.

Hope attempted to be unobtrusive as she tried to catch a glimpse but could only make out a smattering of words underlined three times.

She wanted the words to be *brilliant, incisive,* and *astute,* but suspected they weren't. It made her cringe to picture the profile he undoubtedly was working up for her, the scholarly article forming in his head. She could see the abstract now: *Tiger parenting leads to chronic nightmares, alcohol abuse, and excessive intake of processed carbohydrates.*

"Anyway," Hope said quickly. "I graduated, moved away, got therapy. Threw myself into work."

"And what work was that?" Stark asked.

Hope started to provide an answer, but found she didn't have one. "I . . . I'm not sure."

Stark nodded, seemingly unconcerned. "And your later relationships?"

"Nothing serious, for a long time. Until . . ." She turned her face to the window. "Not for a long time."

Dr. Stark did not look up. "Shall we talk about Dr. Salinger?"

This had been a favorite tactic of Dr. Emerson's as well: meandering through conversations with interested concern, and then lobbing some grenade to throw her off. Talking about Tony was one thing; she'd hadn't been that person for decades. But Luke was different.

"What about him?" Hope tried once more to see what he was madly underlining, though still no dice.

"Regardless of the circumstances, it's normal to miss him. Do you?"

What a ridiculous question. Missing Luke had become a lifestyle. She carried the ache of missing him with her always, like scar tissue.

Hope inspected her hands, fingertips raw and nails bitten. An image came to Hope, of sitting in a nail salon chair while Charlotte waved a dark blue bottle of polish at her. She wiped a clammy palm over her face.

"You say you have no memory of last year," Dr. Stark said. "But you mentioned sirens last session?"

"I'm sure I didn't say anything about sirens." Hope twisted the hem of her T-shirt into a ball.

"You did," Dr. Stark said. "It's in my notes."

And just like that, Hope felt the same quickening of her pulse, the same pounding behind her eyes that had happened in every conversation with Tony two decades before.

There you go again, rewriting the narrative.

Dr. Stark shifted so the flashy polka-dot socks were no longer visible. He put the pad on the table face down, elbows on knees, fingers laced together. "As I've said, it's important to address the epicenter event of your blocked memories, for closure."

Hope didn't want closure. She wanted to go back to the laundry room and fold towels. She waited for the chime, staring straight ahead. She must have been sitting here for at least forty-five minutes. Why was it so hot?

"Let's try an exercise," Dr. Stark said. "What is your first clear memory after the time you lost?" He sounded like he was speaking from the other end of a tin can.

"Waking up here." Hope gathered her hair with one hand and fanned her face with the other.

"Are you feeling all right?" Dr. Stark spoke softly.

The space between Hope and the doctor seemed to widen. His words came in short bursts, louder and softer, as if someone were messing with the volume in her head.

"I'm really warm." The words came to her mouth in slow motion, from somewhere deeper, somewhere that wasn't her brain. "What were we talking about?"

"You were telling me about first waking up at Wilder. Where were you?"

"In my room," Hope whispered.

"And when you woke up, was Dr. Salinger there?" Dr. Stark asked.

Hope released her hair and let it fall against her sweaty neck. She nodded, remembering waking up at Wilder. Remembering the last time she'd seen Luke.

LAST DECEMBER, HOPE had opened her eyes to see Luke sitting in a stiff black chair, watching her, an ankle crossed over his knee. The socks she gave him last birthday, peppered with little kangaroos, peeked out beneath his charcoal pants. He wore her favorite shirt, the smoky blue one, and no tie.

Luke smiled, but it was flat, disingenuous. "Good, you're awake. How do you feel?"

"Hungover." She kicked the blanket off, sliding her arm under the pillow and noting the unfamiliar ceiling. "I was dreaming about the tram that goes to the top of the mountains, remember? You wanted to go, but I was wearing sandals and there was snow." The dream of being with Luke, their cold noses touching, kissing and laughing, slipped away. "I wish we'd gone. Maybe today?"

Luke frowned a little. "Not today."

Hope peered at her surroundings. She was in a room, though not any room she'd ever seen. It was sparse and bare: a utilitarian pine desk against the wall, a window, a nightstand. Outside Hope could see only a bloodless white, the sky obscured by a thick layer of clouds, without a speck of blue. At ceiling height a TV monitor was attached to the wall, near a framed print of a bridge. *Don't look back*, it said. *You're not going that way.*

Hope sat up.

Her hair tumbled down her back, which was odd because she put it up at night, piled on top of her head.

"Where are we?" she asked. "What's going on?"

"What's the last thing you remember?" Luke asked.

Hope tried to think, but there was a buzz in her head that made it difficult. "Waffles," she finally said.

"Impressive," he said.

She stretched against the pillows. "Did we make a pinky promise?"

Luke displayed the first genuine smile Hope had seen since waking, but it disappeared so quickly, it may have been her imagination. "What else?"

"Being in the backyard, under the blanket," she said. "A million stars . . ."

Hope glanced furtively at Luke. It was Luke, but it wasn't. He didn't have that look in his eyes, the one he got when she was flirting: delight and embarrassment, but far more of the former than the latter. He seemed so far away, even though she could reach out and touch him.

Hope pushed the hair from her face and left the bed. She needed to wake up. It would be better after a cup of coffee and a cigarette, and after she got a rubber band for her hair.

"What are you doing?" Luke asked.

"Having a cigarette," Hope said, scanning the empty room for her purse. She surveyed herself: bare feet, gray sweatpants, a T-shirt she'd didn't own.

"What the hell am I wearing?" she asked Luke. "These aren't my clothes. Where's my purse?"

"You should sit down."

Hope crossed to the door and tried to open it. She jiggled the handle, at first tentatively and soon frantically. The clacking echoed into whatever lay on the other side, bouncing back against her ears.

"Sit down," he said. Then added, "Please."

Hope returned to the bed, pulling her feet under her, studying Luke. His shirtsleeves were rolled up on his forearms, something he knew made her giddy. He was so handsome. Every morning she could never quite believe he was real.

She extended her hand in the gesture she'd performed hundreds of times: palm up, fingers extended, crooked downward at the wrist. It meant, hold my hand, and it was always accepted. But this time, he didn't take it, didn't envelop it in his fingers, didn't kiss her palm. He made a split-second movement and Hope thought he was going to, knowing when he did at least everything would seem safer. But he was only shifting in his chair. Hope held her hand there for a time, in the rigid, stale air, before returning it to her lap.

"Luke," Hope whispered. "What the fuck is going on?"

"Hope," he said, crossing his arms. "Ms. Nakano. I'd really prefer if you weren't quite so . . . familiar with me." He cleared his throat. "*Dr. Salinger* is more appropriate for our situation."

"What situation?"

Luke—Dr. Salinger—continued, "I'm afraid you've recently suffered a significant trauma affecting your memory. He gestured around the room. "I realize this is frightening, but Wilder is here to help."

⁂

"Hope?" Dr. Stark's voice made her jump. She pulled at her shirt, which clung to her back as if coated in syrup. She was uncertain anything she'd remembered was spoken aloud.

"When you woke, was Dr. Salinger there?" Dr. Stark asked.

She chewed on her bottom lip, which felt tingly, like lidocaine wearing off after a filling. Then she nodded.

"And what did he say to you? Can you remember?"

Hope tried to feign serious thought, to pretend she was thinking back, to pretend she hadn't recited the words in her head for six straight months. "'Purpose is but the slave to memory,'" Hope said tonelessly. With all the things she'd forgotten, Hope wished she could have forgotten that.

"Anything else?" Dr. Stark leaned forward.

Hope took another long drink, hoping the water might cleanse the words in her mouth, to somehow sanitize them into something far more palatable. "He said, 'We can help you remember. If that, in fact, is what you want. The question really is, Do you truly want to remember?'"

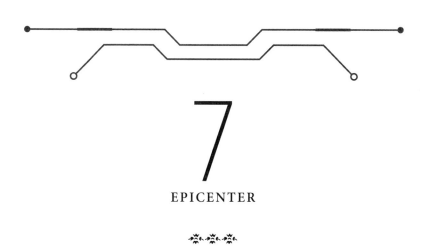

7

EPICENTER

✦✦✦

HOPE
The Wilder Sanctuary
Rancho Mirage, California

TWO MASSIVE GLASS doors slid smoothly on their rails, parting with a gust of air as Hope arrived for her prescribed time with ViCTR.

ViCTR was a place rather than a person. To be more precise, he was the entire third floor of the Wilder campus. While the doctors had anthropomorphized the facility into a "he," ViCTR was an acronym for virtual cognitive therapy retreat. Wilder loved to tack on classifications such as *retreat, sanctuary,* and *refuge* for places which were aggressively the opposite.

The technician at the kiosk, Fernando, hastily returned his phone to the pocket of his cranberry scrubs and grinned at Hope. In general, Fernando was a hot mess. He was tall and round, with hair that was disheveled in a not-on-purpose way. Unlike Jonah, Fernando's scrubs were perpetually wrinkled and spotted with the remnants of whatever his last meal was. He was also frequently being scolded by someone for leaving a door unlocked or his key card on a table. Even so, Hope liked him. Noncelebrity residents were predominantly invisible to staff, and Fernando was one of the few who treated the rest of the Wilder Weirdos like actual people. Although Hope still wasn't sure if he was deliberately nice or simply not savvy enough to know better.

Fernando moved his index finger over the recessed screen on the kiosk. "Arkham is being glitchy, as usual," he said. In a break from tradition, all the rooms in ViCTR had strange, non-wellness oriented names. "Go ahead and use Hestia. Oops, no, I meant Essex."

He pushed a small black touch pad forward. The screen read *Epicenter Event Reconsolidation*. Hope placed her thumb on the pad and a glass door swung open ten feet away. She pushed her hair from her face and headed along the corridor toward the door.

Inside the Butterfly Box (nickname courtesy of Quinn) it was dark, though thin runners of LED lights illuminated as she stepped across the threshold. The wall was covered in crisscrossed acoustic foam tiles, with hills and divots like the foam pad she'd used on the mattress in her first apartment. The carpeted floor was dark and industrial, with white lines swooping through. Save a leather armchair in the center, the room was empty.

A hook on the wall held a black vest. Hope reached for it and then snapped it closed across her chest and her waist. Dangling from the vest were large black goggles, a padded headset, and black mesh gloves with silver lines running along the fingers. Hope unhooked each accessory before she lowered herself into the armchair. She placed the pile in her lap, gripping the holes in the armrests, wondering briefly why Wilder would purchase chairs with drink holders. She would kill for a Negroni.

Being in the Butterfly Box unsettled her, despite its intended purpose of supporting relaxation. Hope ran her pinky across the headset as she stalled, tracing the word *Maelstrom* printed along the bottom edge.

Eventually, Hope pulled on the bulky touch feedback gloves and wiggled her padded fingers. She added the remaining accessories one by one, adjusting the headpiece until she could see clearly.

An undulating keyboard appeared, prompting Hope to enter a password. She typed and the keyboard vanished, replaced by silver letters spinning like a tornado before spelling out ERLEBEN with a flourish. A stylized butterfly fluttered across the screen next, flying like it could land on her face. In the early days, Hope used to jump in alarm whenever the butterfly showed up. It eventually came to rest over the name, angled so its wings covered the letter *B*. Hope supposed 'Butterfly Box' was as good of a nickname as any, since none of the patients knew what Erleben meant, how to pronounce it, or what the hell it had to do with butterflies.

A woman's voice came through the headset, soothing and velvety. Wilder must have commissioned studies to find a voice that inspired maximum calm. "Welcome, Hope," the voice said. "Please select your destination."

Six scenes in square boxes floated in front of Hope, each wiggling slightly for her attention. Hope barely looked at them. "Two," she said into the microphone.

"Enjoy your visit to the Island of Eleuthera. Be well."

Hope exhaled.

"Be well, Hope," the voice said again.

Jesus. "Be well, Morena."

Morena was merely the voice interface, a computer-generated personality like Alexa, only minus the dad jokes and trivia questions. Her name wasn't even really Morena. Quinn had named her over lunch one day, because her voice sounded like his favorite actress.

Lilting piano music swelled, gradually eclipsed by crashing waves and the occasional call of a seagull. The therapy sessions for phobias in the Butterfly Box required walking and movement, as did the yoga programs. The barriers in the virtual world mirrored the walls of the room, presumably to keep patients from ending up with a face full of acoustic foam. Across the hall, Necropolis and Hestia were triple this size and used for people with social anxiety. Meditation sessions didn't require movement, thus Hope had been given one of the smallest, most claustrophobic rooms.

"The air smells of salt and your favorite suntan lotion," Morena said.

Hope could only smell the pungent air of Wilder. But she followed Morena's directions dutifully, as she was guided to breathe and empty her mind. She watched waves crash and realistic palm trees sway, white sand sparkling in the manufactured sunlight.

In her early days at Wilder, Hope was astonished by how genuine this artificial world felt. Now, the real world and the virtual world were the same.

She closed her eyes for only a moment, but in that time the cresting waves fell silent. The cloying Wilder odor disappeared, and a strong, earthy smell of dirt and grass filled the room. Hope opened her eyes, adjusting the headset and focusing her vision, to find Eleuthera Island no longer before her.

"Morena?" Hope said, standing. "Where are we?"

From somewhere, Hope heard the wail of a siren.

It was dusk now, white sand nirvana absent. Hope stood on a winding dirt path, patches of moss growing sporadically along the sides. Bare aspen towered high above and stretched for miles, silent and imposing, white as bone, their brown holes staring at her like eyes. The detail was incredible, even for the Butterfly Box, and instantly recognizable as the Shade from Spooky's bedroom wall.

Hope took a small step forward onto the crudely cleared road. The trees shifted around her, knitting close together, stretching their limbs up to obscure the sky.

"Exit program," said Hope.

The moss and ivy vanished, but the program didn't end.

Surrounding her now was a ring of body parts. They were mostly hands and feet, severed crudely from their hosts and placed end-to-end on the ground in a rough but accurate circle, as if planted there so more parts would sprout and grow. Silver bells and cockle shells.

Most parts were a sickening gray-green color, blood long since dried into a rusty dark brown. A few were still the color of living flesh, their blood a bright arterial red. Every few feet along the circle lay an organ—a heart, or a liver maybe, a pile of intestines—also in varying stages of decay. A path of pink glass candles was on either side of her, the type you buy in a convenience store for a dollar, sticker of a patron saint struck to the side.

The candles guided her toward a table in the center of the circle. A white sheet covered something underneath.

"Exit," Hope whispered. "Exit program."

Instead, the candle wicks ignited in unison. The body parts and pieces of flesh burst into flames, a rising column of fire encircling her. It hadn't been particularly frightening in here thus far, even with the grotesque environment. She'd still known she was in the Butterfly Box, still had the control to end the session.

But now, Hope felt her throat closing.

Her surroundings shifted so the table was now directly in front of her, unavoidable. It was waist height, wider than it appeared from a distance, six feet long. And it wasn't a table, but a hospital gurney.

A ripple of dread spread through her, yet Hope was unable to look away or move. Sirens wailed in her ears.

The cloth on the gurney began to flicker, fading in and out until it finally disappeared.

A body, small enough to fit within the bounds of the stretcher, lay in the middle. It was curled into a fetal position, knees bent, face contorted into a grimace. The body was charred, or in the process of being burned alive. Wisps of smoke curled from it; bits of fiery flesh dripped from the blackening bones onto the surface below before disintegrating into ash. A horrible smell rose into her face, much worse than eucalyptus: the smell of burning skin, of smoke, of ashes.

Hope covered her face with her hands and screamed.

And then she was in the Butterfly Box once more, Wilder uniform sticking to her skin, body mashed against the acoustic foam wall.

Hope slid to the carpet below and pulled the gloves from her slick, trembling hands. She stared at the blue lights along the edge of the ceiling, blinking like stars in the sky.

"I hope you feel centered and refreshed," purred Morena. "Would you like to restart?"

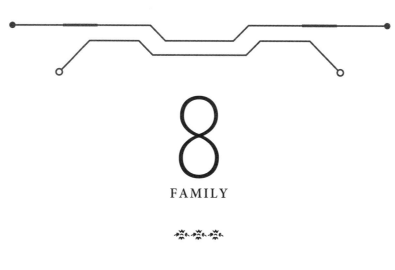

8

FAMILY

✳✳✳

HOPE
The Wilder Sanctuary
Rancho Mirage, California

V ISITING DAY AT Wilder occurred on alternate Sunday mornings and was the sole event that ever managed to fill the dining room. Friends and family, along with a smattering of agents and powers of attorney would arrive at eleven on the dot and be ushered to their tables, seated with their loved ones as if meeting for a business lunch at Spago. The kitchen staff spared nothing for these dining experiences, adding white tablecloths and flowers in mint julep cups, placing gold chargers under the china plates, piping classical music through the speakers. The food was fantastic on Visiting Day, so delicious even Hope didn't long for chili cheese fries.

On these Sundays, some staff ate with residents, joining VIPs for a course or two. Doctors would inevitably arrive in the room to find, serendipitously, an open seat with one of Wilder's red-carpet celebrities. They were always willing to glad-hand loved ones and rave about the unbelievable improvement their guests were making. So much progress. One more month should do it. If you were exceptionally famous, CEO Jack Copeland himself might make an appearance, although Hope hadn't seen him in months.

Following their three-course meal, everyone was encouraged to visit the Zen Garden or play games in the recreation room. Since no one ever came for Hope, she in turn avoided the families. It was too depressing to watch them dealing out limp playing cards, all wearing identical expressions of anxiety mixed with forced positivity, laughing too heartily at nothing.

Visiting Day was a bit like a staged house: orchestrated to give you a glimpse at what could be possible without the pesky detritus of real life, like garbage cans or dirty dishes or toilet brushes. A little too much shine to be wholeheartedly believed.

Hope often wondered why residents went along with the smoke and mirrors of Visiting Day. Perhaps they felt guilty about the high price tag, or maybe they wanted to believe what the doctors were saying: they were making progress.

From her table for two, Hope watched as Spooky and his family made their way through the dining room.

Spooky's brother Henry was in the lead, chatting with Dr. Emerson, smiling and gesturing with his slender arms. Henry came without fail every Visiting Day, driving from UCLA, where he studied engineering. Sometimes he had their mother in tow, sometimes not. Spooky's father rarely came. He was a scientist or a researcher, sequestered someplace far away.

That day, the whole family was here. Spooky's mother, with her chic pixie cut and ivory Max Mara suit, stayed close to Henry. His father moved stiffly, as if each step needed to be precisely calculated prior to execution. Spooky shuffled a few feet behind with his head bent.

Dr. Emerson gushed over his mother's massive Louis Vuitton bag before leaving the table. Doctors never came to sit with Spooky's family, perhaps because there were no successes to report. Spooky had been the same sullen, twitchy person since day one. He needed a lot longer than a month. Henry often brought Spooky little gifts when he visited, usually art supplies like charcoal pencils or gum erasers. He passed a spiral notebook across the table, BRUINS stamped across the front in gold lettering.

Spooky pushed it back to Henry. "Page twenty-seven," he said. "'Residents are allowed two paperbound journals. No metal is allowed.'"

"Crap, I'm sorry," Henry said, patting Spooky on the back. "I forgot. Next time."

Hope once read that brothers alone were incomplete, two halves of one whole, an inseparable pairing of light and dark. With Henry, it was easy to tell where the physical and psychological bisections differed from Spooky. Tall and dashing, with gelled-up short black hair and stylish clothes, Henry radiated confidence, and possessed all the charm and polish and store of social skills his brother lacked.

"Oh good, Henry's here," Quinn said, dropping into the seat next to Hope. "I needed some eye candy today."

Henry gave a whoop of laughter and they both looked over. Their mother was laughing, hand delicately covering her mouth. Even their father looked moderately pleased. Spooky's face held an uncertain expression, resembling a kid who was being told they were laughing with him though beginning to suspect they weren't.

"How was the Butterfly Box last night?" Quinn asked Hope. He cut his rectangle of butter into a square and discarded the unwanted edges onto Hope's plate.

"Last night?" Hope said. "I had the Butterfly Box?"

"That's how you got out of 'game night,'" Quinn said, making air quotes. "Stark sent you to the Butterfly Box. Mindfulness charades was an epic fail, by the way."

Hope tried to think back. She had a brief flash of candles and a whiff of smoke, but they quickly evaporated. "It was a program I'd never been in, but I can't remember anything," she said. "I think it was in that forest, the one from Spooky's room. I should ask him."

"I wouldn't right now. Looks tense over there." Quinn jutted his chin at Spooky's table.

"Spencer needs a haircut," Spooky's father growled in Mandarin. He didn't address anyone, rather it seemed his chicken marsala was to blame.

His wife reached across the table, pushing the hair out of Spooky's eyes with three French-manicured fingers. "I think it's fine," she said timidly, also in Mandarin.

"It is fine," Henry said, a little defiantly, in English. This was their pattern, with the parents speaking in Mandarin and the kids replying in English. It had been this way in Hope's house too, long ago.

Henry rifled through one of Spooky's notebooks and held a spread in front of his brother's face. It looked like the cover of a comic book: characters in capes fighting each other, flying blackbirds, swirls and lines indicating action and violence and movement. "Love this one. Very *Sandman*. Is it new?"

Spooky cast a nervous glance at his dad and nodded.

Their father took a sip of his tea and addressed Henry. "What is that? More pictures?" He said *pictures* as if he'd found meth under the mattress.

Spooky's shoulders slumped even more, and Hope felt a painful sympathy for him. Growing up, Hope had experienced this with her own parents often: suspecting you'd stepped in it, yet too late to course correct.

"You should look at them, Ba. They're really good." Henry offered the notebook across the table, but his father stopped him with a single shake of the head. Henry placed it in his lap, then passed it to Spooky under the table. Spooky gripped it in both hands like a life preserver.

"Spencer should not be wasting his time on garbage." Now he was glaring at their mother. Her hand fluttered to her own hair and in the direction of Spooky, and then to her teacup and back again, not resting anywhere.

"Why don't you guys ever talk to him?" Henry asked, nostrils flared. "He's sitting right here. He has his own opinions. And feelings."

Hope now felt sorry for Henry, because she could easily tell by his father's posture what was coming. But she had to admire his pluck.

"Do not speak disrespectfully to me." Spooky's father spoke quietly but set down his fork with enough force to rattle the glasses. Then he launched into a rapid-fire tirade, as three pairs of eyes quickly focused on their lunches.

"What are they saying?' Quinn asked sotto voce.

Hope pointed her fork at him. "Because we all speak the same language?"

"Don't get all Asianer-than-thou," Quinn said. "I'm not a philistine. I know you're fluent in Japanese and Mandarin, and they're speaking Mandarin. Now translate, or I'll go ask."

As she listened, Hope pushed her chicken around, moving mushrooms out of its curving path. "His mom is trying to downplay everything. Changing what everyone says to sound better." She listened a bit longer. "His dad says art is an embarrassment that won't make any money. He says Spooky should be applying to graduate school instead of drawing pictures. He's squandering his future."

"What future?" Quinn scoffed. "Spooky's going to be in here forever, just like us."

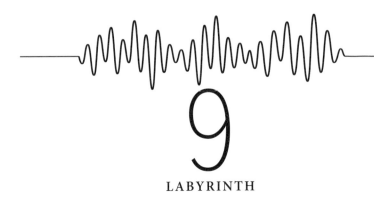

9

LABYRINTH

CARTER

The Wilder Sanctuary
Rancho Mirage, California

CARTER HAD SEVERAL ideas about what the Labyrinth might be. Maybe it was a ten-foot hedge maze, with sphinxes asking you to solve twisted riddles and a host of man-eating plants. Perhaps its location was in an even more high tech part of Wilder. Maybe you had to battle mechanized rats, with discs like the Users had in *Tron*. Or perhaps it was a *Westworld*-type, more metaphorical labyrinth. Maybe seeing it would make him realize he was an android, programmed to do someone else's bidding with no free will of his own. Carter smiled, thinking sentient robot soldier was the current most desirable scenario.

He supposed he could have asked someone about what to expect from the Labyrinth, but Carter tended to avoid people as his default. The celebrities at Wilder lived in their own untouchable bubbles, and the remainder of the "guests" were either guarded or unpredictable or both. He felt as if they might lash out at the slightest slip, which compounded Carter's habit of forever saying the wrong thing. His first week, he'd noticed a young kid with some *D&D* magazines and had tried to make conversation. But Carter must have scared the crap out of him, to the point where he kept reciting rules from the patient handbook.

And then Quinn acted friendly, but who could tell? Carter figured in a place like this, appearing normal probably masked a much worse issue than the people who wore it all out there.

Take Nina, for example. When he first got to Wilder, Nina was really nice to him, giving him little rundowns on all the patients. But after the scene at breakfast a few days ago, he realized Nina was a full-fledged psycho. And then there was Hope. He'd noticed her immediately, on his first day at dinner. And there had been more than a few occasions where he thought Hope was watching him too: at meals, during yoga, at goal setting. Yet each time Carter turned to look, she never was. Maybe that meant he was just as much of a lunatic as everyone else.

So Carter rode to the Labyrinth in a bright red golf cart with a lightbulb painted on the side, armed with no information about what was to come. They drove far beyond where he'd been before, past the Zen Garden and yoga, past the sprawling meditation area, past the pond home to some brown ducks and the two resident swans, Joel and Clementine.

"How long have you been here?" Carter asked the driver. "I'm sorry, I forgot your name."

"Jonah," he said, eyes on the road. "I've been here since Wilder opened."

"And what did you do before that?" Carter asked.

"I was at Copeland-Stark," Jonah said.

"Yeah?" Carter said. "My company—my old company—makes technology for them."

"I know," Jonah said.

They drove in silence for a while. Jonah didn't seem the chatty type. Typically, Carter wasn't either. He much preferred solitary comforts: algorithms, lines of code, finding logical solutions to complicated problems.

After Carter started Maelstrom, Jordan had forced Carter to up his political game, a charge he'd hated every minute of: securing funding, wooing clients, pitching investors. Schmoozing was Jordan's gift, not his. Jordan could sidle up to a billion-dollar investor during dinner and have a check in hand by dessert.

"Do you like it here?" Carter asked. Maybe his nerves were making him talk so much.

"I love it here," Jonah answered, so quickly it sounded like he meant the opposite.

"What did you do at Copeland-Stark?"

The expanse of grass gave way to patches of desert cactus. Jonah made a left turn onto a narrow path barely wider than the golf cart. "I interned with my sister."

"What does she do?"

"Sonogenetics. Um, brainwave manipulation using ultrasound." The muscles in Jonah's dark brown forearm contracted as he moved the gearshift. The cart groaned.

"Wow," Carter said. "Where did you go to school?"

"Johns Hopkins," Jonah said.

It seemed like Jonah spent most days waiting for someone to tell him what to do. He didn't act like a scientist with a fancy degree, manipulating brainwaves. Carter attempted to formulate a way to ask about it that didn't make him sound like a dick.

He was still thinking when they pulled up at a low wall made of beige bricks, surrounded by pink flowered bushes. In the middle of the wall was a red door.

"Thanks for the ride." Carter hopped from the cart.

Jonah drove away without a wave.

Carter stood for a moment, and a few moments more, until he was absolutely positive he had to go inside. Then he waited a few minutes longer. When even less choice remained, he approached the red door and couldn't locate a doorknob, or a latch, or a doorbell. He pushed at it. He knocked.

He wondered if this was a test of his worthiness. Maybe they were all watching him from a hidden camera, taking notes on their clipboards about how he handled stressful situations. So Carter gave up and waited for something to happen, sitting cross-legged on the pavement in front of the red door.

A woman eventually opened the door and smiled at him. It was well over 100 degrees outside, but she was wearing a long-sleeved sweater under her white lab coat. Carter found the heat in Palm Springs suffocating, and just looking at her outfit made him feel hotter.

"I'm Dr. Green. Glad you're here," she said, extending her hand.

He'd never seen Dr. Green before. What was it with the women in this place? She was gorgeous also, with long, curly brown hair. And while she seemed warmer than Dr. Emerson, it didn't make her any less intimidating. She still looked like a runway model. Carter tripped over his sneaker as he rose to shake her hand, pumping it longer than necessary. Dr. Green quickly pulled her sleeve down, but not before Carter noticed the thick, reddish ridge of a scar on the inside of her wrist.

Dr. Green indicated he should enter ahead of her, but he did the same, and so an awkward exchange of starting to walk and stopping ensued, continuing until it bordered on the absurd. At last Carter went through the doorway, bumping sideways into Dr. Green and mumbling an embarrassed apology.

The short path turned toward a single-story building past an ornately carved stone fountain with a topless mermaid on one side and a phallic obelisk rising up from the middle of it, water dripping out from the top onto the mermaid's face in an embarrassingly suggestive way. Carter blushed, averting his eyes. Dr. Green scanned her badge at the doorway.

She held the door for Carter, who entered without incident this time. The waiting area was painted a deep scarlet, with a single framed poster matching the ones around Wilder. It was a black-and-white photo of ocean water splashing over rocks. *Purpose is but the slave to memory.* Two chairs flanked a sturdy wooden end table in the corner, a less pornographic fountain sitting on top.

Dr. Emerson emerged, seemingly from nowhere, in a white lab coat over her tangerine dress. She split her long ponytail in two and pulled on the ends, then held out a tiny paper cup with an orange pill inside.

Carter swallowed it.

"Ready?" Dr. Emerson spun on a heel and headed for a set of glass double doors. Dr. Green scanned her badge on the red wall, and the doors swung open like in a supermarket.

Outside the space was considerable, at least a few acres. It was vast and square, with a cactus-lined dirt path leading to a tall hedge, taller than Carter. An opening was cut into the middle of the greenery, to what he had to believe was the Labyrinth.

Truthfully, he was disappointed. It was basically a big, underwhelming garden. Carter resolved to expand his knowledge of the world beyond sci-fi when he left Wilder. "It's a maze?" he asked. "I find my way to the end?"

"There's only one path," Dr. Green said. "You don't have to worry about making a wrong turn or running into any hosts." She gave him a little wink and smile, and he decided he might be in love with Dr. Green.

Dr. Emerson cleared her throat and Dr. Green lost her grin. "Labyrinth therapy has been around for some time as a meditation tool. There are three phases you will experience—entering, centering, and exiting. As you walk, you'll purge your negative thoughts, reconcile those thoughts to center yourself, and finally achieve harmony and a positive mindset." Dr. Emerson sounded as if she were reading from a brochure.

"The first part can be disorienting," Dr. Green said, gesturing. "It's meant to make you feel isolated so you can focus on your thoughts. The second stage is outside and you'll be able to see the path."

Carter tried for a game face, but he only understood half of what they were saying. And what he heard sounded like a bunch of New Age bullshit.

He'd been thinking about the goddamn mermaid in the fountain, who now had the alternating faces of the two doctors.

Dr. Green said, "The third stage is again isolated, and—"

"You'll see," Dr. Emerson interrupted. "It is designed to help solidify the memories related to your epicenter event."

Carter realized a beat too late that the explanation was over. Shit. Now he was required to say something that didn't make him look like a moron.

He regarded the two doctors, his brain catching up with the present at long last. "So I'm supposed to walk. And think about Rohan and Nadia."

"In essence, yes," Dr. Emerson said. "What's different about our brand of labyrinth therapy is that we give you support to speed up the process." She reached into the pocket of her lab coat and pulled out a small black object.

Carter's heart skipped at the mere glimpse of a piece of technological equipment. He wasn't allowed to use Erleben here, and he missed it. *Here it is,* he thought. *One-way ticket into the OASIS, baby. Time to take the red pill.* He actually got a little excited.

Except, much to his dismay, it was a compact wireless headset with earphones and a foam-encased boom mic, the kind telemarketers wear. He had tons of these at Maelstrom for their product developers and focus groups: $7.99 at Costco. Cheaper if you buy in bulk.

"When you first walk the path, we'll be giving you guidance," Dr. Green said. "We'll ask you questions and provide prompts. Sometimes we might tell you to stop and perform an exercise."

Carter pictured himself in a maze, the ones they used to go to in high school around Halloween. Immense corn hedges out in the middle of nowheresville, dudes stoned out of their minds, stumbling around in the dark among the squeals of teenage girls. He pictured himself doing jumping jacks in that maze or tapping his head three times while standing on one foot.

"An exercise?" he asked.

"A mental task," Dr. Emerson said. "To help interrupt memory attachment during reconsolidation. We may show you images, play sounds, and have you interact with them."

The word *reconsolidation* made the hairs on his neck rise. Carter flashed back to his last session with Dr. Emerson, where she talked about bridges and embarrassing moments while he focused on her legs. The stupid mermaid flashed into his mind again.

"Right now," Dr. Green said gently, placing a hand on his arm. "All we need you to do is put the headset on and walk into the opening. We'll help you through the rest. You won't be alone."

Carter tried to shove his hands into his pockets, reminded for the hundredth time he was wearing stupid sweatpants with no pockets. He stepped on the stone path and took a deep breath. After a brief hesitation, he forced himself to move through the narrow opening. It was dim in the maze, with small, inlaid lights on the ground his only source of illumination. The smells he'd become accustomed to at Wilder were much more powerful in here, and his nose filled with a tangy scent like furniture polish. He instinctively reached his hand out to touch a branch, and it felt thick and plasticine.

Carter adjusted his headset. "Ground control to Major Tom."

"Are you ready?" It was Dr. Emerson's voice, bordering on irritated.

He cleared his throat, embarrassed. "I'm ready."

"The propranolol should start working shortly, if it isn't already," Dr. Emerson said. "As you walk, we're going to ask you about other memories so we have a baseline on your recall ability." She paused. "You may begin. Can you tell us about your first memory of arriving at Wilder?"

Carter stepped cautiously. "I woke up in my room. Dr. Emerson was there." Waking up to see Dr. Emerson had made him certain he was still asleep. Carter shook his head to clear it. He was so much better at thinking about what he wasn't supposed to be thinking about, instead of the reverse.

"You said I experienced a trauma," he said. "That it affected my memory. Wilder was going to help me remember."

"Remarkable," said Dr. Emerson. She sounded so pleased, like she might drop a dog biscuit out of the hedge to reward him. *Good boy, that's a good lunatic.* "You really do have a surprisingly adept recall."

Carter stumbled over an uneven patch in the path and grabbed for the hedge. He felt his stomach dip, like he'd missed a stair. When he took another step he felt dizzy, so he stopped again.

"Please continue walking," said Dr. Green. "Tell us a little about what you did before Maelstrom."

"I . . . I was at Cal," Carter said. "I was getting my degree when I met Jordan."

"But even in college you were already quite accomplished," Dr. Emerson said. "You'd created and sold some programs, won many awards."

"I've always loved computers," Carter said.

"An affinity that got you in some trouble in your adolescence, didn't it?"

"Trouble?" Carter stumbled again, making a sizeable dent in a plastic hedge.

"Someone hacked the school's website," Dr. Emerson said. "Multiple times."

As a teenager, Carter hadn't exactly been the most upstanding citizen. His mother always said he was too smart for his own good, and maybe she was right. He'd loved learning, but he hadn't needed to try very hard to excel in school. In high school this meant free time most kids didn't have, time that allowed him to make more than a few regrettable choices. Except those records had been sealed.

"That was all . . . a misunderstanding," Carter said. "How did you even know about that?"

"We can revisit that in a future session," Dr. Emerson said. "Let's test some other facets of your memory."

Carter relaxed a fraction as the doctors peppered him with a stream of questions. At first the questions were straightforward, and his answers came quickly: his dog's name (Luna), his first game (Magic Words), the interview he'd given to *The 415* ("Sloane Shark"). Others were related to pop culture events like the Oscars or the latest Mad Hatter attack or the winner of the 2022 NBA Finals. Some were trivial and impossible to answer, like listing the juices at breakfast or the number of families last Visiting Day.

He eventually reached an opening in the hedge. Carter stepped through and blinked in the jarring sunlight. A giant maze was laid out on the stretch of dirt and dry grass before him, the curving path delineated by thousands of jagged stones. In the center of the maze was a small building with another red door.

Even though he could feel the sunburn developing on the back of his neck, Carter felt cold and clammy. Something in him didn't want to walk along that path. A small box ascended from the ground on a pole, clacking like a rising roller coaster. A metal door popped open. Carter jumped, and his headset crackled.

Dr. Green said, "The desert can be very dehydrating."

Carter peered into the cubby and took a cup printed with pale green flowers. He knocked back the shot of water and crumpled the waxy paper. The door shut and descended into the ground.

"For this part of the path," Dr. Emerson said, "we'd like you to walk and center your mind."

Carter tried to take a brisk pace around the path, having no idea what actions could cause him to center his mind. He just wanted to get this whole mess over with. Carter moved from the outside of the maze inward, kicking up grainy dust that turned his sneakers brown. But the faster he tried to walk, the less ground he seemed to cover.

He was feeling stranger with each step, much like final exams in college, when he'd pull an all-nighter and drink too much coffee. Wired, buzzy.

The path eventually ended at the red door, and Carter leaned a shoulder against the brick wall. He definitely didn't feel centered; he felt hollowed out. Empty.

"We'd like you to think back to the night for which we are surfacing memories," Dr. Emerson said. "Picture the bar, with Rohan and Nadia. Close your eyes as you access the memory and visualize that time."

He thought closing his eyes would be a welcome relief, but it only made his dizziness worse. He was so thirsty, and so he tried to focus on the bar, on the beer taps lined in the front and the bottles and glasses along the shelf in the back.

Carter didn't know how long he'd been there, leaning against the wall, when Dr. Green spoke again. "Please open the door and enter the building."

He ran his tongue over his teeth to try and clear the unpleasant tingle in his head. Carter pushed at the door and a blast of cool, dank air greeted him as he walked inside. At least it was out of the sun.

He stood motionless in the corridor. Carter couldn't see anything but could sense the walls around him, the low ceiling, a hum of machinery from somewhere. He wasn't usually sensitive to enclosed spaces, but like the maze outside, this place felt wrong.

"This part is purposely dark, but there are no obstacles," Dr. Green said.

Carter extended his hands. It wasn't merely dark, it was an oppressive, suffocating black. Invisible hands seemed to close around his neck. Carter bent his arms and stepped carefully, taking deep breaths to keep from bolting out.

"Please keep walking and tell us about that night," Dr. Emerson said.

Carter tried his best to visualize, as he'd been dutifully practicing. "There were a lot of people, talking, playing pool. Singing. Nadia sang "Take on Me." I told her she had a great voice."

Again, the doctors took turns asking questions. Each time he answered he stopped walking, as it had become an effort to perform more than one action simultaneously.

"What kind of beer was it?" Dr. Green asked.

Carter stopped again. He thought they'd already asked him this. "Tecate. No, it was a Modelo." He looked down, as if he'd be able to see it in his hands.

"Which one?" Dr. Emerson asked. She sounded frustrated, and it made Carter's pulse speed up. "Tecate or Modelo?"

"Negra Modelo," he said, and in his mind he could see it clearly: the brown bottle, the black-and-gold label, the raw, serrated edge where he'd struck it on the corner of the bar. "I'm sure now."

"Very good," Dr. Emerson said. Now she sounded pleased.

"Please open your eyes," Dr. Green said. "Here are some photos taken that night."

A huge screen illuminated before Carter, and he pressed himself into the wall. It was a photo of Rohan and Nadia, standing at a pool table among other Maelstrom staff. Nadia's mouth was open in mid-laugh, Rohan was pointing outside of the camera's range.

Carter was in the background, leaning on the bar and watching the pair. It reminded him of a commercial for TGI Fridays or Applebee's or something. Too much polish, too shiny. Almost like a stock image.

Next flashed a montage of photos and social feeds: Nadia singing, Rohan with his knee up on a chair, a Negra Modelo, Rohan whispering into Nadia's ear, people playing pool, a puddle of shattered brown glass on a dirty concrete floor.

"Please close your eyes once more." He didn't know which doctor was speaking. "Tell us how you were feeling."

Carter shook his head. "I . . . I don't remember."

"When you feel vulnerable and exploited, when people are laughing at your expense, anger is a very normal reaction," someone said. "Did you feel angry?"

"I was angry," Carter agreed.

"Was it anger, or was it rage?"

Carter swallowed. "Rage."

"And what did you do with that rage?" Dr. Emerson asked.

"I called Nadia a bitch. I shoved Rohan. Can I sit for a minute?" He didn't wait for an answer and slid down, back propped against the wall, knees bent into his chest. "I told Rohan to leave. He wouldn't. I grabbed his beer and hit it against the bar."

"You attacked Rohan," said a soft voice, which he thought was Dr. Green.

"I attacked Rohan." Carter's fingers flexed around an imaginary bottle. He could see it now, cutting into Rohan's skin, Rohan on the ground, the Ferragamos Jordan made him buy striking Rohan's back, his stomach. "He fell. He had his arms over his head to . . . to protect himself. I kept kicking him, harder and harder."

Carter couldn't speak anymore. He pressed his cheek against the cold concrete wall.

"This is fantastic progress," Dr. Emerson said. "I'm so proud of you."

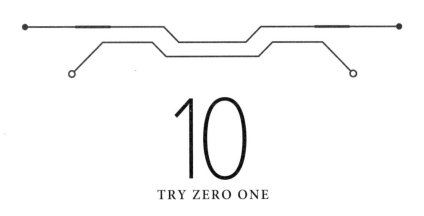

10

TRY ZERO ONE

HOPE

The Wilder Sanctuary
Rancho Mirage, California

T HAT NIGHT, HOPE was assigned to Necropolis, the largest room in the Butterfly Box. This time Morena skipped any guise of meditation entirely and dropped Hope directly into the Shade. It was like someone watching her on Netflix had pushed pause from her last visit: same path, same endless white trees, same moss. In her left ear she heard a fluttering, though the leaves surrounding her were still.

Hope held out her arms and gave her avatar the once-over. Jeans and black boots. Black fingerless gloves, white tank top, motorcycle jacket. It had been an eternity since she'd worn actual clothes, so it was nice to show up clad like a badass. Even if that badass was Joan Jett, circa 1984.

Every few feet, at her eye level, a small piece of paper was attached to a tree trunk. The closest one vibrated, as if it were trying to fly away from the nail holding it in place. The paper was yellowed and a few inches wide, with raw edges like tape torn from an old cash register.

There were three numbers on it: 26-17-22. The next paper had two more sets of numbers: 2-6-17-3, 3-13-6. Each subsequent paper repeated the same thing: 26-17-22, 2-6-17-3, 3-13-6.

For at least twenty more trees, Hope walked and paused, until at the last tree she found a person, pounding another note into the bark with a flat rock.

It was Spooky, his Wilder uniform also absent. He was sporting some sort of complicated armor, complete with shoulder pads and golden breastplate and a long maroon cape, chains and metal pieces clanking together. He looked ridiculous, though admittedly, Hope wasn't in a position to cast any judgment.

"Did you bring me here?" She looked around. "Is this the Shade?"

Spooky didn't answer, and Hope waited another minute. "I thought patients couldn't use the same program together. Quinn tried to take me into his Studio 54 program once, but it didn't work." She added, "Thank God."

Again, Spooky remained silent. Perhaps he wasn't here after all, merely a part of the program. If so, he was some quite advanced CGI.

"Is this the epicenter thing Dr. Stark was talking about? For my memories?" Hope wasn't sure why she kept talking when Spooky clearly wasn't.

At last, Spooky stopped pounding and turned to her. "You're late." He sounded irritated.

"Sorry," she offered. "I don't have a lot of control over when I show up here. Which is where? Is this Mirror Gate?"

"This is not Mirror Gate. And actually, you have a great deal of control when you show up here." Spooky's voice was different in the VR world: confident, sarcastic. He even made eye contact. Still, it was going to take a little time to get used to Virtual Spooky and his judgy attitude.

"Try zero one?" Hope gestured at the notes. "How do you know this code?"

Spooky made a sweeping motion through the air with his left arm. "What does it mean?" Hope asked.

He pointed into the trees, past a grove of birch. As she watched, a section of the forest flickered into large pixels and then smaller ones, then faded until it disappeared entirely.

Spooky and Hope were now standing on a slip of land between a body of inky water and a looming limestone lighthouse. Periwinkle wildflowers bloomed all around, growing through the sand in patches. Hope knelt and dipped her hand in the water.

She had another surge of memories: of sitting outside on a still summer night with two glasses of good single malt and a black sky dusted with stars. Of Luke's fingertips resting on the nape of her neck.

"Serpent's Bay," Spooky said, evaporating her memories.

Hope removed her hand from the water and shook it, out of habit. "I guess that's better than Maggot Gulf. Or Slug Sea."

The lighthouse beam swept across Spooky's stern face.

"Did you make this whole program?" Hope asked. "It's impressive. The movement, the details . . . way better than the ones I've used in the Butterfly Box. I keep forgetting it isn't real."

"Some," Spooky said. "But not all."

"Then who?"

Ignoring Hope, Spooky reached into one of the multiple layers of his costume and removed a stack of what looked like gift cards. He set each card in midair, on a shelf only he could see. Even for VR, it was a pretty cool trick.

Hope examined the cards. Each had a number on it, though different than the "Try zero one" she'd deciphered. She tried to translate and soon realized it wasn't their code. The numbers were too large.

"I can't read this," she said, nevertheless committing the numbers to memory. "I don't understand."

"Help is coming," Spooky said.

Something began to flicker nearby, and Hope took a surprised step sideways. The flicker turned into an outline of a person, then a shadow, shimmering until the mess of pixels finally resolved into Carter.

"Hi," Carter said. "Hope, right?"

"Yes," Hope said. "And you're Carter. But are you real or fake?"

"Real, as far as I know." Carter smiled. His head turned from the lighthouse to the water, and back to Hope. "Where are we? This isn't mine."

"It's called Serpent's Bay," Hope said.

"How are we together?" Carter asked. "There's only one experiencer allowed at a time."

"Ask him," Hope said, pointing at Spooky. "This is his party."

Carter looked at Spooky, who turned and began collecting the plastic cards from his invisible shelf.

"Wait," Hope said, putting out a hand to stop Spooky. "I didn't get it all. I thought you brought Carter to help me."

Spooky paused, but he didn't return the cards still in his gloved hand.

Carter moved to look over her shoulder. "Are you writing software? Like in the seventies?"

Hope spun around. "What do you mean? You can read it?"

Carter laughed. He had a nice laugh. It triggered another flash: a shattered glass, a black card like the ones Spooky had just collected, a rainy sidewalk that didn't seem familiar.

"Of course I can read it," he said. "I'm a programmer."

"I'm confused," Hope pointed at a blue card: 33-31-20-33-32. "It's a programming language?"

"Time's up," Spooky said.

"Wait," Hope said again. "I haven't memorized enough. Another few minutes." She returned to the cards, repeating the strings of numbers to herself. But they'd already begun to flicker, and after a blink, the home screen hovered before her.

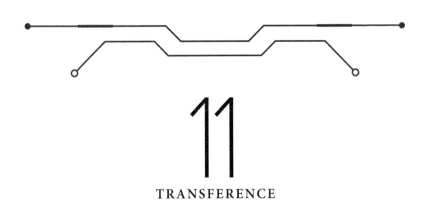

11

TRANSFERENCE

HOPE

The Wilder Sanctuary
Rancho Mirage, California

JONAH HIT THE brakes on the golf cart as a tiny kit fox darted across the dirt road and stopped in the middle. Hope clutched her seat. It was sweltering, and Hope's sweaty skin squeaked against the fake leather.

"Sorry," Jonah said.

"No problem," Hope said. "My blood pressure was already up."

The fox stared at Hope before scurrying off into the grass. Jonah moved forward again, though slower this time.

"Can I ask you something?" Hope watched the scenery roll by, trying to breathe through her apprehension. Nothing about Jonah's movements indicated he'd heard, but she continued anyway. "Do you drive me back to Wilder? When I'm finished with the Labyrinth?"

Jonah nodded, keeping his eyes on the road.

"What am I like, after?" Hope asked.

Jonah gave a half shrug. "Pretty out of it."

"Do I talk to you?" Hope asked.

"No one talks after. No one can," Jonah said, idling in front of the low red door, where Dr. Green was waiting. "Be well, Hope."

Hope slid from her seat and pulled her T-shirt from her body. Even the thin cotton seemed too heavy for this temperature.

Dr. Green tapped her clipboard lightly on the hood. "You'd better get back to campus, Jonah."

The two women watched the cart bump along the path. Hope gathered her hair away from her sticky neck and glanced at Dr. Green. She was wearing a long-sleeved designer blouse, her style and polish making Hope acutely conscious of her own shabbiness.

"Aren't you hot?" Hope asked.

"Shall we go in?" Dr. Green pulled at her silk cuffs. They walked through the red door, past a creepy mermaid fountain near the flat stucco building, and into the lobby.

Dr. Emerson stood against the registration desk, clipboard in one arm, white lab coat starched and spotless.

"Excellent to see you, Hope," she said. "Ready?" She used the fake voice of a preschool teacher, one who didn't enjoy their job but knew how to go through the motions. Now we're going to sing the Cleaning Up Song. Won't that be fun?

Hope fixed her gaze through Dr. Emerson.

After a few more uncomfortable beats, Dr. Emerson handed Hope a small paper cup with two pills, a green capsule and a circular orange tablet. She didn't recognize the green one but swallowed them anyway.

Dr. Green handed her headphones and said, "Come on, Hope. It'll be okay."

Dr. Emerson scanned her badge at the double glass doors, and they walked onto the path to the Labyrinth. The hedges rose on either side of the opening.

"You know the drill, Hope." Dr. Emerson had abandoned the sing-song tone.

Hope nodded, even though she didn't remember anything.

"The purpose of this visit is to surface your memories of the epicenter event that brought you to Wilder. Have you been visualizing as Dr. Stark instructed?"

Again Hope nodded, but she could tell even Dr. Green knew it was a lie.

She cast one final look behind and stepped into the hedge. Hope let her eyes adjust to the dimness as the headphones crackled. She heard the muffled rumble of conversation, periodic snaps and pops and brief silences. Hope craned her neck to the sky, as if doing so would bring in additional light. She felt simultaneously sluggish and jittery, each movement requiring extreme focus.

At last the snapping ceased. "We'd like you to walk for a few minutes," Dr. Emerson said. "The propranolol should start working shortly if it isn't already. As you walk, tell us what you remember just before coming to Wilder. Please begin."

"What was the other pill? The green one?"

"Please try to be as detailed as possible," Dr. Emerson said.

"What was the other pill?" Hope asked again.

"We're testing medications to help your episodic memory," Dr. Green said. "To make what you experience in the Labyrinth stick."

"What if I don't want it to stick?" Hope asked. A sharp smell like the white flower oil her parents used to give her for stomachaches.

"Please try to be as detailed as possible," Dr. Emerson repeated.

Hope began walking. "I woke up in my room. Dr. Salinger was there, sitting in a chair next to my bed. I didn't know where I was. It smelled awful. Like it smells now."

"Let's go further back," Dr. Emerson said. "What are your memories of how you arrived here?"

"I don't know how I got here." Yet as she said it, Hope saw a bed in a white examination room and a tray of random items, like the memory game they used to play at birthday parties: tiny bottles, strange-looking tools, a picture of Hope in the backyard at sunset, their decoder rings, paperbacks with flags jutting from the pages. Someone in red scrubs. She tried to make sense of the images, but the harder she focused, the more indistinct they became. "Was Jonah there?"

"It will come in time," Dr. Green said soothingly. "Let's test some other facets of your memory."

Hope plodded along, continuing her slow shuffle, like an elderly woman using a walker. She was asked a series of entirely random, ridiculous questions: What was your best friend's name as a child? Who is the vice president? What's the capital of Sweden? Who is the head of the Mad Hatters? What sauces were served at lunch last Thursday? Where is the Salton Sea? What was the name of your first pet? How many people visited Spencer last Visiting Day? Where was your first kiss?

"Are you trying to hack into my bank account?" Hope asked.

"We're gathering information to compare to the baseline," Dr. Green said. "Like a lie detector test."

"There's a baseline?" Hope asked. She could now see light around the corner of a hedge.

"What are your memories of Dr. Luke Salinger prior to arriving at Wilder?" Dr. Emerson asked. "Specifically, your therapy sessions?"

There was a growing time delay between the sound in her headphones and Hope's comprehension. "What therapy sessions?"

"For your nightmares," Dr. Emerson said.

Hope made it through the suffocating hedge maze and reached the sunlight outside. Even the stale summer air was a relief; at least it smelled like air. She sank to her knees, palms flat on the hot ground. A metal box about the size of a shoebox rose out of the earth, a creaky door popping open.

"We thought you might be thirsty," Dr. Green said. "A side effect of propranolol is extreme thirst. It can be unpleasant."

The box held a large red cup, the type synonymous with kegs of beer and frat parties. Water sounded delicious, even cucumber water.

Hope drank it all and returned the empty cup to the box. The metal door closed, and the pole disappeared into the ground.

"We're going to give you some background from the time you can't remember," Dr. Emerson said. "Please continue to walk and listen. Periodically we may ask you to pause and close your eyes, to help you visualize."

Hope tried to stay in the middle of the craggy rocks as she stumbled through the dirt toward a squat building in the center. Despite the openness and unobstructed path, something about the walk through the concentric circles was unnerving.

"You began treatment with Dr. Salinger two years ago." Dr. Emerson's voice was buttery smooth. "Through this period you developed an attachment to him, which increased in its intensity over the course of your sessions. Despite his rebukes, you persisted."

"Rebukes?" Hope stumbled once more, picturing Luke in the backyard, feeling his hands in her hair, fingertip tracing her earlobe.

"It may be comforting that this type of situation is incredibly common," Dr. Emerson said. "Women frequently fall in love with their psychiatrists. It's called transference."

"I can't image how anyone would find that comforting," Hope said, reaching the end of the path. She flattened her hands against the wall of a small building, head bowed against its red door.

"It's time to enter the last part of the Labyrinth," Dr. Green said. "Though this part is purposely dark, there are no obstacles."

Hope straightened. It took her three tries to open the door. She walked into the black, hands extending to the side instinctually, disorientation washing over her.

Her palms ran along the smooth walls of the dark corridor. It was still so hot.

Hope wanted to lie on the floor and curl into a ball.

Dr. Green's voice was almost like Morena from the Butterfly Box. "Please relax and take a few deep breaths. We'd like you to perform some visualization. Close your eyes, still your body and your mind. In a moment we'll play you a recording."

Hope did as she was instructed. She counted to ten a few times and began to feel slightly better.

But then, Luke's voice.

"Patient self-esteem appears fair, no reported sleep disturbances, and no reported changes in concentration or memory. Patient currently denies suicidal ideation."

Hope's hands stretched out into the darkness as if she could somehow bring him closer. She hadn't heard his voice in so long, deep and baritone, with a slight raspy edge. Whenever Hope couldn't sleep, Luke would read to her, sometimes from books, sometimes from research he was peer reviewing. It never mattered; she would have listened to him read a grocery list.

Memories flowed through her like faded slides from an old Kodak carousel, with a little whir and buzz before fading to white and advancing to the next picture. Hotel key cards. A party on an estate. Luke's backyard and a red desert sky.

"The patient's acute recall of false memories continues. She is now able to recount events paired with vivid, multisensory details: vacations, parties, moments . . ." At this, Luke paused and cleared his throat. "Moments of perceived intimacy."

Hope slid to the ground, legs bent, nails scratching at the concrete floor. Once again she was twenty-two and engaged to Tony, insisting she hadn't left the front door unlocked, that the dinner was Friday and not Saturday, that she'd paid the insurance bill. At least she'd started out insistent, until Tony twisted it all around.

I believe you *believe it happened that way.*

"Stand up please," Dr. Green said. "Open your eyes and tell us who you see."

Hope braced herself against the cold wall to stand. The TV ahead of her lit up, bathing her in its harsh glow. Her eyes slowly adjusted to the image on the monitor: a pretty young girl in a pink hoodie with a high ponytail and a wide grin.

"Charlie." Hope smiled, reaching out once more.

"Who do you see?" Dr. Green asked again.

"Luke's daughter." Hope pushed further into the wall, feeling her equilibrium slipping. "Charlotte Salinger."

"And what can you tell us about Charlotte?" Dr. Emerson asked.

Hope moved her hands from the sides to the front, groping blindly, but nothing made the vertigo any better. "Charlotte's almost eighteen now. She likes baking and reading. Graphic novels and fantasy." Hope's elbow bumped against the wall. "We both love French fries . . . and milkshakes." She had another flash: of hands in the shape of a heart. Of Luke's voice. *She's got you wrapped around her finger.*

"How did you meet Charlotte?" Dr. Green asked. "Do you remember?"

"She came home early from her friend Maya's. We were eating breakfast. I wasn't fully dressed. I mean, I was wearing Luke's blue shirt . . ." Hope smiled, but it hurt. "I thought he was going to faint. But Charlotte pretended not to notice. She sat down and ate like she'd known me forever."

"Are you certain that happened?" Dr. Emerson said.

"Of course," Hope said. Yet suddenly, she wasn't.

"That isn't what Dr. Salinger has conveyed to us," Dr. Emerson said.

"But it's true," Hope whispered, in the same defeated tone that had always brought a smile to Tony's face.

"Our minds are incredibly susceptible to accepting truths that suit what we desire," Dr. Emerson said. "And the more we repeat this to ourselves, the more we think it's fact."

There you go again, rewriting the narrative.

Hope clenched her hands together, squeezing until it hurt. Her nails were ripped from the concrete floor and cut into her skin. It made sense, suddenly. Why Luke hadn't come to see her, why Charlotte hadn't emailed. Why she couldn't go home. Because there had never been a home to go to.

"Hope," Dr. Emerson said. "It's time to talk about the night of Charlotte's death."

"The night of . . ." Hope's hands fell to her sides. "What did you say?"

Another picture appeared on the screen: Luke's house, his High-lander in the driveway, the red front door, like the door in the main building. The longing to run inside his house pierced through her, sharp and fine.

Then there was a click, and the image was replaced with Luke's home at night, black smoke rising out from the roof like a cartoon, scarlet flames churning from windows in massive plumes.

Click.

A house in the daytime, blackened in places, surrounded by piles of ash, windows missing.

Click.

An ambulance.

Click.

Paramedics wheeling a stretcher down the driveway, a white sheet pulled tight. Onlookers. Neighbors she didn't know.

Click.

The slideshow ended. The pervasive black returned.

Hope flailed her hands out, scrabbling for something to steady herself, finding nothing.

She slid to the floor. "What the fuck was that?"

"Hope," Dr. Green said. "Try to stay calm. Take some deep breaths."

Dr. Emerson cut in: "You went to Dr. Salinger's home, uninvited. You broke into the house, presumably to wait for him. You didn't know Charlotte was asleep in her room."

"Charlie," Hope whispered.

"You were on the living-room sofa," Dr. Emerson said. "You consumed nearly an entire bottle of Jack Daniel's and blacked out with a lit cigarette in your hand. They believe the remains of the bottle spilled and the cigarette ignited a fire. Dr. Salinger arrived home in time to save you, but he didn't know Charlotte was there. She perished in the fire."

A pungent odor flooded Hope's nostrils now, the smell of burning, of ashes and fire and metal.

Hope put her wet face in her hands. The taste of too much whiskey, of stale cigarette smoke, of bile. The melting little body under the sheet in the Shade. She pitched forward onto her hands and knees, sobs echoing along the dark corridor and bouncing back at her.

"No," she said. "I couldn't have done that."

"I'm sorry," Dr. Emerson said. "But you did."

I'm not the villain here, you are.

12

SITUATION ROOM

LUKE
Copeland-Stark Headquarters
La Quinta, California

A T THE GATE, Luke rolled down his window, extracting his badge from the center console where it was caught. It dangled from its scarlet lanyard, COPELAND-STARK in white letters repeating along its length.

The logo was a stylized lightbulb with a lightning bolt instead of a filament. It was a ridiculous graphic, as if a fourteen-year-old kid had drawn it in a paint program circa 1992. Luke was never certain what it was intended to symbolize, other than monumentally shitty ideas.

"Morning, Dr. Salinger," Marco said. He lowered the volume of his sports broadcast and gave Luke a salute. "Early today."

"Too early," Luke said. He inclined his cardboard coffee cup to Marco. "And I haven't had enough coffee to face this meeting."

"Don't think there's enough coffee in the world for working on the weekend." Marco laughed and raised the gate arm.

Luke waved and sped along the winding road leading to Copeland-Stark. There were no cars at this hour, and he slowed near the sprawling stone-and-glass building. Surveying the designated spaces, Luke found he was the last to arrive. That would be noticed. He drove past Jack's shiny black BMW and, as he did most mornings, briefly thought about smashing into it. He pulled his Highlander next to Elliot's Tesla, plugged into one of the charging stations. Luke killed the engine, finished the last cold inch of his latte, and let out a loud, protracted sigh.

The Cure's "Charlotte Sometimes" played from his phone as Luke was stepping out of the car. "You're up early, darling daughter."

"I have a presentation due," Charlotte said. "On recombinant DNA. And it's terrible."

Luke returned to the driver's seat. "I'm sure it isn't."

"Daddy, it *is*." Charlotte's voice became the level of indignant teenage screech that soon only a dog would be able to hear.

"I can help you later," Luke said.

"What do you know about DNA?" Charlotte sounded suspicious.

"It might surprise you I have other talents besides being a giant embarrassment." Luke laughed. "Like, I did have to take a few million science classes in school."

"Okay," Charlotte said slowly, hysterical edge abating. "Can I come tonight instead of tomorrow then?"

"Of course," Luke said. "You know you can come anytime you want. As long as it's okay with—with your mother." Even after all these years, saying his ex-wife's name still gave him an ulcer.

"Great," Charlotte said, though her voice sounded sad.

"Is there something else bothering you?" Luke asked.

"No, it's just . . ." Charlotte exhaled. "Hope used to help me. She's more patient than you are."

"I know." Luke put his forehead on the steering wheel. "I'm sorry. I miss her too."

"No, I'm sorry," Charlotte said. "Thanks for helping me. I'll come after breakfast."

"I'm at work right now, but my meeting shouldn't last long." Suddenly reminded of his purpose, Luke stepped out onto the pavement, closing the car door and heading toward the building. "I'll text you when I'm finished."

"Great," Charlotte said. "And I'll make butterscotch cupcakes."

"It's a deal," Luke said, scanning his badge at the glass doors. "I love you, kiddo."

"Love you too."

Luke stood at the open doorway of Copeland-Stark, hand on the glass door.

Play nice, he reminded himself.

LAUGHTER RANG THROUGH the corridor as Luke stepped into the foyer. Jack Copeland and Liz Emerson were in an alcove, heads bent together, conversation animated. They didn't notice Luke as he quietly hurried in the opposite direction and stopped at Jericho.

They called it Jericho because Elliot insisted, even though the acrylic sign mounted to the wall said Conference Room 3. Stark had a preternatural affinity for superheroes, dating back to high school, possibly even long before.

Elliot and Luke had been one of a handful of town kids in a school of mostly entitled assholes. Elliot's older sister was Luke's year, but she was pretty and popular and Luke had not been one of the cool kids. Elliot had been the same: shy and nerdy, always buried in a comic book. But despite a few shared science classes, Elliot and Luke had only interacted once back then.

Walking home from his job at Shake, Rattle, and Roll one Friday night, a teenage Luke inadvertently crossed paths with a group of jocks leaving a house party. There were eight of them, coked-up and looking for a fight. And Luke happened to be that fight.

Then Elliot drove by with his high beams flashing and horn honking. The kids scattered, leaving Luke panting on the curb and holding his bloody nose.

He spent that night at Elliot's kitchen table, icing his face and talking about *Final Fantasy VII*. Just before dawn, Elliot gave Luke a loaner shirt so he wouldn't have to explain the fight to his mother. They never spoke again, though Luke had always been grateful for his act of compassion.

And then, over a year ago, Luke received an email from Elliot with the subject line *Golden Opportunity*. He hadn't recognized the name and almost deleted it. But within weeks he was wooed and then employed at Copeland Laboratories.

Now Luke wished he had deleted the email.

Luke scanned his badge and entered, almost toppling Jonah and his breakfast cart. "Got you out of bed too, Jonah? Dr. Stark too important to make his own coffee?"

"Funny, Salinger," Elliot called.

Jonah moved plates and mugs to the conference table, transferring a heaping serving platter of various pastries from the cart, adding creamer and pastel packets of sugar substitutes. "I don't mind," he said. He steered his cart toward the door. "Be well, Dr. Salinger."

"Yeah, be well," Luke mumbled. He pulled out a chair across from Elliot as Liz Emerson entered, placing a laptop and a stapled packet of paper in front of him.

"Finally," Luke said, opening the laptop. "You've had this forever."

"You'd better thank me for not telling Jack," Liz said. "You know how he feels about cybersecurity. Did you see Julia Liang's piece in *The 415*?"

"Silicon Valley Bank?" Stark asked, smiling. "I love Julia Liang. She's absolutely ruthless."

"No, today's article," Liz said, placing packets at each seat. "'Curiouser and Curiouser.' In fact, these are the newest set of protocols because of it."

"More security protocols? The Mad Hatters are an urban myth," Luke said. "Like Area 51."

"Just because you're paranoid . . ." Jiang Lu said wryly. He had a deadpan sense of humor, rarely smiled, and almost never laughed unless he was talking to Liz.

Luke tapped the laptop and turned to Dr. Emerson. "Is it going to be faster now?"

"Should be." She massaged her neck. "I added a higher capacity SSD. Why do you need so much processing power?"

"I'm working on something." Luke grabbed a croissant. "Top secret."

"Side hustle for the Mad Hatters?" Jiang asked.

Several people laughed.

"Don't let Jack hear you say that," Liz said. "He'll take you off the Security Breach Response Team."

"How would I survive the heartache?" Luke asked.

More staff entered and settled into chairs, opened laptops, unpacked files from briefcases. Luke exchanged greetings and nods.

"If you get fired, can I have your level-one clearance?" a coworker called out. "I want courtside seats at Chase Center too."

"Be careful what you wish for," said Amelia, sitting down next to Luke.

Among all the big egos in the room, Dr. Amelia Green's mousiness was out of place.

But Luke knew Amelia Green hadn't always been so timid. When they were in graduate school together, Amelia was a different person. She'd been talkative and confident, usually the first one to challenge a professor's assertions or take a fellow student to task around some faulty piece of reasoning.

After earning their doctorates, Luke and Amelia interned togeth-er at several Southern California labs. Then Amelia married Taye, at roughly the same time Luke divorced and moved to the Bay Area. They lost touch for years, until he took the job at Copeland Labs and found Amelia and her brother Jonah working there.

In those intervening years, Amelia had become almost unrecog-nizable. Dr. Green now reminded him of the cat Luke had growing up, the one that bolted under the bed whenever there were guests or someone vacuumed. Skittish and withdrawn.

Luke had always wondered what transformed the friend he'd had in college, but never asked.

He considered Dr. Green now, staring at her lap, sleeves gripped tightly in her fingers, looking like she wanted to be anywhere but in her own skin.

"Jack's entertaining investors tomorrow evening," Liz said, draw-ing Luke back to the present. "Clubhouse at the Vintage. He's expect-ing you and Elliot."

Luke groaned. "I have Charlotte this weekend."

"I'll be there," Elliot said. "But I quit drinking. Losing my svelte figure." He patted his stomach.

Amelia caught Luke's eye and raised her eyebrow.

Luke also wondered how long Elliot's latest period of prohibition would last. He'd attended enough happy hours and investor-wooing cocktails to witness Stark's happy buzz make a sharp turn with little warning.

Several months earlier, Jack had rented a private dining room at La Spiga to charm a few potential investors. Elliot had arrived drunk, then downed a six-hundred-dollar bottle of Giuseppe Quintarelli. By the time the branzino was served, he'd come close to revealing infor-mation in violation of his NDA at least a dozen times. Luke saw them arguing in Jack's car as he left that night, and he hadn't seen Elliot take a drink since.

"I'll cover for you at the dinner," Elliot said to Luke.

"Thanks," Luke said, returning to his laptop. He sifted through a giant backlog of emails, scanning and archiving and ignoring the ones he didn't want to think about.

After what seemed like thousands of emails, an old one from Hope rose to the top of his inbox. It was sent nine months ago, an unexceptional two lines about where to eat for dinner. And then a PS: 1 14-3-19-6 22-3-21. Hope could practically speak in their code, but Luke had never memorized it. This one, though, he knew. *I love you.*

Luke smiled, thinking about all the goofy ways they used to communicate: the decoder ring, messages left in Magic Words, even one particularly nerdy period sending chats in binary. Hope had framed one of those notes and hung it on their bedroom wall. They always tapped it when they left the bedroom, for luck.

"Your email can't be that funny," Jiang said. "None of my emails are that funny."

Luke looked up, the happiness from his memory vaporizing. "Sorry, Dr. Lu, you don't have enough clearance for funny emails." He tilted his screen forward and reached for the bronze carafe. "Why do all these damn war room meetings have to take place on the weekend?"

Like a ninja, Jack Copeland appeared. "Apologies for interrupting your important life with your job, Dr. Salinger."

Jiang snorted, and Liz made a poorly muffled clucking sound. Elliot threw Luke a sympathetic look.

"Sorry." Luke rearranged his face into one of pleasant compliance. *Play nice.*

Jack Copeland placed both palms on the glass table, face stony to silence the room. Jack always ran meetings as if they were in the White House situation room.

It took all of five seconds for the room to fall silent. Jack liked to play the grandfather role most of the time, with his boisterous laughter, off-color jokes, and firm handshakes. He predominantly kept his good-old-boy bigotry in check, though it was only because the drive to make money eclipsed any ideologies he might hold.

"Now, with Luke's permission, we'll get started," Jack said. "Dr. Emerson?"

"I just shared the link with all of you. Julia Liang is reporting that the cyberterrorist group calling themselves the Mad Hatters has attacked another company," Liz said. "This time, it's Zenith Financial."

A low buzz circulated through the room, which Jack quelled with another death stare.

"The CEO is a friend," Jack said. "Everything Julia Liang has reported is true, though he has no idea who her source is. He says it will take months to determine the scope of the damage. They suspect the breach happened over six months ago and were unaware the entire time. This is the end of Zenith. They're in free fall."

"Our analysts believe the Rogue is just getting started," Liz said. "The recent attacks are increasing in size and frequency, hitting companies that were previously thought untouchable."

"No one is untouchable," Jiang Lu muttered.

"Yesterday IT identified some unusual activity in our logs, dating back quite a while," Liz said, holding up her hands at the new swell of murmuring. "We won't know anything definitive for another week. But in an abundance of caution, we're enacting new security measures."

Amelia Green raised her hand like a kid in school and waited to be called on. "Seems like a departure for the Mad Hatters. They usually target individuals, not entire companies."

"While I maintain they're a myth," Luke said, "I agree with Dr. Green. The Hatters don't steal passwords and bank account numbers."

"Except this time they did," Liz said.

"Maybe, but their stuff all has a vigilante justice feel: Kent Rousseau's sexual assault convictions a few months ago, Frank Carr's campaign finances . . ."

"I don't care if the Rogue is Robin Fucking Hood himself," Jack said. "We're at DEFCON 5."

Luke gave up and nodded, fighting an internal battle to keep from telling Jack he meant DEFCON 1.

"These protocols are nonnegotiable." Jack paused, taking his time making eye contact with each person at the table. "*Fortius quo fidelius.* Everyone at this table has a duty to protect our secrets."

13

UNHINGED

HOPE
The Wilder Sanctuary
Rancho Mirage, California

"**B**EAUTIFUL, BEAUTIFUL," AMI crooned. She extended her arms languidly above her head, hands together, fingers pointing at the vast, cloudless sky above. "Be in the here and now. Breathe. In . . . and . . . out."

All the Wilder Weirdos followed suit. Twenty-two pairs of hands in the air, twenty-two inhales and exhales in unison.

Ami bent forward like a taco, arms outstretched. Again, the residents mimicked her movements, though with varying degrees of success. She rose and traversed the grass in her bare feet, adjusting here, praising there. "Excellent, Hope," she said. "You're a natural."

Hope kept her face buried in her mat. It smelled like industrial solvent and those plastic jelly shoes that were all the rage when she was a kid.

Ami was profoundly irritating. She was too perky, too healthy, too squeaky clean. She had the personality of a jar of cupcake sprinkles, and the spelling of her name—Ami with an *i*—made Hope picture a great big bubble floating over it, like the artfully arranged bun currently bobbing on top of her perfect little head.

Quinn alternated between pronouncing her name in French and calling her the Minx. One of his favorite pastimes was to spin Ami's backstory: she was a secret dominatrix, working at an S & M parlor in Cathedral City, slapping rich guys into submission. She wrote crappy online porn on the side, calling it women's erotica, under the pen name of Antoinette La Chatte. Or, she was a drug mule, swallowing condoms full of smack and transporting them across the border to her kingpin boyfriend, Diego "el tiburón" Silva.

Ami stood over Carter, who was bent over himself next to Hope. He resembled more of a lumpy burrito than a taco. Ami pushed on the small of his back, and he groaned. "Acknowledge your limits today," she said brightly. "There is always a tomorrow." She threaded her way toward the front once more.

"I think tomorrow I'll also be acknowledging my limits," Carter muttered.

Hope snickered. Carter lifted his head an inch to grin at her. Hope turned away as the same series of images flickered through her mind: broken glass, a shiny black card, a dark sidewalk in the rain.

"The light in me honors the light in you," Ami said. She placed her palms together and bowed her head. She inhaled and exhaled, opening her arms and extending them, calling down all the splendor. "Namaste."

Participants rolled up their mats and tossed them into a pile. In clumps of two or three, but mostly solo, identically gray-clad soldiers plodded along the paved road leading toward the main building.

Quinn was near the front, speaking animatedly with Nina. Hope wanted to maintain a wide berth around that circus and kept her distance from the others. Carter threw his mat in the pile and jogged a little to catch up to Hope.

"Hey," he said.

Hope slowed. "Enjoy yoga today?"

"Sure," Carter said. "I love being told I suck in a really nice way. It's great for my path to perfection."

"'Perfection is an illusion based on our own perception,'" Hope said automatically. After a beat she smirked, and Carter relaxed.

"Men's bathroom," Carter said.

"Pardon?"

"It's a poster in the men's bathroom, right above the urinals." He gave a sideways glance. "I guess that's when a man is most likely to need a little boost."

"That explains why I've never seen it." Hope laughed. "It's a channel on the TV though. I watch it when I can't sleep. No real TV here."

"I miss binge-watching," Carter moaned. "All those finales I'll never see."

"You think you'll be in here a long time?" Hope asked.

"Until I'm cured." Carter shrugged. "How long have you been here?"

"Six months," she said. "It's starting to feel as if I've only lived here and nowhere else."

"Why are you here?" Carter asked.

Hope bit her bottom lip.

"You don't have to tell me," Carter said quickly.

"I can't really remember last year at all. I know I did something . . . bad. They're helping me remember. But it's not working. I never remember anything."

Hope didn't share personal information with anyone here, not even Quinn. In a place like Wilder, it was wise to keep to yourself. So she wasn't sure why everything came tumbling out with Carter, why he somehow seemed safer.

"I did something bad too. But unfortunately, I do remember," Carter said, and his face tightened. "Is that everyone's story here?"

"Memory is Copeland-Stark's cash cow," said Hope. "But from what I know, and all I know comes from Quinn, most people are here for substance abuse or regular old self-sabotage. They're mostly celebrities, after all."

Despite their slow pace, she and Carter caught up to the Wilder group.

"I've been trying to work up the nerve to talk to you for days," Carter said. "But I'm not great at talking to people." Carter ran his hands through his hair, cheeks pale pink.

"Me neither," Hope said. "It can get pretty lonely at Wilder if you don't have anyone to talk to. If it weren't for Quinn, I probably wouldn't say anything."

They neared the crowd ahead, where the residents were gathered in a clump.

"Have you ever been to Sweden?" Carter asked.

"No," Hope said, disappointed. He'd seemed so normal for a while.

A commotion ahead drowned out Carter's next words. Nina and Quinn were together in the middle of a circle created by Wilder onlookers, like high-school kids fighting in the quad.

Nina was in another rage, arms flailing, skeletal fingers curled into claws. Quinn crouched like a sumo wrestler and sprung for her wrists, causing Nina to kick out and scuff Quinn's shiny white sneakers. That wasn't going to go over well.

"You little piece of shit," she shrieked at Quinn.

Code Five.

Hope clenched her hands. She'd never been outside when a code was called, where there were no bars to block the windows. What were the procedures? Where was Spooky to recite the patient handbook?

From the direction of Wilder, Dr. Stark came running with Dr. Emerson trailing, stilted by her strappy heels.

Fernando, the nice tech from the Butterfly Box, followed close behind.

"Get away from me, you fucking psycho!" Nina kicked out at Dr. Emerson.

Fernando wrapped his arms around Nina from behind and pulled her away. Quinn put his hands on his knees and bent over, panting theatrically.

"Nina." Dr. Emerson took a step forward. "Let's go inside and talk."

"I'm not talking about shit with you." She turned to Dr. Stark, chin pointing at Dr. Emerson. "Watch out for this one, Elliot. She's one crafty fucking bitch."

Nina's hair came loose from her ponytail and fell into her eyes, flopping as she cursed. She wiped spit on her shoulder, swaying a little, and faced the crowd around her. "Y'all think you're here on vacation, don't you? Eating fancy food, yoga poses, painting pictures." She didn't pronounce the *c* in pictures. "It ain't a goddamn party. Y'all gotta wake the fuck up!"

Residents began to peel off, resuming their walk toward Wilder. It was almost lunchtime, and the Nina Show could be cool but not cool enough to miss lunch.

Hope, Carter, and only a few others remained. Quinn came to stand next to Hope.

"Wait!" Nina called at the retreating backs of the Wilder Weirdos, though none did.

Nina turned to Carter and Hope, eyes narrowing before her face cracked into a wicked smile.

"Sucker for a damsel in distress, aren't you, Mr. Maelstrom? Believe me, Hope doesn't want your saving," she said to Carter. "I wonder what Jordan Lin would say about you two. I know you don't take a shit unless she says it's okay."

"How do you know Jordan?" Carter pushed at his glasses. Nina leaned in and whispered something in his ear.

Hope took a step closer in an attempt to hear Nina, but Dr. Stark got between them.

"Nina." Dr. Stark moved forward, hands out, palms up. His voice was soft, as if Nina were a child who'd pulled the puppy's tail. Gentle, gentle. "Let's use one of our coping strategies. Come on, deep breaths. Fernando, it's all right."

Nina locked eyes with Dr. Stark. After a minute, she closed her eyes, chest heaving.

"That's it," Dr. Stark said. "Let's visualize. How about Oscar night?"

Like magic, Nina straightened regally, as if she were onstage, still and dreamy. *I'd like to thank the Academy.*

Dr. Stark put an arm around Nina and guided her up the path.

"Wow," Quinn breathed. "He's like the Freak Whisperer."

Dr. Emerson turned. "Fernando, take Quinn to a processing room so we can be certain he is in a centered state of mind. Also, please wear your key card at all times."

Fernando nodded, pulling his lanyard from his pocket and yanking it over his head. He gestured to Quinn to follow.

Dr. Emerson smoothed her hair and surveyed the remaining residents. "Off to lunch. Be well."

The stragglers chorused, "Be well, Dr. Emerson," and headed up the path to the main building. Hope glanced at Quinn, who winked at her.

✦✦✦

Lunch was "burgers." Burgers at Wilder were, not surprisingly, extremely disappointing. Hope wanted a real cheeseburger, served in a red basket on waxed paper, grease and chili dripping off the sides. The burger on her plate this afternoon was a black bean and quinoa concoction, served with turkey bacon and avocado puree on whole-grain buns, kale chips on the side.

It was like community theater on a plate: passable in content, but slightly tragic in execution.

"These actually aren't terrible," Carter said, after taking a cautious bite and chewing on it as if it were a math problem. "I just wish they didn't call it a burger. It's misleading."

"You're being generous," Hope said. "They're terrible."

"You know," Carter said. "Nina's not wrong. Sometimes the food, the yoga, everything about this place makes me forget why I'm really here."

"They do that on purpose, to keep you complacent," Hope said. "Positive mindset helps your reconsolidation. Don't worry, people don't freak out often. Nina is probably the most unhinged. Overtly, anyway."

"I guess," Carter said. "But she knew stuff."

"What stuff?" Hope asked.

"My company, Maelstrom. My business partner, Jordan," he said. "How would she know those things?"

"Your company?" Hope thought about the VR headset, the word Maelstrom etched along the band. "You made the Butterfly Box?"

"Butterfly Box?" Carter's eyes sparkled. "I like it. Way better than Erleben device." He pronounced it *air-leh-ben*. "The butterfly is for the butterfly effect. You know, the smallest changes making the biggest impacts?"

"Did you do the Shade?" Hope asked.

"Nope." Carter pushed his glasses up his nose. "And I'm not technically allowed to visit."

"So who did it?" Hope asked.

"I had the same question," Carter said, chewing on a kale chip. "So I went to talk to Spooky. Have you seen his wall? He's got serious talent."

"I've seen it," Hope said.

"I had questions for him. Technical questions. Even though I designed ninety-five percent of Erleben, he's doing things with it I didn't program. Things I didn't know it could do."

"I don't get it." Hope pushed her fork through her avocado puree. "Spooky made it? And he's bringing us in there together?"

"Hellooooo, party people!" Quinn pulled out a chair and set his plate next to Hope's. "How about that prison brawl today? Psycho is the New Black, *n'est-ce pas*?" He flexed his bicep at Carter, refusing to stop until Carter gave it an embarrassed squeeze of appreciation.

Quinn winked at Hope and began to cut his burger into equal bite-sized pieces.

"What happened with Dr. Emerson?" Carter asked.

"Oh, the usual." Quinn waved a hand through the air dismissively. "I had to type everything out and then fingerpaint my feelings."

Hope crossed her arms. "You're going to make us ask, aren't you? Just to prolong the drama."

Quinn's face was a mask of innocence. "Ask?"

"The fight," Carter said. "What happened?"

Quinn spread tomato puree onto a chunk of burger with his knife, back and forth like a bricklayer. He loved to spin a tale, and his favorite thing in all the world was a captive audience. He chewed laboriously before speaking again.

"It was crazy!" He paused and regarded Hope and Carter in turn, solemnly. "No offense."

Carter laughed. Hope didn't. It was one of Quinn's favorite lines, and it was only funny the first time. If it were even funny then.

"I really don't know what happened," Quinn continued. "Honestly. It's not a great story. One minute we're talking, about how her big break is coming, how she has an audition playing Jake Gyllenhaal's love interest. Or Ryan Gosling's. I always mix those two up." He ate another forkful of burger and patted his mouth with the corner of his napkin. "All BS, by the way. But anyhow, the next minute she's scratching my eyes out."

"You're full of it," Hope said to Quinn. "What was the last thing you said to her? Before she started beating you up?"

"To clarify, she didn't beat me up. She did get dirt all over my shoes, however." Quinn lifted his now scuffed sneakers as proof. His brown eyes gleamed, a corner of his mouth curling into a smirk. "I *may* have asked her if she'd ever consider returning to her other screen career."

"I knew it," Hope groaned at Carter. "Quinn says Nina used to be a porn star."

Carter considered that, before blushing again and attacking his burger with gusto. Hope had never met anyone so easily embarrassed.

Quinn shrugged. "Just another day in Cuckoo Castle."

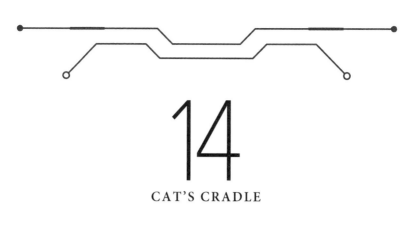

14

CAT'S CRADLE

HOPE
The Wilder Sanctuary
Rancho Mirage, California

AFTER THE LOVE Addiction/Love Avoidance group on Thursdays, residents were allowed thirty minutes online. Six months ago, Hope looked forward to Thursdays, but she never used her full time anymore. And truthfully, it wasn't exactly internet. After running through an extensive series of filters, only the most insipid websites remained: videos of kittens, cooking videos on superfast speed, quizzes like "Which K-Pop Star is Your Soulmate?"

Regardless, all the Wilder Weirdos coveted this time, as no computers or phones were allowed otherwise. The single exception was a resident Hope had never spoken to: Royce.

Royce was a big-time Hollywood agent. Before Hope arrived at Wilder, she didn't even think they made people like Royce anymore. Even Quinn just called him Royce, admitting he couldn't come up with anything more elitist if he tried. Royce was a character from a Bret Easton Ellis novel, a time traveler appearing straight from the eighties and skipping all the decades in between. Royce constantly paced around on the patio or the Zen Garden, shouting demands into his cell. He was working on kicking all three of his addictions simultaneously: premium vodka, high-class sex clubs, and the best blow in Beverly Hills. Even his proclivities were dated. There was some sort of teenage trauma buried in there too, though Quinn didn't know exactly what. But Royce still needed to fire people and close billion-dollar deals now and again, runny nose notwithstanding. And when you were worth what Royce was worth, you could have your Wi-Fi at Wilder.

So Royce was predictably missing from the group that day. Yet Nina was also absent, and no one had seen her for a week. At breakfast, Quinn had speculated about the possibility she'd been kicked out of Wilder for good.

Hope did enjoy being in the library, or the Multimedia Resource Center, as stated on the door. She wasn't sure if three desktop computers made it multimedia, but she nevertheless loved the space. It was in a corner of the Wilder complex, boasting high ceilings, a vast skylight, and endless shelves of books. Several dream interpretation books were stacked on the scratchy cloth sofa next to Hope, *Dreams from A to Z* by S. Groess currently open in her lap. Spooky was on an adjacent chair, his papers spread out on a low table.

Tess, a small, mousy little thing with stringy dishwater hair, leaned against a shelf on the other side of Spooky. Tess mainly just stared through people with her vapid, glassy eyes. She spoke in morose, dejected tones and seemed to only be happy when others were not. Even so, she didn't stand out as one of the stranger residents at Wilder.

That day Tess was playing a game of cat's cradle with her hands, minus the yarn. Her short black fingernails were somehow mesmerizing.

"Page fourteen," Spooky said, watching Tess. "'Nail polish, polish remover, or synthetic nail products are prohibited as they can be misused as inhalants.'"

Tess ignored Spooky, continuing to contort her fingers into odd angles. Hope flipped through her dream book, past a technicolor picture of an insect with a disturbingly human face and another of a hairy spider, until Tess's low humming broke her concentration. Her melody was eerily saccharine, like a freaky child in a horror movie.

Tess trailed her fingers along the books like she was playing a harp, then looked directly at Hope. "It should be here in the library. Somewhere."

"What's that?" Hope asked.

"Jiang's book." Tess rubbed her nose with the palm of her hand, gaze drifting off. "Dr. Jiang Lu," she said again, so loudly that everyone in the library looked up, but then quickly down again. Spooky closed his notebook and took off.

"Great. I'll look for it." Hope had no idea what Tess was talking about, but it seemed like the fastest way to end the conversation.

"You used to know," Tess said. "Before."

"Before what?"

Tess pursed her lips. "Before we came to Wilder. You talked about it."

"I talked about it?" Hope closed *Dreams from A to Z*. "Tess, you were here when I got to Wilder. We don't have a before."

"In my father's living room. By the glass dogs."

She had no memory of ever being close to a glass dog, much less more than one. For a brief moment Hope saw images of people, dressed up for a party or a wedding. But their faces were indistinct and quickly vanished.

Hope pushed herself further back against the scratchy sofa. "I don't know your father, and I think I would remember a house with glass dogs."

"You just choose not to remember," Tess said.

Hope wanted to laugh. For six months, she had endured sessions in the Butterfly Box, weekly therapy, and visits to the Labyrinth, all to recover her lost memories. If remembering were a choice, Hope would already be home.

Tess selected a book, Sylvia Plath probably, and wedged it under her arm. The macabre humming commenced again, and Tess lowered herself to the floor. Fortunately, it seemed their exchange had concluded.

Hope left to join Quinn at the computers. He was scrolling through celebrity gossip sites, practically drooling on the keyboard. She opened a browser and a counter projected prominently on the wall, counting down her thirty minutes in bold, red numbers.

At her terminal Hope opened the Wilder email program, unsurprised to see her account empty. She clicked on her sent folder, a chronological record of the myriad emails she'd sent to Luke and Charlotte. Dozens of letters, all without a response. She closed the browser.

"The Mad Hatters have done it again," Quinn said, not turning away from Buzzfeed. "This time the Rogue took down Zenith Financial, big-time. It seems their CEO has a thing for young girls, says Julia Liang."

"Horrible," Hope said. "What do you know about Tess?"

"Not a lot. Schizoaffective, depressive," Quinn said. "Hallucinations and delusions."

"Sounds fun," Carter said, taking a seat. His own counter clicked on.

"She basically needs to carry a creepy doll around all the time to complete the trope." Quinn moved his mouse. "Holy shit, check this out." He swung his monitor so they could both see.

Adult Film Star Kitty Diamond Found Dead in Her Home

LOS ANGELES, CA — Nina Hart (nee Nina Hartwell) was found dead in her La Canada home in the Silver Shores Community early this morning from an apparent drug overdose.

Hart's agent, Charles O'Kane, called police when she did not appear as scheduled for an audition and had not returned calls or texts by the following evening.

Hart began her career in adult films at the age of 19 under the name Kitty Diamond. She appeared in over two hundred adult films during her decade in the industry. Hart also appeared on Season Three of the reality television program Extreme Divas. *It is reported that shortly after appearing on* Divas *she developed a drug addiction and, according to O'Kane, had spent the last three years in and out of rehabilitation clinics across Southern California and Arizona.*

"She was a good kid," said O'Kane. "Troubled, but a good soul. She'll be missed."

The coroner has not yet ruled out suicide as the cause of Hart's death, authorities report.

Hart is survived by her father, Duane, and a younger brother. She was 41 years old.

15

MIRROR GATE

HOPE

The Wilder Sanctuary
Rancho Mirage, California

THE SKY IN the Shade was a baleful gray, artificial wind whipping leaves and pebbles around Hope and Carter. A torrent of rain fell, and Hope tilted her head to try and feel drops on her cheeks. In the desert, rain is a welcome revelation, even virtual rain.

Hope's eighties outfit was absent. Spooky or Morena, or whomever programmed this world, clad her in black leggings and Luke's blue shirt. It was an odd sensation, standing in a mud puddle, not feeling the rain pouring around her. At least Hope wasn't cold or uncomfortable, which was a perk of life in the Shade.

There were no symbolic markers that had quickly become routine. No lighthouse, no notes nailed to anything, no cards, and no Spooky. Only more aspen, more jagged rocks, more endless white forest.

"Did you think we'll get the code again today?" Carter asked. He pushed his glasses up his nose, though his avatar wasn't wearing any. "Why is it so important?"

Hope couldn't tell Carter what she desperately wanted to believe. It would sound absurd if she said it aloud, to the universe. And if she said it, Carter could dispel her fantasy that the message came from Luke.

"No idea," she said instead. "It's a mystery."

"Cool, a quest. I'm all about the quest." Carter picked up a small rock and launched it. It flickered before it vanished against the wall of trees.

The forest began to disappear, moss and trees transforming into a shimmering gray-blue barrier, curved and tall, stretching to the ceiling. It surrounded them in a corner of the Butterfly Box, reflecting their faces back.

"I think we're at Mirror Gate," Carter said.

The wall's surface began to flow and shift, almost as if it were breathing. Their reflections were also moving, faces rippling into small waves.

"It's beautiful," Hope said, poking her hand into the hypnotic curtain.

"Jesus!" Carter pulled her back, shaking his head. "It's like a horror movie. You don't leave the teenagers alone to have sex, you don't get in the car without checking the backseat, you don't answer the phone when you're alone. Also, you don't reach out and touch the shiny thing in the middle of a quest. It's like Role-Playing 101."

"Fine," Hope said, dropping her hand. "But aren't people supposed to do something during a quest?"

"Fair," Carter said. He inspected the wall for a moment and finally shrugged. "Upon deeper reflection, I've determined we have to walk through."

He extended his hand to her, and Hope took it. Lately, she'd found herself looking forward to stolen moments of conversation with Carter, and the prospect of extended time in the Shade. They'd quickly fallen into an easy, companionable rhythm, as if they'd known each other far longer than a few weeks. He was clever and sweet, but also utterly guileless, which was refreshing in comparison to Hope and Quinn's endless vortex of sarcasm.

"Ready?" Carter asked.

Hope nodded, and they stepped through together into a circular room surrounded by an enclosure of water.

"You're late," Spooky said. He sat at a desk like Stark's in the center of the room, placidly observing their entry, fingers steepled in a Sherlock Holmes pose. Spooky had shed his wizard attire, wearing only jeans, a faded *Firefly* T-shirt, and red Chucks.

"What's it going to be tonight?" Carter asked. "Maiden sacrifice? John Hughes movie reenactment?"

"Pretty in Gray?" Hope suggested. "Bit derivative."

"Agree, but undeniably a moneymaker," said Carter.

Spooky silenced their snickering with a withering stare, as if they'd ruined the punch line of his joke. Then he resumed his pose, looking like he should be stroking a cat and wearing a monocle.

"Let's begin."

The wall moved and warped, contracting and reforming until it became the walls of a bedroom. To her right was a picture window framing a mountain range she knew by heart. On her left was a black-and-white poster of a whale with the words *Don't Panic* printed across the bottom.

Luke's bedroom. Their bedroom. Hope turned to the doorway and the poorly hung full-length mirror on the bedroom door. She could almost see Luke getting ready for work, speaking to her in the reflection. She could almost feel his tie in her hands as she knelt on the edge of the bed to fix it. Hope missed the seemingly insignificant things most—throwaway moments like tying his tie or sharing a soda or riding in the car.

"Cool, *Hitchhiker's Guide,*" Carter said, eyeing the poster. He looked at Hope, and his grin slid away. "What's wrong?"

Hope tried to answer, but no words would come. She wiped her face and felt the scratch of haptic gloves, a jarring reminder she was still in the Butterfly Box and not at home.

Spooky pointed at a frame above the light switch. In the air he spread his fingers apart, and the frame grew until it was magnified to the size of the former door.

It was a blue Post-it note, with strings of zeroes and ones written in Luke's blocky writing. Hope stared at it, remembering when he'd stuck it to the bathroom mirror. Remembering how she deciphered it and framed it for the bedroom, so Luke would see it on his way out each day. How they would tap it every morning, for luck.

"It says 'I love you.'" Her voice was hoarse. "I'd . . . forgotten."

"No, it doesn't," Carter said, eyebrows knitting together. "It says one, fourteen, three—"

"That's because it's coded from my code into binary . . ." Hope turned to Spooky. "Holy crap. 'Try zero one.' Binary. It's coded twice."

Spooky waved dramatically through the air like an orchestra conductor, and Luke's bedroom disappeared. They had returned to the circular room, with rows and rows of numbers undulating on the Mirror Gate wall.

"We have fifteen minutes left," Spooky said. An enormous red timer, far bigger than the library clocks, hovered above.

"Can we take a screenshot?" Carter asked, surveying. "I'd be finished a lot faster."

Spooky set his sneakers on the desk, crossing his legs at the ankles.

Hope and Carter digested the seemingly endless panel of numbers, which were still nonsense to Hope.

"You said it was a programming language?" Hope asked.

Carter nodded. "It's ASCII."

The timer beeped once, like a microwave: 14 minutes, 30 seconds.

Carter swiped his finger across a section of numbers: 051 049 051 057. As he did, the sequence illuminated. Then he drew over them, as if he were writing on a whiteboard. The string disappeared, replaced with only two numbers: 31 and 39.

"Thirty-one and thirty-nine," Carter said to Hope. "What's that in your code?"

Hope shook her head. "Nothing. Mine's a substitution cipher, for kids. Between one and twenty-six only. Could it be backward? Thirteen is L, but there's no ninety-three."

Looking confused, Carter turned back to the wall.

Hope held her breath.

"What's nineteen?" Carter asked.

"V," Hope said.

Carter groaned and turned to Spooky. "ASCII to Hex? Come on."

Spooky, from behind the desk, shrugged.

"It's coded three times," Carter said to Hope, making a mark over the *31 39*. It disappeared, and a *V* popped up in its place with a satisfying trill of digital sounds, like a slot machine.

Hope watched as Carter performed the same ritual of staring and talking to himself, highlighting, then replacing the line of numbers with more numbers. As the numbers turned into her code, Hope followed behind, writing each letter.

The microwave beeps continued to count down.

They only had a moment to stare at the finished message. It disappeared with the final beep, timer and numbers vanishing, returning once more to the silent, shimmering mirror.

"'Verb a lover shadowing memory mechanic'?" Carter said to Hope. "Does that make sense to you?"

"Another code?" Hope suggested. "Or an anagram?"

Carter didn't answer, and when Hope turned he had disappeared, along with Spooky and Mirror Gate. She was back in the Butterfly Box, head pressed into one of the gray foam walls.

16

HEAD GAMES

HOPE
The Wilder Sanctuary
Rancho Mirage, California

N ONE OF THE doctors mentioned Nina. There was no announcement, no solemn moment of silence or meditation, no grief counselors to offer support. The absence of any acknowledgment that Nina disappeared one day and subsequently died—accompanied by Quinn's penchant for dishing the best Wilder dirt—meant everyone knew within hours.

For days, the noncelebrity residents buzzed with increasingly outlandish rumors about Nina's death. Some thought the Wilder doctors were behind it, and that Nina was now buried in the Zen Garden. Others suggested she was a Russian spy (or a government-controlled robot), ultimately taken out by a CIA assassin. Others eschewed the entire article as a hoax, believing Nina faked the whole thing, with plans to make a splashy comeback for publicity.

Though all the A-listers detoxing at Wilder had industry connections, they kept their distance from the gossip. Even Royce, the only resident at Wilder with internet access on top of colleagues in the biz, refused to engage. But as all things do, the stories were eventually exhausted. Nina was rarely mentioned again, except as a cautionary tale never to cause a Code. No one wanted to end up as Soylent Green.

The only person who wouldn't let it drop was Carter. Any moment he was with Quinn and Hope, the conversation inevitably returned to Nina.

Hope would rather be spending her energy figuring out the message. *Verb a lover shadowing memory mechanic.* For the first time in half a year, she had a purpose. A quest, as Carter liked to call it.

But Hope couldn't be observed writing, or for that matter, appearing too interested in anything. She rarely had time during the day with Carter alone, and only a small stretch at bedtime before the medication took over—though at night Hope had tried scrambling the letters, writing them backward, even trying to find a new code buried within. So far, nothing.

That morning she and Quinn sat on the main lawn, backs to each other. Hope stared out at the mountains, at the sky that would always tether her to Luke. Periodically she would take a deep breath and let it out, chest heaving.

Quinn divided his attention between the granite fountain and a pacing, muttering Carter.

"You're killing my Zen vibe," Quinn said finally. "I don't know whether to watch you or the fountain."

Carter stopped short and seemed surprised to see them. "Sorry," he said. "I'm still thinking about Nina."

"You need a new hobby," Quinn said. "Nina was a junkie. Junkies OD."

"I guess." Carter resumed his pacing.

The water from the fountain dribbled over the sides of its three nesting bowls, trickling into the pebbles below. Hope trailed her fingers in it. "I think the Labyrinth is getting to you."

"It's not that. And obviously Nina was a tweaker." Carter threw himself onto the ground. He pulled out a few blades of grass and tossed them to the side. "What about all the stuff she said? How did she know about Maelstrom? About my partner, Jordan?"

"When did she say all that?" Quinn asked.

"You were standing right next to me," Hope said. "After your fight with her."

"I don't remember," Quinn said, standing and stretching. He raised one leg and mimed an exaggerated yoga pose to the sky.

"And it's not just Nina, there's—" Carter broke off his sentence as Royce wandered onto the lawn. As always, Royce was shouting into the phone pressed to his ear.

Hope scrutinized Carter. His expression was grim, hands clenched at his sides. Lately, he seemed to shift from excited to introverted in moments, his silences long and heavy.

He still made jokes, still bantered with Quinn, but Hope could sense a growing anxiety underneath.

"Let's go," Quinn said. He must have noticed it also, or perhaps Royce's swearing tirade was killing his Zen vibe as well. "Carter needs a visit to Planet Funkotron."

⁕⁕⁕

THEY CALLED IT Head Games, the rec room at Wilder. Or maybe it was only Quinn who called it that. It boasted a Ping-Pong table, a pool table (at least that's what Hope thought it was, until Carter told her it was for snooker), and bookshelves of unopened board games. The game boxes were colorful and new, tokens still in baggies or attached to their original casements, as if waiting for some kid to twist them off their little plastic prisons and put them into play.

An ancient Sega Genesis console lived in a corner, the sole piece of technology at Wilder that wasn't cutting edge. No one ever played it except Carter. The Sega came with a paltry offering of nineties games like *Lemmings* and *Batman Forever*, but Carter always played *Toejam and Earl*. Hope and Quinn never played, but both enjoyed watching. Quinn loved the game's groovy soundtrack and hot tub, and Hope liked the hamster in the big ball.

"What I was starting to say," Carter said, fingers flying across the controller, "is that Wilder knows stuff about me they shouldn't know."

"Oh, do spill," Quinn said.

"It's nothing," Carter said. "I have a juvenile record, from getting into some trouble in high school, low-level stuff. But I used to be sort of a delinquent with my computer skills."

"I'll be damned," Quinn said. "The Boy Scout has a rap sheet."

"My point is, those records are sealed," Carter said. "I've never told anyone about it. So how does Wilder know?"

Hope let Carter's words sink in. "And if they do, what else do they know?"

"I'd tell you," Quinn said. "But all the files are locked up in the Wilder dark web and I can't see them anymore." He tapped a deck of cards on his thigh, *California* spelled out in an arc, each letter filled with a landmark or monument.

"What do you mean, dark web?" Carter asked.

"What do you mean, anymore?" Hope asked, at the same time.

"Where do you think my intelligence comes from? You think Wilder Weirdos just tell me everything?" Quinn shuffled the deck, fingers moving swiftly and with precision, blurring the cards.

"Yes," Hope said. She was starting to believe Carter wasn't overreacting after all. "That's what I did think."

Quinn balanced the cards on his knee and took a deep breath, preparing to hold court. Hope reclined on her elbows, legs bent, staring at Quinn.

"As you both know, I'm quite charming," Quinn began. "Wendy, the chippy at the front desk, adored me. She also loved sharing her boyfriend troubles, of which there are a staggering multitude. And I'm always ready to offer advice about the inner workings of the complex enigma that is the male mind. Anyhoo . . . Wendy had a proclivity for texting sexy things to her Sancho, then turning away from her computer. I can't help if the 411 from Intake Days is just out there while she's sending tit pics."

"When's the next Intake Day?" Carter demanded.

"It doesn't matter. Stark fired Wendy when he found out about the sexting. *Adios* Wendy, hello Morgan."

"So make friends with Morgan." Carter's voice rose an octave.

Quinn shook his head. "I'm trying, but she isn't very talkative. She does everything Dr. Stark says. Also, she's one of those people that says 'Right?' to end every sentence. But have patience, my pet. It'll happen."

"We need to get in a different way," Carter said. He set the Sega controller aside as Toejam entered an elevator. "Soon."

"Impossible," Quinn said. "There's no other way."

Hope studied Quinn for a moment. "Q, have you read my intake file?"

He winked. "Your secrets are safe with me."

"I don't have any secrets," Hope said.

Quinn chuckled. "Whatever you say, Hopeless."

"Why can't we get in?" Carter asked.

"Because, darling," Quinn said, "Wilder is on some übersecure, unbreakable system. All the technology is connected to the vents and the Butterfly Box. Even the washing machines. That's how they track us and listen to our conversations. It has to do with the underground tunnels and the funky smells we're inhaling all the time. And no one ever truly leaves because they get turned into tofu scramble."

Carter let out a laugh. "You're full of shit."

A chime rang, signaling yoga was about to begin. Carter shut off his game and the trio left Head Games, ambling onto the path toward the Zen Garden.

"Of course I'm full of shit," Quinn said, jogging to catch up to Carter. "That part was embellished, for a more dramatic denouement. But what's true is the . . . whatever . . . the system at Wilder—"

"The network, you mean? Or the infrastructure?" Carter asked.

"How the hell am I supposed to know?" Quinn said. "Just trust me. It's crazy secure, like Pentagon secure. Like even the Rogue couldn't crack it."

"I can crack it," Carter said, with an uncharacteristic smugness.

"I like you, Carter." Quinn laughed. "You're scrappy. Mad respect, but you're overestimating your talent."

"I'm not especially talented," Carter said. "But I did write the software. And I left myself a couple of back doors."

17

ABSOLUTION

HOPE
The Wilder Sanctuary
Rancho Mirage, California

T HE WHITEBOARD FEATURING the Responsibility Framework
(aka Crappy Chores Chart) outside the dining room was supposed to be updated weekly, though in Hope's experience that
never happened. After breakfast, she'd begun walking with Quinn toward the laundry room as usual, when Jonah stopped her, pointing
to the chart and escorting her to the Library for Inventory Care. He
locked her inside and left without a word.

Inventory Care turned out to be a Wilder term for cataloging books.
According to the page of directions left for Hope, each book required
a stamp in red ink (*Property of The Wilder Sanctuary: A Division of
Copeland-Stark*) on the inside cover. She was then to place a sticker on
the spine and enter it into the system with a barcode scanner.

Hope soon learned more about the library than she'd ever wanted
to know, including that Wilder housed thousands of scientific journals
and research papers on neuroscience. Each title she encountered was

duller than the last: *Applied Cognitive Psychology, Retrieval Practices and Behavioral Therapy, The Unexplored Hippocampus.*

Wilder curated self-help guides and an expansive collection of fluffy fiction for the residents. There was a definite chick lit epidemic happening in this new influx of books. In fifteen minutes, Hope had stamped four stacks of candy-colored covers adorned with shopping bags, stiletto heels, lipstick kisses, and curly typefaces, all with titles like *Living in the Moment, Successories, Smooth Operator.*

Hope's next book had a big, white male hand pointing at her from the cover. *You Control YOU!* it demanded, in bold sans serif. She opened the volume, carefully stamping in a straight line across the inside, fanning her hand over the wet ink.

The mindless repetition and order of this process was comforting. It was peaceful sitting in the cavernous library, smelling the books, alone. Many of the Wilder residents, mostly the celebrities, avoided the solitary chores whenever possible. But Hope knew being alone could be a gift.

Near the end of her darkest days with Tony, he could sense Hope was pulling away. As a result, he rarely left her side. For years, the shroud of his personality had woven a taut, low-grade tension through everything in the apartment, through the air, through Hope. *Have you accomplished anything today? Productivity isn't your best asset, is it?*

She spent those years with Tony at attention, perpetually waiting for an order to stand down, which she knew would never come. In the rare moments they were apart, the world seemed lighter, as if the walls themselves let out a collective exhale of relief at his absence.

When she first moved in with Luke, Hope still held herself in the same manner, ready to bolt as soon as that feeling returned. Yet it never did. As Hope gradually allowed herself to relax, she discovered she missed Luke when he was away, felt a giddy anticipation at the sound of his car in the driveway, smiled when she heard his keys in the yellow front door. And while she'd always understood it was possible, Hope had only experienced it firsthand with Luke. She'd been able to love him, completely, because he'd let her breathe.

A loud knocking punctured Hope's thoughts and the stillness of the library. She set the scanner on the table and went to open the library door, head poking into the hallway.

"Hey," Carter said. "I finished in Creative Connections, so I came looking for you."

Hope smiled, and Carter followed her to the table.

"How come they let you stay in here by yourself?" Carter asked, plunking himself into a chair and shoving a pile of science journals aside.

"Jonah let me in and left," Hope said. "I think he wanted a break."

"Can I help?" Carter asked, cleaning his glasses with the hem of his shirt. Without them, he looked even more like a boy, though the circles under his eyes were darker than ever.

Hope slid the journals back. For a time, the only sound was the clacking of the stamp and beeps from the scanner. Carter stamped furiously, as if he were running a race or getting paid for each finished book.

"You have to wait for it to dry or it will get all smudgy," Hope said.

"Because the throngs of people who are reading"—he closed his book and reviewed the cover—"*Verbal Overshadowing* by Dr. Jiang Lu, will be offended that it's all smudgy."

"Suit yourself." Hope laughed.

Carter's foot rested on the table, chair balancing on two legs as he tilted back and flipped through the volume.

Sticker, *beep*, paper, *beep*.

"Listen," Carter said. "It says they've done studies where people who try to talk or write about an experience actually lose accuracy. Because our brains can't translate visual images or feelings to language, so we simplify. Details get lost that way. Overshadowed."

"Makes sense," Hope said.

Beep, beep.

"So why do we always write or talk right after things happen here? Like the fight with Nina, remember? Quinn had to go 'process' right after. And yesterday, Quinn didn't remember what Nina said about me."

"I dare you to ask Dr. Emerson, next session. Tell her you've been reading"—Hope glanced at the cover—"Dr. Jiang Lu, and you have some thoughts on her treatment decisions."

Carter laughed. "I'm just saying it seems counterproductive."

"Maybe that's what they want," Hope said. "For us not to remember."

Carter returned to reading, but Hope stared at the cover. The way the author's name jangled something in her brain from the last time she was in the library. With Tess.

"The message in the Shade," Hope said. "It wasn't 'Verb a lover shadowing.'"

Carter closed the book on his finger. "Holy shit," he said. He opened the book and then closed it once more, as if the title might have changed.

A chime rang.

Hope stood, placing the scanner on the counter and the stickers in a neat bundle next to it. Carter followed her to the door, shoving *Verbal Overshadowing* into the waistband of his sweatpants.

"What do you think it means?" Hope asked.

"Let's find out," Carter said, holding the door for her. "Is there anywhere we can go? Alone?"

Hope smiled. "Lacuna."

MEDITATION WAS ENCOURAGED as often as possible and wherever possible at Wilder. Lacuna was usually deserted, as the walk was up a steep hill in the full sun. Yet Hope always felt the trek was worth it for the idyllic pond ringed with desert ferns and a view of miles of sky. As a bonus, if you turned at a certain angle, only a small corner of Wilder was visible.

Hope lay on the prickly grass, taking in all the blue. Looking at the sky made her somehow feel closer to Luke, as if he might be seeing it too. Carter sat cross-legged next to her, thumbing through *Verbal Overshadowing*, occasionally sharing a sentence or piece of terminology aloud.

"Nothing on a memory mechanic?" Hope asked.

"Nope," Carter said. "But there's a chapter missing." He held the book open to Hope, displaying a gap between some of the pages. He flipped to the front. "'Chapter 12: Resistance and Resistants.' Whatever that means." He set the book on the grass.

"Is it true you created Magic Words?" Hope asked.

"A long time ago." Carter collected pebbles from the grass and cupped them in his hand.

"Was that before or after you got yourself arrested?" Hope asked.

"That was in college, so I was reformed," Carter said. "Although I still dabble in the hacking world from time to time. At least, I used to."

"Like with the Mad Hatters?" Hope asked.

Carter smiled, as if sharing a secret with himself. "Not exactly, gray-hat stuff primarily. Slightly unethical, but never malicious."

"And then you invented the VR stuff," Hope said. "Erleben."

"*Air-leh-ben*," Carter corrected, turning his head to stare at the pond.

"I can't begin to imagine what you'll invent next," Hope said.

Carter looked uncomfortable, then stood and moved to the edge of the pond. He launched each pebble as far as it would go. "It's going to sound crazy."

Hope gestured in the direction of Wilder. "Not exactly a spoiler alert."

"A few years ago, I visited a small AI company in Stockholm called Minnes," Carter said, holding a pebble in his palm. "Their CTO is a college friend, and they were doing amazing things but didn't have the capital. Maelstrom eventually acquired them. Anyway, their research was with neural interfaces, something called the Eos Ribbon. It's basically a technical interface implanted in your brain. I volunteered to test it."

Hope sat up, horrified. "What do you mean? You put a computer inside yourself?"

"It's not like that," Carter laughed. "It's called a BCI, a brain computer interface. It's basically a bunch of tiny electrodes. They're primarily used for people with neurological injuries. It can help someone who's paralyzed move a prosthetic just by thinking about it."

He squatted near the pond's edge, trailing his hand through the water.

"You're right," Hope said. "That's insane."

"When the robot overlords show up, you'll want one too." Carter smiled.

"Trust me, I won't," Hope said.

Carter turned sideways, like a baseball pitcher, and skipped the last pebble across the pond. It bounced a few times before disappearing into the water with a satisfying plop.

"That's how you're getting into the Butterfly Box," Hope said.

Carter nodded.

Hope considered this. "Does that mean you could use this thingy to get into our patient files?"

"Eos Ribbon. Nope," Carter said. "Before I came to Wilder, I was working on a BCI capable of two-way communication. Right now, BCIs can interpret signals from the brain. They can't send signals back. So I can get into Erleben, but that's it. To get those files I need to do some regular old hacking."

Hope propped herself on an elbow and studied Carter. He was much older than Charlotte, but they shared the same earnest determination coupled with impatience. Charlotte had been that way about everything: school projects, redecorating her room, dyeing her hair, making cupcakes. And Hope had been more than willing to go along. Maybe she was willing to indulge Carter because he reminded her of Charlotte.

"What about on Thursday? Using the library computers?" Hope asked.

"I thought about that because I need Wi-Fi. But it's not something I should do in public," Carter said. "You think Dr. Emerson will let me use her tablet?"

"Probably not," Hope said, thinking. "But Royce might."

Carter posed like a diver and fell onto the grass next to Hope, his arms in a push-up position. "You're a genius."

"Ask Quinn to help you," Hope said. "He has a gift for persuading people to do things. And he loves shenanigans of any kind."

She expected Carter to laugh, but he didn't. His grin had slipped into something solemn again.

"What's wrong?" she asked. "I thought I just solved our problem."

Carter took off his glasses and folded them in his hand. "You need to know something about me first."

"Beyond the fact you're a hacker delinquent and an android cyborg creature?" Hope gathered her sweaty hair on top of her head, wishing for a rubber band.

"Something I learned in therapy," Carter said. "Why I'm here."

"You're not supposed to talk to anyone about what you're trying to remember," Hope said. "It hinders the reconsolidation process. Dr. Emerson would shit a squirrel."

"I don't care." He rolled over, staring at the sky, fingers drumming on his chest. "I hurt someone. He's in a coma. A kid I hired, a friend. Rohan Kapoor. He may never wake up because of me. It's my fault he might die."

He reached out across the grass between them, taking her hand. It was the first time outside of the Shade, and it felt different out here.

"I'm sorry," Hope said.

"At first, I didn't remember any of it. It didn't feel real until the last time in the Labyrinth."

Hope turned to the pond at a splash. Clementine, one of two big white swans, had landed in the water and was now gliding across, sapphire water rippling behind her tail.

"Now I'm sick, knowing I'm capable of that," Carter said, holding her hand tighter. "But I needed you to know: under this geek there's a monster." He said it flippantly, but his face was like a child's. Expectant, searching. As if Hope could provide him with absolution.

"You're not a monster." She felt old, much older than the decade separating them. "At least you feel remorse. At least you take responsibility for your actions." She flicked at a blade of grass. "There are people who cause pain and feel entitled to do it."

I'm not the villain here, you are.

A white mass soared overhead, and they lowered themselves closer to the grass as the other swan flew exceptionally close. Hope could feel the wind on her arms in his wake, soaring by and landing with a splash next to Clementine.

"I think I did something worse," Hope said, almost into the grass, suddenly quite cold. "If I ever remember, I'll tell you."

Carter slowly ran the pad of his thumb across each of her fingers. It felt surprisingly nice, the physical contact, the close proximity to another person. But at the same time, it made her ache for Luke more acute.

Hope gently withdrew her hand.

Carter began cleaning his glasses with his shirt. "Is it Luke?"

"How do you know about Luke?" Her voice was steely sharp. Hope knew she'd never spoken his first name aloud, never called him anything but Dr. Salinger here.

Carter held his palms up, facing Hope. "Nina. After the fight with Quinn."

"Nina?" Hope snapped. It didn't make any sense. "What the fuck would Nina know about Luke? What did she say?"

"She said I didn't have a chance with you, because you were in love with Luke," Carter said, inching back. "But that you . . . made him up."

Hope felt the breath leave her body, as if she'd been kicked. She could feel Carter's eyes on her, but she didn't look at him.

A chime sounded from Wilder, across the grass and to the pond that had seemed so private moments ago.

"I don't want to talk about him," Hope said, standing. She took a deep breath, counted and exhaled, focused on the mountains, and felt no better. Though she suddenly did share in Carter's urgency to find out what else Wilder knew about them. "Come on, let's tell Quinn about this heist."

Carter didn't move. He was still watching her, skeptically.

Hope tried to smile, holding her hand out to help Carter off the grass. Eventually he took it, but everything felt different now.

18

OPERATION GRAY HAT

HOPE
The Wilder Sanctuary
Rancho Mirage, California

I N THE BUFFET line, Carter had barely uttered ten hushed words before Quinn held up a finger to silence him. "Say no more, Toots," he said. "I fucking *love* a caper!" He promptly swept up his pea tendril salad and grilled portobello mushroom, whisking away to join a startled Royce for dinner.

Carter and Hope sat at an adjacent table, both trying for detached nonchalance, both turning around every thirty seconds.

"Why do they put all this stuff in the water here?" Carter made a face.

"I try not to drink it," Hope said. "Especially cucumber."

"I don't know why we can't have regular old water. Or a good IPA."

Hope cut a piece of portobello mushroom, dipping it into the mango sauce on her plate and pushing it around in swirls.

"What does the two mean?" Carter asked, pointing at her plate. "You always make a two with your fork." Then he slashed his hand through the air, as if brandishing a sword. "Or is it a *Z*, for Zorro?"

Hope laughed. "Aren't you a little young for Zorro? Even I'm too young for Zorro."

"They remade it, in the nineties. Don't you know? Everything's just a reboot of the past," Carter said. He observed Royce and Quinn for a moment, then turned back to Hope. "Should we talk about earlier? I know you said you didn't want to, but . . ."

"But we're going to do it anyway?" Hope set her fork on the table and looked out the window.

Outside the summer sun was setting, painting the sky in amethyst and indigo. This was the kind of view that made Luke drop everything and grab his camera, coax her outside to see it too. *Before it disappears,* he'd say.

He'd snap twenty photos of the sunset, of Hope with the sunset. He'd upload the photos afterward, hundreds of them, but Hope never bothered to look. Now she wished she'd taken the time.

When Hope arrived at Wilder it was winter, as much winter you can get in the Coachella Valley, at any rate. She'd been at Wilder for over six months.

Hope wondered how many more summers she would experience from these picture windows, how many more sunsets and sunrises in isolation. If it was time to stop waiting.

"I didn't make him up," Hope said.

"I didn't think you did," Carter said. "Did Luke write the note at Mirror Gate? The binary?"

"I want that," Hope said. "But I haven't heard from him since I got here. I used to email every week. He's never replied."

"But you still love him," Carter said.

Hope weighed her options. Was there a point in lying? It felt wrong to lie to Carter. Or somehow a waste of energy. She nodded.

"Does he love you?"

Hope had to swallow a few times before she could speak. "Not anymore."

Quinn breezed by their table and flashed a thumbs-up. "Asset secured," he stage-whispered. "The eagle has landed. Await further instructions."

Carter returned the thumbs-up, then continued to press. "So what about us?"

"Us?" It felt foreign on her tongue, the idea of Hope ever belonging to an us again. "We're friends."

"We don't have to be," Carter said. "Just friends, I mean."

Ever since watching *Say Anything* in her formative years, Hope had always been a sucker for the Lloyd Doblers of the world. But as sweet and nerdy as he was, Carter was a kid. Most of all, though, he wasn't Luke.

"I'm a lot older than you are," she said.

"Not a lot older," Carter said. "And who cares? Smart women are sexy."

Hope laughed. "It's still impossible, for a lot of reasons."

Carter pointed to the wall behind Hope with his knife, and she turned to the platitude poster of a forest.

It was nothing like the Shade, instead lush and emerald green, a canopy of vibrant leaves bowing and twining together. *When nothing is certain, everything is possible.*

Hope snorted. "I'm not making life decisions based on a fortune cookie. More importantly, we aren't at Wilder because we've got our lives all put together."

"That's exactly why we need each other right now," Carter said, staring at his salad. "Sometimes it's only because I know I'll see you that I get out of bed. But maybe that's just me."

Hope understood.

Admittedly, a small slice of the abyss Luke left with her was beginning to lessen with Carter, and a part of her welcomed the distraction.

"It's not just you," Hope said at last.

﹡☙﹡☙﹡☙﹡

QUINN SPENT THE next few days serving as liaison between Carter and Royce, darting about, spouting meaningless spy phrases behind his cupped hand. Elvis has left the building. The crow flies at midnight.

"Based on my recon, these are the specs for Operation Gray Hat." Quinn folded a towel with his usual precision, stacking it perfectly on top of the last three. "And this is ears only. We'll have four total operatives: Snowman, the Lynx, Black Mamba—"

"Wait," Carter said. "Who am I?"

"Black Mamba."

"I'm Kobe Bryant?" Carter asked.

"Don't be gauche," Quinn said. "*Kill Bill*. What kind of geek are you?"

"Okay, so who am I again?" Carter asked.

"You two have seen *Reservoir Dogs* too many times," Hope said. "No one actually talks like that."

"How would you know, Lisbeth Salander?" Quinn asked.

Hope returned to her folding. "Code names just seem excessive."

"That's preposterous," Quinn said, waving a dismissive hand. "As I was saying, Snowman, the Lynx, and . . ." He gestured to Carter.

"Cowboy."

"Cowboy Carter will be in the book depository. We'll have one sleeper agent on the outside. That's me, Penetrator."

"Hard pass," Hope said. "I'm not calling you that. Change your name or I'm quitting."

Carter laughed, his hair flopping into his eyes. Quinn was being the pinnacle of camp even by Quinn standards, but it was nice to see Carter smile. Carter had three visits to the Labyrinth last week, and Hope could see the toll they were taking. She had a sudden urge to reach over and push the hair out of his eyes, to touch his face. But Carter caught her looking, and Hope returned to folding.

"I'll be Mata Hari, then," Quinn said, dropping sheets on the metal table.

"Mata Hari was a double agent, you know," Carter said, reaching for the pillowcases.

"Will you lunatics stop worrying about the code names and let me talk? The Lynx will gain access to the book depository. TBD will remain on surveillance in case Honeypot or Straightlace show up. Snowman will make the drop to Cowboy, and we will review the dossiers together, inside the depository."

"You didn't tell Royce everything, did you? About why we want his laptop?" Hope asked.

"Of course not. Didn't you hear the ears only part?" Quinn said.

Jonah entered the laundry room, pushing a squeaky cart piled high. He kicked at the rubber stopper on the door and began tossing the towels and grays, one by one, into the washer.

Quinn and his agents returned to their laundry folding.

By the time the chime sounded, Jonah had made little headway through his painstaking washer loading.

"Thirteen hundred hours, agents," Quinn whispered, as they left the laundry room. "You have your orders."

They loitered in the hallway for ten more minutes, unable to access the elevator without Jonah and his key card.

"Should I help Jonah?" Carter asked, at last. "I'm starving."

"I'll go," Quinn said, turning.

Hope and Carter stared at the elevator doors in silence. Since being at Lacuna there had been an unsettling energy between them. Hope felt it again now.

Electric and unpredictable, like a live wire.

"Maybe we should go too," Hope began.

But Carter turned to her suddenly, pressing into her, pinning her against the wall. He pushed Hope's hair away roughly and held her face in both hands. His eyes were an inch from hers, sandy hair falling forward onto her cheek. He smelled sweet, like soap and something spicy.

Hope put a hand on his chest. She could feel his heart through the thin cotton of his T-shirt.

Carter placed his lips on her neck just below her ear, breath burning her skin, and for a second Hope wanted to give in, to push her ache for Luke somewhere far away, somewhere to be addressed later.

But the sound of Jonah and Quinn pulled them apart. In a moment, Carter was standing at the elevator door, as if it never happened.

✹✹✹

HOPE SAT AT the same library table as the previous week, trying to scan books but failing. She'd risen to open the door six times in the last five minutes: once to assure Quinn she was inside, and then five more times for him to report that Royce, aka Snowman, had not yet arrived.

The seventh knock brought Carter instead. He grinned at her. "T-minus five, Lynx."

"Not you too." Hope smiled back, and moved aside to let him in.

Carter leaned against the library return cart, reaching for a chick lit book called *Kisses and Tells*, with a lavender shopping bag on the cover and the *i* in kisses dotted with a hot-pink lip print.

"Some light reading?" Hope asked.

Carter laughed as he fumbled the book. He took a step forward, closing the space between them. "Hope," he said quietly.

"We're in the middle of an operation," she said. Though without thinking, she brushed the hair from his face. He closed a hand around her wrist as she did, sending another tiny jolt through her.

"I don't really care about the operation at the moment," Carter said.

Again Hope felt unmoored so near to him. The intensity between them in the hallway still lingered, the feel of his heartbeat, the way he'd smelled, the heat. But even so, she knew Carter wasn't Luke and never would be. Some holes were too big to entirely fill.

"We can't," Hope said. "I can't. I'm sorry."

Carter let go of her hand and backed up against the library cart. "Can't or won't?"

"Both," Hope said, as a series of taps came from the library door. "Can we talk about this after?"

Carter turned to the door, but this time Hope pulled him back.

"To be continued, okay?" Hope said.

Carter stopped short, dropping *Kisses and Tells* on the floor. He stared at Hope with the same expression he'd had deciphering the code at Mirror Gate, as if he were unraveling a puzzle.

"What's wrong?' Hope asked.

"Nothing." Carter shook his head, then gave a small smile. "To be continued."

Hope opened the library door to Quinn's impatient face. Royce was lurking in the hallway a few feet behind.

Quinn handed the laptop to Carter. "Password is foxtrot, 7, 5, Charlie, echo, shit—what's N?"

"November," Hope said, surprised at the ease this fact came to her.

"November," Quinn repeated. "And how do you say an asterisk?"

Carter groaned and opened the device. "How about just say asterisk? Can you tell it to me without the military lingo?"

Quinn made a face but repeated the password. Carter began typing with one hand as he walked away.

Hope held the door as Quinn directed a finger-on-nose-earlobe-pull maneuver at Royce, who looked confused but gave them a nod and retreated. They waited, watching opposite ends of the corridor until Royce turned a corner.

"How's Cowboy?" Quinn smirked at her.

"Inside, Mata Hari," Hope said. "The mission, remember?"

"Oh, *now* you're all about the mission," Quinn called, but Hope was already halfway through the library.

At the table, Hope couldn't determine if Carter was making progress. A black window with tiny lines of multicolored code was up on Royce's screen and a clock in the corner counted down instead of the one on the wall. It was at 26:42.

"I figured we should try and get out of here before rec time, to be safe, so I set a timer. And we already lost time waiting for Royce," Carter said, still typing.

Hope sat at a nearby table and scanned a few books. Quinn paced the stacks, drumming his knuckles nervously on the shelves, swiveling his head from Carter to the closed door. Carter's hands flew over his keyboard, adding to the discordant tapping in the room.

At 15:41, Hope set the scanner on the table. "Sit down, for God's sake," she said to Quinn. "You're making me crazy."

"That ship has sailed, Toots." But Quinn stopped pacing and stood behind Carter, poking him on the shoulder. "Are we in yet? Are we in yet?"

"Stop," Hope said, glancing at the door. "Let him work."

At 11:01 Carter let out a breath. "I think I did it."

Quinn and Hope moved behind Carter. In the window were two folders: Wilder: Active and Wilder: Deactivated. Carter clicked on the Wilder: Active icon. Rows and rows of file folders appeared in the window, all titled in the same format: 09003-BKC. 09093-LSC. 26050-JCC. 00727-SSE. 16043-SSE.

"Patient numbers?" Hope said. "But there are so many."

10:28.

Carter clicked on the first folder, 0908-SSE, revealing dozens of documents.

"Bryan Herrera. Who's that?"

"No one here, unless it's an alias," Quinn said. "And I've never seen files like these."

Carter opened another of Bryan Herrera's files labeled "Treatment Record." Inside was a spreadsheet listing pill dosages with a much larger variety of drugs than even Hope had been prescribed, blood draws and transfusions, time logs for something called the Tank.

"We don't have time to open all of these," Quinn said, eyeing the clock.

7:08.

Carter removed his glasses and pulled the right earpiece from the frame. At the end protruded what looked like a tiny silver key. He wiggled it free, then inserted it into the laptop.

"What is that?" Hope asked.

"It's a thumb drive," Carter said.

"In your glasses?" Quinn asked, giving Carter's shoulder a squeeze. "Best. Spy. Ever."

Hope leaned closer to the screen. "That one," she said. A single file did not follow the patient numbering system. It was labeled Clearance Level One.

Carter clicked it open, and the three began reading what looked like a legal contract. He scrolled through a dozen or more pages of the same set of legal forms, for patients they all knew at Wilder. And at the end of the forms, signatures of authorization that were far too familiar.

"What the hell?" Quinn said. "Nina was Dr. Stark's sister?"

"Q," Hope said, turning. "There's someone named Tomás on the Copeland-Stark board of directors. Is that your Tomás?"

Quinn's face paled as he read. "What the fuck? We were just—?"

"That's why we're all here," Hope said. Her mouth was dry. "They put us in here."

I'm not the villain here, you are.

"So they could have a seat at the table," Quinn muttered. "We're fucking insurance."

"Copeland-Stark doesn't call it that." Carter pointed at the screen. "They call it collateral."

19

FORTIUS QUO FIDELIUS

LUKE
Copeland-Stark Headquarters
La Quinta, California

L UKE SAT AT a glass table in Sokovia, also called Conference Room 2. Jack and Elliot's heads were bent together in conversation across the table. He hadn't been invited to join in, which was just as well. Stark was spotless as always: collar and pocket square pressed and cuff links shined. Jack looked like himself, weathered and no-nonsense.

Elliot and Jack fell silent when Dr. Frank Sato poked his graying head inside. "You wanted to see me?"

Jack pushed his chair back with a scrape and stood, hand outstretched.

"Come in," Elliot said, gesturing across the table. He felt around on the side of the desk, and the windows darkened as the brightness of the overhead lights increased a level.

Dr. Sato sat, hands tightly clasped on the tabletop. "What's up?" His voice was light and tone affable, but Luke could practically smell his nervousness.

"Dr. Sato," Jack said. "You've been a loyal, trusted employee. While I can't ignore the setbacks in production last year, I also realize it was a result of your personal matters. Though we trust that's been resolved."

Frank Sato nodded. He placed a finger under his collar and tugged at it. Luke felt sorry for him. He didn't know Dr. Sato well, but thought he was a straightforward, all-business guy. He also came with an impressive CV: doctorate from the University of Tokyo, research fellowships and professorships all over the world. He'd also collected a major neuroscience award every year for a decade until last year, when he'd basically disappeared from the scene.

Elliot pushed a sheaf of papers forward, a dozen translucent "Sign Here" flags protruding from its pages.

Dr. Sato swiveled the packet to read the cover page, with the Copeland-Stark logo watermarked across it. "Dr. Frank Hitomi Sato," it said. "Clearance Level One Agreement. Confidential Documents Enclosed."

"Level one? I thought . . ." He let out a breath. "Honestly, I thought it would be a separation agreement." Dr. Sato sifted through twenty pages of legal language Luke knew too well: enumerating that everything developed would now belong to Copeland-Stark, forbidding him from starting his own biotech company and taking any clients with him. A strongly worded reminder from the attorneys about the NDAs he'd signed when hired.

When he reached the last page, the page with the list of perks and the salary line, Dr. Sato let out an audible breath. Just as Luke had, less than a year ago.

"I'm speechless," he said. "Equity shares?"

"You just have to sign." Elliot pushed a pen toward him, smiling. "This is going to open doors you didn't even know existed."

Dr. Sato read carefully through the pages once more, slower this time.

"You're welcome to have your attorney take a look, though it's mostly boilerplate," Elliot said, nodding at Luke. "We've all signed one."

Luke watched as Dr. Sato initialed here, signed there, dated in other places. With an inhale, he signed the last page and passed it to Elliot, who signed and passed it to Jack, who did the same. At last, Frank Sato leaned back in his chair, looking like he'd just finished giving birth.

Elliot moved to a side table and poured four glasses of amber liquid. He knocked back one and refilled it, then returned to the table with the glasses and a wide smile. Apparently he'd started drinking again.

"Welcome to the family," Jack said. He reminded Luke of the fox from the fable, convincing the gingerbread man to get on his back. Hop on. I'll take you across the river, no problem. Climb on my nose.

Frank Sato tipped his glass at Jack and took a drink.

Elliot pressed a button on the speaker. No answer from the other side, only a beep and a crackle. "We're ready to talk terms," he said.

The men sipped in silence, a shadow of confusion on Dr. Sato's face. Luke knew why. He thought they'd already talked terms. He'd just signed twenty pages of terms.

After a moment Liz Emerson entered, mouth set in a thin line, laptop tucked under her arm. She set it, closed, on the table and smoothed her ponytail. "Congratulations on your clearance," she said.

Dr. Sato smiled. "Thanks, Dr. Emerson."

"You understand the document you just signed is permanently binding and irrevocable. Level one provides you with virtually unfettered access to Copeland-Stark, its research, projects, and patients. The agreed-upon nondisclosures and noncompetes, from the inception of your employment, forbid you from discussing anything Copeland-Stark deems confidential in perpetuity."

"I know," he said.

"Excellent." Dr. Emerson's tone was brusque, as if wanting to get her speech over with. "Now that you've cleared the final hurdle, I need to inform you of additional internal agreements. These agreements are mandatory."

Sato nodded, still looking baffled.

"As I said," she continued. "This is mandatory, and it ensures company integrity remains bulletproof."

"Due respect." Dr. Sato eyed the table. "I just signed a contract promising I can't even think about my research without checking with you first."

"Our research," Elliot corrected. "Your research is Copeland-Stark's now."

"Our research," Sato repeated.

Jack wiped his mouth and spoke over the rim of his glass. "Dr. Sato, why did you become a scientist?"

He rubbed at his chin. "It sounds clichéd, but honestly, to make the world better."

"And?" Elliot asked. "Have you done that?"

"I believe so," Sato responded, a little defensively. "My research, ah—our research—has the potential to give millions of stroke victims their normal lives back. The potential alone for BCIs—"

"That's the point," Jack interrupted. "Potential. We don't want to wait ten years for potential to crystallize when the world needs it now."

More like Jack Copeland wants the money now, Luke thought.

"We have the capital," Liz Emerson said. "And we have the brains, with talent like Luke here, along with Dr. Jiang Lu and Dr. Amelia Green. And now you round out our dream team."

"Best of the best," Elliot said.

"Which is why we were more than willing to help you navigate your little . . . hiccup . . . in Osaka last year," Jack said. "Because you're family."

Dr. Sato paled, then looked at Luke and Liz in turn. "I appreciate that. A lot. My daughter Kumiko . . . she got into some . . . bad trouble last year. Really bad. She narrowly avoided prison."

"I'm sorry," Luke said. That explained Sato's missing year. "I have a daughter also. I hope Kumiko is getting help."

"All in the past," Jack said, waving a dismissive hand. "It demonstrates we know your value. And we'll do whatever it takes to ensure your success, because your success is our success. The only thing we need in return is your loyalty."

"I'm starting to feel like I'm meeting with the Corleones." Sato laughed nervously and looked around the table. No one joined in. He tapped the sheaf of papers with a finger. "I think I've proven my loyalty since I've been here. I've signed your NDAs and your clearance contract. I'm committed. What else do you need to be assured?"

"One more thing." Liz Emerson opened her laptop and swiveled it to face him.

Luke watched as Dr. Sato leaned in to read the document, the one that until quite recently had been triple-encrypted. The one that they never printed out or emailed.

He wanted to tell poor Frank Sato what he wished someone had told him a year ago: that the one more thing Copeland-Stark needed was your soul.

❧❧❧

THE SUNSET WAS beautiful, the sky lit up in pinks and purples. Luke leaned against the frame of his sliding glass door and sipped a scotch. He thought about getting his camera, but he couldn't bring himself to move. His eyes roved through his backyard, where he hadn't stepped since December. A blanket was still folded over in a heap on the patio lounger, as if Hope had only recently peeled it back and stepped away.

He hadn't touched almost anything of Hope's since December. Her laptop was still on the desk in the living room, the cup of pencils she never wrote with but rather stuck into her hair still sharp. Everything was preserved, frozen in tableaus around the house. Sometimes he would stand in the closet door and run his hand along the row of clothes: the dress she'd worn to Jack's party, the pink bathrobe that made her look like a Peep. Sometimes he would put his face in her black sweater, where a whiff of Hope's perfume still clung.

Luke reached the bottom of his glass. He shut the patio door and poured another, reminded of the meeting this afternoon and Dr. Sato's level-one clearance.

Then he remembered his own reaction when he'd been the one in that chair, a mere six months ago.

⁂

"WHAT THE HELL is this?" Luke had asked, after Liz Emerson presented him with the same document she'd shown Sato. "Collateral?"

Liz was grim. "That's the term Copeland-Stark—the term *we* use—for the additional security measures required by all investors, all board members, and all staff with level-one clearance. Anyone with enough power and access to compromise company health and reputation. This, as of ten minutes ago, includes you."

Luke scrolled through and back up again several times, dumbfounded.

"We need you to identify your contribution," Liz said. "And we'll take care of the rest. The paperwork and alibis will be ironclad."

"My . . . contribution?" Luke could barely speak over the pounding in his head.

"The most logical choice is Charlotte," Jack said.

Luke whipped around to face him. "Out of the question."

"We know this is a shock," Liz said. "But Charlotte makes perfect sense. She's young, and you know Wilder is a first-rate facility. And in two years, if you want to trade her for someone else, that's fine."

"Trade her? Charlotte's my daughter, she's not a fucking car. Are you insane?" He glanced around the table and found, yes, in fact they were all batshit crazy. "How can you be doing this? How can you be getting away with this? Elliot? Say something."

But Elliot Stark only sat, face pained, avoiding eye contact.

"Luke." Jack leaned close enough for Luke to smell the whiskey. The genial grandfather Jack wasn't in the room. This was the real Jack Copeland, the one who built an empire on avarice alone. "You've signed an agreement. *Fortius quo fidelius.*"

It started to finally sink in, just how fucked up this whole thing was. Some golden opportunity.

Luke looked at Jack. "I couldn't care less about your fucking agreements," he said. "Do what you want. Ruin my reputation, fire me, I don't give a shit." He slammed the lid of Liz's computer, shoved it across the table, and stood. "I'm out."

Jack laughed, but it was mirthless. "This isn't a request."

Elliot put a hand on the laptop, stopping its slide and speaking for the first time.

"Give him a little time. Luke doesn't need to sign today," he said to Jack, giving Luke a pleading look. "He'll come around."

LUKE DROVE FOR at least an hour, too fast and in aimless circles. Elliot had texted and called no less than twenty times on the drive, which Luke ignored.

He was in in the strip-mall parking lot in front of Swiss Donut, hands gripped tightly on the wheel, a pink box of donuts on the passenger seat. The donuts had smelled delicious when he'd walked in, but now their aroma was making him queasy.

Suddenly, Amelia Green rapped on the passenger-side window.

Luke briefly considered starting the engine and gunning it, but instead he unlocked the door.

"How did you know I was here?" Luke said.

Dr. Green opened the door. She got into the passenger seat and placed the box of donuts on her lap.

"Come on," Amelia said. "You have a Copeland-Stark cell."

Luke glanced at his phone in the cup holder, once again feeling spectacularly naïve. Of course he was being tracked.

"Stark sent you?" Luke asked, but he didn't need to look at Amelia to know the answer.

"I was ignoring his texts for a reason," Luke said. "There's nothing any of you can say to change my mind. My job is to protect Charlotte, not throw her to the wolves."

"Then don't send Charlotte," Amelia said. "Send Hope. Elliot said they'd approve her."

Luke unclenched his jaw. "Are you listening to yourself, Amelia?"

"Luke." Amelia took a deep, stuttering breath. "I want to tell you something. About how I got my clearance."

Luke waited, fingers still gripped tightly around the steering wheel.

"You remember Taye, don't you?" she asked. Her fingers picked at the tape on the donut box in her lap.

"Of course." Luke nodded, a little surprised. "I was at your wedding."

"That's right. It seems so long ago," Amelia said, with a sad smile. "Seven months after the wedding, our son Kamari was born."

Luke wasn't sure what to say. They'd lost touch after Amelia got married, but it still seemed like he should know she had a child.

Amelia pulled out her phone and clicked around, then handed it to him. Luke scrolled through pictures of a young boy, the perfect blend of Amelia and Taye: peeking out through a play structure at a park, eating a giant ice-cream cone, riding on Jonah's shoulders with his mouth wide open in delight.

"Kamari," Luke said. "Beautiful kid."

"It's Swahili. It means 'moon.' At least that's what Taye's uncle told us."

Amelia stared at the image of Jonah and Kamari for a full minute before dropping the phone into her purse.

She continued, "When I had my clearance meeting, they wanted Taye. And I did what you did. Specifically, I told Jack to go fuck himself."

Luke gave a rueful smile. "So you get it—"

Amelia cut him off. "I came home and told Taye. I mean, it took time to sink in, but eventually it did. We decided to move, uproot everything, change our names. Get away from Jack Copeland for good. But a few days later, I was sent a separation agreement. I was of course forbidden to say anything publicly about the company. But there was an enormous severance package, and we needed that money."

Luke felt the knot in his stomach loosen just slightly, because things like separation agreements and NDAs lived in the world of above-board business.

"Taye and I decided it was a gift," Amelia said. "We didn't have the power or money to fight Jack Copeland. We could pay off our debt and even save for Kamari's college. I signed it, and we celebrated."

"Copeland-Stark can keep their money too," Luke said. "I don't want anything to do with it."

"Let me finish," Amelia said, and Luke could see she was fighting tears. "Two months later, I woke up and the house was empty. The car, all of Taye and Kamari's things, gone. And Taye left divorce papers on the dining table, suing for full custody of Kamari."

"Why?" Luke asked. "Taye had a change of heart?"

"I thought so, at first," Amelia said. "Maybe he couldn't stand walking away after all, knowing what had happened and not speaking up. But he wouldn't return any calls or texts. I didn't see him until our first mediation. And to make a very long story short, he said I abused Kamari. That I'd done drugs and had affairs and was a negligent, unfit parent."

"Believe me, I know what a custody battle is like," Luke said. "My ex did her share of lying to suit her narrative."

"You don't understand. Taye wasn't lying," Amelia said. Her fidgeting had removed the tape from the donut box now, and she rolled it between her thumb and forefinger.

The shock must have been plain on his face because Amelia hurriedly waved her hand through the air. "What I mean is, Taye *believes* I did all that. He believes those horrible things actually happened," she said. "Even though none of it did."

"I don't understand," Luke said.

"Luke," Amelia said. "Copeland-Stark made him believe it. Those are Taye's memories now."

"Christ." Luke placed his forehead on the steering wheel.

"I haven't seen Kamari since," Amelia said, her voice quiet and thin. "My little boy was four when they left. He wouldn't even remember me now."

"I don't know what to say," Luke said. "There aren't words for it."

"There aren't," Amelia agreed. "But I'm telling you, so you don't fuck up like I did. Play nice. Sign the papers. Give them Hope so you can keep Charlotte safe. She'll understand."

The silence in the car was absolute. Luke couldn't fathom how anyone could understand. He certainly didn't.

"Can I have a donut?" Amelia asked. "I'm starving."

It was such an odd thing to say that Luke laughed out loud. Then he looked at the cardboard box and laughed more, realizing how ludicrous it was to think a conversation with Hope would go easier if only he gave her a maple donut first.

He nodded. Amelia chose her donut and set the box in the backseat.

"How do you live with yourself?" Luke asked. "That's not a criticism. I'm truly asking."

Amelia sighed. "Right after, I took a bottle of pills. But instead of waking up in the ER, I woke up at Copeland Labs. That's when I knew they were always watching, and they'd never stop." Amelia finished her donut and wiped her hands on her jeans. "And then my mother died. That left just me and Jonah, and I can't do that to him. We're all we've got. So now, I just cope."

Amelia removed her cardigan and extended her bare arms toward Luke. "Obviously I can't show this to a therapist."

Luke drew in a breath.

He'd had dozens of patients who engaged in self-injury through the years, but he'd never seen a case this severe. Jagged scars crawled up both of her arms, deep and ridged. Luke suspected they continued well beyond the short sleeves of her top, and he'd see much of the same on her legs.

His eyes rested on Amelia's inner forearm, where KAMARI was etched deeply into her skin, like initials carved into a tree.

⁂

THE RINGING OF his phone startled Luke back to the present. He was still leaning against his sliding glass door, but now the sun had fully set and the patio was black.

"Dr. Salinger?" The voice on the line was young and full of energy, making Luke feel even more exhausted. "This is Rohan Kapoor, from Maelstrom. I work for Carter Sloane."

"Thanks for returning my call," Luke said. He opened a drawer and removed a tattered notebook.

"Sorry it took so long," Rohan said. "Things have been crazy here."

"I'm sure," Luke said. He lifted his glass. Once again, he'd downed another two fingers of Macallan without tasting it.

"Look," Rohan said. "I know this sounds weird, but there's a password? I want to be cautious."

"Right," Luke said, feeling slightly foolish. "Chaotic stupid. You want it in Leet?"

"No that's good enough." Rohan laughed. "How can I help?"

"I had some questions about the software you manage." Luke lowered himself onto one of the blue kitchen stools, his, the one with the divot from Charlotte's spastic vacuuming. Hope's seat, where she used to sit and watch him cook, was pushed under the countertop. "Don't hold back on the technical details."

"Okay, shoot," Rohan said.

"Let's start with how and when you push updates." Luke flipped to a blank page. "More specifically, I'm looking for a way into the Erleben device."

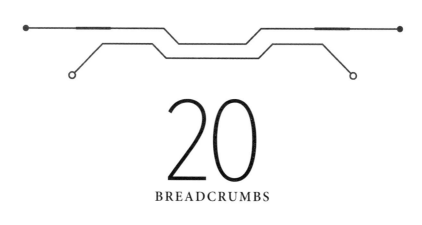

20

BREADCRUMBS

HOPE
The Wilder Sanctuary
Rancho Mirage, California

THE PEBBLES OUTSIDE Mirror Gate, virtual or not, were starting to hurt her ass. Mirror Gate was no longer porous, instead almost insultingly the opposite. Hope rested against the unyielding surface, waiting, though for whom or for what she was unsure.

She examined the thick fleece bathrobe covering her avatar, the one Luke bought when she complained about how cold the house was. On her feet were pink slippers with bits of feathery pink fluff, the high-heeled kind fifties housewives wore.

Tonight, Hope wanted to be back in the meditation program on the white sand beach. She'd even pretend to smell suntan lotion if it would stave off the confusing tennis match of thoughts bouncing from Luke to Carter and back again.

"Exit program," Hope said, getting to her feet.

The room flickered, and though Mirror Gate was still there, now so was Spooky. His sneakers were bright green that day, vibrant purple socks beneath the frayed ends of his jeans. Hope thought about who Spooky might have been before Wilder, when he sold comic books at Fortress.

"Look who's late now," Hope said, standing.

"Something unexpected happened," Spooky said.

"What happened?" Hope asked. "Are you okay?"

Spooky gave a flick of his wrist and the Butterfly Box morphed. The Mirror Gate wall was replaced by a room with black wood paneling and exposed brick, bursting with every conceivable knickknack. Mounted on the walls were things from a reality-television-level hoarder: discolored photos in gilt frames, license plates, a Fender Stratocaster, an antique Clark Nova typewriter. There was a massive Eiffel Tower in the corner next to the row of pinball machines, lit up like Christmas. A distressed metal sign was to her left, with BELIEVE spelled out in lightbulbs. A few broken bulbs buzzed intermittently, like a bug zapper. In the room's center was a diner booth for four, made of cracking red vinyl patched with duct tape, white piping along its edges.

Hope followed Spooky to the booth.

The table was one you would find in any diner, grooved metal running around its edges, topped with a beige lattice-patterned laminate, chipped in places, stained with coffee. On the tabletop was a silver jukebox and the usual accoutrements: salt and pepper shakers, generic ketchup bottle, container of sugar packets, squat chrome napkin holder, its smiling mouth ready to produce little brown napkins.

"Is Carter coming?" Hope asked.

"Very doubtful." Spooky moved the salt and pepper shakers, lining them up in the exact center, much like Quinn would do.

She glanced at the door and the broken Exit lightbox suspended above it. "He isn't coming to help?"

"Don't count on it," Spooky said.

"Carter and I found the book, *Verbal Overshadowing*, but it didn't tell us much. There's a chapter missing."

"Yes," Spooky said.

"All these visits, all these breadcrumbs." Hope paused, tracing her customary *2*, or *Z* for Zorro, on the laminate with her pinky. "Who's the memory mechanic? Is that Dr. Jiang Lu?"

Spooky's hands contracted. "I can't tell you now."

"Screw this." Hope stood. "If you're going to be a Magic 8 Ball all night, I'm done."

"I have a new message for you. From Dr. Salinger."

Hope wanted not to care. She wanted to have the courage to rip off the headset and never visit the Shade again. Instead, she swept her hand across the table. The pepper skittered into the salt, and the shaker tipped and spilled.

"Why are you so angry?" Spooky looked genuinely confused. He pinched a bit of virtual salt and threw it over his shoulder.

"We found out something," Hope said. "A lot of us were put in Wilder on purpose, like hostages. Copeland-Stark calls it collateral."

"Things aren't always as they appear," Spooky said.

"You don't understand," Hope said. Her voice was hard, despite how much she wanted things to be other than they appeared. "Dr. Salinger basically put me in here to get a better parking space. How would you feel if someone you thought loved you did that?"

"Terrible," Spooky said. "But there's always more to the story." He pulled a napkin from the dispenser and smoothed it on the table. Then he folded it, *Blade Runner* style, into a perfectly angular kangaroo. He made a wiggling motion with his index finger and the kangaroo rose, stretched its tiny paws, and hopped past the salt and pepper shakers toward Hope.

She held out her hand and it jumped into her palm, wiggling its pointy paper tail.

Hope's tears stung her eyes. "Kangaroo sanctuary," she murmured. She watched it for a while, until the little kangaroo hopped off her hand and settled itself down near the salt.

Spooky pushed a menu toward her, yellowing paper encased in a cracked plastic sleeve. A black clip-art picture of a smiling chef with a puffy white hat and handlebar mustache stared at her. He was brandishing a platter, though of Belgian waffles rather than a burger and fries. Accent lines were drawn around it, presumably to show how exciting they were. Hope smiled, despite herself. The Waffle Brothel.

The message on the menu was yet another string of nonsense numbers. Hope tried to decipher it, but they weren't her code or the one from Mirror Gate. She felt like Matt Damon in *Good Will Hunting*, only without the whole genius at MIT part. "How am I supposed to read this? And don't you dare tell me 'reply hazy.'"

"Concentrate and ask again," Spooky said, deadpan.

Hope flung the menu at Spooky. The kangaroo hopped a few inches to the left with an annoyed shake of its tail. She lay her head on the table with a Quinn-level sigh, flicking angrily at the knob on the jukebox, the selection of songs flipping back and forth.

Hope lifted her head. Their titles weren't songs, but the books she remembered from cataloging in the library: L-12: *You Control YOU!* (Chip Novak), H-3: *Verbal Overshadowing* (Dr. Jiang Lu), M-9: *Dreams from A to Z* (Samantha Groess). Rows of ivory buttons ran across the bottom, letters and numbers for selecting the song. Hope's eyes narrowed, as while the letters progressed dutifully from A to Z, the numbers didn't.

"That's the cipher," Hope said. "Right in front of me."

Spooky set the menu before her again, then removed another napkin and busied himself with folding.

Hope matched numbers to letters, periodically glancing up to check her work on the jukebox. While the code formed words this time, the sequence seemed mismatched. Hope read and reread, unable to make meaning, reluctant to believe it was truly from Luke.

"What in the hell does this mean?" Hope said. "Escape is sweet? Time is twisted?" She read it once more, memorizing.

Spooky stood. The Exit sign over the door was now flashing bright green. "We have to go."

Hope stood as well. "Is that really all the information I get?"

"As Carter would say, it isn't a quest if I do it all for you." Spooky placed a flawless napkin palm tree on the table.

❦❦❦

HOPE REMOVED HER headset and peeled the gloves from her hands. The Butterfly Box was bathed in a pulsating green. She opened the door and found she was caged behind steel bars, the faint sound of sirens coming from the floor below.

"Hello?" she called out through the bars. "Spencer? Is anyone here?"

Fernando's large frame lumbered down the corridor. As usual, he looked like he'd been through battle in his dirty scrubs and bed head.

"Can you let me out?" Hope asked.

"Crap." Fernando put his hands in his pants pockets, then patted the front of his shirt. "Left my key card on the desk. Just a sec."

Hope watched Fernando jog out of sight and return, out of breath when he reached her. He placed his key card on the pad, but the bars remained in place.

Fernando's eyebrows came together as he shoved his lanyard into his pocket. "It must be a Code Nine," he said. "The bars will go back up when it's over."

"What's a Code Nine?" Hope asked.

Fernando glanced at the green lights and shifted on his feet, scrunching his nose. "Not allowed to say."

Hope wrapped her hands around the bars, like a prisoner. "Who else is here? On this floor?"

"Nobody." Fernando's bushy eyebrows came together. "Just you."

"But Spooky . . . I mean, Spencer, was with me." Hope investigated the empty room, running her shaking hands through her hair. "We've been together all night . . ." Her voice trailed off as Fernando stepped back, perhaps just realizing he worked in a mental institution. The key card fell from his pocket.

Fernando's phone buzzed. He fished into the breast pocket of his scrubs and held it to his doughy face. "Yes, Doctor . . . just one . . . Hope. Yes, I'll be here."

"Dr. Emerson is on her way. You're supposed to wait here," Fernando said. He turned from Hope.

"Your key card," Hope said.

Fernando looked at the key card on the floor and grinned, though he didn't retrieve it. "Yeah, it drives her crazy when I do that."

Hope watched Fernando retreat back down the corridor, liking him even more in that moment.

She gave the bars another shake, then sat cross-legged on the industrial carpet, staring at the flashing green lights, repeating the new message in her head:

It's when certain options fail, escape is sweet.
More proof adds other motives.
Remember truth flows beneath obvious memories and time is twisted.
False efforts often alter beliefs as I sleep.
Could everyone be lying?
Your Luke.

She attacked the message, trying to discern meaning. Everyone was lying to them, she was at least sure of that. But was Luke telling her to escape Wilder? Stop sleeping? Nothing about the words felt like Luke, least of all the signature.

He never signed things 'Your Luke,' as if he were a Civil War soldier writing missives by candlelight.

Hope repeated the words until even the sound of heels on tile was welcome. Dr. Emerson placed a card against the wall and the bars slid into the ceiling. "I've opened the door for you," she said, as if it weren't abundantly plain. "We've installed another security update and needed to reset the system. We were unaware anyone was on this floor."

Dr. Emerson bent to retrieve Fernando's key card with an annoyed cluck and turned, pace brisk as she moved toward the double doors.

Hope jogged to catch up. "What's a Code Nine?"

Dr. Emerson paused at the kiosk and dangled Fernando's key card from her pale wrist. "There's a reason we have these on lanyards, Fernando."

"Sorry, ma'am." Fernando took it sheepishly and placed it around his neck.

"This way," Dr. Emerson said to Hope. "Patient elevators don't work when a code is active. We're taking the service elevator."

Hope followed the doctor to an elevator she'd never noticed. As they waited, she saw Fernando remove his lanyard and shove it into his pocket. He winked at Hope.

The elevator was cramped, and Hope found herself uncomfortably shoulder-to-shoulder with Dr. Emerson.

"What's a Code Nine?" Hope asked again.

Dr. Emerson tugged at the hem of her lab coat. "It's a critical patient issue."

"Which patient is having the issue?"

With a ding, the doors slid open. Dr. Emerson stepped out first. They moved through the empty hallway, Hope's hands over her ears to muffle the noise.

As they reached Hope's door the sirens stopped, though the lights remained green.

Dr. Emerson reached into her coat pocket and produced a plastic baggie with three unfamiliar pills. "You missed meds this evening," she said, holding them out to Hope.

Hope snatched the baggie and stepped into her room.

"Hope," Dr. Emerson said. "I'll watch you take those."

An ill-tempered sigh escaped. Hope ripped open the baggie and tipped the pills into her mouth, swallowing them all at once. She opened her mouth wide, tongue waggling grotesquely.

"That won't be necessary," Dr. Emerson said, with a step back. "Good night. Be well."

Hope shut the door.

21

SELF-INFLICTED

HOPE
The Wilder Sanctuary
Rancho Mirage, California

H OPE SLEPT THROUGH the chime to wake up, the chime to be ready, and the chime signaling breakfast. Eventually a continuous knocking penetrated her slumber and she forced herself out of bed, dragging her bare feet across the floor.

Jonah was waiting for her on the other side, looking unduly concerned. "You missed breakfast."

"I did?" Hope yawned. From somewhere still veiled with sleep, she remembered the sound of sirens and the staccato of heels. Green lights. She rubbed her face and yawned again.

"Don't look so worried," Hope said. "I'm up."

"Community goal setting starts in ten minutes and attendance is mandatory." It was the longest sentence Jonah had ever uttered to her.

"Isn't it always mandatory?" Hope asked, opening her single drawer for a clean set of Wilder grays.

"Today it's extra mandatory," Jonah said.

He stepped aside to allow her to enter the bathroom and leaned against the wall.

Hope slid the pocket door closed. She peed, changed, and brushed her teeth in a sleepy haze. In the mirror, a significantly paler and thinner version of the person she used to be stared back at her. There were circles under her eyes, and her hair had become lank and stringy. *Smart women are sexy*, she thought, and laughed out loud.

Jonah gave a tap on the door.

"Coming," Hope said, hastily. She tried a smile at her reflection, then gave up.

❧ ❧ ❧

COMMUNITY GOAL SETTING was held in the Bloom Room, so named because of the mural on the wall. It was a floor-to-ceiling garden of psychedelic flowers, painted in a forced perspective which made you feel like Alice in Wonderland. The black calligraphy across the top commanded: *Bloom Where You Are Planted*.

The Wilder Weirdos were gathered in a semicircle in front of the trippy flowers. Quinn and Spooky were seated in front of a six-foot white lily. Quinn patted the empty seat between them and Hope slid in.

"Overslept," she said. "That's never happened. And I feel hungover, which I know hasn't happened in at least seven months."

She scanned the room. No Carter yet. The newest Wilder Weirdo, Kumiko, sat on the other side of Spooky. Royce wasn't there either, though he never had to follow the rules. They were going to need more chairs.

"Where is everybody?" Hope asked Quinn. "Jonah told me this was extra mandatory."

Quinn placed his hand over hers and squeezed tight.

The doctors entered in a line and turned to face the semicircle. Dr. Emerson wore a plum-colored dress under her lab coat, her pointy fingernails painted to match. Dr. Stark's skin looked sallow in his salmon-colored polo. He held a tin of Altoids in his hand, repeatedly clicking it open and closed with his thumb.

Dr. Green came last. She shut the Bloom Room door and stood for a few moments. When she finally turned, she walked stiffly, trademark long sleeves gripped in her clenched fists.

Usually goal setting was run by a single doctor, but never everyone at once. Fully awake now, Hope registered their somber faces and the anticipatory hush in the room.

Dr. Emerson cleared her throat. "We have some unfortunate news."

"It's come to our attention rumors were circulating at breakfast. We want to make certain you have accurate facts," Dr. Stark said, pocketing his Altoids.

Hope dug her nails into Quinn's hands. She closed her eyes, counting to ten, exhaling, wishing she were back in the Shade. Whatever it was, she didn't want to hear it.

"One of our guests, Carter, died last night," Dr. Emerson said. "His death was self-inflicted, as a result of ingesting a lethal dosage of several different medications, resulting in cardiac arrest."

Dr. Stark spoke. "In other words, he overdosed."

A chill spread through Hope, numbing her fingers and toes, her lips. She tried to move, to stand and leave the room, but her body wouldn't comply. She felt Quinn's arm around her, but it felt suffocating and she shook it off.

Tess raised her hand, and Stark acknowledged her. "How did he get enough pills?" Her voice wasn't apathetic at all this morning.

"They have . . . we have determined he is—he had . . ." Dr. Green's voice shook. "He'd been taking pills from other patients since he arrived, as well as saving his own. To take all at once."

The Wilder Weirdos whispered to one another soberly. Hope wasn't fooled. This news was prime gossip, and there was no mistaking the morbid curiosity behind the sympathetic murmurs.

Hope could hear someone making a kind of horrible, anguished sound, a moan or a cry or a strangled scream. At first she thought it was Nina, and it took a second to remember Nina was dead. Like Carter. She wanted to tell the person to be quiet; Hope couldn't hear what the doctors were saying with that racket going on. She needed to concentrate on the doctors.

"We'll be conducting a thorough investigation into how this happened." Dr. Stark looked at Dr. Green, who said something that Hope couldn't hear over the awful wailing.

She turned to find the source of the sound to tell them to shut up. But when she looked around the room, everyone was regarding Hope as if watching a mildly interesting documentary.

That's when Hope realized the sound was coming from her.

She pressed her fists against her mouth, trying to shove the noise back inside.

"Hope," Dr. Emerson stepped forward, voice deceptively calm. Hope focused on the doctor, in her designer shoes and flawless manicure and patronizing sneer. A sharp pain pounded behind her eyes.

"You knew," Hope said. "You knew the Code Nine was Carter last night, but you didn't tell me. Those pills knocked me out, but they didn't make me forget."

Dr. Emerson set her mouth in a thin line, red lipstick disappearing. In general, her favorite rebuttal for the truth was to pretend it hadn't been uttered. "It looks like you need some time to process," she said. "Let us help you."

"No fucking way." Hope was able to stand now, so quickly and with so much force she knocked over her chair. It fell with a clatter against the giant flower mural.

"I know you believe you two were close, but Carter was struggling," Dr. Emerson said. Her tone was like spun sugar, saccharine and empty.

I believe you *believe it happened that way.*

"It's all lies," Hope said. "You're lying. Carter never would have done that."

"He did," Dr. Emerson said. "And unfortunately, it isn't uncommon."

"Uncommon?" Hope's laugh was hysterical, and it rattled hollowly in her chest. "Are you telling me the Wilder Sanctuary, where people pay hundreds of thousands a year for wellness, expects patients will kill themselves? You need to rethink your fucking PR strategy."

"That's quite enough," Dr. Emerson said. She shot Dr. Stark a look.

Dr. Stark approached Hope slowly, as he'd done with Nina. "Everything you're feeling right now is normal. This is a tragedy. Jonah's going to take you back to your room and give you something to help you rest. And then we'll talk."

Hope whipped her head around. She hadn't even noticed Jonah was in the room, but now he was coming toward her. She stepped away and grabbed for Quinn, who put his arms around her.

"Page twenty-two," Spooky said, looking directly at her. "'Code Four. In the event a resident may cause harm to oneself or others, physical restraint will be used.' Page twenty-seven. 'Patients may be placed in protective isolation when deemed necessary by staff.'"

"*Mi'ja*," Quinn said softly. "Spooky's right. You have to calm down or they'll call a code. They'll lock you up."

"I don't care." Hope put her face into Quinn's chest. "Those bastards did this to him. You know it."

"I know," Quinn whispered into her ear. "But don't give them a reason to do something to you. Don't make trouble."

Hope tried to protest, to conjure some of the fury she'd had seconds ago. But it just wouldn't come, and now it was a struggle to form words. Quinn was right. If she didn't play nice, she'd be next.

She let Jonah lead her away.

22

ESCAPE IS SWEET

HOPE
The Wilder Sanctuary
Rancho Mirage, California

HOPE'S NOTEBOOK LAY open on her chest, though her pen had rolled underneath the bed hours ago. There was nothing to see out her bedroom window. Windows were dimmed by eight, turned a slate gray, straining against any light clamoring to get in. When Hope woke, the wall of gloom was the only clue it was night.

She pulled the thin duvet around her neck. Hope hadn't been able to get warm for days. It didn't matter the weather was 110 degrees, not that she'd been outside to know. She wore one of the utilitarian Wilder sweatshirts provided in winter and two pairs of socks. Still, she shivered.

For three days, Hope had sequestered herself here. She wouldn't leave for meals, eschewed yoga, ignored her sessions with Stark. She refused to let Quinn coax her out of bed, and now he'd stopped trying. She rose only to visit the bathroom and avoid her face in the mirror. The days passed like a movie, she the single stationary character in the frame, others moving in and out in fast motion, light growing and dimming.

On the first day, Jonah let himself in after she patently ignored his knocking. "Breakfast," he said.

Hope was curled in a ball, blankets pulled tight to her nose. "Not hungry."

Jonah shifted, rubbing his neck. "What should I tell the docs?"

"Whatever you want," Hope said. She felt like a high schooler again, refusing to go on the senior field trip. "Can you turn up the heat?"

But no guards escorted her to breakfast and no doctors appeared. Trays of food were left in her room three times a day. Hope would note their existence periodically, eat a bite and gag, then spit it out and return to sleep. Later the food would be changed out with something new. Jonah returned on the second day, but this time he sat in the chair by the bed.

"Hope," he said. "They aren't going to let you do this forever."

"What do you care?" Hope asked, with an ire that sounded a lot like Charlotte.

"I do care," Jonah said, and Hope was momentarily distracted by how disheartened he sounded. "You have to play nice."

"Play nice," Hope repeated slowly, the words making her feel sick. "Isn't that all I've been doing?"

Jonah stood, shaking his head. "I don't want something to happen to you when they run out of patience."

But once again, Hope ignored Jonah and turned to face the wall.

On the third day, Hope woke to see a book on her nightstand. It was *Kisses and Tells*, the book Carter had been holding in the library, a memory that felt like decades ago. Finding the collateral files with him had carried so much weight at the time, and now it seemed utterly insignificant. She shoved the book under the mattress.

On the fourth day, Hope tuned the television to a loop of rain falling into a brook. It made her feel even colder. But she watched for a time, letting the patter descend into white noise, ignoring yet another knock.

The door opened anyway. "May I speak with you?" Dr. Emerson asked.

There was no point in a response; Dr. Emerson never requested permission for anything.

The doctor entered as predicted, perching on the chair as if it were a dirty park bench.

"Your desire to isolate yourself after the news of Carter's death is perfectly normal," she said, adjusting her patterned accent scarf.

Hope's eyes fogged at her words, but she blinked rapidly to send the tears away.

"Mindset is the key to your recovery. And frankly, we believe your relationship with Carter was a damaging distraction. While it may sound harsh, his death may have been a blessing."

"My God," Hope said. "Do you even hear yourself?"

"I only have your best interests at heart," she said. "We all do."

Hope contemplated the ceiling. There were so many things she wanted to say, about Luke, about the collateral. But down deep she knew Quinn and Jonah were right. If she made trouble and something happened to her, she'd never learn what really happened to Carter. She'd never get the chance to make them pay.

"Whatever you need to tell yourself to sleep at night," she finally said.

The silence following stretched for a full minute, and when Dr. Emerson spoke again her voice was clipped. "We've given you ample space to grieve. Tomorrow you will return to your routine, including an extended session in the Labyrinth this week."

"And if I won't?" Hope asked.

"Then we'll have no other choice but to force your compliance." Dr. Emerson stood and adjusted herself once again, splitting her ponytail in two and pulling it tighter. She tapped the tray of food on the nightstand. "Eat your dinner." She spun on her heel like a boarding-school matron and left.

Admittedly starving, Hope pulled the tray of food onto her lap and removed the silver dome. It was an unappetizing piece of chicken breast, surrounded by a reddish sauce that made it look like a murder scene. She replaced the dome and groped under the bed for her pen.

Hope paged through her notebook until she came to the section where she'd printed Luke's message from the diner.

It's when certain options fail, escape is sweet.
More proof adds other motives.
Remember truth flows beneath obvious memories and time is twisted.
False efforts often alter beliefs as I sleep.
Could everyone be lying?
Your Luke.

Hope spent thirty minutes trying to decipher the message. She tried the first letter of each word, and the last letter. She wrote the entire message backward. She wrote every other letter. She moved the punctuation around. She translated the letters back into numbers and moved those around.

Nothing worked, and her stomach rumbled as she frustratingly turned past her pages of cross outs and muddled phrases to the diary she'd been keeping since December.

For the first time in seven months, Hope reread from the beginning. Numbers tumbled and blurred together, mixing into one big puddle like the rain on her monitor. Medication dosages, Labyrinth visits, sustainable salmon and acai bowls. *Laundry w. C, library w. C, C looks tired, C looks worse. To be continued.*

Hope started a page in her notebook for Carter. Rather than her numerical shorthand, she wrote a descriptive narrative. Carter, his sandy hair and glasses falling down his nose, the smell of soap, his hazel eyes. His quirky sense of humor. The blushing. The moment in the hallway, the rhythm of his heartbeat. The look on his face when she'd said, "I can't."

When she finished, Hope wondered why she was taking the time to memorialize it. So she could look back and wonder if it ever happened? And what if writing would cause Carter to distort and disappear faster, à la Dr. Jiang Lu? Would she trust herself if she read it again?

Her stomach made another loud grumble. Hope pulled the plate nearer and removed the cover, then poked at the chicken with her fork. She cut off a sliver and pushed it through the sauce. She cut and swirled and chewed mechanically, staring at the plip-plopping brook on the monitor. It wasn't until her last bite of chicken that Hope stopped, now noticing the number she'd left in the remains of the sauce.

Hope shoved the tray aside and grabbed her notebook again. This time, she extracted the second letter of each word.

23

ALMOST ENOUGH

HOPE
The Wilder Sanctuary
Rancho Mirage, California

F ERNANDO ASSIGNED HOPE to the largest Butterfly Box, Hestia, because Arkham remained glitchy and she didn't have an appointment. Inside, with the virtual keyboard floating before her, Hope felt foolish typing W-A-F-F-L-E-S into the air.

The undulating squares vanished, and Hope looked around slowly, feeling dizzy. She stood on a familiar flagstone walkway, outside the one place she'd ever felt was truly home: Luke's little white house. A low brick wall extended to the right, the little dwarf palm tree they'd named Chuck planted to her left.

Hope took two steps closer to the front door. She loved that door. Long ago it had been a fading red she despised, painted poorly by a previous owner. It had drips of red stain in parts, which is why they named it the murder door. In one of Charlotte's sudden brain waves one weekend, she and Hope had sanded and repainted the door a sunny yellow.

The door shimmered now, moving from static to pixels and back again. When it cleared, the pixels sharpened into a video of Luke, his face close up and slightly at an angle, like he was on a conference call.

Hope stared, transfixed. Even in the Butterfly Box, even knowing he wasn't real, Luke was beautiful. Maybe this wasn't entirely her Luke, but it was the closest she'd been, was the closest she would ever get. It was almost enough.

But then he locked his eyes with hers. "My God," he said. "Hope."

Hope put a hand over her mouth.

"Finally," he said. "I can't believe it."

She dropped her hand, whispering around the lump in her throat. "Is it really you?"

Luke was a little grayer than before, with shadows under his eyes that mirrored her own. He was pale and exhausted but also perfect. More perfect than she could ever imagine someone looking. Hope stared at him, into the stormy blue of his eyes, and the ever-present longing she'd been carrying all these months threatened to consume her completely.

"It's me," he said, with the smile Hope hadn't thought she'd ever see again. It felt like a trick somehow, impossible. But in that smile was the Luke she adored, the Luke she trusted unconditionally. He'd explain everything, make things right, as he always did. He'd take her away from this nightmare and they'd go home: through the yellow front door, back to the kitchen stools and waffles and Macallan under the stars. Back to Charlotte.

"I don't have much time," Luke said. "I'm piggybacking on a signal."

"I don't know what that means," Hope said. Her lip was trembling, and her words came out in stutters.

"I don't really either, but it doesn't matter." Luke's face came closer to the screen as he looked at her. "Christ, I miss you like hell. Have you been hurt?"

"No," Hope said, knowing it wasn't entirely true.

Luke's eyes roved around her. "What on earth have you done to Erleben?"

Hope looked over her shoulder. Even though the front door remained, the rest of Luke's house had disappeared. She was standing a patch of moss, aspen all around. "It's called the Shade," she said. "But I didn't do this. One of the patients here . . . he created it."

"Carter H. Sloane," Luke said.

"You know Carter?" Hope asked. She'd never known his last name. "Carter H. Sloane" sounded so important.

Luke looked uncomfortable. "If it weren't for Carter, I wouldn't have been able to get in here. Not him, specifically. One of his engineers, Rohan Kapoor. He works at Maelstrom, Sloane's company."

Hope's head began to pound. Rohan Kapoor. A kid I hired.

Hope tried to remember the conversation at the pond, but the details were mixing together. She felt like she was in a session with Stark, her mind filling with syrup. "But Rohan's in the hospital. That's why Carter was at Wilder."

"No he isn't," Luke said, rubbing the stubble on his chin. She'd seen this gesture so many times, and now it hurt to watch from so far away. "Rohan texted me a few minutes ago. You can tell Carter. Listen, there isn't time for this—"

"I can't," Hope interrupted. Her hands began to shake. "Carter is . . . they said he committed suicide."

"Fuck." Luke's camera tilted. Hope could see the *Don't Panic* poster on the bedroom wall, a corner of the nightstand on her side of the bed.

"I'm sorry," he said, righting the frame and reappearing. His picture flickered. "Did you find the book?"

"Yes," Hope said. "Who's the memory mechanic?"

Luke's image flickered once again. He swore, then said something else, but Hope could hear only every other word. She could see his fingers move as if typing.

"Can you still hear me?" he asked.

"Luke," Hope said. "I need to know. I saw these files—"

The picture disappeared entirely for a few seconds before returning.

"I'm sorry, I really have to get off this signal," Luke said. "I'm just glad you're okay. I needed to see for myself."

"But I'm not okay," Hope said. She pushed her hair away, the neoprene of her haptic gloves scratching her cheeks. She wanted it to end, this unreal virtual world. The mystery, the constant clutching for answers but never quite gaining any purchase. "Something isn't right here. You need to come get me."

"Hope." Luke's jaw was set, and Hope saw his eyes cloud before he looked away. He ran his hand over his bowed head. "I can't."

Comprehension dawned on Hope like droplets of ink in a glass of water. It twisted and expanded and diffused slowly, spreading out its tendrils until it was entirely black. At last she understood—he wasn't her Luke anymore. Maybe he'd never been.

There you go again, rewriting the narrative.

"You can't?" Her mouth had an alkaline taste, like burnt coffee. "Or won't, because your position at Copeland-Stark is more important?"

Luke shook his head.

"All these months, wondering why I never heard from you. Then finding your signature on an agreement that put me in here. Explain how you could do this to me," Hope said. "I need to hear it from you."

"Hope, I can't," he said again.

"Luke," Hope said. "Or wait, is it Dr. Salinger again?"

"Please," Luke said, leaning in, eyes bright. "You have to trust me a little longer. Trust in us."

"Us?" Hope asked. She pulled off the headset and threw it to the ground.

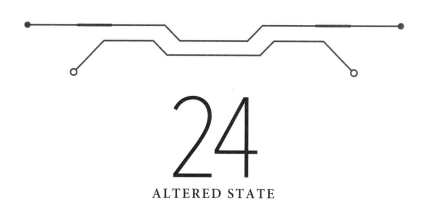

24

ALTERED STATE

HOPE

The Wilder Sanctuary
Rancho Mirage, California

"THESE ARE POSSIBLY the weirdest huevos rancheros I have ever eaten. Tía Lucia would roll over in her grave if she saw me eating this." Quinn inspected his fork with a wrinkled nose, then popped it into his mouth anyway. "Never make good food out of healthy shit."

Hope had to agree, even though she didn't have a Mexican relative, dead or alive, to offend. The "chorizo" was a sad combination of turkey and tofu; the cheese didn't taste like cheese. The eggs were poached perfectly, so that was something. The whole thing was piled on a fake tortilla made of pulverized cauliflower. Crunchy, passable, but overall wrong.

Quinn had evidently decided to act like Hope had been on a vacation for the past five days rather than mourning in a hole.

". . . and so Tess lost her shit. Full-on Carrie style, without the blood. She kicked over all of Ami's crystal bowls and threw a tuning fork at her. Complete disruption to my sound bath."

Hope smiled, because she was expected to. Her time with Luke in the Butterfly Box had been on continuous replay in her head since it happened: *Hope, I can't, Hope, I can't,* on an unrelenting loop. Her meds had never been more welcome last night.

"I thought Ami was going to cry," Quinn continued. "Honestly, I think not having Carter being shitty at yoga is taking a toll on her chakras."

Hope looked into her mug, gripping it tightly.

"I'm sorry, *Mi'ja*. I wasn't thinking. I'm . . ." Quinn sighed and rolled his shoulders. "I had the Labyrinth yesterday. And today—"

"It's fine," Hope said. Quinn spent so much time being the upbeat one at Wilder. It was easy to forget he was a patient, and things like the Labyrinth drained him as much as everyone else. She patted his hand.

"I'm just all Tom Cruise on *Oprah* right now." Quinn shook his head from side to side, like a dog leaving a swimming pool. It gave her a headache to watch.

Quinn considered her as he folded his napkin corner to corner. "You're going to be fine, little Hopeless," he said.

"That's a pretty big ask, considering where we are." Hope let the steam from her tea rise over her nose, beading in tiny droplets on her upper lip.

"We can fix you later," Quinn said. "But today we have much bigger fish to fry."

Most residents had cleared from the dining room, having already placed their plates in the metal bins and shuffled to goal setting. Jonah hadn't shown up to chivy the last stragglers on to their next activity, so Quinn leaned in. "We need to plan our next steps."

"Q," Hope said. "We don't even know how Carter got those files. And even if we did, I don't want to ask Royce for help again. I don't trust him."

"Royce is gone too." Quinn raised an eyebrow. "Coincidence? Right after he helped us? The body count is growing."

Quinn unfolded his napkin and returned it to his lap. He poked at his egg, and the yellow insides flooded his cauliflower tortilla. He tipped his plate back and forth, so it covered the entirety of the inside rim. He was extra fidgety today, almost manic.

"We're going to find out where the nefarious place is," Quinn said. "I'm going to call it Wilder with a Vengeance. No, wait . . . Bizarro Wilder."

Hope ate a piece of egg white. It was rubbery and cold, and she chewed until she thought she might gag. She pushed her plate away and took a gulp of her tea, scalding her mouth in the process. She desperately wanted to be back in her room, warm under the bedspread, staring at the rain on TV. She turned to the window.

"Hopeless, keep up. Wilder 2.0. The secret lair. Where is it?"

"What lair?" Hope turned back, but it took an effort to focus on Quinn.

"Let's recap," Quinn said. "The files in the Active folder? How many people are at Wilder? Maybe twenty? Thirty?"

Hope shrugged. "Sure."

"But not a hundred. You said it. Why are there so many active files? Where are they?" Quinn asked. "It has to be close by, drivable, wouldn't you think? Do you think it's downtown?"

"They built a super-secret compound between Melvyn's and the Best Western?"

"You're right. See? Your investigative mind is why you're a critical operative for Operation Find the Horde. No, that's a stupid-ass name." Quinn leaned closer. "The point is, what if Nina didn't really die? What if Carter didn't either?"

Quinn suddenly had Hope's full attention. "You think Carter's still alive?" she whispered.

"Hopeless, do we have any reason to believe what they tell us?" Quinn asked.

She had to admit Quinn's point was valid. Hope shook her head.

"So why should we believe what they said about Carter?" Quinn asked. "What if he's at Wilder 2.0 instead, with the other people?"

The idea was so painfully seductive. Hope wanted to dismiss it, to live in the world of facts and objectivity as was her nature. But there it was, dangling just within her reach, daring her to believe it.

"You don't know how much I want that to be true," Hope said.

✤✤✤

PROMPTLY AT 11:15, Hope knocked on Dr. Stark's door. At 11:20 he still hadn't answered, though she could hear movement inside. Three minutes later he opened the door. A corner of his rumpled shirt hung out of his waistband, and his usually styled hair was unruly.

"Did we have a session this morning?" Stark asked, passing a hand over his bloodshot eyes. "I'm so sorry, I've double-booked myself. I'm late for a meeting." Stark stepped into the corridor and shut his door, walking briskly away as he tucked in his shirt.

So Hope arrived early to the dining room, *Kisses and Tells* tucked under her arm. Then she spotted Quinn, alone at a larger table set with six sparkling place settings, and something about his posture made her pause.

He held himself straighter than usual, characteristic slouch and insouciant aura absent. Quinn had the same look Hope used to get at the airport—back in the day when they let you wait in the terminal—craning her neck to spot her father. She tried to catch his eye and he looked through her.

Hope approached the table. Quinn didn't make any motion to indicate she should sit, so she didn't. "You look nervous."

"It's my birthday." Quinn adjusted his fancy place setting so the charger and seven utensils were precisely equidistant.

Hope put a hand on his shoulder. "Why didn't you tell me at breakfast? Happy birthday."

"Tomás is coming." Quinn smoothed his hair even though it was perfect. He held out his hands in front of Hope to show they were trembling. He pivoted toward the door, tapping his foot at the same time.

"I've been up all night trying to think of a legit reason for the coll—" He broke off and looked over his shoulder. "For what he did, why I'm here. Do you think there's anything he could say that would be in the same stratosphere of forgivable?"

Hope wanted to tell Quinn about Luke. About how she'd been clinging to any chance there was an explanation. That even knowing what she knew, Hope still couldn't help loving Luke. That telling yourself a lie is so much easier than accepting the truth of a betrayal.

There you go again, rewriting the narrative.

But she couldn't bring herself to admit those things aloud, and so Hope only nodded. "Sure," she said weakly. "There could be."

"I hate that after all this, I still can't wait to see him," Quinn said.

"I get it," Hope said.

"Will you sit? Keep me honest?" Quinn asked. "I always turn into a marshmallow the second I see him."

"I'll be close." Hope pointed at a table further away. "But this is between you guys."

For a moment, Quinn's face looked as close to angry as she'd ever seen it. But just as quickly it was gone, and he smiled. "Of course. You do you."

❈ ❈ ❈

HOPE ATE HER trout almondine and green beans mechanically, then opened *Kisses and Tells* when she realized she was lonely. She'd become accustomed to Quinn's chatter with every meal.

Instead of the large font and gratuitous exclamation points she'd expected, the book open before her was *Verbal Overshadowing*. Carter had swapped the covers.

Hope looked up to tell Quinn. But his body was still angled toward the door, shoulders slumped. Tomás had not arrived yet.

She returned to the book, reading chapter 10: "The Power of Suggestion."

While we have all seen hypnosis as portrayed in popular media, there is no empirical evidence that a subject can be "cajoled" into an altered state of consciousness. For memory engrams to develop, subjects must be conscious and engaged. Closing one's eyes to visualize activates the imagination centers of the brain. In short, hypnotists are asking patients to fabricate and create rather than recall.

A chime pulled her away from the text, and Hope glanced up. The dining room had emptied completely, leaving only Quinn at his table and Jonah leaning against the back wall.

The extent to which humans can be significantly influenced by the power of suggestion is not only well-documented but also scientifically validated. Cognitive researchers have just begun to realize the potential of inserting false or modified memories into susceptible subjects.[3]

Hope slid a finger to the footnote, squinting at the small print:

3 Dr. Luke Salinger, The Memory Mechanic: *(San Francisco: Helix Press). More: chapter 12, "Resistance and Resistants."*

Hope flipped forward to the gap in the book, despite knowing it was the missing chapter. Though now, taped to the first page of chapter 13, was a familiar item: a thin silver key. The flash drive from Carter's glasses.

Suddenly, Quinn stood and dropped his napkin in an untidy heap on his untouched cake, then stalked toward the door.

"Q," Hope called after him. She pushed her chair back and stood to follow.

Hope was a few feet away when Quinn stopped and gripped a dining-room chair with both hands. She froze as Quinn wound up like a batter and smashed it against the nearest window. He continued to swing, uttering a guttural, primal cry each time. A pair of strong arms grabbed her from behind as Hope took a step forward.

It was Jonah. "What the hell are you doing?" he hissed.

"Helping him," Hope said, wrenching away.

"You can't help. Sit down." His eyes were stony, and his voice held a businesslike authority she'd never heard.

Hope sat.

"We have a Code Four here," Jonah said, finger to his ear. "Hello? Hello?" Jonah swore, then walked quickly to the phone on the wall by the door.

Quinn set his chair on the floor and crossed to Jonah. Hope shrank further into her chair as red lights flashed from the ceiling and sirens wailed. But just before the bars descended, Quinn shoved Jonah through the open door. He stepped back as the bars fell with a slam, leaving Hope and Quinn alone in the dining room. The bars over the window Quinn had been attacking fell an inch, then stopped.

Hope pulled her knees to her chest, wrapping her arms around them. Quinn looked around, though he didn't seem to be seeing anything. Then he picked up his chair and returned to the window.

At the last Code Four, Quinn had held her hand. He'd even kept her from causing her own code in the Bloom Room. Hope thought back to all the times Quinn responded to her distress intuitively. How he'd been there to talk to her, distract her, make her laugh. How she'd avoided reciprocating much emotion, but he'd nonetheless become a lighthouse in the hurricane of Wilder. And here Quinn was now, in his own personal hell. Hope made her way toward the window again. Quinn ignored her. He was like a woodcutter, splitting logs. His breathing was labored, but he gave no indication of letting up. The chairs here were made of a cheap wooden veneer, and Hope wasn't sure if it or the window would give first.

"You've proven you're a badass," Hope yelled, over the sirens. "Don't you think it's time to take a break?"

With each swing, the window vibrated.

"Q, stop and let's talk," Hope said, putting a hand on his arm. "We can walk to Lacuna."

Quinn paused, at last, chair in mid-swing. "Why the fuck should I talk to you? You never talk to me. Just the same sarcastic bullshit all the time." His face was slick with sweat, or tears, or both.

For a second Hope thought he might launch the chair at her, but instead he swung it in another wide arc at the window. It wobbled, and the chair began to splinter.

"I needed you to sit with me, help me deal with Tomás, but you couldn't be bothered," he spat. "You won't tell me what you're doing in the Butterfly Box. Yes, I know you sneak up there. You're nothing but secrets."

Hope opened her mouth, then closed it. He was right. All she had here were secrets.

"You're so fucking selfish." Quinn paused again, breathing in gasps, sweat dripping off his face and his arms. "Do you care about anyone but yourself?"

"Of course I do," Hope said. "I care about you. I care about Carter."

"Bullshit," Quinn panted, hands tight around the chair back. His voice held a venom she'd never heard. "You make me sick."

Quinn raised the chair again, and Hope knew this time he was aiming for her. Her hands went up instinctively, but she didn't move quickly enough. She crumpled to the floor, into darkness.

25

LOSS

LUKE
Palm Springs, California

I T WAS NEARLY midnight, and Luke's eyes were starting to go. He refreshed the feed on his laptop, then stood and stretched his aching back. The screen held the same image it had since his conversation with Hope yesterday: the grainy matrix of Erleben. Empty.

Luke wandered his hallway, turning on lights and standing in each room like a visitor. He paused in Charlotte's ultrafeminine room, eyes roving over her pink bedspread and white furry throw pillows, taking in the sheer amount of fluff and glitter and sparkle. Hope and Charlotte used to love weekend fix-it projects. After pouring over Pinterest for hours, they'd gone shopping and spent two days locked inside this room hanging fairy lights, framing posters, hot gluing jeweled things to other things.

A sharp stab of guilt went through Luke as he inspected a picture of Hope and Charlotte on the dresser, reminded again of how this loss was his daughter's as well.

Luke returned to his pacing. He wandered into his bedroom, pausing at the framed Post-it over the light switch. Then he sat gingerly on Hope's side of the bed, careful not to disturb the pillow. He opened the drawer of her nightstand, which held an eclectic assortment of books, hair rubber bands, journals and pens, and a mess of hotel key cards.

He pinched a rubber band between his thumb and forefinger, thinking about how Hope frequently wore one around her wrist, carried at least ten in her purse. How he'd tease her for spending an hour doing her hair before they went out, but within half an hour putting it up. How he'd gently pull the band from her hair just to see it tumble down her back. Wilder residents weren't allowed items like rubber bands or shoelaces or hairspray, and the thought of Hope without her supply of rubber bands made him disproportionately sad.

He slipped the black band around his own wrist, then collected the key cards into a pile and fanned them out in his hand. Luke could never associate any of their trips with a particular card, but Hope always remembered. Santa Fe, she'd say. Avila Beach. San Francisco.

At least, that's what she used to be able to do.

Luke dropped the cards back into the drawer and shut it, then smoothed the bedspread back into place.

In the closet he ran a hand across her clothes, listening to the hangers tinkle against each other. Luke straightened dress shirts on his side, then pulled a tie from the rack. His good luck tie, a gift from Hope. The last time he'd worn it was for the *Breakthroughs* interview, a year ago. He leaned against the wall, clutching the tie, remembering.

Luke had overslept the morning of the taping. Hope hadn't returned from picking up Charlotte until after midnight, and he'd stayed awake long past, stressing about the interview. He had agreed to meet Elliot for coffee and a run-through of talking points before their flight to SFO, but he was late. Luke raced around the bedroom getting ready, cursing. He swiped his tie off the dresser and draped it over his shoulder. Hope was on the bed reading his book, soles of her feet on the headboard, hair wrapped in a towel. She was wearing his shirt from last night and nothing else, only buttoning the middle buttons. It was hard not to stare; she looked far better in it than he ever could.

He thought about the shower twenty minutes ago. He'd been singing James Taylor with extreme enthusiasm when Hope pulled the curtain and stepped in with him. So focused on the song, he'd jumped when she pressed herself against his back and wrapped her leg around his. It took only seconds to register how good she felt in his arms: steamy, wet, slippery with soap from his skin. How her shallow breathing and those soft, sweet little moans he loved echoed off the tiled walls. How with her lips sliding haltingly down his chest, his nervousness about the day ahead faded away as he gave in—to her fingers, to that sublime tongue, to Hope.

"'Praise for *The Memory Mechanic*,'" she now read aloud. "Dr. Luke Salinger explores the science behind false memories and forces us to ask the chilling question: What if everything we remember never actually happened?" Hope pushed her reading glasses onto her head and waggled her fingers at him. "Ominous."

Luke was still unfocused, trying to clear away the image of the shower, but it wanted to linger.

"Come on," Hope said. "I'm trying to get you pumped. Big day. Game on."

Game on.

Luke stood in front of the mirror, watching Hope as he tied his necktie. "Are you going to put clothes on today?"

She feigned offense. "I have clothes on. Come here, you're doing it all wrong."

"You have my clothes on." He moved to the bed, resting his hand on her thigh. Her skin was impossibly soft. "Not that I'm complaining, but I have to meet Elliot and then get on a plane, and then give this interview. And if you stay like that, I'll have no reason to leave and then I'll be a colossal failure and you'll stop liking me. At which point I'll be left to roam the streets, shuffling in my slippers, muttering your name."

"That's a massive amount of responsibility," Hope said. She moved onto her knees and worked his tie into a perfect knot. "I wish I could come. You know I love it when you get all cognitive." She took the towel off her head and fluffed out her damp hair.

"You'd just make me nervous anyway," he said.

"Will you send me a signal?" she asked. "While you're on camera. A little wave, or something. A secret sign."

"Sure." Luke laughed.

She reclined against the headboard. "You might get some backlash after this, when people find out what Copeland-Stark is doing."

"What do you mean?"

"The manipulation," Hope said, and her voice was strained. "How easy it is to make people think what you want them to think."

"You don't think people should know how susceptible they are?" Luke said. "You of all people know there are innocent people in prison because of shitty interrogation techniques. But think about how easily people are taken in by a clickbait headline or believe a lie because someone sounds like an authority."

Luke held his suit jacket by its hanger and ran a lint brush down it.

"Not to mention the hundreds of patients I've worked with who were paralyzed from trauma, or phobias," he continued. "They couldn't leave the house. They couldn't have a healthy relationship. Through no fault of their own. And now they're unencumbered, free to live their lives." He could feel a familiar rush, the fusion of adrenaline and conviction that always surfaced when he talked about his research.

Luke exhaled and turned to Hope. This wasn't the first time she'd heard this particular sermon, and he expected the serene smile Hope wore when he got "all cognitive." But that day, her face was pale, eyes troubled and far away.

"You know I'm doing this to help people, right?" He shrugged on his jacket and came to kneel by the bed. "I'm not Tony. I would never do it to harm anyone. And I would never, ever do anything like that to you."

It took Hope a moment to return to Earth, but when she did, she placed a hand on his face. "I know. I got one of the last good ones."

"I'm lucky you're crazy," he said, turning his head to kiss her palm.

The shadows left her eyes, and she smiled. "Is that an opinion or a diagnosis, Dr. Salinger?"

"Both," he said, standing.

Hope smoothed his lapels. "So handsome," she said. "Break a leg. And don't forget my special signal."

In the bedroom doorway, he turned to look at Hope. She was stretched out on the bed again, looking remarkably feline, nose in his book. There were times like this, when she was doing the unremarkable, that he couldn't believe his luck. She was like a wisp of smoke: ethereal, fleeting. Luke was overcome with the desire to skip the meeting with Elliot and this ridiculous interview, and barricade the two of them inside his house, forever.

"I love you," he said.

Shit.

It was the first time he'd said it.

He was the first one to say it.

Shit.

"I love you too." Hope didn't even seem fazed. She looked over his book to where he stood frozen in the doorway and started to laugh. "What? Was there any doubt?"

Luke dropped his briefcase on the ground with a thump. He shrugged off his suit jacket and returned to the bed, deciding he cared fuck all about meeting with Elliot.

❃❃❃

His phone vibrated on the dresser, pulling him away from that morning. Luke jabbed at the speaker button.

"What's wrong?"

"Don't freak out," Elliot said.

"What's happening?" Luke couldn't imagine a time where anyone could say those words and have it work.

"Dr. Emerson is with her now, and I don't really know anything," Elliot said. "But there was an incident with Hope and Tomás Romero's boyfriend."

26

JUST US GIRLS

※ ※ ※

HOPE
The Wilder Sanctuary
Rancho Mirage, California

"G OOD, YOU'RE AWAKE. How do you feel?"

Hope thought she was pulling a *Groundhog Day*, waking up at Wilder again on that winter afternoon. But a glance at the window showed it was summer, and Dr. Stark and not Luke reclined in the black chair.

With considerable effort, Hope sat up. "My head is killing me."

"You received quite a blow," Dr. Stark said. "But your CT scan was normal. Any nausea? Dizziness?"

Hope shook her head. Which hurt like hell.

"Do you know what day it is?" Stark asked, stylus poised over his tablet. She noticed Stark was developing a gut.

"Do I ever?"

"Good point," Stark said. He gave her a tired smile. Hope wondered if he was trying to grow a beard. "You've been asleep for almost fourteen hours. What do you remember?"

"Quinn," Hope said. "The chair. He hit me."

"Where were you when this happened?" Stark asked. He was blurring around the edges.

"In the dining room. I was reading . . ." Hope remembered Carter's flash drive and her eyes searched the room, which didn't take long. *Verbal Overshadowing* wasn't on the desk or the nightstand. "Is Quinn okay? Where is he?"

"He's fine," Dr. Stark said. "His behavior was a manifestation of his condition, but fortunately the incidents pass quickly and have no lingering side effects."

"I want to see him," Hope said. After Carter, she was finished believing anything the doctors claimed.

"You'll see him tomorrow." Stark pulled a penlight out of his pocket and Hope followed the light with her eyes. "You don't have a concussion, but you did lose consciousness briefly. Tomorrow you'll be fine as well."

Hope remained unconvinced, but Stark had moved on.

"We haven't been able to meet since Carter . . ." Dr. Stark pulled at his tie. "Took his own life. I apologize again for missing our session. Especially since you've had a rather trying week."

Hope almost laughed at Dr. Stark, always the master of understatement. Of her two friends in the world, one was dead and the other had just bludgeoned her with an IKEA chair.

"It isn't your nature," Dr. Stark said. "But embracing your emotions as you grieve is important."

Hope thought about the insults Quinn had hurled at her, which hurt far worse than her head. "It's not in my nature to feel?"

"Not *to* feel," Stark said. "To admit what you feel, to ask for help. Neither of which are weaknesses." He rested his tablet on his knee and studied Hope. "I'm sending you for an hour with the Erleben device first thing in the morning."

"It's *air-leh-ben*," Hope said haughtily.

"And I'd also like to try additional sessions in the Labyrinth, to help you process," Dr. Stark continued.

Hope blew a gust of air from the corner of her mouth.

"I know it isn't your favorite place," Stark said, again with the understatement.

"Do I have a choice?" Hope asked.

"Not technically," he said. "But it's much more likely to be effective if you aren't fighting it."

Hope turned onto her side. She slid her arm under the pillow and felt something hard, not needing to see it to know what it was. She sat up again, suddenly wanting Stark gone as quickly as possible.

"I'll go."

"Excellent." Stark looked surprised but he stood, steel chair legs scraping against the floor. He kicked at the scuff marks with the bottom of his shoe. "Get some rest. Be well, Hope."

As soon as the door clicked Hope dove under her pillow, but another knock stopped her.

"I'm not hungry," Hope called.

The door opened anyway, as she knew it would. "*Mi'ja?*"

"Q," Hope said, letting out a breath of relief at the sound of Quinn's voice.

"I thought Stark would never leave," he said, shutting the door and pressing his back against it. "I've been lurking around for twenty minutes. He's really letting himself go . . . Have you noticed?" Quinn patted his stomach. "Needs some serious manscaping."

Hope motioned him closer, and Quinn crumpled into the chair. He leaned forward and buried his head in her blanket.

"You okay?" Hope stroked his hair.

"No." His voice was muffled, heavy. "Fuck, I'm so sorry, Hope. I can't believe I let you see me like that. I can't believe I hurt you."

"I'll be fine. Truly," Hope said.

"I'm still so sorry. Please, please forgive me."

Hope scooted in the narrow twin bed as far as she could, squashing herself against the wall.

Quinn climbed in next to her, extending his arm so she could rest against him. He reached for the remote and switched on the monitor, scrolling through the channels, landing on the screen of platitude posters. *The only impossible journey is the one you never begin.*

"You know my favorite quote?" he asked. "If we cease to believe in love, why do we live?"

"I've never seen that one," Hope said.

"It's not here. It's from a very wise woman, a sage." He looked a little more like Quinn now.

"Maya Angelou? Christiane Amanpour?"

"Close." Quinn grinned. "The hot chick in *Vampire Diaries.*"

Hope laughed and gave him a poke. They snuggled together in silence, Hope watching the reflection of inspirational phrases playing on Quinn's brown eyes.

"What's it called?" Hope asked. "What happens to you?"

Quinn tensed. "It's called intermittent explosive disorder. It's characterized by sudden fits of impulsive, violent behavior that are grossly out of proportion to the situation. I'm basically a three-year-old having a supersized temper tantrum in Target. And then it ends, and I feel like I was watching myself the whole time from the ceiling, and I can't remember why I was so pissed."

"I never knew," Hope said. "Because it never occurred to me to ask. I've been a terrible friend."

"Hopeless, what I said before . . . I didn't mean—"

"Q," she said. "I shouldn't have needed to literally be hit over the head, but as Stark says, I have a hard time asking for help. And he's right. I should have trusted you. I'm sorry."

"It's hard to trust anyone in a place like this," he said.

"Wilder isn't why I don't trust people," Hope said. "Or not the only reason. I had a fiancé, a long time ago. He was . . . I've never met anyone more skilled at manipulation. And I let it happen, for years. It almost destroyed me. I swore it would never happen again."

It was a rarity for her to reveal so much truth, to anyone. Hope felt unprotected, exposed. Like a mouse reaching for the peanut on a trap. But she'd opened the floodgates, and everything about Tony continued to tumble from her mouth.

Quinn listened, arm still tight around her, fingers tapping a rhythm on her shoulder.

"And now Luke," Hope said. "I really thought he was different. The worst thing is, I still believe he wouldn't do this to me. Which only shows how little I've evolved."

"I know the feeling," Quinn said. He grabbed for the remote and switched to the screen of rain. "Hopeless, we need to figure this out. We need to find out what they are really doing to us, to all those people. Where they are."

"Where Carter is," Hope said. "I forgot. I was about to tell you, before. I think Carter left this for us." She groped under her pillow and produced *Verbal Overshadowing*, opening it to reveal the jump drive taped to chapter 13.

"Thanks, Cowboy." Quinn smiled. "Now we only need to break into an office, get to a computer, log on without anyone knowing, and get way smarter so we can actually access the files. Where is the Rogue when you need him? Or her? Or them?"

"We need Carter," Hope said, the words causing a tightness behind her sternum.

"It's just us girls, now." Quinn pulled her close. "So it's going to have to be an old-school caper."

Hope smiled. "The best kind."

"Tomorrow," Quinn said. "I have Dr. Green before Creative Connections, so right after. Plus, if they make us do another vision board, I'm going to need to counter it with something deviant."

"Tomorrow." Hope nodded. "I have the Butterfly Box first thing."

"Now"—Quinn removed his arm and swiveled to face her, crossing his legs in a yoga pose—"let's dish. I have more questions."

"Ask away," Hope said. "Better hurry while I'm still feeling sorry for you."

"Start with what you're doing in the Butterfly Box," Quinn said, settling against the pillow and throwing a leg over hers.

"It's called the Shade," Hope said. "But I might need to start a little further back."

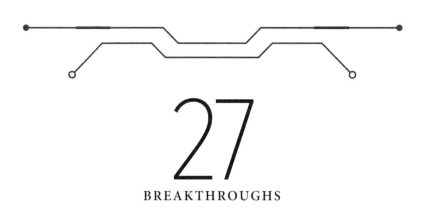

27

BREAKTHROUGHS

HOPE
The Wilder Sanctuary
Rancho Mirage, California

HOPE STOOD AGAINST a wall in the Shade, next to a shadowy outline of Spooky. At her feet, runners of lights like the LEDs in the Butterfly Box illuminated a path ahead.

"Why is it always so unnecessarily dark and creepy?" she asked. "One day can we go somewhere nice, like a puppy farm?"

Spooky motioned with his hand, and an ornate crystal chandelier in the ceiling lit up.

Hope blinked into the brightness of a private screening room resembling the celebrity homes on HGTV. There were two rows of curved armchairs covered in lush red velvet, complete with matching tufted ottomans.

The walls were a deep crimson, accented with gold filigree and dark wood wainscoting. Hope followed Spooky to the front. They sat, facing a massive movie screen flanked by velvet curtains. Spooky snapped his fingers. The lights dimmed as the screen lit up and a sound—one he surely must be too young to have personally experienced—filled the room. But Hope knew. It was the whir of a fan and a faint, continuous clicking like running a fingernail across a comb: the distinctive hum of a Super 8 movie projector.

It reminded Hope of family movies her father used to play, from the dusty box of film reels in the garage. He'd thumbtack a white sheet to the living room wall and turn on the projector, teaching Hope how to make shadows with her hands. Hope could only manage a butterfly, but her father made the best ones: a horse, a bear, a barking dog.

Grainy, off-color footage with little specks and lines played now, running a slideshow of pictures of a party at someone's house. Someone's humongous house. There was an infinity pool in the backyard, complete with waterfall. On the other side of the pool, a six-piece orchestra played. Waiters were scattered among the guests with shots of soup, pointy canapes, shrimp cocktail with enormous tails hanging over martini-glass rims.

"Do you remember where you were?" Spooky asked.

Hope shook her head. "Have I been there?"

Then there were pictures of Hope, the Hope she hadn't been for some time. Hope in a slinky cocktail dress with designer heels and curled hair and makeup. Perched at a high stool near the pool, chatting with a group of people. Turned toward the camera, blowing a kiss. With a bright red drink in her hand, talking to Dr. Emerson. Smiling at a dinner table with her head against Luke's shoulder, hand on his lapel. Mugging for the camera next to two huge glass greyhounds, with Tess.

"The glass dogs. Jack Copeland's house, at the Vintage Club last year," Hope said slowly. "Tess was right. We did meet before. She's his daughter."

Spooky nodded. "What was the party for?"

"Luke's book." Hope swallowed. "He'd been interviewed on TV. It was a big deal."

The slideshow faded out and the set of a talk show faded in: a white leather armchair adjacent to a matching sofa, circular table between with bright blue coffee mugs and a glass bowl of green apples, translucent windowpanes and a silhouette of the Golden Gate Bridge behind. In the armchair was the host, a petite woman with a lot of makeup and five-inch Louboutins.

Luke sat on the couch with Dr. Stark. Between them was a woman Hope didn't recognize. She was Korean, heavyset, older. She wore a conservatively cut suit and black flats, and carried herself with a general air of importance.

"Welcome to *Breakthroughs*. I'm Natasha Chan," the host said, blinking her fake eyelashes. "My guests today are the architects behind an unprecedented breakthrough in the study of memory. I have Dr. Elliot Stark, chief operations officer of biotech giant Copeland-Stark. I also welcome Jordan Lin, co-CEO of Maelstrom Corporation, and Dr. Luke Salinger, known for the book that earned him his nickname, *The Memory Mechanic*."

Hope gripped the armrests.

"Let's dive in," Natasha said. "Tell us how the memory hacking works."

Stark laughed, with a sideways glance at Luke. "First off, we don't call it hacking. That's a Jordan Lin term. In our field we call it reconsolidation."

"I've read the book," Natasha said to Luke. "Call it what you will, but for me it sounds like a fancy term for mind control. And what struck me most is how susceptible we are to believing false memories. Can you take us through the steps?"

"Of course." Luke adjusted his tie. "It's basically about pushing the right buttons, in the right places, but delicately. We want a subject to feel compelled to please. You'd be shocked at how much change happens with even the most subtle nudges toward social conformity. We heap on praise: the subject is commended for how accurate their memories are, how adept their recall. It makes them want to continue to impress."

"As we all do, on some level," Stark added.

"After that," Luke continued, "we introduce the false memory. It has real facts buried within: where they work, restaurants they frequent, names of friends. Obviously, at first the subject is thrown off and dismisses it entirely."

"Nuance is critical here," Dr. Stark said. "Every word counts. Think about how if I say, 'having a light lunch,' it means something vastly different from 'scarfing a pizza.' These details are what allow the alterations to take root."

"We tell the subject that memories are malleable." Luke paused to take a sip from a mug with BREAKTHROUGHS printed across it. "We explain how memories are continually remapped. Then we ask the subject to close their eyes and visualize as we present the false memory to them."

"The key in this," Dr. Stark cut in, "is when the patient is asked to close their eyes, they're accessing areas of the brain responsible for imagination, not facts."

"Right," Luke said. "We then direct the subject to go home and think about it, to practice visualizing the memory. They aren't allowed to talk to anyone about it. That's it."

"That's it?" Natasha Chan asked. "I've seen the footage, but it's still so hard to believe."

"We have over a ninety-nine percent success rate with subjects believing the memories actually are a true recollection," Stark said. "The remainder—we call them resistants—experience little change or none at all."

"Playing devil's advocate here," Natasha said. "Why do it? Surely there are ethical ramifications."

"Anything can be used for evil if it's in the wrong hands," said Dr. Stark. "But what we're doing has erased myriad phobias, cured depression and PTSD for thousands, broken substance addictions."

"Give us an example."

"Think about a substance abuser. We can introduce false memories of being violently ill while using, and they aren't interested in it anymore. Or the opposite: replace it with something positive—a love of exercise, for example," Dr. Stark said.

"Can you plant a hatred of chocolate in me?" Natasha laughed.

"What we're really talking about is helping people move on from and overcome trauma," Luke said, straightening his pant leg. "There are also staggering implications for the justice system: correcting interrogations, ensuring law enforcement doesn't unwittingly force false confessions. And we're also exploring how this research could help patients suffering from dementia."

"Speaking of," Natasha said, "what if there were a memory I wanted to never forget? Like the birth of my son? My first kiss?"

"There's a correlation between the emotional value of a memory and our ability to recall it," Dr. Stark said. "The more attached we are, the more likely we'll remember it."

"And for the average person, there are many memory strengthening tricks, like using mnemonic devices," Luke said, with a quick smile at the camera. "Don't think about kangaroos cooking waffles."

Natasha laughed. "That's an odd image."

"Memory relies on associations," Luke explained. "You hear a song, and it transports you back to a memory of listening in the car, which jogs the memory of who you were with, where you were going, arriving at that place, and so on."

"But the kangaroo?"

"Most people have few associations with kangaroos and waffles, so it sticks out. It forces you to use several parts of your brain to make a wider web of associations. I promise you, a week from now you won't remember what reconsolidation means, but you'll remember the kangaroo." Luke lifted his mug and held it awkwardly, with his pinky outstretched, tapping it against the side.

Hope smiled.

"I'll bet you're right." Natasha laughed, turning to Dr. Stark. "But that's only the beginning for Copeland-Stark, correct?"

Dr. Stark nodded and placed his foot on the parquet floor. "Dr. Salinger's procedure has proven to be highly effective, though over a period of weeks and at times months. We've added additional remedies to cut treatment time to hours"—Stark looked at Jordan Lin—"such as the use of virtual reality to throw memory formation into hyperdrive. Think of having patients *living* their new memories, totally immersed in their environments—smelling, feeling, absorbing—making those multisensory associations rather than merely imagining them."

"That's where we come in," Jordan Lin said. It was the first time she'd spoken. "My partner did almost all the initial programming himself and relied heavily on Dr. Salinger's research to make the world as immersive as possible."

"Your partner being Carter H. Sloane, correct? He programmed an entire VR world by himself?" Natasha asked. "We should bring him on *Breakthroughs*."

"Oh, I don't take him out much." Jordan waved a hand dismissively, as if Carter were a beloved pet that after months of arduous training had finally learned to sit on command. "He's won all kinds of awards, but I had to strong-arm him into starting Maelstrom; he'd never even considered monetizing his talent. If I hadn't come along, he'd still be hanging around on the dark web doing God knows what." She chuckled into her mug.

Natasha Chan turned to the camera. "It's time for a quick break," she said. "When we return, it gets even more interesting. Ms. Lin will discuss Maelstrom's acquisition of Minnes, a Swedish biotech firm creating some revolutionary brain technology. Then we'll learn about Copeland-Stark's newest facility. I guarantee it will make your last vacation pale in comparison. Stay tuned."

The picture faded and the theater chandelier illuminated.

From far away a lighthouse horn echoed, a low, gloomy hum that vibrated their ears.

"Do you remember that now?" Spooky asked.

"I'd forgotten." Hope's eyes stayed on the blank screen. "Or maybe I wanted to forget."

"Why would you want that?" Spooky asked.

"You saw it," Hope said. "Luke's made a career of manipulating people into thinking they did something they didn't do. Or vice versa. I was probably one of those people."

"People can be very selfish," Spooky said quietly.

"That person in the slideshow before? Smiling at the party, blowing kisses? I can barely remember her. I'm so different now." Hope ran a hand through her lifeless hair.

"We all are," Spooky said.

Once again, Hope wondered about the kid who sold comic books and played *D&D* before Wilder. She studied Spooky. "What's your story, Spencer? Who put you here?"

Spooky shook his head. "That's for another day."

28

VIOLENT IMPULSES

✴✴✴✴✴

HOPE

The Wilder Sanctuary
Rancho Mirage, California

QUINN WAS EXTRA punchy when they left Creative Connections the next day.

"I told you, another goddamn vision board," he said, as they headed down an empty corridor toward the library. "I wanted to jab a glue stick in my eye."

"Did you see Tess's board?" Hope whispered. "It looked like a shrine in a serial killer's house."

Quinn grabbed her arm as they rounded a corner, pulling her in another direction.

"Library's that way." Hope pointed.

"This is closer," Quinn said, stopping in front of a door. "And private." He produced a key card from underneath his T-shirt, disentangling himself from the red lanyard and holding it against a pad on the wall.

"How the hell did you get that?" Hope asked.

"It was hanging from Fernando's pocket this morning," Quinn said, opening the door and ushering Hope inside. "Which is how I remembered this room."

It was a large examination room with a curtained-off hospital bed on the right side and a small round table on the left. A speaker device was in the middle of the table, balanced on its three curved legs like a spaceship preparing for takeoff. A long, low shelf divided the room in half. It was filled with baskets of therapy toys: puzzles, clay, stress balls, magnetic blocks. Quinn pointed to a computer and printer on a desk under the window.

"How did you know this was here?" Hope asked.

"It's called a processing room. They brought me here after my fight with Nina," Quinn said, pointing to the bed. "First, they checked me over on that, and then they had me type everything out." He dropped Fernando's lanyard next to the keyboard and hit the space bar. The screen lit up with the Copeland-Stark logo. "No password on this one either."

"What if they catch us in here?"

"I'll beat the crap out of you with a fidget spinner and say I was having another episode," Quinn said. He put a hand over his mouth. "Sorry, too soon?"

Hope pulled the silver flash drive from her bra and put it in the tower. On the screen, the folders *Wilder: Active* and *Wilder: Deactivated* appeared as before, but now there was an additional document, titled *CH12 R&R.*

"The missing chapter," Quinn said, pointing.

Hope nodded as she opened the document. "It's not that long," she said, scrolling. "But too long to read now. Do you think there's another code inside? A message?"

"Print it," Quinn said, reaching over her to click the hot keys.

The printer came to life with a whirring sound. It spit out a page and the whirring stopped, followed with a series of short beeps. Quinn moved to the machine, opening the paper drawer and poking at the console. "PC Load Letter? What the fuck does that mean?"

Hope clicked on the printer icon, though she knew it was futile. Her customary solution for any tech problem was to have Luke fix it.

Quinn gripped her shoulder and Hope froze at the sound of voices coming from the hallway. Voices and an unmistakable click of high heels.

Hope closed the folder, pulled the drive from the tower, and slept the computer. Quinn grabbed the paper from the printer and pulled its plug from the wall. He shoved Hope toward the bed, pulling the curtain closed around them. They crouched on the floor next to the shelf of toys, observing through the gap in the curtain.

The doctors moved into the room with an almost synchronous choreography, opening laptops and setting coffee mugs on the table. Dr. Stark placed a stack of two-prong file folders in the center of the table, near the speaker. He looked even more ragged than he had the night before.

"What's this?" Dr. Emerson paused at the desk. She snatched up Fernando's lanyard with an annoyed expression and scrutinized it, then waved at Dr. Green. "Never mind, go ahead."

Dr. Green pressed the speaker button and dialed. As she did, her sweater sleeve rode up her arm, revealing several angry scars slashed across her inner wrist. Hope was grateful the sound of the ringing phone masked her surprised inhale.

"Give me some good news," said a deep voice from the speaker.

"Good morning, Mr. Copeland," Dr. Green said. "We're ready to brief you."

"Good morning, Jack. Let's get to it," Dr. Emerson said. She pulled a folder from the top of the pile and opened it. "Subject 16012-TRC is demonstrating considerable progress."

Quinn poked Hope, then pointed at himself proudly with both thumbs.

"There is a marked increase in anxiety around established obsessions dealing with contamination and order," Dr. Emerson continued. "As well as the more violent impulses manifesting in the last two months. The subject has had two documented rage incidents since the new treatments. Compulsive behavior has also increased in frequency; however, with this subject, it's difficult to ascertain if the compulsivity is a habit or a manufactured affect, not entirely a result of the disorder. The patient tends to be somewhat . . . theatrical."

Hope almost laughed out loud.

"Regardless, regular intervention is quite promising." Dr. Emerson closed the folder and opened another one.

"Subject 09003-BOC is also making progress, though we are considering a modification to his schedule from the original plan. We will likely be trying a more radical course of treatment measures."

"And 26050-JCC?"

Hope repeated patient numbers and letters in her head, memorizing.

"Also improving," Dr. Stark responded. "Marked increase in mood swings and antisocial behavior. Just today, her vision project was quite disturbing." He looked around the table at the nodding heads.

"In addition," Dr. Emerson said. "With the removal of Subject 57220-JLC, we believe we've dealt a severe blow to the Mad Hatters. There have been no reported cyberattacks since, and we're told chatter on the dark web is chaotic."

"It could be a coincidence," Dr. Green said softly. "It's only been a week."

"We aren't letting our guard down," Dr. Emerson said. "But we're confident we've neutralized the Rogue."

Quinn mouthed *Rogue* at Hope, who returned his confused expression with her own.

"Excellent," Jack Copeland said. The speaker crackled and buzzed. "So, what's the bad news?"

Dr. Emerson adjusted her monitor, fingers flashing in a blur across her keyboard. "This brings us to Subject 09093-LSC."

Hope recognized this patient number. It was hers.

There was a long pause. The doctors stilled. Dr. Stark stopped his fingers in mid-tap on the table.

"Christ almighty. What now?" Jack Copeland's voice was measured, almost fatherly, though it didn't appear anyone in the room was fooled by it.

The doctors exchanged pointed glances around the table, playing a silent game of responsibility chicken with their eyes.

Dr. Stark leaned in now, a sheen on his brow and the bridge of his nose. "The most recent treatment in the Labyrinth produced the same results, despite modifications to the boilermaker cocktail. The subject is moderately responsive during the procedure and experiences the same side effects as other patients: disorientation, loss of some motor control, thirst. However, unlike the others, symptoms all abate within several minutes."

Now Stark looked profoundly uncomfortable. He rubbed at the stubble on his chin. "Within thirty minutes, the subject returns to baseline, experiencing no reconsolidation of new memories—"

"Amelia!" Jack interrupted.

Dr. Green inclined the lid of her laptop and spoke over it. "Yes, Mr. Copeland?"

"Translate. In English."

Quinn snorted softly. Hope flicked him on the knee.

Dr. Green glanced around the room. Dr. Emerson was staring straight ahead, implacable. Dr. Stark was absorbed in his Altoids tin.

"In short," Dr. Green said, "nothing is working. She has no memory of the Labyrinth, any therapy sessions, and zero attachment to the new memories introduced. We also think her intake procedure may have somehow . . ." Dr. Green took a sip of water.

"This is just speculation, Jack," Dr. Stark said, face pinched.

"Let her finish," Copeland said.

Dr. Green pulled at her shirt cuffs. "We suspect the initial wipe may have removed a larger time period of memories than anticipated. In addition, we believe the subject might actually be resistant." She snapped her laptop shut and placed her hands on top.

Hope closed her eyes. The *Breakthroughs* interview, the missing book chapter. Resistant.

"You've got to be joking," Jack Copeland said. "I thought that was one percent of the population or some shit."

"Even less," Dr. Stark said, as Dr. Emerson shot daggers across the table.

The doctors continued communicating via their nonverbal code of eyebrow raises and mouth twitches.

"We do have one more thing to try," Dr. Emerson said. "Dr. Green's sonogenetics headsets paired with the Labyrinth."

"This is the first I've heard of this," Dr. Green said. Hope had never heard her speak sharply to anyone. "The headsets are still in beta."

"Do it," Jack Copeland said.

"But it isn't safe," Dr. Green said, the alarm in her voice growing. "They haven't even gone through human subjects yet."

"You let me worry about that," Copeland said. "What if that doesn't work?"

The uncomfortable shifting, reshuffling of papers, and idle typing on laptops resumed. Dr. Green looked like she was going to puke, and Hope felt the same way.

Again, a hum from the speaker, a disembodied Charlie addressing the Angels. "Dr. Emerson, you assured me she would not become a problem," he said.

Dr. Emerson developed a flush, but her voice was steady. "Dr. *Salinger* assured *us* she would not become a problem."

"Luke Salinger is becoming a liability," Copeland said. "I don't care what level it says on his paperwork."

"He's effectively sidelined, but we need Luke," Dr. Stark said, using the same placating voice he often used with Hope. "He's far more dangerous out of the company than he is in it. And let's remember the PR angle. The Memory Mechanic is the face of Copeland-Stark."

"We could always groom a new face," Dr. Emerson said, but the comment hung in the air and floated away in the silence.

"So let me summarize," Jack said. "The grand plan you promised me would work has failed? I guess the inmates really are running the fucking asylum now."

"Dr. Green," Dr. Emerson said suddenly. She pulled Fernando's lanyard from her neck. "Can you return this to Fernando and ask him to wait in my office?"

Dr. Green looked confused but took the lanyard and left the room.

Dr. Emerson waited at least a minute before speaking again. "I personally think we should move her to the lab. "Subjects 00785-SSE and 36940-SSE in particular have shown great promise with Dr. Lu's techniques, especially the Tank. But Jiang is anxious for more subjects."

Quinn removed a stress ball from a purple basket and mashed it in his hand.

"Done," Jack said. "And I want you to find us a new location for the facility, Elliot. I don't like putting down roots."

Dr. Stark lowered his gaze to the pile of papers before him. "Of course. But I want to say . . ." He flicked the corner of a Post-it. "I'm not entirely comfortable with this."

Dr. Emerson sent Dr. Stark another gut-shot look.

"Well, Elliot," Jack Copeland said, allowing a long, pregnant silence to elapse before he spoke again. "I suggest you find a way to get comfortable fast."

29

CLOAK AND DAGGER

LUKE

The River at Rancho Mirage
Rancho Mirage, California

F OR FIFTEEN MINUTES Luke circled, stalking shoppers and meandering couples as if they were prey, to find this parking space.
Now he was waiting, blinker on, for the soccer mom and her
six kids to load themselves, some screaming, others kicking, into their
silver minivan. He punched the horn and gave the finger to the Tesla
weaseling in from the other side.

"Not today, asshole," he called out the window. A towheaded boy
paused his climb into the backseat to look at Luke and giggle. Luke
gave him a guilty wave as he parked his Highlander.

He strode across the parking lot toward the movie complex, passing the enormous copper pigs in front of the barbeque restaurant,
pausing to give each a pat on the snout as Hope used to. Several restaurants, a chocolatier, and a smelly-soap store swept through his periph-
eral vision before he arrived at the theater. As he entered through the
double doors, the pervasive smell of popcorn made him pause. Hope

loved movie popcorn to an almost ridiculous level of adoration. Even when they watched at home, she would make Luke detour to the theater, this theater, for popcorn. He didn't even know you could buy it without a movie ticket before Hope arrived in his life.

Luke hadn't been to the movies in ages and was momentarily stunned by the ticket prices. Especially considering he wouldn't be watching the movie.

Luke ducked inside Theater Five and chose a seat in the back. The theater was partly full, with couples and families trickling in, balancing cardboard containers of soda and Red Vines and those weird little pellets of ice cream that dissolve in your mouth. Luke scanned the theater several times, but he didn't recognize anyone.

Stretching out his long legs, he alternated between tapping his coffee cup and snapping the hair rubber band he was still wearing on his wrist. He wondered how much the pert brunette spokesmodel got paid for doing these promo spots for coming attractions. The lights dimmed, and Luke watched a confusing advertisement that, in the end, reminded the audience to silence all electronic devices, and another making him wish he'd stopped for a Diet Coke. He took in previews for yet another Nicholas Sparks adaptation, the next installment in a superhero series, and a reboot of a television series from the eighties.

As the music for the feature swelled, Luke rose and ducked out. He skulked along the side of the theater and used the exit to the right of the screen. He paused at the door and looked around before leaning on the long steel bar and stepping out into the evening.

This place was called the River, though the only suggestion of water was a manufactured pond in the middle. Fairy lights were draped over bushes and trees, casting their glow onto the water below. It smelled like an amusement park, artificial and processed, with the barest hint of mildew.

After growing up, getting married and divorced, and living some of his most tumultuous times here in Palm Springs, Luke never dreamed he'd move back. The job at Copeland Laboratories was only slated for a year. But then Hope happened. And he'd stayed because of her, because she loved the desert and had this mystical belief it was somehow their desert. And Luke found that when he looked at the world through her eyes, he could believe it too. Hope could do that to a person. And he knew he would stay a hundred years more if he had to, for her.

Early in their relationship, Hope made Luke revisit all his old haunts around the city. He spent months serving as her personal tour guide through the twists and turns of his memory lane. Some sights elicited laughter, while others were the gloomy parts he'd avoided revisiting long ago. But she'd asked, and all Hope ever really had to do was ask.

Luke drove her everywhere: to the abandoned bridge where they used to get stoned, to several of his older brother's apartments, his old high school, the scene of the fight where Elliot Stark saved him, the country club where he worked graveyard while taking classes during the day. Luke shared feelings and desires he'd never spoken aloud to anyone, even while they were happening. And through it all, Hope listened, forehead pressed against the passenger window or smoking on a bench while he paced. She lapped up every triviality, tale after tale, a kitten inhaling cream from a saucer.

"There were happy times too, growing up," he said, after a particularly morose tour of his adolescence where Hope had remained uncharacteristically quiet. Cathedral City was becoming distant in the rearview mirror. Luke was determined to end this night with a new memory, a good one. The sun was setting, casting long shadows on the blue wildflowers that seemed to be in bloom solely when Hope was in the vicinity. "I guess I just want you to know everything."

They'd left the scattered mini-malls and shopping complexes and liquor stores behind, heading toward the old downtown Hope loved. It made her feel like a 1940s Hollywood movie starlet, like she was in *Barton Fink*.

"I want to know everything," she said, taking his hand. "It's all confirmation I got one of the last good ones."

He'd laughed at the time, but there wasn't a hint of the usual flippancy in her voice. It was simple and earnest, with almost naked honesty, and Luke knew in his bones she meant it.

THE BENCH CREAKED as he sat. "Sorry I'm late. Couldn't find any parking."

Dr. Amelia Green sipped her coffee, fingers drumming on her paper cup. "Did you do what I asked?"

"I left my phone at home. I came here and bought a ticket. I stayed through the previews, and I left through the back exit." Luke pulled a crumpled piece of paper out of his pocket and showed it to her. "I didn't eat the message, and it didn't self-destruct, by the way."

She didn't laugh.

"What's with the cloak-and-dagger routine? You couldn't just text me?"

Amelia finished her coffee and placed it on the bench between them. Her face was wan, eyes bloodshot and puffy. "Did Stark tell you Quinn Mireles had an episode?"

Luke felt his pulse begin to race. "He promised me Hope was fine."

"She is. It could have been much worse, with how much they'd amped him up. But both were back to normal a day later," Dr. Green said. "And you also heard about Jordan Lin's partner, Carter?"

"That was unexpected. It screwed up a lot." His own words registered, and Luke kicked himself. "Sorry, I didn't intend it to come out like that. That's not what I meant."

She waved it away. "What you probably didn't know was that Carter and Hope developed a . . . close friendship in there."

Luke stood for a reason he couldn't explain.

"Sit down," she said. Her voice was tired.

Luke gave a dissatisfied grunt but returned to the bench. He snapped the rubber band on his wrist, a trick he'd suggested to patients to break negative thought patterns. It didn't work. After all this time, he couldn't blame Hope for giving up on him. For choosing a better man.

"They didn't want you to know. Dr. Emerson thought it would make Hope more receptive to treatment if she were happier. You know an open state of mind is critical. That's why we designed Wilder this way."

"I know, I know," Luke said, rolling his eyes. "What was the cause of Sloane's death?"

Amelia used her best Liz Emerson voice. "Extremely high doses of several medications resulting in cardiac arrest. Self-inflicted."

"But Wilder has that system to control the meds," Luke said.

"Yes, it's automated, precise to the milligram." She crossed her legs at the ankles. "Like in a hotel minibar, only a thousand times more sensitive."

"Then how did he get extra meds?"

"That's just it. I don't think he did." Dr. Green held up a hand as if pushing her thoughts clear away. "They thought he was the Rogue, so they got rid of him. The only thing on Jack Copeland's mind is keeping his secrets from being exposed. And he has the money and power to make it happen."

"Those are our secrets too," Luke said. He thought about Amelia taking a bottle of pills when she got her clearance, and the scars he'd seen on her body nearly a year ago. They'd all paid a price to keep secrets.

"I want to help you destroy Copeland-Stark," Amelia said.

Luke stared at her.

"Come on, Luke," she said. "We go way back. I know Jonah's been telling you what's happening at Wilder."

Luke considered this, but he didn't speak.

"He didn't rat you out," Dr. Green said, hands passing over her face. "He's my brother. I know him better than anyone, and I know he hates Copeland-Stark more than you do."

"I doubt that," Luke said. "What happened to playing nice?"

"I've been playing nice for three years," she said, and for the briefest moment Luke saw a flash of the fiery Amelia from graduate school. "Three years ago I took those pills because I wanted to end my life. It was my choice. But Carter Sloane didn't have a choice. He didn't want to die, I'm certain of it. And I can't stand by anymore."

"Have you talked to Elliot about this?" Luke asked.

"Not yet," Amelia said.

"Good, don't," Luke said. "The less he knows, the better. Also I suspect he's started drinking again, which makes him erratic and talkative. I don't want him accidentally telling Copeland anything."

"I didn't put it together," Amelia said slowly. "But he looks like shit. Comes in late and keeps missing appointments. He eats like a box of Altoids a day. Remember the dinner at La Spiga? You think we're in for that version of Elliot?"

"I remember how much it cost Jack to clean it up," Luke said. "And I hope not."

"They're shutting me out," Amelia said. "Liz sent me out of the meeting yesterday on a bullshit errand, so I didn't hear everything. I do know they still haven't gotten the information they want from Hope. They're giving her one more chance in the Labyrinth, but after that . . . I don't know."

Luke stood again, grasping the keys in his pocket.

"What are you doing?" Amelia asked, sitting up straighter.

"Something," he growled. "Something besides sitting at the fucking mall."

"No," Amelia said. "I don't have any proof, of anything I told you. You know Copeland-Stark. There won't be a paper trail, and all records will be perfect. Fabricated, but perfect."

Luke wanted to throw something, but he knew Amelia was right. He sat again, reluctantly.

"I'll stall as long as I can. And I'll be at the Labyrinth and prevent the headsets from working when she goes in," Amelia said. She put her hand on his arm. "Luke, let me help. Please."

After a minute, Luke nodded. He reached into his pocket and pulled out a mini tin of Altoids.

"Jesus," Amelia said. "Not you too, with the mints."

"I've been carrying this around for days, trying to figure out how to get it to Jonah. But it will be less suspicious if you do it. Just one, before she goes in that fucking rat maze."

Amelia glanced around before opening the tin. "Is this Jiang Lu's?"

"Yes," Luke said. "The Vesper."

Amelia snapped the lid, cradling the tin in her palm like it was a bomb. "And he just gave it to you?"

"Hardly. His wife did." Luke fell silent as a couple strolled near, holding hands. He waited for them to pass. "It needs to be dissolved in water, real water, not the boilermaker. And it probably tastes like shit, but you can't mask it with anything."

"I'll figure it out," Amelia said. "If I live long enough."

30

TURNCOAT

HOPE
The Wilder Sanctuary
Rancho Mirage, California

Quinn was stretched out in Head Games, his long legs hanging over one arm of the sofa.

Hope was on the floor, *Verbal Overshadowing* closed in her lap, head bent close to his.

Spooky sat in the far corner, fingers blurring as he jabbed at the Sega Genesis controller, making odd comments into the air as he defeated a steady stream of comic-book villains.

"The graphics are technically impressive for this era," Spooky said. "But the gameplay is beyond sluggish. The onscreen objects are crude and the control configuration is terribly designed."

"Was that the one with Michelle Pfeiffer?" Quinn made a meowing sound. "She was an exquisite feline."

"That was *Batman Returns*, 1992," Spooky said, without turning around. "*Batman Forever* was the sequel, the only film with Val Kilmer. Seal won three Grammy awards for the theme song."

"Good to know." Quinn yawned loudly. "So tired. I think they changed my meds again. I need a little power nap."

"Page nineteen," Spooky said, without turning around. "'Patients are entitled to eight hours of sleep per night. If you choose not to sleep, you will not be allowed to sleep at other times. Furniture in communal areas is not for sleeping.'"

Quinn sighed and reached for the deck of California cards, eyes still closed, and shuffled them on his chest. Spooky finished his game and began another.

Hope opened the book, where she was now also storing the single page they'd been able to print, the last page of chapter 12: "Resistance and Resistants." She unfolded it now, already creased and worn from repeated readings:

> *While we continue to study the possible physiological and chemical factors that may contribute to increased resistance, we have identified (anecdotally) certain commonalities among resistants.*
>
> *Simply being aware of the possibility that memory alteration can—and does—occur disrupts the formation of false memories. Resistants were less responsive to subtle social pressure, denying fabrications even when presented with ultimate confidence. Additionally, these subjects posed an average of 36 percent more questions in an attempt to dispute the "facts" and clarify. When debriefed, resistants were able to identify minor inconsistencies in the narrative, which reinforced their skepticism and strengthened their resolve in their own beliefs (Salinger).*

"Anything new?" Quinn asked. He swung his legs to the floor and dealt himself a game of solitaire.

"Nope," Hope said, folding the page and returning it to the book. "But I don't think it's in code."

Hope ran her finger down the patient numbers she'd jotted in the margin, written in her code in case the page was found. For a time, the only sound was the clicking of the Sega controller and the snap of Quinn's cards.

"The patient numbers," Hope said. "Mine is 09093-LSC. I can't figure out anything with the numbers, but I also think LS is Luke Salinger. And yours, 16012-TRC. Tomás Romero?"

"My little Hopeless," Quinn said, queen of hearts held in his hand. "You're like a walking *Da Vinci Code*. But what about the C?"

"Collateral," Hope said. "Not very inventive, but it makes sense."

"You know what?" Quinn swept his unfinished game into a haphazard pile, bending the cards. "I'm glad that turncoat Tomás hasn't been here. If he ever comes back, he's going to have some 'splaining to do." He shuffled again.

"Q," Hope said. "Carter's was 57220-JLC. Jordan Lin, his partner."

"Okay," Quinn said. "So?"

"That's the number they mentioned when they were talking about the Mad Hatters," Hope said. "They thought Carter was the Rogue."

"The Mad Hatters are an urban legend," Spooky said. "As a result, there is no Rogue."

"But if Copeland-Stark believes they do exist," Hope said, "and the Hatters destroy companies . . ."

"Then they'd want to keep that from happening," Quinn finished. "Do you really think Carter was the Rogue?"

"I already told you," Spooky said, still playing his game. "There is no Rogue."

"He had the skills," Hope said, returning to the numbers on her paper. "The doctors mentioned two patients yesterday, with SSE at the end. And the file we saw with Carter in the library, Bryan Herrera. Also an SSE. Are they connected to the same person?"

"Sonia Sotomayor? Sylvester Stallone?" Quinn offered. "The Thigh-Master lady?"

Hope laughed. "We should look at the files again. See how many SSEs there are. Can you get us into the processing room again?"

"Fernando got canned," Quinn said, frowning. "Probably my fault, for stealing his lanyard."

"But we can't open them in the library," Hope said.

"Hey," Quinn called. Spooky didn't turn or stop playing. "Can you put a jump drive into that thing?"

"No," Spooky said. "This system predates the first USB flash drive by eleven years."

Quinn looked at Hope. "*Mi'ja*, we're striking out all over. No information, no access, and no way to read the microchip."

"It's not a microchip, if it's a flash drive," Spooky said. "While there is a circuit board inside—"

"It was only spy lingo," Quinn interrupted. "And just for that, I'm never going to give you a dope spy name. So there." He dealt another game of solitaire, and Hope settled into her book again.

The impermanence of memory can be a troubling fact for some. As a species, we want to believe our memories are infallible because they make us, us. However, consider the liberation in embracing this fluidity and instead allowing your mind to retain only what is most cherished.

Quinn tapped her knee with the back of his hand. "Give me the microchip. I'm going to ask Morgan."

"Morgan who?" Hope asked, fanning herself with *Verbal Overshadowing*.

"Morgan-at-the-front-desk Morgan." Quinn held out his hand for the flash drive. "I'll get her to let me use her computer. And the timing will be perfect. All the docs will be in sessions."

"Morgan Stark," Spooky said.

"As in Dr. Stark?" Quinn asked. "That's her last name?"

"Morgan Stark is the daughter of Tony Stark and Pepper Potts," Spooky said, as if it were common knowledge. "Iron Man."

"You know, I'm about topped out in nerdiness right now." Quinn held his hand above his head, to show just how topped out he was.

"Stark does have a daughter named Morgan," Hope said. "I never made the connection."

A chime rang. Spooky switched off the Sega and left without a goodbye. Quinn and Hope followed, lingering in the doorway.

"Gimme," Quinn said, extending his hand. "It's worth a try."

Hope reached into her bra and produced the drive. She placed it in Quinn's open palm, closing her fingers around his. "Are you sure? Anyone can walk by."

"Trust me. I know what I'm doing." Quinn dropped her hand, tucking the drive into his sneaker.

"I trust you, but not Morgan," Hope said. "Especially if she's Dr. Stark's daughter."

But Quinn threw up a peace sign and was already sprinting down the hallway. "Have faith," he called. "See you at lunch."

⁂

"The meatloaf is in the oven." Quinn set his plate on the table and slid into his chair.

"It's not meatloaf." Hope pointed with her fork. "I think it's farro."

"Not what I'm talking about," Quinn said. "Morgan wouldn't let me use her computer, so I created a diversion and pulled up the files myself. But she came back faster than I'd planned."

"Did anyone see you?" Hope asked.

Quinn waved a hand to shush her. "Hopeless, there are at least a hundred different active patient files labeled SSE. Definitely not one person's collateral. Even Angelina Jolie doesn't have that much family to pimp out."

"Who are they then? Where are they?" Hope asked.

"They sure as shit aren't here," Quinn said. "Dr. Emerson mentioned a facility. That must be Wilder 2.0."

"Yes," Hope said. She opened her hand under the table. "Give me the drive so I can keep it safe."

Quinn looked uncomfortable. "Oh, that."

"Oh, that?" Hope repeated.

"So . . ." Quinn ran a hand over his jaw. "Stark was right behind Morgan when she came back. I had to pull the drive out and drop it into her pencil cup. Do you ever wonder why everyone has a pencil cup? I've never seen anyone use a pencil."

"Focus," Hope hissed. "So, it's gone?"

"Relax, *Mi'ja*," Quinn said, dismissing her alarm. "Stark was too busy scolding her to notice me. I'll get it after lunch."

"Jesus, Q," Hope said. "You're like the sloppiest spy—" But she stopped talking when she felt someone at her elbow and looked up from her farro.

It was quite possibly the best-looking person Hope had ever seen, which was saying a lot, since she was surrounded by celebrities all the time. This man looked like Lorenzo Lamas from the *Falcon Crest* days, complete with perfect teeth and coiffed hair. He wore a crisp white shirt paired with slim navy pants, tapered at the ankles. His brown leather shoes were so pointy and shiny they could have been a weapon.

At first, Quinn's face lit up at the sight of Tomás, but just as quickly, his expression fell.

"Quinn?" Tomás's voice became tentative. "You aren't happy to see me?"

"*Mi'ja*," Quinn said, turning to her. "This is Tomás Romero. Tomás, my good friend, Hope."

Tomás extended his hand and Hope took it. It was smooth and dry, his fingernails manicured. Hope knew hers did not feel or look the same, and she withdrew her hand quickly.

"How long are you in town?" Quinn asked. His voice was monotone, and he didn't look at Tomás.

"Until late this evening. I have to catch the red-eye to Dubai, and I'll be there for a month."

Dr. Green appeared at the table. "Mr. Romero," she said, smiling and extending her hand. "Welcome. We didn't have you on our list for today."

Tomás tilted his head. "Is that a problem?"

"Not at all," Dr. Green said. "We're having a table set by the window for you and Quinn. And Dr. Stark is on his way from headquarters to join you."

Quinn threw Hope an apologetic glance as he left the table.

31

MINOR INCONSISTENCIES

HOPE
The Wilder Sanctuary
Rancho Mirage, California

T HE GOLF CART hit an uneven piece of pavement every so often, knocking Hope sideways and forcing her to grip the metal railing above the open window. She watched the back of
Jonah's head as it moved, brown hands gripping the steering wheel at
precisely ten and two. He hadn't said a word the entire ride.

They drove past the empty swan pond, its water mirroring the cloudless sky above. With each thud of tires, Hope's mouth became drier.

Hope hadn't seen Quinn since lunch the day before. He hadn't
been at goal setting or sound therapy. This morning he wasn't at breakfast either. She thought about Quinn's face when he first saw Tomás,
the light and the love. She desperately wanted Quinn to have found an
answer that would make everything right.

Too quickly, they arrived at the stucco building with its low stone
wall. Hope stepped out on the dirt, counting, eyes locked on the red
door. Dread crested thorny and hot inside her.

Jonah was still idling, and Hope turned to him. "What's up, Jonah?"

He held out a bottle of water, the tiny kind you get free in a hotel or at a kid's birthday party. Copeland-Stark didn't believe in plastic water bottles, or straws, or anything else that might increase their carbon footprint. Hope hadn't seen a plastic water bottle ever at Wilder.

"Are you thirsty?" Jonah asked.

"Not particularly," Hope said.

"Drink this," Jonah said. "So you won't be thirsty in the maze."

"What maze?"

Johan jiggled the bottle at her and didn't answer.

Hope hesitated, then reached out and drained it in a few gulps. It tasted worse than the water at Wilder, with a horrible aftertaste, like pennies.

"Am I actually starting to like the taste of Wilder water?" Hope returned the empty bottle to Jonah. "Regular water tastes horrible now."

"It isn't regular water." Jonah crumpled the bottle and shoved it into his pocket.

"Then what is it?" Hope asked.

But Jonah had already kicked the cart into gear. It disappeared down the hill, and Hope approached the red door. After a minute, she went inside.

Dr. Emerson stood at the wall, key card poised, as Hope entered. Dr. Stark rose from one of the black leather chairs in the corner. His slacks were paired with a pointy-collared lavender button-down. His clothes were pressed and starched once more, but he was still unshaven and his eyes were puffy.

He held out a cup, and Hope took the two pills and swallowed. "Where's Dr. Green?"

"Off-site," Dr. Stark said. "I'll be overseeing your session today."

He handed Hope a headset, thicker this time, more like the ones in the Butterfly Box. Stark extended his arm to usher Hope out the glass doors. Together, they walked to the mouth of an enormous hedge.

Hope adjusted the earpiece and entered, each step forward compounding the unease in her stomach.

"Tell us what you remember about arriving at Wilder," Dr. Emerson said. "Please be as detailed as possible."

Hope walked. "I woke up in my room," she said. "Luke was there."

"And what did Dr. Salinger say to you?" Stark asked.

"He said I experienced a trauma," she recited. "He said he would help me, if I truly wanted to remember." *Purpose is but the slave to memory.* Hope tugged at the ends of her hair.

"That's excellent, Hope," Dr. Emerson said. "I can already tell this will be productive."

Hope thought about the *Breakthroughs* interview, about heaping on praise and encouraging social conformity. But the last thing Hope craved was approval from Dr. Emerson.

She continued her recitation of that December day until it seemed the doctors were satisfied. Through the hedge maze they lobbed random questions at her, about her former pets, trips, schools, hobbies, jobs.

"What do you know about the cyberterrorist group the Mad Hatters?" Dr. Emerson asked.

Hope stopped walking. "Nothing."

"Nothing?" Dr. Emerson repeated.

"I know they're hackers," Hope said, walking again. "That's it. Kind of hard to follow CNN these days."

"That's fine," Dr. Stark said. "Please keep walking."

An odd series of random questions followed, and the hedge maze eventually ended.

Hope stepped into the sunlight and air. A metal box clicked up from the ground, the little door swinging open.

"We thought you might be thirsty," Dr. Emerson said.

Hope reached for the cup and was about to drink when she remembered she wasn't thirsty. Jonah had given her water.

So you won't be thirsty in the maze.

She tilted the red cup, watching as it splashed at her feet and soaked into the dirt below.

"A side effect of propranolol is extreme thirst," Dr. Stark said. "It can be unpleasant, like cotton. Your throat isn't feeling dry?"

At the mere suggestion Hope felt her mouth drying out more, her tongue becoming like sandpaper. But she shook her head. Jonah had given her water. She swallowed, dust from the dirt path caking her throat.

"All good." She licked her lips.

In her ear were muffled clacks, scraping and shifting, as if someone put a hand over their mic. Then silence. The metal door on the little box closed and returned to the ground.

Dr. Emerson said, "We're going to give you background from the time you can't remember. Please continue to walk and listen. Periodically we may ask you to pause and close your eyes, to help you visualize."

Hope walked between the lines of stone as Luke's voice came through her headphones. "Patient self-esteem appears fair . . ."

It was work, to ignore the ingrained, visceral pull generated by Luke's voice. Hope whispered passages from *Verbal Overshadowing* instead, to keep herself from listening: "'In short, hypnotists are asking patients to fabricate a tale and create, rather than recall . . . Simply being aware of the possibility that memory alteration can—and does—occur, disrupts the formation of false memories.'"

An uncomfortable tingle began in her head as she neared the red door in the building at the center of the maze. It traveled down her neck and into in her limbs, intensifying as it reached her fingers, as if Hope were being slowly electrocuted. She ripped off her headphones and put her head between her knees. Everything stopped.

Hope rested her chin on her knees and inspected the thick black rubber. There was no Maelstrom logo on this headset. Running along the inside edge were three holes, two smaller and one larger, which would have been unnoticeable if they weren't now flashing red and green and white.

She thought back to the meeting she and Quinn overheard. *Sonogenetics headsets . . . still in beta . . . human subjects.*

She heard a buzz through the earpiece and knew the doctors were trying to talk to her, whining like a hive of bees. Hope brought the microphone to her mouth.

"Give me a second," she said. Her throat was still on fire, but her head was clearing.

Buzz, buzz, silence, *buzz.*

After a few gulps of air, Hope returned the headphones to her ears.

"That's incredibly dangerous," Dr. Emerson said, voice harsh. "Don't do that again."

"Hope," Dr. Stark said, sounding breathless. "It's time to enter the last phase. Though this part is dark, there are no obstacles."

She entered the concrete room and groped through the darkness.

"It's time to talk about Charlotte Salinger's death," Dr. Emerson said.

"Charlotte?" The tingling in her veins became unbearable. Hope's teeth vibrated, like being drilled at the dentist. Her vision blurred. "Charlotte's not dead."

A too-bright screen appeared on the wall, and Hope sucked in a breath at a picture of Luke's house, of their cars in the drive. She gaped at the next series of images: Luke's house on fire, the charred remains of the same house, a stretcher with a taut white sheet across it, an ambulance at the curb.

Except, as Hope leaned closer and inspected the screen, she found something off about the pictures. They didn't look entirely real. The front door was still the red murder door. The ambulance looked strange somehow, generic, like the clip-art program she used for presentation decks. It had no license plate.

"'Resistants were able to identify minor inconsistencies in the narrative,'" Hope recited to herself, "'which reinforced their skepticism and strengthened their resolve in their own beliefs.'"

The slideshow ended.

"Why is the door red?" Hope asked. "Charlotte and I painted it yellow."

The same searing pain pulsed though her head and wound its way into her fingertips. Hope dropped to her knees.

"A week before you registered at Wilder, you broke into Dr. Salinger's house," Dr. Stark said. "You didn't know Charlotte was asleep in her room."

Another jolt of pain. Hope tried to call up lines from *Verbal Overshadowing*, to count, to do anything to stave off the burning in her arms and head.

Dr. Emerson continued, "You drank almost an entire bottle of Jack Daniel's before passing out. The Jack Daniel's spilled. You dropped a cigarette into it and set the house on fire. No one knew Charlotte was home. She died in the fire."

Hope shook her head, gasping through the next shock. She hunched over, palms pressed flat on the concrete floor. "No," she said. "No."

"I know it's devastating," Stark said. "But it's the truth."

Hope heard Luke again, though not through a recording in her headset but from his *Breakthroughs* interview. *Don't think about kangaroos eating waffles.* She saw his pinky tapping against the side of his mug, the smile at the camera.

A memory of him singing in the shower, of tying his good-luck tie into a half Windsor. A pinky promise in the backyard and an eighteen-year-old bottle of single malt.

Then she heard Tony's voice in her head. And for the first time ever, it was welcome.

I believe you believe it happened that way.

There you go again, rewriting the narrative.

With considerable effort, Hope pulled herself onto her knees. She placed her hands behind her back and stared straight ahead, head high, like a prisoner awaiting execution.

"I . . ." She took a great lungful of air and let it out, counting to ten four more times before she felt strong enough to speak. "I fucking hate Jack Daniel's."

I'm not the villain here, you are.

Stark and Green were silent.

"Why do you keep repeating the same bullshit each time?" Hope asked, voice thin but sure. "So that I'll finally believe it, or so you will?"

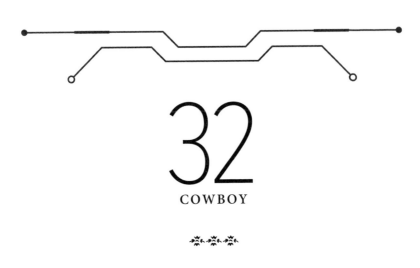

32

COWBOY

HOPE

The Wilder Sanctuary
Rancho Mirage, California

HOPE WOKE FROM a dreamless sleep, head pounding. The sun was high outside her window. She had no idea what day it was, but it was clear she'd missed breakfast and goal setting. She wondered why Jonah hadn't come to rouse her.

Jonah had driven her from the Labyrinth and walked Hope to her room. She remembered leaning against him, barely able to stand and covered in sweat. He'd helped her into bed, pulled up the covers, and exited. She hadn't even thanked him for the water.

For the first time, Hope found she could recall every excruciating minute of her time in the Labyrinth: Stark's singsong tone, the stinging headset, the plastic cup rising from the ground, the photoshopped images of Luke's house, the multiple lies.

Hope leapt from the bed. She hastily changed her clothes, brushed her teeth, and slipped on her sneakers. She needed to talk to Quinn. She wanted to find out about Tomás, but more important, she needed to tell him how to fight the Labyrinth, and to plan a real quest to un-cover Wilder 2.0.

In the dining-room doorway Hope surveyed the bright flowers on the tables, the silver breadbaskets, and the gold chargers.

Dammit. Visiting Day.

The room was nearly empty, so Hope secured a corner table and helped herself to a roll. Fewer tables were set, Dr. Emerson the only administration present.

Spooky's brother Henry came alone that day. Hope noted how much more at ease Spooky seemed, even smiling as they reviewed his latest set of drawings.

Jonah set a plate of eggs Florentine before her, hollandaise drip-ping down the spinach and English muffin. It smelled delicious, and Hope was so ravenous she decided not to wait for Quinn. Jonah filled her water glass.

"Have you seen Quinn this morning?" Hope asked.

Jonah shook his head and ambled away.

Hope returned to her eggs, as Dr. Emerson escorted the new girl, Kumiko, and a man who must have been her father to an adjacent ta-ble. Kumiko was around Spooky's age, with electric blue streaks in her jet-black hair and lots of thick black eyeliner. She must have had a case of eyeliner stashed away, because Hope had seen Dr. Emerson take it away at least a dozen times. When Kumiko first arrived, Quinn's only comment had been, "Drugs. All of them."

"We are tremendously pleased, Dr. Sato," Dr. Emerson said to her father. "Kumiko is making significant progress in a remarkably short time. She's a delight."

Kumiko rolled her eyes to the ceiling, looking less like a delight and much more like Charlotte.

Dr. Sato nodded curtly as he pulled his napkin from the silver ring. His face was pinched, and Dr. Emerson looked momentarily un-comfortable. She gave Kumiko an awkward pat and moved away.

"Dr. Emerson," Hope said.

She turned, red lips preserved in a fake-pleasant smile. "May I help you, Hope?"

"Where's Quinn?" Hope took a drink of water and grimaced. Again, it tasted like pennies.

"Mr. Romero checked him out," Dr. Emerson said, smiling and raising her voice so it could be heard at the nearby tables. "He's made enormous progress and was ready to be released. As I'm sure you will be too, quite soon. Be well."

Dr. Emerson was halfway across the room and through the kitchen door before Hope could ask anything else.

Tomás was in Dubai, for a month. He couldn't have checked Quinn out.

The potato in her mouth turned to dust.

Quinn was gone, and Hope was all alone.

Jonah arrived at the table to clear her plate, despite clearly seeing the 80 percent of her remaining eggs Florentine. He took the plate with so much force it clattered to the ground. The dish didn't break, but hollandaise splattered onto Hope's shoes and sweatpants. She plucked the napkin from her lap and bent over to clean up.

Jonah knelt beside her, pulling a dishtowel from his back pocket. He said two words: "Head Games."

Hope tried to meet his eyes, but Jonah was swatting at the sauce on her sneakers. "Head Games," he repeated into the floor. "Go. Now."

Her shoes left a Hansel-and-Gretel trail of egg yolk all the way to Head Games. Hope pushed open the door, unsure about what would be waiting for her.

At the window stood an incredibly handsome young man, wearing jeans and a fitted black shirt. He had close-cropped black hair, and exuded energy just standing there. Hope wondered fleetingly when in the last decade she began referring to this sector of the world as young men.

He held out his hand. "My name is Rohan Kapoor, Hope. I work for Carter Sloane."

Hope kicked the door closed.

"I told them Jordan sent me to pick up Carter's things," Rohan explained. "Someone's bringing them from Copeland-Stark."

Hope's eyes moved from the clock above the door to Rohan. "Then you probably have about twenty minutes before Dr. Stark shows up. Probably less before the receptionist realizes you aren't in the lobby."

"Then I'll talk fast." Rohan sat on the sofa. "Carter left me a message, but I didn't get it until last night."

Hope sat next to Rohan. "I don't understand."

"I oversee all the software that's used here. Erleben primarily, but also databases, email, the recording system—"

Hope interrupted. "Recording system?"

"They have cameras in some of the rooms here. That's another thing I oversee."

"Which rooms have cameras?" Hope asked. She almost didn't want to know.

"The dining room, most of the hallways, the front desk."

Hope's stomach turned over. The front desk, where Quinn used Morgan Stark's computer.

"The patient elevators, but not the service ones," Rohan said. "Out to the Zen Garden but no further."

"What about our rooms? The doctor's offices? Library?" She gestured around. "This room?"

Rohan shook his head. "Nope. Only those. Well, there are cameras all over, but no feed. Carter never got it working, for some reason. And in some cases, it interferes with privacy."

Hope scoffed. "I find it hard to believe Wilder gives a shit about my privacy."

"You're right, they don't," Rohan said, his face now serious. "But they definitely give a shit about theirs." He tugged on the neck of his shirt. "From the requests I've gotten to retrieve footage, they're more worried about being caught than catching someone else."

Hope glanced nervously at the clock again.

"Anyway, Carter hid three instructions in the Erleben code. First, to start monitoring the data-security software twenty-four seven. Which I have, but everything's been normal. The second was to come to Wilder, find you, and give you this." He reached into his breast pocket and produced a key, exactly like Carter's silver jump drive, only black. He bounced it gently in his hand. "And to tell you to tell— Spooky?—to stay in the asylum when it's time. Is that a person?"

"He's a patient here," Hope said, as Rohan dropped the drive into her open palm.

"This interfaces with Erleben, so you'll have to be hooked up first," Rohan said. "There's a port on the headset, between the first two letters in Maelstrom. Once you get in, you'll need a password, but I don't know it. He just said to tell you it's on planet . . . Funtron?"

"Funkotron," Hope corrected, pointing at the Sega Genesis. "*Toe-jam and Earl*. It's one of the video games we have here."

"Whoa." Rohan laughed. "Antique. But Carter loves those old games. We have a bunch at Maelstrom . . ." He stopped talking and looked at his hands, swallowing. "He loved them, I mean."

"I miss him too," Hope said.

"Yeah." Rohan stood, shoving his hands deep into his pockets and moving to the door.

"Wait," Hope said. "How did you get Jonah to find me?"

"Oh," Rohan paused with his hand on the doorknob. "Dr. Salinger helped with that."

The door opened into Rohan's shoulder, knocking him aside a few inches.

Hope crammed the key under her thigh.

"There you are," Morgan said to Rohan, without so much as a glance in Hope's direction. "We have your things."

"Sorry," Rohan said, smiling. "I was looking for the bathroom and ended up here, accidentally. Then I got distracted by . . ." He cast his gaze around the room for an alibi. Hope wondered what he was going to say. The three unopened boxes of Trivial Pursuit? But Morgan wasn't even listening. She was far too busy goggling at Rohan like he was Ryan Reynolds.

After the door closed, Hope tucked the drive into her bra and made a beeline for the Sega Genesis. She fell to her knees and turned everything on, found the *Toejam and Earl* cartridge, and shoved it in the slot. As the groovy music started, she held the controller in her hands and realized she was utterly out of her depth. She'd only ever watched Carter; Hope didn't actually know how to play.

A chime signaled the end of Visiting Day brunch. Soon, residents would begin arriving to play despondent checkers or depressing backgammon with their families.

Hope unsnapped the plastic case to return the cartridge and noticed the instruction booklet. Luke, who felt instruction manuals were a form of treason, would have teased her about even opening it. Hope took it out anyway. At least she could memorize the directions before the next rec time.

She folded the manual in half to tuck into her waistband. Then she saw it, on Toejam's shoe: a tiny line drawing of a butterfly. She opened the booklet, where six page numbers in the table of contents were circled in blue marker: 3, 5, 7, 18, 22, and 23.

She smiled. *Cowboy.*

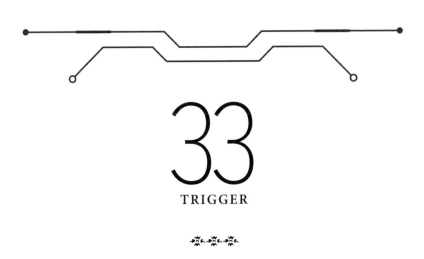

33

TRIGGER

✢✦ ✢✦ ✢✦

HOPE

The Wilder Sanctuary
Rancho Mirage, California

THE TECH IN the Butterfly Box who replaced Fernando, Phoebe, was an irritating overachiever. She sniffily reminded Hope she didn't have an appointment and was reluctant to give her a room, citing the patient handbook rules with an automaticity rivaling Spooky's. But Hope pleaded with her, and Phoebe finally agreed to let her use Arkham, the room that was perpetually on the fritz.

Hope walked the corridor, glancing at the suited-up patients, grasping through the air for things only they could see. A resident was walking the length of Necropolis in large strides with high knees. Occasionally, he would drop to the ground in a crouch and army crawl a few feet. For the first time, it occurred to Hope how ridiculous she must look from the windows outside.

Inside Arkham, Hope inserted the drive as Rohan had directed. She donned the other accessories and pulled the headset on, typing C-O-W-B-O-Y into the shimmering keyboard.

"Welcome back, Carter." Was it just Hope, or did Morena sound extra happy?

The screen flickered and a sprawling space materialized. There were pine desks clumped together in a corner, each boasting a few knickknacks to differentiate it from its neighbor: a plant, a red Swingline stapler, one of those plastic dolls with the enormous black eyes, oblong head without a mouth. Glass doors like the ones at Wilder surrounded her, each blocking off a cubicle containing multicolored tables and chairs.

The room to the left was larger, with a conference table in the center and orange padded swivel chairs grouped around it. A whiteboard to the side was covered in a detailed flowchart. It looked like one of those crazy walls in a police detective show: words circled with arrows and dotted lines and question marks linking them together, symbols and boxes and braces littering all of it.

To her right, enormous screens lined one wall in a grid pattern. Video game consoles and controllers were strewn on the floor below, in front of an assortment of ottomans and beanbags. On the adjacent wall was a pinball machine, and the classic arcade cabinets Hope remembered from her own teenage years: *Spy Hunter*, *Burgertime*, *Galaga*. A nook in the corner held more ramen packages, Red Bull cans, and enormous plastic containers of cheese balls than the Buy More. In the middle of the room stood a pool table topped with purple felt.

Suddenly, the entire room went fuzzy, then black. Goddamned Arkham. Hope was just about to pull the headset off and try again, when it came back to life.

She stepped closer to the pool table. The screen of *Spy Hunter* lit up. The graphics faded, and Carter's face appeared.

Hope walked through three beanbags and the corner of the pool table in her haste to get closer. "Carter, where are you?"

He didn't react to Hope. This Carter was in the same room where she stood, learning casually on the pool table she'd just passed through, only his room was real. He wore a slim blue suit, charcoal striped tie, and white sneakers. Hope couldn't tell if he looked odd because she'd never seen him in anything but Wilder Grays or because he was uncomfortable dressed up. His hair was shorter, bangs no longer hanging in his eyes.

Carter looked so young, brimming with energy. His body was relaxed, hazel eyes without glasses, and without shadow.

"Hey Hope," he said. Carter gathered the pool balls and corralled them into the plastic triangle, swapping them around like he was solving a puzzle. He rotated them with his fingertips until all the numbers were facing up, and put his fingers inside the triangle, tightening the balls together. Then he gestured with his arms wide, at the space behind.

"Welcome to Maelstrom." He smiled like a proud papa. Carter hoisted himself upon the pool table, legs dangling. "We, Jordan and I, modeled this place after Facebook. It was all the rage in startups at the time: open spaces, no walls, play as much as you work. Happy employees make productive employees."

Carter rolled a pool ball, yellow number nine, across the violet surface. It bumped against the side and fell into the corner pocket, making a hollow clunk as it came to rest at the chamber underneath his sneakers.

"Everyone hated it." He laughed, shaking his head. "It sounded innovative, but in practice was just dumb."

Tears came to Hope at the sound of his laugh. She tried to wipe them away, but they fell into her mouth, salty and warm.

"But that's not why we're here." He looked directly at the camera, somehow locking eyes with Hope. "I was planning to do this in person, and much later, but the best-laid plans and all that shit." He launched the red seven ball at the bumper. "You've been at Wilder for about five months, and I hope you've made friends with Spencer. You're going to need him."

Hope felt dizzy. She wanted to sit, but she didn't want to put any additional space between her and Carter. The world around her wiggled and Hope held her breath that Arkham would stay online.

"Do you remember the first time we met? Think about it. I'll wait." He set his palm over the eight ball and moved it back and forth.

"In the Shade," Hope said, feeling foolish. "Serpent's Bay."

Carter tilted his head. "I'm guessing you think it was at Wilder. Maybe even in Erleben. Am I right?"

Hope nodded.

"But you're wrong." Carter was clearly enjoying himself. He launched the remaining balls toward the pockets one by one. The air filled with the sounds of knocking and rolling, balls falling into the tracks. He turned to face Hope, looking directly into the screen, suppressing a grin. "Mind sufficiently blown?"

Carter hopped off the table. "You might want to sit down. The first few times can be really rough."

Hope lowered herself to the ground, trying to brace herself, though she didn't know for what.

"Inara." Carter straightened and spoke in a loud, clear voice. "Activate Erleben Voice version 3.9. Login: Morpheus. Password: UnplugMe." Morena's voice came through Hope's headset, sounding far more affectionate than usual. "Welcome back, Cowboy. I've missed you."

On-screen, Carter's expression didn't change. Hope bit her lip. It was too easy to forget he was only a video.

Carter waited another few seconds before speaking again. "Inara, activate Eos Ribbon Trigger NakanoHope 7-C. Password MakeItSo." Carter swept his index finger exaggeratedly at the camera and grinned.

Despite the strangeness of the situation, Hope had to chuckle. But her laughter was cut short by hot, stabbing pains in her head. The sensation was different from the Labyrinth, localized though far more painful.

"Take a second," Carter said. "Breathe slowly. Keeping your eyes open helps the disequilibrium. It will subside soon."

Hope took a few slow, ragged breaths.

"Let's try again," Carter said. "Do you remember the first time we met?"

The heat intensified, as if her brain were being lit on fire. With each electric jolt, memories flashed into her head: broken pieces of glass, a black card, standing on a rainy sidewalk in Mountain View, a year ago.

"Hope tanaka? sorry I'm late."

Hope set her wineglass on the table and stood. She'd never been on a blind date before and wasn't sure how to behave. Shaking his hand seemed too formal and businesslike, but hugging seemed too intimate.

Thankfully, he seemed to feel the same way, giving Hope an awkward pat on the shoulder before taking a seat across from her.

She'd done her research, but in person he looked much younger. He wore a stylish charcoal suit, Italian and custom tailored by the looks of it, though his posture gave off the aura of a boy playing dress-up. The shoulders of his suit jacket were shiny from the intermittent drizzle that had been falling all day.

"Carter H. Sloane," Hope said. "We finally meet."

"You can drop the H. And the Sloane. Just call me Carter." He shrugged off his jacket and turned to hang it on the chair, jostling the table in the process. Hope's glass tipped over, splashing her sweater before rolling off the table and shattering on the floor.

"I'm so sorry," Carter said, cheeks pink. He stood with his napkin and approached her, then probably realized he shouldn't make an advance at her breasts quite so early in the evening.

"It's fine," Hope said, thankful she'd chosen a dark sweater over a white blouse at the last minute.

Carter returned to his seat and thanked the server who'd come to sweep up the glass, by name. He then ordered Hope another white wine and an IPA for himself.

"I've never been here," Hope said, glancing at the menu she'd read twenty times before Carter arrived. "Any recommendations?"

He looked relieved to be talking about the food. "All the fancier stuff is good, but I come here for the bacon burger," Carter said. "My company is right around the corner, so I eat here a lot."

"That sounds delicious," Hope said, placing her menu on the table. "Your company. That would be Maelstrom?"

"Come on, I know you did a little homework on me," Carter said, grinning.

"Fair enough." Hope smiled back. "But the things I found were old, from when Magic Words came out. The only actual interview I found was 'Sloane Shark.' But I did read it."

"That title is the worst," Carter said, unfolding his napkin and dropping it in his lap. "But Julia Liang is the only person who'll get to interview me."

"Why?" Hope asked.

"I hate interviews, for one," Carter said. "But she's an excellent journalist. She does her homework too. And she isn't shady."

A server returned to the table with their drinks, and Carter ordered for both of them. Normally, Hope would have found that irritating.

But from Carter, it just felt polite. He didn't seem anything like the slick startup guy she'd imagined.

"'Sloane Shark' said you developed a VR device. Erleben?" Hope asked. "I'm sure I butchered that pronunciation."

"It's *air-leh-ben*," Carter corrected, sipping his beer. "It's German. It means 'experience.' In VR specifically, it means an experience that's entirely immersive." Then he smiled, again with a blush. "It sounds totally pompous when I hear myself say it aloud."

Hope laughed. "If what Julia Liang says is true, you've done something pretty remarkable. So maybe pompous is okay."

Carter leaned in, looking more comfortable. "I've never seen or felt anything else so realistic. You truly believe you're there. Do you watch *Star Trek*? It's like the holodeck. Almost." He set his pint glass on the table.

"And you did it all yourself?" Hope asked. "You must know it inside and out."

"I did the majority of the programming," Carter said. "But now it's growing so fast I need to hire a team. We just got a big investor, so I had to hire an engineer solely for Erleben and all Copeland-Stark's needs. And I've got this amazing intern from Cal that I'm snapping up the second he graduates." Carter grinned at Hope. "But I hid a few Easter eggs in there, just for me."

"Oh?" Hope asked.

"All programmers do. The right passwords will unlock a few worlds, and . . ." Carter paused. "Well, there are just some tricks no one else knows about."

An enormous burger on a cutting board was placed in front of Hope, complete with fried egg and French fries in a silver cup. It was a far cry from the Stoner Shack.

"Have you been into technology your whole life?" Hope asked.

"Lots of coding camps growing up. Then I started branching out on my own," Carter said. "In high school, I found out a few staff members were doing shady things, like stealing money from PTA donations or changing grades for influential parents. So I got into the district website and posted it on the front page. I did it for two years before I got caught." He took a huge bite of his burger and nodded appreciatively.

"You were quite the vigilante," Hope said. On the table, her phone buzzed. Hope silenced it and dropped it into her purse.

"I'm reformed now. But it bothers me when people are taken advantage of," Carter said, blushing again. "I can't believe I told you that. I guess I didn't want you think I'm an übernerd. And I guess after just one beer I'll say anything. Sorry, this is really boring, isn't it?"

"Not at all," Hope assured. "Did you say Copeland-Stark? Big Pharma, right? The memory people?"

"That's right," Carter said.

"What's virtual reality got to do with memory drugs?" Hope asked.

"Therapy," Carter said. "VR Therapy has been around for a while to help phobias, but Copeland-Stark wants to explore how it can help people recover lost memories. Don't ask me how."

"That's fascinating," Hope said. "So are they going to use it at the new hospital they're building?"

"Wow, you keep up with the news, don't you? It's not a hospital, exactly," Carter said. "It's called the Wilder Sanctuary. It's going to be a high-end wellness treatment facility. Very high-end. I've only seen pictures, but it's pretty unbelievable."

"Maybe I should check myself in," Hope said. "I could use a little break from the world."

"Start saving now," Carter said. "Jack Copeland told me they're charging over fifty thousand dollars a month."

"That's slightly out of my price range," Hope said. She swirled a fry in the egg yolk on her plate. "What's Jack Copeland like?"

"I've met him a few times," Carter said, making a face. "My partner, Jordan, usually takes care of the business end of things so I don't have to."

"They call him Maverick Jack," Hope said.

"That's because he does whatever he wants and makes millions doing it," Carter said, wiping ketchup from the corner of his mouth. "I mean, he doesn't look like your average CEO. He never wears a suit, and he doesn't do any schmoozing. But he has a huge ego and he's completely focused on making money. I'm pretty sure he doesn't realize there are people on the other end of those drugs he makes. Would you like another drink?"

Hope nodded, and Carter signaled the server.

"Once I asked Copeland if he thought they'd be able to cure dementia," Carter said. "And you know what he said? 'Curing patients is an unsustainable business model.' Isn't that awful?"

"That's pretty disgusting," Hope agreed.

On the table, Carter's phone lit up and he glanced down. "Crap, I have to take this. I'm sorry." He held the phone to his ear. "Hey Jordan, I'm at dinner. Can I—" Carter stopped talking and nodded a few times, then signaled the waiter. "Okay, fifteen minutes. Tell Rohan not to touch anything until I get there."

Hope finished the last of her wine and wiped her hands. "That didn't sound good."

"I'm so sorry, something's melting down at work," Carter said. "I have to go."

The server came to the table with the folio, and Carter handed him a black Amex without even looking at the check.

"I really enjoyed this," Hope said, reaching for her purse.

"Please let me pay," Carter said. "It's the least I can do when I monopolized the entire conversation. I promise I'm not a narcissist."

"I don't think you're a narcissist." Hope laughed. "And I learned a lot."

The server returned the Amex with a wide smile. Hope followed Carter to the front of the restaurant and out the door. The drizzle had turned into rain, and they ducked under an awning.

Hope put a hand on Carter's arm. "Look. I need to tell you something." She glanced up the street and moved closer. He took a small step back. "I really like you, but I don't want you to get the wrong idea. I'm not looking for a relationship. And also, my last name isn't Tanaka."

"I know," Carter said, then laughed at Hope's expression. He had a nice laugh.

"I did my homework on you too, Hope Nakano," Carter said. His phone beeped, and he retrieved it from his pocket. "Sorry, I really have to go. But I'll call you tomorrow. That is, if you want to see me again."

"I think I do," Hope said slowly.

Carter leaned in and for a moment Hope thought he was going to kiss her. But instead, he put his mouth near her ear. "To be continued," he said. Then he turned on his heel and walked away.

THERE WAS A noise, like a needle being dragged across a vinyl record. Carter and the sidewalk were gone now, and Hope was back in Maelstrom. *Spy Hunter* showed a poorly rendered car moving up a wide street, but that quickly faded to black. The world around her flickered and stretched, until her usual meditation selections hovered before her, stuttering into pixels every few seconds.

"Shit," Hope said, pulling off her headset.

"Arkham has gone down," Phoebe said, entering the Butterfly Box. She registered Hope's expression and added, not at all sincerely, "Sorry."

Hope slipped the key from the headset as she followed Phoebe out the door.

34

SAVING THROW

HOPE
The Wilder Sanctuary
Rancho Mirage, California

HOPE PACED THE empty hallway, rubber soles squeaking each time she changed course. For the twentieth time, she read the print on the wall. It was tinted to look like an older photo, or as if it had used a fancy filter on Instagram. A rosy sky with fluffy clouds and an out-of-focus bird in flight, wings stretched outward and upward. *If you're waiting until you're ready, you'll be waiting the rest of your life.*

She approached the door once again, took a breath, and knocked twice before entering. Graph paper and magazines were spread across Spooky's desk. Hope watched him for a time, scrawling notes on the paper, occasionally shaking his head and muttering words like, "critical fail," "saving throw," and "skill monkey."

"Spencer," she said, as softly as she could.

Spooky's pen fell to the floor and he bent to retrieve it, hair masking his face.

"Can I come in?"

Spooky rubbed his palms together and shoved his hands between his legs, sandwiched between his clamped knees. His chin dipped, once. Hope took in the Shade on Spooky's wall. It was all there now, incongruous yet harmonious at the same time: the forest, Mirror Gate, Serpent's Bay with its limestone lighthouse, the movie theater, a nondescript building that must have been Maelstrom. And still, a few parts unfinished, an area of matte-black paint and then a path leading to Hollow of the Moon.

Artistically, the Shade was magnificent. It was hard to believe so much life could exist in a flat rendering, in a picture drawn entirely from cheap white chalk. She could almost see the water of Mirror Gate rippling, the leaves at the tops of the aspen swaying in the wind. It was so lifelike, so dimensional.

Hope lowered herself onto the edge of the bed. "You really are a sensational artist."

"Thanks." Spooky gave a small smile. He kept his hands gripped tightly between his closed legs.

"I was just in the Butterfly Box," Hope said. "Carter's friend came, gave me a password. I saw a video of Carter. He did something—unlocked something—that helped me remember, a little, from my lost year. Like what happens when we're in the Shade together."

Spooky's sock feet tapped on the wooden floor. He didn't appear surprised, but then again, Spooky never seemed shocked about anything.

"Carter's friend brought me a message for you too: 'Stay in Wilder when the time comes.' What's that mean to you?"

"Nothing." Spooky shook his head.

Hope gripped Spooky's bedspread in her hands. "People are disappearing. Nina, Carter, Royce, and now . . ." Hope swallowed.

"Quinn's gone too," Spooky said. Hope couldn't determine if it was a question or an affirmation.

"What if you're next?" she asked. "What if I'm next? Carter said I would need you, and I know he's right. Because who's more suited to a quest?"

Spooky's lips twitched, a smile forming, disappearing, and re-forming several times. He seemed to be waging an inner battle with his mouth.

"Please," Hope said. She stood from the bed and knelt on the floor in front of him. "We need each other out here. I can't do this without you." She put a hand on his, surprised when he didn't jump twenty feet into the air. "I also have a suspicion you knew this conversation was coming. That you've been preparing yourself for it."

Spooky placed his palms flat on his thighs, rubbing them as if he might rub the gray right out of the cotton polyester blend. His mouth moved in a soundless prayer.

"I don't know what happened to get you here," Hope said. "But whatever it was, I know it was bad."

Spooky stopped fidgeting, eyes on Hope. "It was," he said. His voice was raspy and soft but without a tremor.

"You can tell me," Hope said. "I'm listening. I want to know."

They sat for a time, Hope kneeling on the floor, as Spooky stared intently at the Shade. When he finally spoke, his voice wasn't Shade Spooky's, but it was close. "I'd like to show you."

35

SACRIFICES

HOPE
The Wilder Sanctuary
Rancho Mirage, California

T HE SMELL WAS ghastly. It hung in the air like mist, seeping into Hope's nostrils, mouth, and pores. The Shade sun was high in the sky, beating down on her neck with ferocity, Hope praying her suit had Virtual SPF 75 at least. Spooky was nowhere. He'd only told her to go to the biggest Butterfly Box available, use the password *BartleTest*, and wait.

The terrain was flat, a wasteland of dirt and sand sprawling around her, dotted with the occasional green runty bush or a rusty utility pole, sagging power lines extending into nowhere. Broken-down wooden structures of unknown purpose abounded, forlorn and nondescript. Far off in the distance were mountains she recognized, but they were blurry shadows against the blinding blue sky.

Hope was on high alert for a horde of undead to spring out, gangrenous legs dragging along behind them, craggy faces melting off their bones.

To her left was a rotting wooden lean-to and what might have been a camper, perhaps thousands of years ago. It looked like an Airstream, with its curved corners and shape like a homemade loaf of bread. It was sunken about two feet into the sand, layers of metal and paint disintegrated to its original state. To her right was a dirt lot with dozens of abandoned cars, their tires and windows missing, in various stages of sinking into the ground and rusting. Sprinkled among the cars were carriages that looked like they came from a carnival ride. A trapezoidal sign with a flashing yellow arrow boasted "Bombay Beach Drive-In" in retro lettering like *I Dream of Jeannie*.

Spooky appeared from behind the sign, adorned with buckles and boots up to his knees. He really had a thing for leather and shoulder pads. His hair was slicked into a roguish style and gelled solidly in place. He had a hardened, I've-been-fighting-bad-guys-in-the-desert look. Mad Max, the Asian Version.

Hope reviewed her own avatar's nondescript outfit, evidently made for an extra in any number of post-apocalyptic movies. The cloth was weathered, in various shades and multiple gradations of dirty. An arm of her shirt was torn off, the neck an unraveling scraggle of cloth. Dystopian chic, Quinn would have called it.

Hope's stomach clenched at the thought of Quinn, of what may have happened to him, of what was happening to him now. She simply refused to entertain any more permanent alternative for Quinn. Or for Carter.

"This is by far the most realistic place you've ever taken me," Hope said. She surveyed the wasteland around her, wrinkling her nose again at the stench. "But can you do something about the smell? I could do without that part of the reality."

"I spent the most time on this one," Spooky said. He waved his hand through the air in a lazy arc. The smell disappeared, and the sickly floral scent returned. Hope wasn't sure which was worse, dead people or dead flowers.

Her feet made crunching sounds, like the icky but slightly satisfying feeling of stepping on a snail. She knelt, finding they weren't shells but bones, the skulls and fins and pointy protrusions of fish skeletons. A carpet of bones with hollow, vacant eyes and gaping mouths revealing broken teeth. Still icky, but fish bones were better than human ones.

The scene flickered once more, and the drive-in was replaced with a ramshackle clapboard house. Like the rest of the buildings, it was sinking into the ground on dirty brick pillars. An armchair that may have once been upholstered in leather sat on a sagging front porch, springs and yellow stuffing jutting out from the cushions. The sign above the door was old and broken, an *F, R,* and *S* the sole letters visible, written crudely, like a clubhouse sign painted by kids. It hung from the rafters by a chain at an odd angle, squeaking as it swung in the nonexistent breeze.

Spooky walked up the steps and stood on the porch near the armchair, tapping his boot. Hope followed. The rusty screen door let out a pitiful moan and then slammed behind them like a gunshot.

Hope expected a haunted house. Perhaps even a few skeletons sitting at a kitchen table, still posed as if they were eating breakfast, drinks in hand like the characters in the *Pirates of the Caribbean* ride. Instead, she stood on a scuffed linoleum floor in a cluttered bookstore. Before her lay rows of wooden shelves, glass cases filled with toys and action figures, large glossy posters of superheroes suspended from the ceiling.

"So this is where you used to work?" Hope asked. "Fortress?"

Spooky bent his head forward, as if hoping his hair would conceal his face, but it was too styled to fall this time. He pointed a finger at the Chinese boy behind the counter wearing a careworn maroon T-shirt with the words *Don't Piss Off the Dungeon Master.* This kid was laid-back and confident, with a wide smile on his face. It was hard to believe this Spencer in the Fortress would someday become the Spooky of Wilder.

The other employee behind the counter was much older, with three days of beard growth and a tweed newsboy cap. The Manga emblem on his T-shirt was stretched tight across his paunchy belly, revealing an inch of hairy pink skin. He bore the superior, geek-shaming vibe you could only get from a comic-book store staff member. Or tech support.

A bell tinkled, and the Spencer behind the counter waved at the tall boy entering. Hope recognized him at once as Spooky's brother, though a slightly less polished version than Henry of today.

Spencer-of-old joined Henry at a table piled with cardboard boxes. Henry immediately began slitting the containers open with a box cutter.

"Dad's pissed again. But what else is new?" Henry said, setting the razor, open, on the table. His elbow displaced a pile of comic books onto the floor.

Spencer shook his head with a flash of annoyance, kneeling to straighten the fallen magazines, flipping them over and adjusting their covers. He returned the cutter to its housing. "Because you need to get off your ass and apply to college. Mom and Dad, especially Dad, will never let it go. You can't work here forever."

"But Gopal says I can take over someday." Henry gestured around Fortress. Hope followed his hand and so did Spooky, but she knew they weren't seeing the same thing.

"No way," Spencer said.

"Why not? You work here too. You're the one that got me this job."

"Only when I don't have school," Spencer said. "I like it, but it's just a job. I'll be graduating soon and—"

"Heard it. You'll be running some zillion-dollar startup in Silicon Valley." Henry's edge of bitterness belied the good-natured grin on his face. "Spence, maybe running this business *is* for me. I did get a B-plus in economics."

"Asian F," Spencer said. "Unacceptable."

"We can't all be you." Henry kicked at a table leg with the toe of his sneaker. "I can't be you."

"I get it." Spencer squared his shoulders. "But you can't expect the kind of parents white kids have. It's just what you do." Spencer didn't sound bitter, instead merely resigned. "I wanted to be an artist."

"You're a terrific artist," Henry said.

"Maybe," Spencer said. "But I won't be one. And you won't skip college and run a comic-book store. You may as well tell Dad you want to be a teacher."

They both laughed. Henry hefted another cardboard box onto the table and opened it, revealing a gross of thin plastic sleeves.

"School isn't for me. I'm not book smart. Cool, new *Weatherman*." He set the comic aside and gave it a loving pat.

"You are smart. You just don't try that hard," Spencer said.

Henry rolled his eyes. "You sound like Mom."

The two brothers busied themselves with placing a thin sheet of cardboard behind each comic book and ushering both book and cardboard into a plastic sleeve.

"I'm scared," Henry said finally. "I don't know what Dad wants to do with me. I don't want to go there."

A shadow crossed Spencer's face, an expression Hope was more than familiar with. He put down a stack of *Vampironicas*. Henry took one off the pile.

"You aren't going," Spencer said. "I am."

Henry stopped his perusal of *Vampironica*. "Spence," he said.

Spencer didn't look up. "Let me take care of it."

Something passed between them, as if an agreement had been made, but Hope didn't understand what it was. Two halves of the same whole, one made of light and one of darkness.

Spooky nudged Hope and pointed to a door behind her. The red-and-white metal sign bolted onto it read "Storage: Employees Only."

Hope should have known it wouldn't be comic-book storage beyond. It was an old warehouse, with floor-to-ceiling casement windows to her left and ugly mustard-colored paint on the walls. But gleaming industrial tables stood out against the drabness, peppered with test tubes and microscopes and appliances resembling microwaves and deep fryers. There were rolling carts filled with rows of tiny bottles and vials, mysterious medical equipment, brand-new examination tables.

On a swiveling stool, a man in a white lab coat sat with his back to them. He alternated between looking into a machine filled with vials, peering into a microscope, and typing. He had jet-black hair graying at the temples.

A door opened with a metallic thud, and Spencer sauntered in as if he'd followed them from Fortress, though he now wore a fitted waffle-weave shirt, a beige hoodie, and designer jeans. This Spencer moved with assurance as he dropped his backpack on the floor. The man didn't look up. Spencer jumped onto a stool, winding his yellow Chucks around the leg and using the countertop to rotate in slow circles.

"Where's Henry? What are you doing here?" the man asked in Mandarin.

Spencer responded in English. "I'm doing it." He thrust his hands into his hoodie pockets.

"Nonsense." The man's tone was gruff, and he gave a shake of his head. He took off his red rubber gloves and threw them in a red basket, placing his plastic safety goggles on the tabletop. While he looked different in a lab coat, Spooky's father still exuded the same closed-off severity that he did on Visiting Days. "The equipment is calibrated for Henry." He went back to tapping on his keyboard. "And your degree is nearly complete. In addition, you have that internship. It's an opportunity not to be squandered."

"That's an even better reason it should be me. Henry has a longer way to go. So calibrate it to me, or whatever." Spencer stuck out his leg to stop the spinning, face turned toward the ceiling. "Also, if anything happened to Henry, Mom would die. He's her favorite."

His father didn't protest. Like Hope's own parents, he didn't seem the type to say anything merely to make someone feel better. And also like Hope, Spencer didn't appear to expect anything different.

"It's fine, Ba. Let's just get it over with. I have my last midterm tomorrow afternoon."

His father closed his laptop and rose to a metal examination table topped with a rubbery blue cushion. Nearby were several rolling shelves of machinery, tubes and cords extending from them at all angles. A silver medical tray with a scratchy brown paper towel on top, ten or more syringes of varying sizes lying in wait, like an obedient little battalion.

One syringe had a plunger thicker than any Hope had ever seen. It looked almost comical, like a prop or a toy.

His father gathered caddies of small silver-topped bottles, shaking a few, holding some up to the light as he read their names. He looked like a discerning grocery shopper, tapping on a watermelon, squeezing an avocado in his hand. He gestured at the table with a wave, two caddies hooked onto his fingers.

"Let's get started, then." He sounded almost impatient, as if he were waiting for his toddler to finish a run on the slide so they could leave the park.

Spencer hopped on the table in one practiced move, eyes darting to indeterminate points on the ceiling, fingers drumming on his chest.

His father depressed a small syringe at the nape of his son's neck and Spencer cried out.

"That's the numbing agent," his father said brusquely.

There was a rap on the door and everyone pivoted, including Hope and Spooky.

Dr. Emerson entered, trademark blond ponytail sleek and tight, patent-leather heels tapping on the dusty floor. A tan file folder was tucked under her arm. Her WASP-y Barbie-doll perfection made the space look even dingier.

"Hey Liz," Spencer's father said with a smile.

"Jiang," Dr. Emerson said. "Dr. Stark wants an update. We've got a lot scheduled after this run."

"I'm on time." He smiled, and Hope realized she'd never seen him look happy before. He gave Dr. Emerson a mock-impatient look, tone easy. "I am *trying* to get started."

"Great," Dr. Emerson said. She noticed Spencer, prone on the table. "Hello Henry."

Spencer propped himself up on one elbow, a charming smile blooming across his face. "I'm not Henry, I'm Spencer."

"Oh, of course you are. Spencer." Lines appeared on her forehead. Dr. Emerson seemed put out at the possibility Spencer might know his own name. She brushed off her lab coat, dismissing the idea with a swipe down the crisp fabric. "You boys are both growing up so quickly." She placed the file folder on the table. "I'll leave you to it, Dr. Lu. Elliot will be ready for Spencer when you finish."

"White ladies," Spencer said, after the door shut. "They think we all look alike."

"Be respectful of your elders." Dr. Lu's face resumed its customary stern expression. He raised the syringe, squirting a little liquid out and flicking it with his fingers. "Close your eyes and think about a happy event in your life, something that gives you pleasure. Something recent." He spoke in English now, in a singsong voice, as if telling a bedtime story.

Hope gritted her teeth. He sounded like Stark, and Emerson. And Luke. He sounded like all of them.

Dr. Jiang Lu chose another vial, scrutinizing the label once more before inserting a syringe into the top. He took Spencer's arm, wiping it off and deftly inserting the needle on the first try. Spencer closed his eyes and straightened out his legs. His fingers ceased their tapping.

"Do you have it? Your happy memory?"

Spencer swallowed twice, and when he spoke, he wasn't flippant or confident anymore. "Ba? I don't feel right."

Dr. Lu's thin voice continued, "When you have your happy memory, tell me about it, in as much detail as you can. You have an excellent memory, so I know you will have many details."

Spencer's voice was already more sluggish. In the last few minutes he'd changed from the Spencer in Fortress to the Spooky of Wilder.

"I drew this picture for Art 301. I only used Blackwing pencils. No one could believe I could make those kinds of shadows using just graphite."

Dr. Lu pursed his lips. It was clear, script or not, that talking about his art wasn't making a happy memory for his father.

Spencer added quickly, "I got full credit for it; my professor said it was the best in all his courses."

Even in this state, he knew his memory didn't wholly count for happy in his father's eyes. Hope got it completely; it's what she would have said to smooth things over with her own parents. If you have to be a loser, at least be the head loser.

Dr. Lu grunted his approval, if a little grudgingly, upon hearing that. He selected the next syringe from the tray, the strange, big one. "Remarkable. Impressive. Describe it to me."

"It was a forest." Spencer's voice was croaky now. "Trees as far as you can see, a winding path. Shadows and light. It even has a backstory. It's called the Shade—"

The walls blurred and refocused. Spooky and Hope were back in the desert where they had begun. Fortress was gone, as was the drive-in. They stood together, staring at the fault lines in the dirt.

"Your father," Hope said at last.

"All in the name of research." Spooky kicked at the ground. "Groundbreaking research."

"He experimented on his own kid?" Hope felt sick.

"His own kids," Spooky corrected. "Henry too. Thought experiments, sleep experiments, mind manipulation. All kinds of new technology. He's been doing it since I can remember, probably even before. I wouldn't be surprised if he tried things when my mom was pregnant." Spooky looked over his shoulder, as if expecting his father to appear and scold him.

"It's reprehensible. It's . . ." Hope was stuttering, finding it hard to express her horror and her fury. Spooky was just a boy, barely older than Charlotte. Defenseless. "How could . . . how could he?"

Spooky's jaw was tight. "My father is a very driven man. He entered into a commitment with Copeland-Stark, and he takes his commitments seriously. *Fortius quo fidelius.*"

Hope knew she'd heard that phrase before, but its meaning was a mystery. "It doesn't excuse it. His own sons—"

"In here, I can look at it more objectively," Spooky said. "Out there, I'm still upset about it. Visiting Days are the worst. I can't even look at my father then."

Hope took his hand. "You saved Henry. You made a tremendous sacrifice."

"Henry is my little brother." He shrugged. "There was no other choice. And sacrifices aren't really sacrifices unless they hurt."

Hope gazed at the postapocalyptic expanse of land. The dirt was cracked in a herringbone pattern, symmetrical and mathematically beautiful. "Thank you for showing me," she said.

"You and I made sacrifices," Spooky said. "But we don't yet know the consequences."

36

HANDLED

LUKE
The Vintage Club
Indian Wells, California

J ACK COPELAND LIVED in a nine-thousand-square-foot, sprawling estate off the eleventh hole at the Vintage Club. The manicured backyard featured two pools and a waterfall, and the
kitchen and dining room opened into a Carrara-marble-tiled indoor
patio, semi-enclosed and furnished as if it were still inside. The patio
boasted even more marble and a zinc bar bigger than most restaurants,
as well as three fireplaces flanked with high-end furniture.

It wasn't the first time Luke had been at Jack's, but he hoped it would
be the last. The entire staff of Copeland-Stark was voluntold to turn out
for this event. Luke wanted to be home, staring at Erleben in case Hope
returned. He wanted to be anywhere but here, but he had to make an
appearance. His whole life had become about appearances, after all.

Elliot Stark was utterly in his element, having been invited to play
nine holes with Jack and some of the investors. They stood by the marble fireplace now, laughing with Liz Emerson.

Luke skulked by, headed to the bar and too late to recalculate his route.

"Dr. Salinger!" Stark called to his retreating form. He raised his glass at Luke.

Luke inclined his head toward the bar. "Getting a drink," he said.

"Come and talk to us after," Copeland boomed. He sounded jovial, but Luke wasn't fooled. He was being summoned.

There was a full bar and a few bartenders, of course. Two men nearby were engaged in deep conversation, acknowledging Luke with a nod. Luke had been around enough to tell they were both researchers. One was tall and ferrety, wearing a short-sleeved button-down and khaki pants. His buddy was stocky and round, wearing an argyle sweater and slacks. They wore that pasty, fidgety, rabbity aura researchers carried: not enough sunlight, and more experience with rats than people.

Luke ordered a Guinness and loitered for as long as he could before walking back to the team. Stark raised his martini glass at him.

"I thought you quit drinking," Luke said.

"This is a special occasion," he said. "Jack knocked it out of the park. We may have locked in another angel investor." Stark whispered in Luke's ear, sloshing his martini over the side of his glass, droplets falling onto the pristine floor. "You should introduce yourself. Logan Hu, CEO of Omnia, is over there talking to Jordan Lin. Logan's got a startup in San Francisco and is interested in biotech, especially the Eos Ribbon."

"Maybe two investors by night's end," Copeland said, pointing with his beer. "She's a venture capitalist also."

The group turned to the bar. The woman was tall and curvy, with long red hair and large green eyes. She was chatting with the two researchers, Ferret and Argyle. They looked positively giddy, as if they'd recently crawled out of their warrens to find a field of lettuce.

Stark let out a low whistle, then stumbled back and almost knocked over one of the gaudy glass dogs Jack had on display.

"Down boy," Copeland said, clutching the teetering statue.

"She's quite attractive," Liz Emerson said. She looked as if she'd eaten something that didn't agree with her.

"Luke, you should go talk to Logan Hu," Stark suggested. "His father is Dr. Charles Hu, the one building that city of the future, Perception. But make sure his wife isn't around."

"Who's his wife?" Luke asked.

Dr. Emerson pointed across the room. "Julia Liang," she said. "*The 415* reporter. So watch what you say."

"Elliot is right, go do your magic," Copeland said. "We stand to make a shit ton of money out of this deal."

"We already have a shit ton of money," Luke said. But he held his Guinness in a toast and forced a smile. "But I'll go make us more."

�֍֍֍

LUKE STOOD AT a cocktail table with Jiang Lu, his wife, and Amelia Green. The two women were deep in conversation. Jiang stood next to them, nursing a beer.

"I didn't know how to motivate him," Mrs. Lu was saying to Amelia Green. "I couldn't even get him to apply to college. With Spencer it was so easy. Straight-A student, early admission to UC Berkeley, 4.0 in computer science. He had an internship secured months before he graduated. We never had to worry about anything."

"Except we could never get him off that computer," Jiang said. "And he spent every penny he earned on more equipment."

Mrs. Lu looked at her husband for a few moments, eyes flashing. "I miss my son," she said quietly.

"All Henry needed was a good swift kick in the ass," Jiang growled to no one.

Dr. Green looked sympathetically at Mrs. Lu. "Spencer is doing well," she said softly, patting her on the hand. "Soon, I'm sure."

A tuxedoed waiter breezed by. For lack of anything better to do, Luke took a small plate of cocktail shrimp and an array of mysterious tartlets. He added another item to the mental list of why he hated parties like this: tiny goddamned food.

Stark sidled up to Logan Hu and made introductions. Luke searched for a graceful exit, and when he could find none, searched for a non-graceful one he'd gladly seize. Still no dice.

"Dr. Hu wants to know about the Eos Ribbon," Stark said. "Of course, a great deal is proprietary, but Jiang can give you the broad strokes."

Jiang smiled, his lousy mood seeming to have lifted. "The Eos Ribbon is a BCI, which stands for brain computer interface. The technology, the idea of mapping the brain to control computer functions, has been around since the late nineties. Research has grown exponentially since. Though we're still several years from the truly groundbreaking applications, or mass distribution."

"Mass distribution?" Logan Hu said. "Intriguing."

"Right now, BCIs are being used widely for people with neurological injuries," Jiang said. "Paraplegics, for example, are now able to move their prosthetic limbs simply with the power of concentration."

"Amazing," Logan Hu said, and Stark looked elated, bouncing around on his feet.

"We see endless potential in the Eos Ribbon," Jiang said, ramping up. "Although at the moment it's still in the early testing stages for our human subjects—"

"Thank you for the concise summary, Dr. Lu." Stark clapped him on the shoulder. "I'm going to stop you before we get into trade-secret territory."

"Elliot," Luke said. "Can I talk to you when you get a moment? Privately?"

"Of course," Stark said. "I need to introduce Logan to Dr. Emerson first. But I'll find you."

Jiang finished his drink and took his wife to the bar for another. Stark and Logan Hu followed.

Luke stood next to Amelia and sipped his Guinness, surveying the mountains. "I didn't know we'd started testing the Eos Ribbon on human subjects."

Dr. Green looked grim. "Neither did I."

Luke crossed the endless main foyer and crept along one of ten hallways. Stark, despite his increasing inebriation and affability, had been avoiding Luke all night. He and Jack had disappeared up the stairs over ten minutes ago, and Luke had decided to follow.

As he rounded a hallway corner, Luke banged his knee on a massive credenza. He swore colorfully as a metal bowl containing weird, artsy balls of wooden yarn wobbled. Several fell from the bowl and off the table, rolling slowly down the corridor.

Luke chased after the spheres, feeling like a sitcom character. He knelt on the marble floor to fetch one that had rolled under a console table. Jack Copeland's voice came from behind a partially closed door, and Luke straightened quickly, trying to avoid being caught balls out. Literally.

"And I'm just hearing about this now?" Copeland was saying. His voice was the low, threatening rumble that always signaled trouble. "How the fuck could you let this happen?"

"I'm still investigating," Stark said. "Look, it's fine. The flash drive we found is destroyed, and the only remaining copy is on the secure network. Only the three of us have access. I double-checked with Jordan Lin. It's all handled."

"How did Tomás Romero take it?"

"He's not happy with us," Stark said. "To put it mildly. But he understands. I'm not worried about Tomás."

Luke stepped closer to the door, his back pressed against the wall separating him from Jack and Elliot.

"I have to tell you, Elliot," Copeland said. "I have reservations about letting you bring your daughter in as employee rather than a patient. It's a deal I wouldn't have made with anyone else."

"You made it with Dr. Green," Stark said sharply.

"That was a special circumstance," he snapped. "As you well know."

"This had nothing to do with Morgan," Stark said. "You're over-reacting."

"Someone has to," Copeland said.

Stark replied, too quiet for Luke to hear. He took a step closer to the door.

"This place is becoming like Swiss cheese," Copeland said. "We can't afford any more mistakes. And now we have to worry about Amelia Green?"

"Amelia's a mouse," Stark said. "And I have a plan for Hope. Like I said, handled."

There was a small snap, and Luke looked at his hands. He'd been gripping the spheres so tightly he'd broken off a piece. Luke stepped silently into the bathroom, moving behind the open door and peeking through the crack. Stark's head extended into the hallway, looking slowly left and right before it disappeared.

"Good news, got a text," Stark said. "We're good to go on the new location for the lab."

"Where?"

"An old aviation center," Stark said. "Twice the size. Not optimal, distancewise. It's just shy of the Arizona border. But the inconvenience is a necessary trade-off."

"Great," Copeland said. "Start moving immediately. Have them work around the clock until it's done."

"We should get back," Stark said. "Before we're missed."

Luke waited until Jack and Elliot left the room and disappeared around the corner, then forced himself to wait two minutes more. He dropped the wooden balls into the bowl, moving quickly down the stairs, through the main foyer, and out the front door.

37

CRIMINALLY INSANE

HOPE

The Wilder Sanctuary
Rancho Mirage, California

A T LUNCH, HOPE found Spooky at a corner table on the patio, hunched over his graph paper. It was a scorching desert afternoon, and no one else wanted to be outside, least of all Hope. She'd had a headache for days, and the oppressive heat was only making it throb more.

She slid into the seat across from Spooky, dropping *Kisses and Tells* onto the table. Hope waited for a break in his concentration, watching the arugula on her plate droop sadly.

After five minutes, there was no indication Spooky planned to acknowledge her existence. Hope cleared her throat, and he dropped his pen with a small sigh to look at her. Hope held up the book.

"Not my genre," he said.

"That's just the fake cover," Hope said. She opened to a page with a dog-ear and turned it toward Spooky. "This is your dad's book. Have you read it?"

Spooky peered over his nose to read: *The Eos Ribbon: Nexus between Mind and Technology,* and shook his head. "I don't have to. I lived it."

"This was published over a year ago. At the time, the Eos Ribbon was being used on patients with paralysis and neurological trauma. But then it goes on to talk about the potential for more horrific uses, though it says no human testing has occurred in those areas." Hope tapped the book with her index finger. "But that's not true, because it's what your dad was doing to you. Implanting one of these ribbons."

Spooky nodded.

"You have one, and Carter had one. He thought it was how you got into the Shade without going into the Butterfly Box."

Spooky nodded again.

"Your dad talks about things like the Butterfly Box and the Labyrinth and those goddamn headsets—which were incidentally invented by Dr. Green, did you know that? It's called sonogenetics, controlling brains with ultrasound. They tried it on me a few days ago, in the Labyrinth."

"I know what sonogenetics is," Spooky said. He picked up his pen once more.

"But he writes about all these things like they're still theoretical. And maybe they were at the time he wrote it, but I doubt it." Hope fanned through the pages. "There's a lot in here that your father "speculates" about as ways to mess with someone's memory: blood transfusions, experiments on identical twins, implants, all kinds of psychotropic drugs. There's a whole chapter on subjecting people to weeks of sensory deprivation, strapped into a thing called the Tank, with no stimulus at all."

Spooky's face had grown shades paler since Hope had begun speaking. His hair fell forward as he looked down at his map, sweaty hands making ripples in the paper.

Hope leaned closer. "Only he wasn't speculating, was he? He and Copeland-Stark have been doing these experiments on people for a while."

Spooky looked at Hope, his black eyes sharp. "Like I said, I lived it," he said again.

"Why didn't you tell anyone?"

"I never remembered anything, right after." Spooky shrugged, picking at a hole in his map. "And when I did, I was already here. Who would believe it?"

"I believe it," Hope said.

"So?" he said. Hope had never witnessed anger from Spooky, but now his voice was brittle. "You're crazy, like me."

"We need to tell someone," Hope insisted. "It's immoral. It's—"

"Who?" Spooky emitted a wheezy sound, which Hope realized was a laugh. "We don't have proof. No one cares my father wrote a book about unethical science experiments that haven't been performed."

"There is proof," Hope said. "In the Copeland-Stark files. The ones Carter found. Hundreds of patient records that are labeled *Active,* for patients that aren't at Wilder. The SSEs."

"But we don't have those either," Spooky said. He pulled out a fresh piece of graph paper and a charcoal pencil and began a new drawing, freehand, sure and dark.

"We did," Hope said. "Quinn had it. He left it at the front desk. The last time I saw him, he was getting it back." She put her chin in her hands, fingers pressing into her temples, pushing against the pinpricks. "Nina was telling the truth, and she vanished. Carter found their files with Royce's help, and now they're both gone. Quinn talked to Morgan and supposedly left with Tomás, but he didn't."

"You believe everyone is still alive," Spooky said. "They aren't."

"You can't be sure," Hope protested. "They could be at the other place. Wilder 2.0."

"It isn't called that," Spooky said. "It doesn't have a name. They call it 'the other facility' or 'the lab.' And they were extremely careful so I wouldn't remember where it was."

Hope dropped her hands.

"The warehouse with your father. In the Shade."

Spooky titled his paper at an angle, brushing light strokes with his pencil.

"But you did remember, because you recreated it, in the Butterfly Box," Hope said, trying to call up any landmark from the Shade that would give her a clue to where it was. She combed through the scattered fragments of information she had, trying to form it into something that made sense: the patient files, *Verbal Overshadowing* and the Memory Mechanic, *Breakthroughs*. Carter's message and Rohan Kapoor's visit.

"Did you ever figure out what Carter meant?" Hope asked. "About staying in the asylum?"

Spooky's pencil lead snapped and rolled off the table. "You never said that. You said, 'Carter's friend brought me a message for you too: Stay in Wilder when the time comes. What's that mean to you?'"

"Right," Hope said. "That's what I said."

"That's not the same," Spooky spluttered. "What was the message, exactly?"

Hope thought, then spoke carefully. "'Tell Spooky to stay in the asylum when it's time.'"

"The Elizabeth Arkham Asylum for the Criminally Insane." Spooky looked like he might explode. "It first appeared October 1974, in *Batman* number 258."

"I'm not following," Hope said.

"Arkham," Spooky said.

"As in the broken room in the Butterfly Box?" Hope glanced at Spooky's new drawing, then snatched it from the table. There it was: the lot with the rusting cars, the abandoned Ferris wheel seats, and the trapezoidal sign: Bombay Beach Drive-In.

"Christ," she said. "That's it, isn't it? Wilder 2.0."

Spooky took the drawing back and placed it at the bottom of his stack. "It's the closest landmark I remember."

"So, where the hell is that?" Hope asked. "Bombay Beach? Is that even in California?"

"I don't know," he said, carefully lining up the edges of his artwork. "I can find out though."

"Go for it." Hope tapped her head. "Do your robot magic. Fire up that ribbon you have."

"I'll Google it in the library, after my session with Dr. Emerson," Spooky said. "I'm not a smartphone."

Hope refilled her water glass and took a long, coppery drink. "I need to tell you something," she said. "Quinn and I heard the doctors talking about me. They said if I didn't do better in the Labyrinth, they were going to move me and let your dad experiment on me. That was almost five days ago, and I didn't perform well."

Spooky looked directly at her, face now fearful. "That's bad," he said.

"They won't kill me," Hope said lightly, although she felt nauseous.

"They might not," Spooky said. "But you'll wish they had."

The sliding glass door opened, bringing a welcome gust of air-conditioning and a less-welcome Dr. Stark. He knelt at the side of the table.

"Spencer," Dr. Stark said. "Dr. Emerson was called away, so your session will be postponed."

Spooky continued to draw, nose bent over his paper.

Stark hoisted himself up and turned to Hope.

"I'd like to see you for a session tonight, Hope. Please come to my office after dinner."

"We've never met at night," Hope said.

"Can't be helped," Dr. Stark said. "Be well, both of you." He was gone in another gust of air.

"What makes you think they won't kill you?" Spooky asked, as if Dr. Stark had never interrupted.

"I think I'm leverage," Hope said, putting the lukewarm glass to her forehead, "for making Luke behave. They still need him, because he's the Mechanic . . ."

Luke.

"We do have a connection to the outside," Hope said, standing. "Go find out where Bombay Beach is and see if the jump drive is still at the front desk. Then meet me in Arkham."

38

DOWN THE RABBIT HOLE

HOPE
The Wilder Sanctuary
Rancho Mirage, California

NSIDE ARKHAM, HOPE suited up as quickly as possible. The virtual keyboard floated in front of her, wiggling, a few keys shimmering as she typed W-A-F-F-L-E-S once again. The dark foam walls of the Butterfly Box vanished. Millions of stars surrounded her, blanketing the ceiling in a glorious wash of tiny sparkling gemstones. An enormous golden moon hung in the middle of the night sky, dipping down so close you could stand up and grab it with both hands.

"Hollow of the Moon," Hope whispered, face turned to the ceiling.

She stood on a tiny square of concrete, uneven and cracked. To her left was the backyard lounger, complete with lime-green cushions. She moved closer, fingers hovering over the blanket she'd snuggled under on so many nights, standing over it as if it were sacred.

"Luke?" Hope said. "Are you there?"

The biggest cushion lit up with lines, stretching and stuttering until Luke's face appeared.

"Hope," he said. "Listen to me."

"No." She shook her head. "You listen. Copeland-Stark has another facility somewhere. My friends are there. But they have other patients too, maybe a hundred. And they're performing those experiments in *Verbal Overshadowing* on them."

"Yes, human subjects," Luke said. "I found out last night."

Hope didn't understand, but she didn't have time to care. "We don't know where it is. Spooky is searching for somewhere called Bombay—"

"I looked it up," Luke interrupted. "I overheard a conversation between Jack Copeland and Elliot Stark. It's an aviation center at the Arizona border, about three hours from here."

"I have the proof, in the patient records. At least I will, soon." She didn't add, *fingers crossed, if Spooky gets the drive.*

"Thank God." Luke let out a long, relieved breath, but Hope didn't know why. His eyes shifted from hers, and she could hear rapid typing. "Now we need you all the way back."

"What are you talking about?" Hope asked. "Back from where?"

Luke ignored her, eyes fixed on another window, speaking like he was reading from a cue card. "Inara, activate Erleben Voice version 3.9. Login: Morpheus. Password: UnplugMe."

"Welcome back, Cowboy. I've missed you." Again, Morena's voice rang through Hope's headset, very nearly purring.

Luke spoke again. "Inara, activate Eos Ribbon Trigger Nakano-Hope 9-C. Password: RedPill."

"Thank you, Cowboy. Enjoy your visit down the rabbit hole."

The dull throb in Hope's head became the same hot, stabbing pain as with Carter.

She slid to the floor.

"Our last Christmas Eve together was the day you came to Wilder," Luke said. "Do you remember?"

Hope closed her eyes.

"No," Luke said. "Look at me. We're not imagining anything. Keep your eyes open. Remember."

Hope opened her eyes and focused on Luke, mesmerized by the most impossibly beautiful blue eyes she'd ever known. More memories came to her as the pinpricks of heat pulsed: a white room, a tray of objects, a window made of diamonds.

❋❋❋

FROM SOMEWHERE FAR away Hope heard Luke, but it was an effort to make her body comply. She felt a kiss on her forehead, gentle and scratchy, as he reached across to snap open her seat belt. She wrapped her arms around his neck, eyes still closed.

"Wake up, Sleeping Beauty," he said. "We're here."

Grudgingly, Hope opened her eyes. She was so groggy, but she willed herself to rally. She felt like she might be coming down with something.

The flu, maybe. It was going around work.

Luke kept his arm around her waist as they walked. They crossed a circular driveway and went past a gurgling fountain to a large, modern building with glass windows and manicured landscaping.

"Where are we, again?" Hope felt stupid asking. She should probably know. He must have told her.

"We have an appointment," Luke said. With one hand still holding her close, Luke fished in his pocket for his phone and typed a text with his thumb. It took him a few tries, and he eventually let go to use both hands. The door clicked, and Luke swung it open as he helped Hope to the other side.

They faced a wide, empty hallway lined with even more doors, an almost dizzying amount. Hope stepped onto the shiny floor. It was dark, and the hallway seemed to stretch on into forever. A sickeningly sweet smell was in the air, like decaying flowers.

"It doesn't look like anyone is home," Hope said. Her words came sluggishly to the surface, slower than they sounded in her head.

"This is the back entrance," he said. "There won't be many people here. It's Christmas Eve."

"Merry Christmas," she said brightly, then laughed. And then she wondered why it was so funny.

Luke's phone buzzed in his pocket as they continued down the hallway. A few lights on the floor lit up. She stepped purposefully, mesmerized by each step on the floor and the timing of the lights. She felt like Michael Jackson in the "Billie Jean" video.

Hope licked her lips a few times, noticing how odd her tongue felt in her mouth, how big and dry. "I don't know what's wrong with me today."

She looked into his face and sought his eyes; a few tears fell on his right cheek. She reached up and wiped them away.

"Why are you sad?" she asked. She wondered if she made him upset. It made her heart hurt.

"I'm not sad." He kissed her again on the forehead. "But now, I need you to do something for me."

"Anything," she said. "Why are we whispering?"

They reached the end of the corridor and stopped at a door. This one had a window in it with thin crisscrossed silver lines. Hope touched one of the diamonds. They were pretty.

"Shhhh . . ." Luke placed a finger over her lips. "We're going to see a friend of mine. But I need you to keep your head down. Don't talk, and . . . you can't hold on to me. Can you do that?"

Hope tucked her hair behind her ears. "Of course I can." She was trying to keep her voice quiet, so she didn't know if the sound came out. She put a hand to her lips where his finger had been.

The door opened. She kept her head bent, as she was told, Luke walking in front and Hope shuffling behind. Luke stopped to talk to someone. Hope wanted to see who it was, but she didn't dare.

"Dr. Salinger." The man spoke gruffly. "Jonah just told me you were coming. We weren't expecting you."

"No worries, Isaiah," Luke said. "I forgot to call. Christmas Eve, you know? I guess I drew the short straw."

"Me too," the man, Isaiah, said. "No one else here but me and the crazies."

They laughed. Luke sounded like everything was fine, so Hope relaxed. If they were laughing, it must be okay. She felt like she was going to fall again but didn't reach out for Luke. She gripped her jeans in her hands.

"Can I help you with anything?" Isaiah asked. There was a pause. "Wheelchair?"

Hope wanted to laugh, but she willed her mouth closed. Why would Luke need a wheelchair? She bit her bottom lip tightly, so hard she tasted blood.

"Later, probably. Thanks," Luke said. "But right now, I need a room for an hour, and then we'll head upstairs."

Hope chanced a look. Isaiah was huge, like the Incredible Hulk. He unlocked a door—another diamond-patterned one—with a card around his neck.

Isaiah gestured around. "Take your pick."

Hope lay on a flat examination table in the room Luke chose, a thin rubber pad underneath her. It was sort of like a doctor's office, though not like any she'd ever been in. Everything was metallic and shiny, as if it were brand new. There weren't any pictures on the walls, no dog-eared issues of *People*, no plants. She lay against the waxy covering on the table, like the paper from a butcher shop.

Luke was unpacking things onto a tray. He pulled items from a bag he must have brought, though Hope only noticed it right now.

When he returned to her side, Luke placed the tray on the table near her face.

"What's all that?" The tray was full of random items: Luke's book. A stack of photos, the top a picture of Hope in the backyard, in front of the sunset. Some plastic key cards. Was that his decoder ring?

"Just some tools." Luke rolled up his shirtsleeves. She absolutely loved when he did that, could never resist running her fingertips along one forearm. Luke let her, for a minute, before he picked up her hand and returned it to her side.

He bent over Hope, and she reached for him. She felt a tightness across her chest and looked down. Luke had wrapped something blue around her, tightly, across both her arms and legs too. She couldn't move.

For the first time, Hope was scared. "What's happening?"

Someone in red entered the room. He was young, with dark brown skin and a grave expression on his face.

The man in red handed Luke something. Or maybe Luke handed him something; Hope couldn't be sure.

Luke bent to kiss her forehead, raising his hand close to her face. "Shhhh," he said. "It's going to be okay."

Hope felt a sharp pain in the nape of her neck. It stung and grew hot, pulsating, like when she snuck out to the mall in seventh grade and got her ears pierced without telling her parents. Hope cried out, trying to cover the burning spot, but her arms were pinned.

Luke swept his phone through the air, as if looking for a signal. He glanced at the man. "Fifteen minutes?"

The man in red didn't look happy. "More like five."

Luke's eyes widened. "How the hell am I supposed to make sure it worked?"

He didn't respond, instead leaving as silently as he'd come.

Hope tried to think, but her brain wouldn't cooperate at its normal speed. They were in a hospital. Luke had given her a shot. "Am I sick?" she asked.

Luke looked sad again, and Hope wished she hadn't said it. She hated to see him upset.

"Yes," he said. "But I'm going to fix everything, so you aren't sick anymore." He pushed the hair off her face, running his fingers through its length, his blue eyes bright.

Hope closed her eyes. His fingers felt so nice. "Okay," she said sleepily. Luke would take care of her; he always did.

She felt his lips on hers, and his mouth near her ear.

"I love you," he said. Even so close, his voice sounded miles away. "Still, and always."

She thought she said *I love you too*. She must have, because she did love him. Luke was every single star in her universe.

But she wouldn't remember.

39

PARTLY THROUGH

HOPE

The Wilder Sanctuary
Rancho Mirage, California

"P AUSE."

With trembling hands, Hope pulled off the headset.

Spooky lay prone on the floor at her feet, eyes closed, fingers moving rapidly on his chest like he was playing a piano.

"Spooky," she said, voice hoarse. "Spooky!" She knelt and gave him a shake.

After a few seconds, he opened his eyes.

"Did you get the drive?" Hope asked.

Spooky shook his head. "It wasn't there. I'm trying a different way."

"I thought you said you weren't a smartphone," Hope said.

"I'm not," Spooky said. "I'm better."

Hope traced the word *Maelstrom* along the headset's edge.

Spooky propped himself up on an elbow. "Are you finished?"

"I don't think so." Hope shook her head.

"Are you remembering?"

She nodded.

"But you don't want to go back in?"

Hope bit her lip.

"What have you learned?" Spooky asked.

Hope put a hand to the nape of her neck. "Spencer, do I have one too? An Eos Ribbon?"

"Go back in," Spooky settled himself on the floor once more. "No way out but through. And you're only partly through."

"No way out but through," Hope repeated. She pulled the headset over her ears. "Resume."

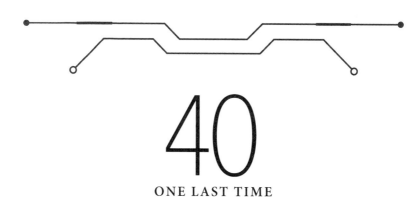

40

ONE LAST TIME

HOPE
The Wilder Sanctuary
Rancho Mirage, California

L UKE WAS PACING, in and out of the frame of the green cushion, when Hope returned to the Shade.

His face centered when he noticed Hope. "What did you just remember?" Luke asked. "Our last day together?"

"I don't know." Hope shook her head. "I don't want to know." But she did know what happened last Christmas Eve, even if she willed it to be untrue. "All this time, I trusted there was more to the story. I trusted you. Us. Even when you were strapping me to a bed. I still had complete faith in you."

"I know," Luke said, a catch in his voice.

"Did you wipe my memories?" Hope asked. "You're the reason I can't remember?"

Luke's face was drawn, his eyes dark. "I did."

"Why?" she whispered. Hope wished for anger, to conjure up some of the indignant fury from watching Spooky and his father. But she wasn't angry; she only felt heartbroken, emptied. Consumed. Her mouth was dry, much dryer than it had been in the Labyrinth. Hope backed into the fence, which must have been a wall of the Butterfly Box. Her feet were in the black bark, trampling the virtual blue wildflowers.

"I had to," Luke said. "I didn't have a choice. You—"

"We were . . . you were supposed to be different. The last good one. I loved you," Hope said, tears spilling from her eyes. She slid to the ground, face in her scratchy gloved hands. "I still love you."

"I love you too," Luke said.

"You don't," Hope said. "You couldn't, to do all this."

The world dimmed around them, flickering for a few seconds before returning.

"Listen to me," Luke said. "There's more."

Hope wrapped her arms around herself. "I can't take any more."

"You have to. I put the most important part the deepest, but you have to find it all now." He ran a hand over his chin, then looked at her. "Have faith in me, one last time."

Hope put a hand on her headset, but she couldn't will herself to pull it off.

"I made you a promise," Luke said, holding up his pinky. He gave a doleful little smile. "We made promises to each other."

Hope looked at Luke, at his pinky held before her. One last time. She dropped her hand and nodded.

Luke spoke louder, again methodical and careful. "Inara, activate Eos Ribbon Trigger NakanoHope 12-C. Password: ChaoticStupid."

"I'm sorry," Morena said. "Incorrect password. Please reenter your password."

Luke swore, reading it once again, even louder and slower this time, as if Morena were somehow mentally challenged.

"I'm sorry. Incorrect password. Please reenter your password. You have one more attempt."

"Something's wrong. I guess we have to do this the old-fashioned way," Luke said, adjusting his camera and leaning in. "The day before Christmas Eve. I'd just been offered level-one clearance."

Hope's head pulsed again, sharp and hot. The images flashing though her were too fast and confusing to focus on, so she focused instead on Luke. "You brought home donuts," she whispered.

"I did." Luke smiled.

DEC 23

EIGHT
MONTHS
EARLIER

41

PROVIDENCE

LUKE

Palm Springs, California

"WHERE'S CHARLOTTE?" LUKE burst through the yellow front door and dropped his briefcase. The pink box fell from his hands, donuts spilling onto the runner in the entryway.

Hope was on her laptop, her back to him. She wore cut-off sweatpants and his old *Firefly* T-shirt, tied in a knot at her waist. The setting sun streamed in from the window, casting a pink haze onto her neck. Her hair was piled on top of her head, with a Dixon Ticonderoga pencil stuck into the middle of it.

"Charlotte's at Maya's," she said, through another pencil gripped between her teeth. "I said it was fine. She might stay overnight. She said she would text you." Hope scratched her knee absently, still glued to her screen. "But she made waffle batter for us, for tomorrow. Isn't that sweet?"

The normalcy was overwhelming. Luke's head started to pound.

"Do I smell donuts?" There was pure joy in her voice.

Luke tore down the hallway, calling out as he ran. "Hope, we're leaving. Text Charlotte and have her come home right now. Forget it, don't do that. We'll get her at Maya's."

He burst into their bedroom, pulling the suitcases from under the bed and clothes from the dresser.

"Hope! Come in here and start packing your shit!" He flung open the closet doors and seized whatever he could: his tie rack, Hope's pink bathrobe, his tuxedo . . . wait, what the fuck was he doing? He needed to make a plan.

They needed to make a plan.

Luke took a deep breath and ran back into the living room to find Hope still typing away, eating a maple donut.

"This isn't a joke," he said. "We're leaving. Now. Tonight."

Hope wiped her sticky fingers on her shorts, and she typed for another minute before closing the lid. Rather than seeming alarmed, or scared, or any number of the reactions he'd imagined on the drive home, he found her face resigned. Hope rose from the desk, licking her fingers. She picked up her wineglass and crossed the room to sit on the couch.

"I thought I had a few more weeks, at least," she said, taking a sip. It was the only glass she ever used, the first gift he'd ever given her. Oversized, with a small chip on the bottom of the base. And etched on its side: Novinophobia: The Fear of Running Out of Wine.

"Look," he said. "I know this sounds crazy, and it is. It's a shit show. But we're leaving."

"And where are we going?" Hope took a sip of wine.

"I don't know. Anywhere. The Bahamas." Luke held his hand out. "We're opening the Waffle Brothel."

Hope laughed, patting the seat next to her. "We're not going anywhere." She emptied her glass and set it on the coffee table, pulling the pencil from her hair and letting it spill down her back. She rubbed her face with her palms. "I assume Jack Copeland gave you level-one clearance today?"

Luke's hand dropped. He swallowed. He seemed to have lost the power of speech. He may have nodded.

"And," she continued, "I'm your collateral."

LUKE WATCHED HOPE light a cigarette and blow a plume of smoke into the air. It hung for a moment before dissolving into the dark sky.

They were on the lounger in his backyard, as they'd been a hundred times. Watching the moon above the mountains, Hope's head on his shoulder, her legs slung over his. But this time, he was perched on the edge of the seat, arms crossed over his chest. Hope was on the other side, eyes dry but rimmed with red, hugging her knees.

"Copeland Laboratories got tons of press a few years ago, remember?" she said. "An essentially no-name company becomes Fortune 500, almost overnight? And for two years, everyone watched as Jack cut his R and D budget to nothing and bought up companies who already had drugs manufactured and patents secured. Then he'd raise the prices through the roof—three and four hundred percent more—literally the day the deal closed.

"There were people who got sick and lost everything because of Jack Copeland, because their insurance wouldn't cover the price increases for their medications. People died, because Jack Copeland gamed the system and convinced the world he was helping them. And meanwhile, Wall Street is calling him a genius, an innovator: Maverick Jack."

Luke heard all the words, from somewhere far away. He focused on the tip of her lit cigarette. He'd brought out a bottle of Macallan and two glasses as they came to the backyard, out of habit. Or perhaps from a need to do something normal, if only to keep from passing out.

"It got to the point where there were so many different types of fraud going on that MacMillan-Howe felt like something had to stick. So they brought it to the SEC, but they got nothing, because Jack Copeland is as cagey as they come. He's like John Gotti. Teflon."

Hope stood and walked to the side of the house, where they hid the ashtray so Charlotte wouldn't find it. Like a robot, Luke reached for the whiskey. He opened the bottle and filled the glasses methodically.

"That's when MacMillan-Howe brought me in to take over the investigation. And for a while, it was just another fraud case. Just another greedy corporation," Hope said. She didn't sit when she returned, merely lit another cigarette and took a glass when he didn't pass one to her. "But then I discovered a pattern in the drugs they were buying and the staff they were hiring. They all had one thing in common: memory. Copeland-Stark started building Wilder and made the single biggest investment in company history for a VR startup. I couldn't find a connection, but I knew there had to be one. Jack Copeland doesn't do anything by accident."

Hope took a long drink and put the glass to her forehead. "We needed information from someone on the inside, but no one would talk to us. *Fortius quo fidelius*, and all that cult bullshit. I was ready to give up. And then . . ." Her voice stalled, and she swallowed. "Then I was sent an article about you joining Copeland-Stark, a flyer for a lecture you were giving, and a draft of your book."

"What draft?" Luke asked, mentally trying to construct a timeline. "Who sent it?"

"The Rogue," Hope said.

"As in the Mad Hatters? I don't fucking believe this," Luke said, although he knew the real problem was that he did.

"I'd already read Jiang Lu's book. And then I read yours. It made me furious, what you were doing. Implanting false memories. The power you had to manipulate people."

"How *I* manipulate people?" Luke said. "Are you even listening to yourself? I told you I'm not Tony."

"I know you're not Tony," Hope said. "Now. But back then I didn't."

Luke clenched his hands together.

"Being their Memory Mechanic made you indispensable to Copeland-Stark." Hope swirled the Macallan around in her glass, back still to him. "The more I learned, the more I realized you were the right asset: single dad, squeaky clean on paper, rising in the company but not totally on the inside yet. You were the only one who could get me the proof I couldn't get. My last chance."

Every word fell like shattered glass onto his skin. Luke couldn't reconcile this Hope. It was like she didn't even care what she'd broken. He had never seen her this cold or this calculating.

"I wasn't an asset. I was a mark." Luke poured another two fingers, pausing only an instant before making it four.

Luke thought about the night they met, after his lecture in San Francisco. About their first kiss in the deserted corridor outside her hotel room, her hands on his face.

He'd never been kissed like that before, at least in no memory, recent or otherwise. He'd never been kissed like it would change the world, and in that singularly perfect moment he didn't know it actually would.

And all this time, he'd thought it was providence.

"A flyer for a lecture," Luke repeated. "It was all a fucking con."

"That's how it started," Hope said, facing him. "But the second I heard you speak, I knew I was utterly wrong about you. I fell in love with you that first night in North Beach. And every night after that." She knelt before him, and in that moment she looked like his Hope again. "And I fell in love with Charlotte."

Luke considered Hope, bathed in moonlight, more beautiful and now even more out of reach than ever. Every bone, every muscle, everything in him wanted those words to be true. But he took inventory in his brain, flipping through all the facts in a mental Rolodex. Past the omissions, past all the times she would close her laptop abruptly when he came in, past the phone calls taken outside, past the texts she would get at odd hours of the night from "C."

"I wish I could believe you," he said.

"Remember when I first moved here?" she asked. "And you drove me all around?" She smiled sadly. "I listened to you tell all your stories, and I thought, 'He's like me: broken in places too, working to be better than his past.' And I wanted to do that with you. Together."

Luke remembered her hand in his, the look in her eyes. *I want to know everything.*

He cringed at all he'd told her, all he'd been more than willing to reveal. Because despite his motherfucking doctorate in cognitive psychology, he'd believed she loved him.

"I knew in the end," she said, "there would be too many lies to recover from. You would always wonder what I was hiding. You would look at me like you're looking at me now."

Hope stood and climbed up next to Luke, sitting at a distance. She didn't swing her legs over his. "I betrayed you. And I know those scars run deep. I'm so, so sorry. But I don't expect or deserve forgiveness," she said. "For what it's worth, I started to tell you, about a million times. I really did. But beyond my own selfishness to not lose you, I also knew you'd quit Copeland-Stark."

Luke took a drink. "Well, you're right about that."

Hope's eyes narrowed, a new determination on her face. "He wouldn't have let you. That's not how Jack Copeland works. I'm not kidding about the John Gotti thing. He thinks like the mafia. He doesn't kill you; he decimates the people you love. He brutalizes them. And I won't let anything happen to Charlotte."

"Charlotte," Luke swallowed. He felt like he was in some cut-rate spy movie. He was a scientist, and things like this didn't happen to scientists. But Luke thought back to Jack today, and what Amelia had suffered through. What she was still suffering through. And he knew Hope was right.

Hope lit another cigarette. "I'm going to do the rest of this without you. I just need you to tell them I'll be your collateral." She added, "Please."

Luke set his glass on the table. "What the hell are you talking about?"

"I'm going into Wilder." Hope leaned over to flick ash into the ashtray.

"You're going to what?" Luke said. "Are you crazy? No."

"You know what's going on now, how far Jack Copeland is willing to go. You were there today," Hope said. "The Hatters can only get me so much. I need to find out what's going on; I need incontrovertible proof. And you need to keep Charlotte safe. Just play nice and let me handle it."

"You're wrong," he said. "There has to be another way."

"There isn't." Hope turned her face to the sky, to the few stars hidden by the clouds. "I promise, there isn't." She slid off the lounger, taking the ashtray and disappearing once more around the side of the house.

Luke put his spinning head in his hands. Spinning from the whiskey, from the meeting with Jack, from the panic about Charlotte, from Hope. He heard her come back, saw her feet on the cracked pavement, but he didn't look up.

"I'd better go," she said quietly.

"Go?" He lifted his head. "Go where?"

"To a hotel," she said, taking her whiskey glass off the table. "I don't think I should stay here tonight. Or . . . anymore." She stood for another moment, then turned and walked to the sliding glass door. It let out its usual hiss and swish as it opened. When she spoke again, her voice shook. "I love you, Luke. I didn't know, until I met you, what was missing all this time."

Luke watched her place her glass carefully in the dishwasher and push in her stool, hand resting on the back for a moment. Then she turned on the hall light and disappeared around the corner.

After another minute, he followed.

LUKE LEANED IN the bedroom doorway. Hope was at the bed, sifting through the piles of clothes he'd thrown there a few hours ago.

"Your panic packing is a little alarming," she said quietly, returning his tuxedo to the closet.

Luke gave her a half smile, which hurt to produce.

She folded her bathrobe and placed it on the bed. "So you'll tell Jack and Elliot?"

"Yes," he said.

"Thank you. And I can get all this . . . soon. In a few days." She waved vaguely around the room, not meeting his eye.

Luke's chest tightened. He watched as she returned her cocktail dresses, still in their plastic, to the closet, followed by two pairs of his dress shoes. At the bed she reached into the suitcase once more and stopped, hands still inside. She stood in the same position for at least a minute, head bent.

Luke walked to the bed and put his hands on Hope's shoulders, turning her around gently. Her body trembled, and she kept her head bent over his good luck tie clutched in her hands. Luke placed his thumb under her chin, lifting her face. Hope's eyes were wet and bright. He tried to take the tie, but she held tight.

"I can't seem to let it go," Hope whispered.

Luke swallowed, holding her gaze. Then he ran his fingers through her hair, tracing her earlobe. He couldn't help it. It was like he was built that way, as if there were unseen wires connecting them together, winding in and around all their spaces between.

Hope's tears fell for the first time, then turned into heaving sobs.

Luke took her into his arms, and she buried her face in his chest, soaking him with her tears.

HE WOKE A few hours later. It was almost a quarter past two, and Hope wasn't in bed. The half-packed suitcase was still on the floor, her jewelry still on the nightstand. He checked the bathroom, which was empty. In the kitchen, her phone was charging on the counter, with texts from "C" he didn't even try to read.

Luke went to the sliding glass door, spotting Hope on the lounger under the blanket, head tilted at the sky. He watched her from behind the door, breath making a foggy cloud on the glass. Then he stepped outside, chilled in his T-shirt and boxers.

"What are you doing?" he asked, shifting in his bare feet. "It's so cold."

"I couldn't sleep. There's still a lot to plan," she said, peeling back the blanket. "It's warm here."

Luke got under the blanket with her. Hope curled herself into him like a kitten.

"You can't do this alone," Luke said. "Let me help."

Hope nodded into his chest.

"Promise me I won't lose you forever," Luke said.

"I promise," she said, hooking her pinky with his, under the blanket. "I love you," she whispered.

He stroked her hair, and she traced a finger slowly up and down his forearm. Eventually her eyes closed, and her hand rested on his arm.

"What if loving each other isn't enough?" Luke said into the air, knowing she was asleep.

But Hope opened her eyes again, alert.

"It is," she said. "It's all that matters. There isn't anything else."

Luke put his arms around her, and Hope twined her legs with his. They fell asleep together outside, under the blanket, under the stars, and under the December desert sky.

THERE USUALLY WEREN'T days better than Waffle Saturdays. That day, not so much. Luke and Hope sat at the kitchen counter, on the tall blue stools, in silence. Hope had a copy of Jiang Lu's book open next to her plate, highlights throughout and Post-its jutting from the pages. Her phone rested on top of *The Memory Mechanic*, also full of little flags. She hadn't touched her waffle.

"I'll have to take it all," Luke said, breaking the silence. "Jiang's technique, it wipes much more than recent memories. After that I'll have to add some false memories, so you won't figure it out. You'll be left with confusing fragments." He watched her over the rim of his coffee mug. "Tyrell Corporation," it said. "More Human than Human."

"I understand." Hope swallowed. She was so pale.

"Hope." Luke faltered. What did he want to say? Thanks for taking one for the team?

"Don't," Hope said, shaking her head. "This is the only way." She stared out the window, as if memorizing the mountains and the sky. Then the shadow of fear was gone, the resolve from last night flooding her face once more.

"You can't come to Wilder, ever," Hope said. "And even if they let me contact you, don't respond, no matter what I say. There's no telling what they're going to try and make me believe." She pulled her robe tighter. He would miss seeing her in that fluffy monstrosity. He'd miss everything.

"We'll go tomorrow," Hope said, glancing at the calendar on the wall. "Christmas Eve. Charlotte will be at her mom's for a few days."

"Best Christmas ever," he said grimly.

"I won't remember, so it doesn't matter." Hope tapped the small silver case on the table. "And you can put this ribbon thing in me?"

Luke nodded. "I know how, technically. But I've never done it."

"Right after, you have to convince me. Then leave and don't come back. Because if for a second I think any of us is still there . . ." Hope cut a piece of waffle but she didn't eat it. "And you have to act like everything is normal, at work."

"I know." Luke pushed a strawberry around in swirls on his empty plate. "Play nice."

"I trust you," she said.

"There will be drugs also," he added. Hope never liked taking pills. Even when she had the flu, she wouldn't take ibuprofen. "They'll affect your memory, your clarity. I'll need to give you what they call the boilermaker in the morning. Before we go."

"I love a good cocktail," Hope said.

Luke's stomach clenched. "Essentially, it's a roofie. A supercharged roofie."

"It's fine," Hope said, chewing on her bottom lip. Her hands were tight around her mug, and Luke knew nothing had ever been further from fine.

"We're flying blind," Luke said, getting up to pour more coffee. "I know very little about what goes on at Wilder."

"But now with your level one, you can start finding out," Hope said.

Her phone buzzed on the table. Hope checked the caller ID and pressed the pulsating phone icon. "Hey, C. You're on speaker. Luke is here."

"Hey," said a male voice Luke didn't recognize. "Jordan's still the last holdout. She wants to string Copeland along for the sweetest possible deal. It could take months."

"You heard this directly from her?" Hope leaned closer to the phone.

"Last night at Le Vallauris. You will not believe how much it cost for a plate of foam and a shot glass of soup."

"Wait, you're here? In town?"

"Flew in last night," the voice said. "But I'm at the airport now. I need to get back for a meeting."

"Too bad," Hope said. "And who is Jordan's collateral?"

Jordan Lin, Luke realized. Which meant C must be Carter Sloane, the boy genius, the giant behind Maelstrom.

"Not positive," Carter replied. "But she has a brother in New Jersey with two kids and a single sister. It's probably her."

"Interesting," Hope said.

"Good news. They've agreed not to try and save the VR experiences."

Hope leaned forward. "Really?"

"When Copeland saw the price tag for all that storage space and bandwidth, he pulled the plug. I also may have padded my estimates. That guy's an actual billionaire, but he's crazy cheap. That's how you stay rich, I guess."

"I guess," Hope said.

"They can still watch Erleben in real time, don't forget that. So if you have to contact me, I suggest you start brushing up on your ASCII: 111 107," Carter said. "That means 'okay' for all the losers out there."

Hope laughed.

"Also," Carter continued, "I've disabled as many cameras as I could get away with, and I've added everything from your list into Erleben. The kangaroo took me a whole week. What the hell is that?"

Hope glanced at Luke, a melancholy smile on her face. "It's just important stuff. Important to me. But there's no rush, you still have about six months."

"Look, six months sounds like a lot to you, but this stuff takes time to do it right. I want to bring in someone else to help. My intern from Cal, Spencer."

"An intern?" Hope said. "You can't be serious."

"You don't understand," Carter said. "He's an actual genius. Ten times smarter than me. I've never seen anyone do what he can do."

"You're sure you can trust him?" Hope asked.

"I'm positive," Carter said.

"Okay, then I trust you," Hope said.

"I'll talk to him this week," he said.

"Anything else?"

"Hope," he said. "Are you still sure?"

"Come on, it'll be like a vacation. I'll be eating like a queen, meditating, cleansing." Hope put her forehead into her hands. Her voice was light, but her face was strained. "I'll bet I even get shot glasses of soup."

"I bet you don't," he said. "And you, meditating? Please."

"Thanks, C," Hope said. "I'll text you later tonight. To be continued."

"To be continued," Carter said. There was a pause. "Be careful, Hope."

She hung up.

"You're friends with Carter Sloane?"

"The Rogue set us up on a fake blind date over a year ago," she said. "Carter's the one who got me the Eos Ribbon."

"We were already together then," Luke said.

"I said fake date," Hope said. "I realized I'd need the person who created Erleben, and that person might also know more about Copeland's plans for Wilder. But I wanted to make sure I could trust him first, without raising any suspicions with Jordan Lin. So, blind date."

Luke wondered when, if ever, this disequilibrium would end. "What did you mean he had six months?"

Hope fidgeted with her phone. "I told Carter to wait to activate the Eos Ribbon. Six months from when I go in," she said.

"Are you out of your mind? That's an eternity."

"This is the long game, Luke. Six months is enough for them to know the procedure worked. Liz Emerson is scrupulous. But they'll relax when they realize I'm a zombie." Hope tapped a finger on her phone. "Carter will be monitoring it the whole time, from Maelstrom. He knows what to do. Also, it's safer if you don't contact each other. I trust him completely to follow the plan. And the less you know, the better."

"Plans can go wrong," Luke said. But it wasn't about the plan. It was about Hope stuck in that place, alone. "What did he mean about the kangaroo?"

"I've memorized it." Hope tapped his book. "Especially the chapter called 'The Emotion Factor.' Memories with high emotional value aren't as easily forgotten. So I had Carter add things that would remind me of you, of us."

"Kangaroo Sanctuary," Luke said. He added two sugars and poured milk into his mug, stirring absently with a knife. "Memory's a funny thing, though. You can't just cut and paste. But maybe . . ." He ran his hand through his hair. His mind kicked into research mode, mentally identifying options and sorting things into orderly columns. "But I can try and leave you some . . . breadcrumbs. Triggers that guard against the procedures. It may make them think you're resistant, which is good. It will send them down a different trail."

Luke returned to the table. "But if I tell you what they are now, it won't matter. They'll be gone tomorrow."

"I'm not worried." Hope bent her hand toward him. "You're pretty hard to forget."

He took her hand, pressing her palm against his cheek and then his mouth, lingering far more than usual.

Hope glanced at her plate. "Don't leave me breadcrumbs," she said, picking up her fork and pointing it at Luke, a real smile on her lips. "Leave me waffles."

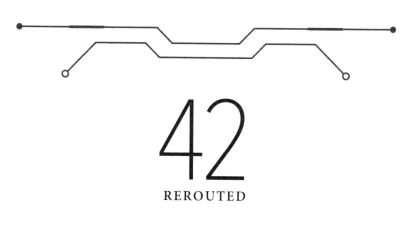

42

REROUTED

HOPE
The Wilder Sanctuary
Rancho Mirage, California

"WAY TO BURY the lede," Hope said.

Luke laughed, and Hope let the familiar sound wash over her. Then she was plunged into an all-encompassing blackness which felt like the third phase of the Labyrinth.

"Something's wrong with the video feed," Luke said. "Still there?"

"I'm here," she said.

"I'm coming to Wilder right now and getting you out of there," Luke said.

"No way," Hope said. "Not until Spooky gets the files."

"Why's it spooky?" Luke asked.

"Spencer. Spencer Lu," Hope said. "He's getting the files of all the patient records right now. Without those all this will be for nothing. You need to go to that place, the one in Arizona. If they discover we've got their files, the first thing they'll do is shut it down."

"That's three hours from here," Luke said. "Three hours away from you."

"You work for Copeland-Stark," Hope said. "You have credentials, and you know what to say without making anyone suspicious."

Luke sighed. "Then you need to get somewhere safe in the meantime, under the radar. Find Dr. Green or Jonah, you can trust them," Luke said. "Or Stark, but only as a last resort."

"Luke," Hope said. "Be careful."

"Always," he said. "Pinky promise."

The Maelstrom headset was yanked unceremoniously from her head. Hope blinked into Spooky's placid face. "Did you finish?" she asked. "Did you get the files?"

"Not yet. But I got into the network. Carter didn't make things easy. There were a lot of hoops to jump through. Also"—Spooky glanced at the ceiling—"I had to improvise."

Red lights flashed, and Spooky shoved Hope backward into the corridor just before the bars crashed between them. Spooky's face appeared and disappeared, in time to the flash of the red lights above.

"What's going on?" Hope asked, hands gripping the bars.

"I tripped a Code Eight," Spooky said, looking slightly smug.

"Code Eight? A Security Breach?"

"Page thirty-one," Spooky quoted, "'In the event a data breach is detected, all access will be suspended, and network traffic will be rerouted. All servers will remain offline until the Breach Response Team can perform a thorough investigation and address all vulnerabilities.'"

"And you did this on purpose?" Hope asked.

"Think," Spooky said. "Repeat."

"All access will be suspended and network traffic will be rerouted," Hope said slowly, and then she smiled. "To Maelstrom. To Rohan Kapoor. That's why Carter wanted him to monitor the data-security software. And now they can't use the cameras or the computers. So how are you doing it?" Hope tapped her head. "Your robot brain?"

"Arkham is the only room not connected to the rest of the network," Spooky said. "That's why it's never working. And also why Carter wanted us in here."

"How much longer?" Hope asked.

"Two hours." Spooky shrugged, as if he had all the time in the world. "Maybe less. You'll know."

"How will I know?" Hope asked.

"You have your own robot brain," Spooky said.

"Clear. No guests."

Hope and Spooky turned. Jonah was running up the corridor, phone in his hand and index finger on his ear. He ripped the earpiece out as he reached them, throwing the springy cord on the floor, grinding it into the tile with a large black sneaker. On his other foot was only his white athletic sock.

"I bought you five more minutes, but that's it." Jonah reached into the pocket of his scrubs and placed his lanyard in her palm. "Take the service elevator," he said. "Dr. Green will meet you at the Roofie Room and get you out of here."

"But . . ." Hope looked at Spooky.

"I'll wait and take him myself, don't worry," Jonah said. "Get going."

Hope nodded.

"And Hope." Jonah jerked his head to the side, and she saw his sneaker wedged between the door and the frame. He lowered his voice. "Haul ass."

As directed, hope hauled ass. She slipped through the door and headed toward the service elevator, scanning Jonah's key card on the pad. She barreled in as it opened, nearly knocking over a tech and narrowly avoiding falling into his cart.

Before the elevator doors fully opened, Hope had already sailed past the tech and into the main hallway. Slipping in her crappy sneakers, she ran past the Bloom Room and the menacing row of quiet rooms they used when someone caused a Code Seven. As she rounded another corner toward the Roofie Room, a Man in Gray emerged from a doorway. Hope slowed her run. It was Isaiah, the giant tech she'd seen in her memory with Luke.

"Code Eight," he said, his voice deep. "Everyone is to report to Creative Connections."

"I have a session with Dr. Stark," she said. And before Isaiah could block her path, she backed away and continued walking, keeping her head down and periodically casting glances behind. Isaiah remained in the hallway, watching her.

Hope had no choice but to head in the direction of Creative Connections, along the corridor that would take her past the doctors' offices. She didn't dare breathe as she passed Dr. Emerson's office, its glass doors thrown wide open but the room empty. But steps from the infirmary, she heard the sound of heels on tile.

The infirmary door opened, and Dr. Stark stepped into the doorway, waving her inside. "Get in here quick," he whispered. "Luke just texted me."

Hope let out an exhale and followed. But before she could close the door all the way, it was blocked by Isaiah's shiny black boot.

Dr. Stark let him in and shut the door. Isaish locked it and stood in front, arms crossed like a bouncer.

Hope looked around the infirmary. Dr. Green was sitting in a chair under the window. But then Hope saw Jonah, and the look on his face told her everything had gone to shit.

Dr. Stark took Hope's arm and inserted a syringe. "Methohexital. It will only last a few minutes, but I don't have time to fight with you."

The room blurred and shifted. She tried to keep her eyes open, but everything slipped into oblivion.

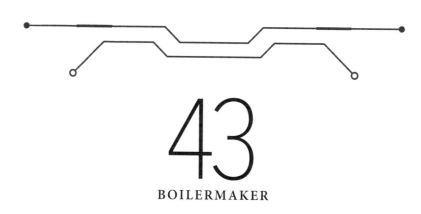

43

BOILERMAKER

HOPE

The Wilder Sanctuary
Rancho Mirage, California

H
OPE WOKE TO Dr. Stark's face gazing down at her, his pink dress shirt crisp and perfect under his lab coat. "Good, you're awake," he said. "How do you feel?"

She lifted her head. Hope was strapped to the bed, harnessed in place by a six-inch blue mesh belt. It crossed her stomach and secured her arms in one unforgiving panel.

Another panel held her legs in place. Hope bucked against her restraints, but it did nothing.

Dr. Green hovered, shifting from side to side, eyes darting. Isaiah remained in front of the door, though this time Hope noticed the .45 pistol on his waist. Jonah was in a chair under the window, hands clasped on his knees.

"Code Eight," Dr. Stark said, producing a syringe from his coat pocket. "They've called in the cavalry."

"Elliot," Dr. Green said. "What the hell are you doing?"

"Amelia, think. It's a data breach. In twenty minutes this place will be crawling with lawyers and investigators, exactly what we've been trying to prevent for months." Dr. Stark looked at Hope. He looked wild, eyes manic. "The response team has to review everything. They're going to find things we don't want them to see, and we don't need Hope talking to Luke on top of it all."

Dr. Green put a hand on his arm. "What's in there?"

"Boilermaker," he said.

"Undiluted? You can't give her that," Dr. Green said, clearly alarmed. "You just gave her Methohexital."

"It's not going to kill her," Dr. Stark said. "I just need her to answer some questions."

"Elliot, are you hearing yourself?" The skin around Dr. Green's mouth paled as she pressed her lips together, eyes flicking to Jonah. "Stop. This is all Jack's fault. We can stand up to him, fight back."

"Oh Dr. Green, forever the optimist." Dr. Stark shook his head. "This isn't a movie. The good guys aren't going to win, especially when none of us are really good anymore." He removed the cap from the syringe and set it on the table.

"You've lost it," Dr. Green said. She went to the phone on the wall and put the receiver to her ear. "Morgan, get me—"

In a second, Dr. Stark was at the wall. He replaced the receiver and grabbed Dr. Green, then pushed the needle into her neck. Dr. Green flailed her arms and kicked, landing a decent smack on Stark's mouth. He spat blood onto the floor. Jonah lunged at Stark, but the Man in Gray had stepped between them. He grabbed Jonah and pushed him against the wall, face first. He produced a zip tie from his pocket and wrapped Jonah's wrists in one smooth motion, then held him tight.

"Fuck." Dr. Stark dropped Dr. Green into the chair, and she struggled, eyes turned on Jonah but unfocused. Everyone watched Dr. Green as her eyes drooped, then closed. Her head fell against the windowsill.

For a minute, the only sound was Dr. Stark's breathing. Then he turned to the Man in Gray. "Isaiah, you and Jonah go to the Roofie Room and get me another bottle. He knows where it is."

"Can't sir." Isaiah shook his head. "The breach—we're in lock-down."

"Fuck," Stark said again. He turned as if he were going to leave, then spun around and lowered himself onto the end of Hope's bed. He looked terrified and crazy, muttering to himself and tapping his thumb against his bloody teeth. Then he bounded up again and stared out the window, swearing and talking under his breath.

With a loud exhale, Dr. Stark turned from the window, hands brushing down his pant legs. He adjusted his tie.

"We have to go, all of us," he said, moving to the bed and unfastening Hope's straps. "Before the response team gets here. I'll sort it all out when we get there. I just need some time to think."

Hope gripped the metal rails as Dr. Stark tried to pull her from the bed, gritting her teeth and wrapping her feet around the posts. Stark was built like Spooky: thin and wiry. He grunted in frustration at Isaiah, who shoved Jonah to the ground and pulled Hope off the bed effortlessly, holding her in place.

Dr. Stark crossed the room to the phone, smoothing his hair as he waited for an answer on the other end. "Hi Morgan, it's Dad." He paused. "That was Dr. Green. She's not feeling well, and I'm going to run her home. Can you send a town car to the back entrance? And tell Mr. Copeland I'll be delayed when he arrives?"

Hope tried to catch Jonah's eye, but he was staring at Dr. Green from the floor, face ashen.

Dr. Stark hung up and turned back to the group. "Everybody ready? We're going on a little field trip."

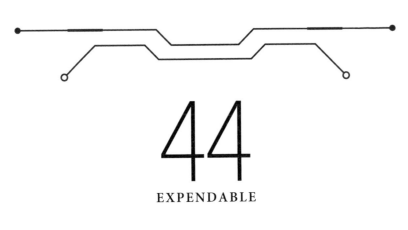

44

EXPENDABLE

HOPE

Somewhere on 111 South
Imperial County, California

T HE SLEEK TOWN car made its way past small, nondescript cities
and casinos. The sun was setting, with patches of blush and
lavender airbrushed across the darkening sky.

For the past thirty minutes, Jonah and Hope had sat without speaking, knees occasionally knocking into each other. Hope spent the drive
alternately trying to read road signs and scanning for headlights, for
any sign Luke was behind them. But the highway was empty, as it had
been for nearly an hour.

Stark was across, arm slung casually across the seat, fingers tapping. Isaiah watched a fixed point out the rear window from his perch
next to Stark. Periodically, he would straighten his scarlet tie or pull
on his pant leg.

It would have been like the limo Hope took to her senior prom, if
not for Dr. Green, splayed across a bank of seats, covered sloppily in
a sheet.

Dr. Stark opened a faux wood-paneled cabinet and mixed another drink. He'd been pouring steadily from a full bottle of Nolet's Reserve since they left Wilder, decreasing the amount of club soda each time.

"I'd offer you some," he said to Hope, tipping his glass in a toast. "But I don't want to risk any interactions with your medications."

Hope looked away.

"Why so quiet?" Stark asked. "Where's that Hope Nakano sass I've come to love?"

Hope glanced at Jonah, whose eyes were glued to Dr. Green, a muscle in his neck twitching.

"I'm not sure what you think you're going to get out of Jonah." Stark rubbed at the stubble on his face.

"Goddamn sociopath," Jonah said quietly. He didn't look at Stark.

"What's that?" Stark tilted his head, seriously considering Jonah, though his eyes seemed to have trouble focusing.

"You pretend to care about people," Jonah said, eyes now on Stark. "My sister trusted you. Amelia told me you were helping us. But all you care about is yourself."

"Technically, we use the term antisocial personality these days." Stark gave Hope a wry smile, as if they were sharing a private joke at Jonah's expense. "Which I'm not. I'm protecting my family. Surely you can understand." He was beginning to slur his words.

"Morgan, maybe," Jonah said. "She got off easy. But Nina didn't."

"Nina." Dr. Stark gestured with his glass, looking disgusted. "I've been cleaning up Princess Nina's goddamn messes since I was ten. Her entire life was a wasteland of drugs, abusive boyfriends, and unwanted pregnancies. I stopped enabling Nina when I turned sixteen." He drained his glass and opened the cabinet for another refill.

"Wait until Morgan finds out what her father really is," Jonah said, and turned to Hope. "You know his last name isn't even Stark? He changed it so people would think he was a superhero."

At a green sign reading "Mecca," the passengers lurched as the town car slowed abruptly for a car at the crossroad. Hope couldn't help craning her neck to see the driver, willing it to be Luke's Highlander. Willing Jonah to have gotten him a message somehow. But with a squeal of tires, it turned left in front of them, speeding along the lonely road in the opposite direction.

"I hate to break it to you Hope," Dr. Stark said. "Luke isn't coming to save you. I caught him eavesdropping at Jack's party the other night. So he's halfway to Arizona, only to find an abandoned aviation center that isn't actually abandoned. And where we aren't."

Hope's skin grew cold. Luke had been certain Wilder 2.0 was near Arizona. And she hadn't told him about Bombay Beach.

Stark dropped a few more ice cubes into his glass. He clinked them around, then shook off his fingers. The bottle of gin was now half empty.

She turned to the window and watched the desert she loved spreading out before them, mountains bold and barren. For fifteen minutes the only sound was ice against glass.

"Here we are," Stark said. "Welcome to the Salton Sea."

The town car slowed, and they turned into the dirt driveway of a sprawling, nondescript building with several floors. The gate in the chain-link fence was wide open, a single floodlight illuminating the front walkway. As if they were expected.

THE CORRIDOR SMELLED strongly of pine disinfectant and bleach. Stark kept a hand on Hope's shoulder as they walked, and Isaiah held Jonah tightly at his side as they went through a door and descended a stairwell, then through another door into another hallway.

This facility wasn't anything like the gleaming glass hallways of Wilder. Hope couldn't determine what it might have been before—

perhaps a warehouse. The walls were covered in peeling mustard paint, the dusty floors may have once been mint colored but were now a grayish brown. Panels of fluorescent lights hung from the ceiling above, some buzzing and brightening intermittently. Single lightbulbs were mounted to the wall every few feet, housed in small, rusty cages. They bathed the hallway in a sallow glow, casting jaundiced shadows.

Hope could hear the clang of doors closing on the floor above, the sound of machinery humming and grinding. Yet they hadn't encountered another soul since they entered.

Two more turns led them into a large room with high ceilings and the same fluorescent lights. From somewhere a fan whirred, although Hope felt no air circulating. Stark flipped a lever on the wall and the lights came on a few at a time, flooding slowly across the ceiling as they buzzed, until they illuminated a familiar lab.

Mirroring Spooky's memory exactly, there were shiny examination tables, monitoring equipment piled onto shelves, trays with threatening metal instruments laid upon them: syringes, scalpels, forceps, a speculum. Straps hung off table edges, the same blue polycarbonate mesh as at Wilder. A lone aloe vera plant sat on a shelf in a small terra-cotta pot, a single, incongruous sign of life.

"Open a few windows," Stark said to Isaiah. "It's hot as hell in here."

Against the wall, underneath a gigantic clock, was a wooden stick. It had a metal hook on the end, like her third-grade teacher used to use in the old classroom with no air-conditioning. Isaiah hooked it onto a high window, cranking it open. It moaned back.

Just then Jonah made a lunge for Dr. Stark, tackling him and pushing him to the ground. The Nolet's fell from Stark's hand and rolled away but didn't break. Isaiah dropped his hook and joined in, pulling Jonah away and punching him in the stomach. Jonah collapsed on the floor, gasping and spitting, as Isaiah kicked him repeatedly with his big black boot.

"Leave him alone!" Hope yelled.

Dr. Stark rose to his knees and then stood. "Enough!"

The Man in Gray stepped back, pulling the .45 from his holster.

"Put that away," Stark said. "We can get this done with minimal fuss." He gestured to an examination table like a spokesmodel. Show her what she's won.

Isaiah grabbed Hope and roughly deposited her on the table, where she banged her head on a metal railing. He held her legs still with one forearm as he attached a strap to her left ankle, tightening the buckle, before moving to restrain her left arm.

"It isn't too late," Hope said. "You don't have to do any of this."

"You're mistaken," Stark said. "It's the only way out."

"What about all the people in here?" Hope asked, eyes fixed on the clock. "More collateral?"

Stark raised an eyebrow and Hope's stomach dropped.

"I see your memory is returning," Stark said, then smiled in a way that gave Hope chills.

"They aren't collateral," Jonah wheezed from the floor. Everyone turned. "They're lab rats. Copeland-Stark doesn't have enough board members and executives and assholes with clearance for all the experiments they want to do. They can't use celebrities that keep coming back for the food and yoga."

Jonah tried to stand, but Isaiah left Hope on the table and landed another kick. Jonah fell forward onto his hands.

Hope took a few deep breaths, listening for any sign of help, though she knew it was futile. Luke was in Arizona now. The only sound was Jonah's gasping and the second hand of the wall clock. Jonah pulled himself to his knees, slower this time. He wiped the blood from his face, smearing it onto his already filthy scrubs.

"They started taking people from around here to experiment on," Jonah said, through heaving breaths. "Only they call it research. Meth heads and people without families to miss them. People who are here without visas and have no one to turn to for help." He spat a great glob of scarlet onto the floor at Stark's feet. "Because if you're poor or brown you don't count as a real person. They call them expendables."

SSE, Hope thought grimly. *Salton Sea. Expendable.* With Stark and Isaiah still watching Jonah, she silently undid the strap on her left arm, pulling the mesh over the thick prong of the buckle and repositioning it to the largest hole.

Stark moved to Jonah's side, squatting. "I'm sorry about this, Jonah." Stark looked at Isaiah. "Take him to one of the rooms. And then go get Amelia too. Keep them apart. And don't use that gun unless you absolutely have to."

Isaiah nodded, then pulled Jonah to his feet and dragged him across the floor.

Hope looked at the clock. Fifteen minutes had elapsed, on top of the fifty and change it took to get there. Two hours, Spooky had said.

The heavy double doors clanged shut, and Stark straightened himself. He tipped the Nolet's into his mouth and then set the bottle on a table. Then he moved to the mobile cabinet at Hope's right, removing a selection of tiny glass bottles. Hope squinted as he switched on an overhead light, like at the dentist, though far brighter.

"I apologize to you as well, Hope. For what's about to happen," he said, setting a bottle on a tray. "But I know you understand. Parents will do anything to protect their children, and I'm protecting Morgan."

Dr. Stark sat on a wheeled black stool. He unbuttoned the cuffs of his shirt and methodically rolled up his sleeves. Then he began filling syringes, holding bottles to the light and inserting needles into the tops, pulling out their plungers with practiced hands.

Hope pushed the hair from her eyes out of habit, which was when Stark noticed she wasn't completely tethered to the bed. He capped a syringe and stood hastily, fastening the buckle on her right hand, then her right ankle. Hope strained her legs against the braces.

"Morgan's the receptionist," Hope said. She cast a glance around her, for anything that might be a weapon, but nothing was nearby. "She isn't incarcerated like we all are."

Hope looked at the wall. Twenty-five minutes. Her head was throbbing from being whacked on the bed.

"Yes, she's the receptionist, and I intend to keep it that way," Stark said. "Just as you would, just as Luke would. That's how I knew he would give you up to save Charlotte, and you'd go willingly for the same reason. Even though you were the one we wanted all along. And once I get what I need from you, Morgan will stay safe for good. Jack gave me his word."

"What else could you possible need from me?" Hope asked. "I've been here for seven months, walking through your fucking maze and drinking your fucking boilermakers. That wasn't enough?"

Stark swung the tray partly across Hope's chest and lined the syringes, scalpel, and metal instruments in a perfect line, like Quinn might have.

"I need to know what you discovered about Copeland-Stark, and who you've told."

"I know about the collateral," Hope said. "That's it."

"Bullshit," Stark said.

Hope glanced at the clock once more, and Stark followed her gaze.

"It is getting late, and we've got a lot ahead of us tonight." Stark put his face closer to Hope's, close enough for her to smell the gin. "I tend to get a little chatty when I drink."

Stark held a bottle to the light, squinting at the small print. "We know MacMillan-Howe has been after us for years. And we know you enlisted the Mad Hatters to help you, but that ended when you came to Wilder. With the Rogue out of the picture, you're our last loose end. Jack needs to know the extent of the damage so he can control it. It's in your best interest to tell me everything."

Hope looked at the syringe in Stark's hand and felt sick.

"What makes you think this drug will work on me when nothing else has?" Hope asked.

"The meds we keep at Wilder are aboveboard, for the most part," Stark said, extracting liquid from the tip of the syringe. "Jiang's cocktails aren't quite so gentle. I won't sugarcoat it; this will be painful. Or you can just tell me everything MacMillan-Howe has on us."

Hope gritted her teeth and looked at the clock again.

"Your choice," Stark said, shrugging. He placed the syringe in the bottle and pulled out the plunger. "Just remember, I'm not the villain here." He said it calmly, head angled, as if he were deciding on the pinot over the fume blanc.

Hope thought she'd never repeated any of Tony's words to Stark, but she wasn't certain. She couldn't be sure if he knew how that particular turn of phrase would affect her, if he used it to rattle her even more. Either way, it worked.

"You can apologize all you want, justify yourself by using Morgan," she said to Stark. "But you and Jack are the villains. And in a few minutes, it isn't just me who will know. Although I can't take the credit. Carter did most of the work."

Stark paused, syringe suspended.

Hope's stomach twisted, just as she felt a concentrated, now-familiar heat pulsing through her skull.

"Carter found your files, of your expendables. 19478-SSE. 20095-SSE. 06825-SSE. Do you want to hear about them all? There's over a hundred," Hope said, testing her left arm. "Maelstrom has them now, and all your dirty laundry is being sent to every news organization and government official in the world."

Dr. Stark's face changed into one of bemused confusion, as if the aloe vera plant on the shelf had burst into song. "Nice bluff. We destroyed the drive Quinn left at the front desk."

"But the Code Eight wasn't an accident. It was so Spencer could get into the network, using a back door Carter left. And Spencer knows where this place is because he's been here, with his psychotic father. And by now he's told everyone, including, I suspect, the Hatters." Hope looked at the ceiling. "I'm curious though, how certain are you that the Rogue was neutralized? Are you absolutely sure Carter was the Rogue?"

The smirk slowly slipped from Dr. Stark's face.

"Either way," Hope said. "You're fucked. But if I were you, I'd probably run."

Dr. Stark looked like he just might take Hope's advice, although Hope had already pulled her left hand from the loose buckle and wrapped it around the speculum. She hit Stark full force in the face with one smooth motion. Stark stumbled forward onto her, blood dripping from his nose. She hit him again, against the side of his head, and the speculum slipped out of her hand.

Hope grabbed the next thing she could reach, a scalpel. But she'd gripped it by the business end, and when it neared his face Stark clasped her hand, closing his fingers tightly around hers. She felt the slice in her flesh and screamed, and scalpel fell to the ground.

She bit down, hard, into the side of Stark's closed hand. He released her with an irritated yelp. Hope lunged for the first syringe she could reach. She stuck it into Stark's neck, pushing the plunger with her thumb. She did the same with the second. She seized a third. Stark staggered backward into a cart of medical equipment. Bottles and instruments and cotton swabs tumbled out across the floor.

She undid the buckles on her right hand and ankles.

"Goddammit." Stark climbed on top of the bed, attempting to pin her legs, but she was already free.

Hope struggled to extricate herself from under Stark. She kneed him in the chin and kicked out. For a split second, they made eye contact. His pupils were huge, eyes feverish.

Stark clamped his hands on her right ankle with both hands as she tried to leap off the bed, twisting it until a sharp pain shot through her leg. Hope screamed, turning to jam the third syringe into his shoulder, pulling it out and doing it again and again, stabbing anywhere, until he let go. She didn't even know what drugs they were, or how much was actually getting into his bloodstream, but at least it hurt.

Bracing against Stark, Hope used all the strength remaining in her left leg to push herself off the bed. She fell onto the floor, hitting her head once more on something hard and made of metal. Stark pulled himself slowly into a sitting position on the bed, swinging a leg over the side.

"Fuck," he said, slowly. He fell back against the mattress.

Hope pulled herself up and stood over the bed. She dug an elbow into his chest and leaned all her weight on him, strapping his right arm in, followed by his left.

He lay prone while she finished his left leg.

"That shit works fast, whatever it was," Hope said, smearing blood across her face. "Or was it the fancy bottle of gin? You really should be careful, mixing alcohol and narcotics."

Hope fastened the last strap, over his right ankle, extra tight. "Why don't you tell me about a happy memory? Please try to be as detailed as possible."

Stark winced and gritted his teeth. His face and dress shirt were covered in blood, his or Hope's, she didn't know. His eyes were alert and narrowed.

Hope picked up the final syringe, pulling off the cap off with her mouth and spitting it at Stark. She pressed it into his neck and pushed the plunger. "That's for Carter," she said. "I hope it kills you."

Stark opened his mouth to speak, but he was interrupted.

"I really wanted to be the one to break his nose."

Hope turned, not expecting the lightheadedness coursing through her at the sight of Luke. She didn't entirely trust it was him, solid and real, in jeans and his beat-up sneakers. For a moment, she could only stare, and for that same moment, no one else existed. She took a step toward him, and a searing pain shot through her right ankle. But Hope barely felt it, even as she stumbled. Luke caught her. She didn't seem to know where to put her hands: around his neck, on his face, gripping his arms or his waist. So she did all of those things. Hope needed to do something to make him stay, to keep him from disappearing.

"I'm here." Luke wrapped her tightly in his arms and she buried her face in his chest, inhaling deeply. The feel of him, the smell of him, the realness of him. Hope allowed herself a small, tentative exhale that came out as a shudder.

Luke brushed the hair from her face and kissed her forehead, one arm still around her. "You're safe. Everyone's safe."

"Everyone?" Hope had forgotten other people were in the room, or the world, for that matter. She lifted her head, still clutching Luke.

Behind Luke stood Spooky, straight and confident. And next to Spooky stood Quinn, uncharacteristically mussed, face drawn and tight.

"You're late," Hope said to Spooky, who smiled.

She turned to Quinn. "Got a little dicey there for a second. I could have used some help."

"Eh." Quinn waved a hand, and Hope noticed a large bandage on his inner elbow. "You got this."

"Is . . ." She almost couldn't ask. "Carter?"

Quinn shook his head. "He isn't here, *Mi'ja*. I'm sorry."

Hope nodded.

Luke pulled a black rubber band off his wrist and handed it to her, pinched between his thumb and forefinger.

Hope let go of Luke just long enough to put her hair in a knot with a satisfied grin, only now noticing the blood smeared on his cheek. "You're bleeding," she said.

"It's not mine," Luke said. "And you're bleeding too." He picked up her hand, inspecting it, wiping away some of the blood with the hem of his shirt.

"It's just a cut," Hope said. "It looks worse than it is. But I think he did hurt my ankle."

Luke stared down at Stark, eyes venomous. In the distance, a wail of sirens drew closer.

Together they peered at the bed where Dr. Stark remained strapped. His teeth were clenched, but his eyes wide and clear, with a glare that could have set the room on fire.

"Good," Luke said cheerfully. "You're awake. How do you feel?"

ONE
WEEK
LATER

45

WORTH EVERY RISK

HOPE
Palm Springs, California

STEAM RISING FROM the sink spread over the bottom half of the kitchen window in a thin layer of fog. Hope placed the rubber stopper in the drain and got carried away with the dish detergent, swirling it in figure eights into the slowly rising water. She let the bottle of detergent fall in, placing both hands in the water, palms on the sink bottom. Suds grew in hills and mountains around her wrists.

"You're supposed to be resting. I can do that."

Luke's voice was jarring, and Hope jumped as he entered the room and dropped his keys on the kitchen table with a clatter. The turquoise stool scraped on the tile as he sat, bending his knee and pulling a worn sneaker off his foot.

"I'm fine," Hope said, fishing out the soapy detergent bottle. She deposited a plate and a mug from the counter into the sink. A knife and two spoons followed the mug into the water, sinking beneath the layer of bubbles and falling on the stainless-steel bottom. She wiped her hands on her shirt, looking at her fingers. They were already pruny.

Hope tried to keep her voice light as she turned. "Can you take me to Wilder today?"

"Why in the hell would you want to do that?" Luke's eyes clouded with a darkness that had recently become familiar, though it was an expression Hope couldn't translate into understanding.

"I want to talk to Quinn. Say goodbye to Spooky." It sounded like a weak reason, and it was. She could have met them anywhere; it didn't need to be Wilder. But she didn't want to say the real reason aloud.

It had been a week since the Salton Sea, and she and Luke hadn't talked about Wilder at all. There were police until near dawn, with a litany of questions. They'd likely still be there today, if Quinn hadn't had a fleet of attorneys on retainer who marched in and magically made the detectives reconsider their positions. And Hope had also seen a doctor for her injuries, a sprained ankle and her cut hand requiring five stitches. All she wanted to do after that was sleep, in Luke's bed, with Luke. That, and hold Charlotte and never let go.

Charlotte had burst into the bedroom on Hope's first morning home, throwing open the door and climbing into bed between them, snuggling under the covers like a toddler.

Hope hugged her tight. She'd cut her long hair short, and Hope put her face close. She smelled like laundry detergent and vanilla and sunshine.

"I missed you so much," Charlotte said. "Dad sucks at homework. And I haven't been to the Stoner Shack in forever. Can we go tonight?"

"Of course," Hope said. "I've been dreaming about it for months."

Charlotte held up her pinky. "Never leave again."

"Nope," Hope promised. "Never again."

Luke got out of bed to make breakfast, lingering in the doorway as Charlotte gave Hope the play-by-play of every event since December. He looked happy, and it seemed like things were returning to normal.

But that moment with Charlotte was an anomalous break from the uneasy air between them now. Luke didn't seem to know how to react to Hope's skittishness, her forgetfulness, the hours she'd spend sitting in the backyard, alone, staring at the sky. And Hope couldn't find a way to reintegrate herself into the life she'd been missing since December.

"How about we binge something tonight?" Luke said now, voice hesitant. "Catch up on some of the shows you missed?"

Hope turned around, Novinophobia wineglass and dripping sponge in hand. "Sounds fun."

His shoulders relaxed. "I can stop at the theater on my way home and get some popcorn."

"You can buy popcorn without actually seeing a movie?" Hope asked.

A shadow crossed over Luke's face as he descended from the stool, a glimmer that had become all too familiar in the past week. The look he'd get when she forgot about things she should know, seemingly mundane things, like popcorn. "You liked . . . before . . ."

Before. Before Wilder. Before Carter disappeared. Before he took her memories because she insisted this was the only way. Before they had the hubris to make sacrifices without considering the consequences.

"I guess I used to know that, huh?" Hope gripped the wineglass a little tighter in her fingers. She tried to say it lightly, but it came out strangled. She willed herself not to cry over something so asinine as forgetting popcorn.

Luke took a step toward Hope, and she backed away. Her elbow bumped into the counter and the wineglass flew out of her soapy hands, shattering on the tile floor.

"Don't," Luke said, walking into the hallway as Hope fell to her knees. "I'll get the broom."

Hope picked up the big pieces of glass with thumb and forefinger, stacking them in her cupped hand. Luke knelt beside her and held out the dustpan. She placed the pieces inside and sat on her heels, wishing for words that wouldn't come.

"It's just a glass," Luke said. "We have lots of other glasses." He rose, sweeping the area for any remaining pieces. He dropped the glass into a paper grocery bag and folded it over a few times.

"Everything feels broken," Hope said.

Luke made a noise, and she knew it hadn't come out right. Like everything these days, Hope felt one thing and said something askew, something that came out in tatters.

He shut the lid of the metal can and grasped the broom handle, as if unsure what to do next.

"I have errands I need to run this morning," Luke said, facing the kitchen window. "I'll drop you off at Wilder and go to the dry cleaners, get stuff for dinner. Then I'll pick you up."

"Thanks," she said.

Hope listened to Luke put the broom away and in a few minutes, the shower began to run. She'd forgotten how much she loved to hear him sing, how long it had been. Hope cocked her ear toward the bathroom door, wondering what was floating through his head this morning.

She stood at the window, staring out past the fence at the desert, until the sound of the shower stopped. Luke wasn't singing today.

✺ ✺ ✺

Yellow caution tape wound its way around the considerable length of the Wilder campus proper, with a stern admonition for those who would dare to cross. Sometimes it said, "Crime Scene," and other times it was twisted and backward, looking a little like her code. Hope was momentarily distracted considering how big Wilder was, and how much it probably cost the city of Rancho Mirage to purchase all that tape to wrap around Wilder Sanctuary. To keep out no one.

Hope reclined on the curb outside the curving sprawl of the Wilder driveway, smoking a cigarette. She'd bummed some Marlboros off the guy threading the tape around the Zen Garden five minutes earlier. He'd opened his pack and kept one for himself, placing it carefully into his breast pocket before handing the rest to Hope with a plastic lighter featuring a neon cannabis leaf. She must have looked like she needed it.

The first hit gave Hope the world's biggest head rush. It wasn't quite as satisfying as she'd been craving for eight months. Yet in a fit of defiance, she'd lit the other one off the dying embers of the first, to prove something—perhaps just her own continuing stupidity—to the universe. Besides, there wasn't anything else she should be doing. It's not like they would let her help move evidence into the CSI vans.

Two workers emerged from the glass double doors, calling directions to each other. One was walking backward, both holding what at first appeared to be a bookshelf balanced between them. As they neared, Hope saw it was a stack of the Wilder platitude posters, at least ten of the black frames, about the best way to live your life.

The workers passed Hope in silence, one giving her a nod. The top poster used to hang outside of Elliot Stark's office: a semicircle of smooth, flat black rocks, foreground in sharp focus. *Each new day brings new choices.*

Hope ducked under the caution tape and limped across the wide pebbled path to the front door. The high reception counter remained in the foyer, but the acrylic display of Wilder brochures was conspicuously absent.

A cottony quiet enveloped the lobby. Workers bustled about, paying no attention to Hope. She instinctively looked for a gray uniform, although the residents had already gone home, and most staff had been evicted from Wilder in a much more permanent type of way.

As she passed Head Games and neared the elevator, Hope knew something was off about the feel of the building. It wasn't until she reached the third floor that she realized it was the smell, or rather, the lack thereof.

The elevator slid open with its familiar ding. Hope tugged at the hem of Charlotte's jean shorts, too short for Hope's liking, though she'd tried to mask them with a white dress shirt of Luke's. The clothes hanging on her side of the closet were now too big, but also felt like they belonged to someone else. Her sprained right ankle was encased in a bright pink boot, making her slow and clumsy. A few days ago, in the doctor's office, she'd thought the bright bubblegum hue might cheer her up or return some of the moxie she used to have. It didn't.

Her boot made a rhythmic, hollow clunk on ViCTR's tile floor. Every cubicle door was open, blue LED lights paving the way along the corridor, the Erleben butterfly flapping at her from the screens in all the rooms. In Hestia, the door didn't close after she stepped through.

Quickly, so she wouldn't lose her nerve, Hope strapped on the vest and attached the other accessories, lowering herself into the leather armchair. The back of her neck grew hot, deep under the skin, and she ignored it.

Hope entered C-O-W-B-O-Y and waited.

Nothing happened.

"Cowboy," she said aloud. "Inara. Anyone, please."

"I'm sorry," Morena purred. "The Erleben Device is offline. Please contact your system administrator for assistance."

She rose from the armchair, stripping off her gear and dropping it into a heap on the carpet. A chime rang, piercing and distinctive. Hope straightened, wondering for an instant if it was time for lunch, or rec time, or yoga.

She paused once more in the doorway as she left.

"Bye C," she whispered. "Thank you."

AT THE WILDER curb, Hope put her elbows on the narrow strip of grass, legs stretched out. She smoked in the stillness, relishing the thought no one could come and tell her she was breaking a rule.

"Smoking, including the use of e-cigarettes, is a violation of the Wilder compact you signed on your Intake Day."

Quinn looked strange without his Wilder grays, in slim shorts and a skintight Balenciaga shirt that probably cost more than a car. Only Quinn. He took the cigarette out of her hand and helped himself to a long drag, executing a few perfect smoke rings before handing it back and lowering himself next to her. "Damn. That shit really does leave your system."

"Second one is way better."

Quinn took another drag and reclined on his elbows, the way Hope had seen so many times. But this was different. Quinn was confident, wiser. A little older. A little sadder.

Hope and Quinn had exchanged a few texts that week and spoken on the phone once. Quinn had yet to tell her what happened to him at the Salton Sea, or mention anything they'd done to him. Perhaps, like Hope, he wasn't ready to relive it just yet. Or perhaps he'd never be ready.

"Dr. Emerson was interviewed on CNN, did you see?" Quinn asked. "Sanjay Gupta laid her *out*."

"I don't know anything," Hope said. "Wilder talk is verboten in my house."

"Dr. Stark—actually I should call him Dr. Hartwell—makes sense; no one's real name is Stark. Anyhoo . . . they threw the book at him: kidnapping, murder, assault, collusion . . . I can't even name them all."

"Good," she said. "Rot in hell."

"Also they raided Copeland-Stark. The whole place was destroyed, everything shredded or taken or whatever. And Jack Copeland pulled a Keyser Söze." He put his fingertips to his lips and then splayed them apart into the air. "Poof."

"Jack Copeland has enough money to be in the wind forever," Hope said.

"That's exactly what Jake Tapper said," Quinn agreed. "And he's always right."

"Thanks for helping Luke out, with the detectives," Hope said. "They were assholes until your lawyers stepped in. And I know they're the reason why press hasn't been camped out on our lawn."

Quinn waved it off. "Fight bullies with bigger bullies, I say."

They watched workers moving furniture out of Wilder like carpenter ants. Three passed Quinn and Hope, balancing a large couch from the library between them. Hope thought about all the hours spent on that couch, reading dream books and staring out at the mountains.

"I suspect I'm not going to be seeing Tomás for a while, what with the whole violation-of-federal-statutes thing," Quinn said. "He was a hot tamale, no question. And the fact that he shit money was gravy. But plenty of other catfish in the sea." He attempted a grin, though the sorrow in his eyes betrayed him.

"Do you need a place to stay?" Hope asked. The thought of Quinn in the house comforted her.

"Nah," Quinn chuckled. "Tomás had the Vintage Club house in my name, believe it or not. For tax purposes. You, Luke, Charlotte, and fifty of your closest friends can come stay with me. In fact, Fernando is there right now. Until he gets back on his feet."

"You're a good person." Hope stamped her cigarette out on the sidewalk. "At least I don't have to worry about you living in squalor."

A red sports car pulled up to the drive, stopping with a squeal of brakes inches short of Quinn. Hope pulled her legs away from the street as purple Chucks stepped onto the concrete.

Quinn popped up to approach the driver's side, no doubt to get a better look at Henry Lu.

Hope put a hand on her forehead to shield the sun. "Hey, Spencer."

He was starting to look a little like the old Spooky she'd seen in Fortress: shorts and a zipped-up hoodie, a new haircut. He sat on the curb in the spot Quinn had just vacated.

"I've been doing a little *D&D* research in my spare time," Hope said to Spooky.

"What have you learned?" He bent his head, as if hoping his now short hair would cover it.

"I learned that the Rogue is a *D&D* character," Hope said. "An important one. The Rogue engages in sneaky combat. The Rogue lays traps. But I'm sure you already knew that."

"In *D&D* it's typically just called Rogue," Spencer said. "There's no article."

"So I should call you Rogue instead of *the* Rogue?" Hope asked.

Spooky smirked. "I'd prefer just Spencer, thanks."

"But I'm right," Hope said. "You're him, aren't you?"

Henry's car squealed away and Quinn returned to the curb, settling himself on the other side of Spooky.

"He's getting coffee across the street," Quinn said.

"Then I only have a few minutes," Spooky said, looking down the long curve of the driveway. "We're on our way to Westwood."

"That's what you're doing, then?" Quinn asked. "Staying with Henry?"

"For now," Spooky said, picking at a clump of grass near the curb. "My brother doesn't know everything . . . how I got to Wilder. My dad made it so he wouldn't remember." He tossed the blades of grass he'd uprooted onto the pavement. "I don't want him to know."

"It wasn't your fault," Hope said. "You know that, right?"

Spooky looked unconvinced.

"Have you seen the articles? More come out each day," Quinn said. "Henry will figure it out if you don't tell him. And it will be much better coming from you."

"I wish it wasn't like this," Spooky said.

They nodded. Everyone wished it wasn't like this.

The trio sat in companionable silence until the car came speeding up the drive. Henry emerged, engine still idling. He was in his hipster best, cuffed khaki shorts and a slim, short-sleeved seersucker shirt with three buttons undone. His topsiders matched his woven belt perfectly.

Spooky stood and Quinn followed, then helped Hope to her feet.

"You guys need a ride somewhere?" Henry asked, as if he were collecting his brother and his dorky friends at the mall.

"No," said Quinn. "Just wanted to say goodbye to Spencer."

Henry pushed his chunky black sunglasses on top of his head, revealing the circles under his eyes. "Okay. Take care, then." He looked at Spooky. "Ready?"

Spooky nodded, unzipping his hoodie. He gave Hope a sidelong glance as she read his T-shirt: In this Style, 10/6.

She smiled.

"Bye guys," Spooky said, with a half wave. He climbed into the passenger side, buckling his seat belt and staring at an unknown point in the distance.

Quinn and Hope watched as the taillights disappeared down the driveway, onto the road, and away. They settled onto the curb again.

"I'm a little choked up at that outpouring of emotion," Quinn said.

Hope snickered. "As expected."

Quinn stretched out his legs and rubbed at a speck of dirt from his huaraches. "What about you? What does the future hold for Hopeless?"

"I wish I knew." She leaned against Quinn. He felt normal and reassuring. "All I've wanted forever is to get back home, get back to Luke. Now . . ."

"Now you miss Wilder."

Hope nodded, grateful to hear it from someone else. "Insane, isn't it?"

"I'm not exactly the pinnacle of mental health right now, but I think it's normal there will be an adjustment."

"It doesn't feel like an adjustment. Luke feels like a stranger," Hope said, scratching at the edge of her boot. "He started getting the newspaper delivered while I was away. There's a huge pile in the garage. Huge. And every morning he opens it, reads one section, and then it goes on the pile."

Quinn looked confused. "You're upset because he's going to start a fire?"

"Of course not." Hope sighed. "We're different now. Things I say disappoint him, and I don't know why. He says things I'm supposed to understand, but I don't. We used to laugh together, all the time. I haven't heard him laugh since I've been back."

Quinn put his hand on her knee. "Have you talked about it?"

Hope didn't answer.

"So, in typical Hopeless fashion, you're keeping it all in the vault?"

Hope lit her fourth cigarette. "I guess I am."

"What scares you most?"

The two Wilder swans soared through the sky, in the direction of the pond. Hope exhaled into the wind, away from Quinn, watching them become smaller and smaller until they disappeared.

"I'm scared too much has happened. Too much to fix. Too many scars."

Quinn took the cigarette out of her hand. "Just tell him that."

Hope tapped the heel of her sneaker on the concrete. "It's easier this way."

"You know it isn't." Quinn blew another perfect smoke ring into the air. "Be honest with him." He gave her a poke. "'If we cease to believe in love—'"

"No more quotes. Ever, ever, ever," Hope interrupted, poking him back. "But you're right, as always."

"Hopeless," Quinn said, taking her hand. "We could have met anywhere today. Why here?"

Hope leaned against his shoulder.

"I wanted to try and get into the Butterfly Box one more time. I know how it sounds, but I thought . . . since they never found him . . ."

"Carter?" Quinn asked.

Hope nodded, then tightened her fingers in Quinn's.

Luke's Highlander appeared in the driveway and stopped in front of them.

Quinn helped Hope to her feet, avoiding her still bandaged left hand, and waved into the car. "So that's the famous Memory Mechanic, huh?"

"That's him."

"He looks like a decent enough bloke." Quinn narrowed his eyes at her. "But if he ever does you wrong . . ."

"Like have me committed?" Hope said, placing both hands over her mouth. "You don't think that can happen twice, do you?"

Quinn laughed. "You put your own dumb ass in there."

"I did." She looked at Wilder and found it difficult to turn away.

"It was colossally, monumentally stupid of you," Quinn said. "Worst caper ever. You have been disavowed."

Hope laughed around the lump in her throat.

"And he was worth all of that, huh? All the risks, the lost memories, the Labyrinth?"

Hope's laugh disappeared. She chewed on her bottom lip, gazing over Quinn's shoulder into the car window. Luke was drumming his fingers on the steering wheel, eyes focused on the San Jacintos.

"He's worth every risk," she said simply.

Quinn wrapped his arms around her tightly, and Hope buried her face in his shoulder.

"I wouldn't have survived here if it weren't for you," she said. "You were like a knight. You saved me."

"Back atcha, Toots." His voice wavered. Quinn locked his bright eyes with hers. "You don't need any knights. You never did. But promise me, no more hiding. Let him love you."

Hope nodded.

Quinn opened the Highlander door, reaching in to shake Luke's hand.

"You need a ride somewhere?" Luke asked.

"No thanks," Quinn said. "I have a car coming."

He helped Hope get in, despite protests she was perfectly able to do it herself. She and Quinn made agreements to keep in touch, to get coffee or lunch soon. But they both knew it was a lie. After today, all the former guests of the Wilder Sanctuary would be working overtime to never think about each other again.

"This one is very important to me," Quinn said to Luke, with a nod in Hope's direction. "Take care of her."

"I will," Luke said. The old Luke would have made a wisecrack about her willfulness or risk-taking tendencies or stubbornness. But this Luke opened his mouth and closed it a few times without saying anything, and when he spoke again his voice cracked. "I'm very grateful Hope found you, Quinn."

Quinn kissed his two fingers, throwing up a peace sign before shutting the door. His long thin legs carried him quickly down the driveway, and Hope watched him, forehead pressed against the window, until he disappeared.

THREE
WEEKS
LATER

46

STILL AND ALWAYS

HOPE
Palm Springs, California

"I'VE MISSED THESE SO much," Hope said, cutting into her second waffle of the morning. "The ones at Wilder were whole grain. And they didn't give you syrup. Just this low-sugar jam travesty."

"I hope they include that in the indictments," Luke said, pushing the syrup across the table. He didn't look up from his new morning ritual of reading the paper. "That should add another ten years to the sentences."

"They should," Hope said, seizing the opportunity to steal the last piece of bacon from his plate.

It was late September now, the summer heat no longer suffocating, the nights cooler. Their recent weeks had been filled with Charlotte and her preparations for college. They'd made hundreds of trips to buy sheets and shower accessories and closet organizers. She and Charlotte had packed, then unpacked, then repacked. And despite the fact that UC Santa Barbara was less than a four-hour drive, it still felt like Charlotte had moved to another planet. The house was quieter now than it had ever been.

Some days Hope had no idea if Wilder had even happened. She was plagued with nightmares once more, ones she couldn't remember in the morning, only the fear.

She would wake gasping for air, clutching at her throat or her hand or her chest. *It's just a dream,* Luke would say, wrapping his arms and legs around her. *I'm here.*

"No bacon at Wilder either?" Luke asked, eyes peering over the newspaper.

"Turkey bacon," Hope said. "Which you well know isn't bacon."

They ate in silence until Luke finished his usual scan of the newspaper and set it on the table.

"Amelia Green finally texted me back," Luke said. "She didn't know of any other facility other than at the Salton Sea. But that doesn't mean there isn't one. In the end, she was kept at arm's length, like I was."

Hope forced herself to swallow the bacon that had tasted so heavenly just seconds ago.

"That doesn't mean we won't stop looking for Carter," Luke said.

"You think it's ridiculous," Hope said, "that I think he might still be out there."

Luke didn't answer, and it was disconcerting to no longer be able to decipher his expressions.

"It's my fault," Hope said. "If I hadn't gotten Carter involved in all of this, he'd still be running Maelstrom. He'd be fine."

"That's not true," Luke said. "Jordan Lin put him in there. And he wanted to help you. He chose to help you."

"I just . . ." Hope twisted her napkin into a ball. "I need him to be alive."

"I know," Luke said. He came to kneel beside her. "That's why we'll do whatever it takes to find him."

Hope put both hands on his face. "Thank you, for understanding."

"Hope." Luke looked up at her, searching for something, though Hope didn't know what. "I just want you to be happy, above everything, above my own selfishness. And whatever—whoever—you want, that will make you happy . . ."

The kiss she gave him was fierce. Hope tried to pour everything she'd been feeling and everything she couldn't say into that kiss. The need, the regret, the promises, the apologies.

As if that one kiss would somehow fix everything to come, and everything that came before.

"Carter is my friend, and I care deeply about him. And I miss him," Hope said. "But you make me happy. Just you."

Luke put her forehead on hers, their noses touching. "Okay then," he said, slightly out of breath. "I think we should celebrate."

"It goes awfully high up," Hope said, reading the sign.

PALM SPRINGS AERIAL TRAMWAY
VALLEY STATION
ELEVATION: 2,643 FEET

"Almost nine thousand feet. But you won't believe the view from up there." Luke took her hand. His face was cautious, searching hers one again.

Clusters of couples and families were gathered in the cramped waiting area, talking and laughing and jostling each other. To anyone else, the dull buzz of conversation would likely go unnoticed, but to Hope the voices were shrill, as if everyone were screaming. There were too many people, their movements and motives unpredictable. She shrank into Luke a little, closing her eyes and counting to ten.

"Why don't you wait for me there?" He indicated a concrete bench twenty feet away. Luke slung his backpack over his shoulder and kissed her on the forehead. "I'll go get us tickets."

Hope threaded her way tentatively toward the bench, avoiding as many bodies as she could. The bright pink boot came off two weeks ago, and though her walking was essentially normal, she was still unsure about each step.

A crowd gathered on either side of the bench, small children chasing each other, distracted parents scolding minutes too late. A young mother with a toddler in mid-tantrum on her hip dropped her enormous plaid diaper bag on the bench, trying to wrestle open a container of Cheerios with her mouth.

"Sorry," she said, through a mouthful of Tupperware. "Did you want to sit?"

Hope shook her head and took an immediate detour. She exited the station and fled down the stairs, onto the pavement and the bright fall sunshine.

It was quieter outside. The few people in the parking lot were unpacking gear from their trunks and herding their children. Hope clutched the stair railing, taking gulps of the desert air, pushing the rising apprehension somewhere safe and secure. She counted to ten again.

Luke burst outside, thick stack of tickets clutched in his hand, face flooding with relief when he spotted her. "Jesus," he said. "I didn't know where you were."

Not for the first time, Hope felt a pang of guilt. "I'm sorry, it's still weird to be with people all the time. I'll get used to it eventually." She desperately wanted to be all right, and she even more desperately wanted Luke to believe she would be all right.

Luke nodded. "I got the tickets."

She inclined her head at the stack of papers in his hand. "How many times are we going up?"

Luke smiled. "I went ahead and bought the whole tram, so there won't be anyone else. Just you and me. I thought you might like that better." He paused. "Maybe it was a dumb idea."

"It was a good idea," Hope said. "And I'll be fine. I'll be with you."

IT WAS A ten-minute ride through the sky, a swift journey in a little round capsule up the six thousand feet in altitude. It was breathtaking. And also slightly terrifying.

"Okay?" Luke asked.

Hope hadn't eased her iron grip around his arm. "Better than I imagined." She leaned into him, Luke's hand on her thigh. They sat in silence for the rest of the ride, watching as the jagged mountains outside came ever closer, rising up and around like the Butterfly Box.

When the tram arrived, they stepped out at the top. It was much cooler up here, and Luke threw his jacket around her shoulders. Hik ers and families roamed along paths, children chased each other. Hope had an overpowering urge to turn and run. But they headed out onto a narrow wooden trail until Luke veered them onto a deserted path. There was the tiniest patch of snow at the end, like icing on top of a green cupcake, dotted with purple and blue wildflower nonpareils. Luke and Hope sat on a flat rock, gazing at the world spread below.

"Didn't I tell you?" he said.

She smiled. "You did."

She felt his hands in her hair, and she closed her eyes, wishing that gesture could make it all go back to what it had been.

"I want to help you," Luke finally said. "And I should know how, but I don't. I know you need your space; I know healing is a process. I know you'll tell me what happened in there, in time. Or you won't, and that's fine too. But I'm scared you'll disappear. Sometimes I feel like you're here, and other times like you're already disappearing."

Hope felt it too. Some nights she couldn't sleep at all and would go outside, where it was still and silent. Hope would lie on the lounger and wrap herself in the palpable hush reserved for desert nights. Or for the Shade.

Last night Luke had come outside, pale from lack of sleep, and curled up with her.

They hadn't spoken, and she continued to watch the sky long after he fell asleep.

"I'm sorry I'm such a mess," she said. "I know how hard it's been on you."

"Be a mess," Luke said, staring into his hands. "Be silent and moody. Cry and scream. Just . . . please don't disappear. Don't shut me out."

Hope stared at the ground. A bright blue wildflower lay near his foot, separated from its patch by someone's heel.

"You once told me we were both working to be better than our past. That you wanted to do it together," Luke said. "Maybe you don't remember."

"I remember," Hope said, eyes still downcast. "It's true."

"Before you, I had Charlotte and work and friends. I thought I was content. But I didn't even know I'd been drowning in loneliness until I fell in love with you. You rescued me," Luke said. He picked up the delicate little flower and set it gently on the rock. "When I didn't even know I needed rescuing."

Hope looked at Luke, her Luke. Every single star in her universe. And she realized, in typical Hopeless fashion, how she was still keeping things in the vault.

"I promise not to shut you out, and I promise I won't disappear," she said, picking up the flower and spinning it in her fingers. "We rescued each other. When I couldn't remember anything, I could always remember you. Even at the very worst times, when they tried to tell me nothing was real, I knew it was. I felt it, even if I didn't have the memories."

Luke let out a breath. "That's all that matters." He sounded like that settled everything.

Hope thought about Quinn's question, about what scared her the most, and she knew she hadn't answered him truthfully. "But what if loving each other isn't enough?"

There, she thought. *That's what scares me the most.*

"It is," Luke said, resolute.

"How do you know?" Hope released the flower and watched it float to the ground. She pulled Luke's jacket around her tighter.

"Because you told me so," Luke said.

"But I'm crazy," Hope said. "I've got papers to prove it."

Luke laughed, for the first time in what seemed like years. Hope let the sound wash over her.

She lifted her face, letting herself be caught up in Luke's smile. Hope couldn't look away from his eyes, infinitely more magnificent than the sky above. And once again, as she did that long-ago night under the stars, Hope wished to be swallowed whole, by Luke, and by whatever lay within.

"I love you," Hope said. "Still, and always."

"Still and always," Luke repeated.

Together they turned toward the surrounding desert, their desert, their mountains, and their big blue sky. Like they were the only souls of consequence, like the whole world had frozen just to accommodate the two of them. For the first time in a long while, the universe seemed like there was a glimmer of possibility again, like if they both tried hard enough . . . maybe they could.

And Hope knew, this time, they would.

"I'm still missing so much," Hope said. "Not all of the memories have come back. What if they never come back?"

"It doesn't matter." Luke wrapped his arm around her, and Hope leaned close. He took her hand and kissed her palm, in that space between her life line and her love line. "We'll keep making new ones."

ACKNOWLEDGMENTS

T O MY INIMITABLE agent Kimberley Cameron, thank you for your tireless championship of *The Mechanics of Memory* and for never allowing my confidence to flag. Your tenacity, wisdom, and unlimited fabulousness are what made this little dream of mine a reality. *Je t'aime!*

Dorian Maffei, you will forever be the best date I ever had. Thank you for listening, reading, and deciding to share my manuscript with Kimberley.

A million thanks to Sue Arroyo and the exceptional team at CamCat Books, who took my words and made them into an honest-to-goodness book with the most gorgeous cover in the history of book covers.

Special thanks to my editor Helga Schier, whose eagle eye and talent for story made *The Mechanics of Memory* far better and tighter than I ever thought it could be.

To Tim Storm, my absolute hero. Your guidance and sheer brilliance helped me turn an octopus of a story into a book. I still can't distinguish between an em-dash, an en-dash, and a hyphen. But that's what I have you for, right?

To my writing club that never quite got off the ground: Sam, thank you for the countless hours logged drinking cocktails, eating chips and onion dip, and strategizing effective ways to kill people. When the FBI shows up, it's all on you to explain that my search history is purely professional. And to Max, for explaining all things technological and for knowing I was a writer long before I did. You can choose the title of the next one. (Just kidding.)

To my brilliant and endlessly talented son Derek: I hope this career detour of mine reminds you to always follow your dreams. You're the most amazing person I know, and I can't wait to see how you change the world in the same way you changed mine. I love you with all my heart. (But you still aren't getting a cut of the movie deal.)

To my husband, Evan, who didn't look at me even a little bit sideways when I announced I was quitting work to write a book. (Sorry, honey, it took a little longer than a year.)

To my writing buddy, Luna, who cuddled on my lap through three years of drafts and continues to provide emotional support through the sequel.

To my sister Kathy, for reading and rereading outside your preferred genre. Someday I'll write one about puppies and rainbows just for you. And for my beautiful book club sisters: Andrea, Alissa, Shelley, and Sola. Can we change our name to the WALNMMs?

To my nieces and nephews (by blood and by choice): Elliot, Emeline, Elaina, Maya, Nina, Marco, and Anja. I love you to the moon and back. The world is in good hands because of you. Go be great.

To those who spent years listening to me agonize, reading drafts, providing feedback and advice, casting the movie, and cheering me on: Joanna (someday *In Between Days* will get its due!), Rebeca, Victor, Summers, Craig, Rick, Alex (Ivan), Jeff, Paul, and Scott.

For Tom Locker, who on one of my darkest days, assured me that life had better things in store.

For two bad ass authors, Jackie Johnson and Meredith R. Lyons. Thank you for helping me navigate these murky waters, for drunken Polos, and for boosting me up every day.

And to Andrea Salas, who was fierce, brave, brilliant, irreverent, and graceful all at once. You left my life way too early, and I miss you every single day.

This book was a multiyear labor of love (and sometimes hate). To identify every single person who contributed to this journey is nearly impossible. So, thank you to all my people, named and unnamed, for believing in me. And in some ways, thanks also to those who didn't.

ABOUT THE AUTHOR

A UDREY LEE BEGAN writing fiction at the young age of eleven, when she and her best friend coauthored a masterpiece about gallivanting around London with the members of Depeche Mode, Wham!, and Duran Duran. Unfortunately, these spiral notebooks have yet to find a publisher evolved enough to understand the genius buried within.

As a result, *The Mechanics of Memory* is her first work of published fiction.

Audrey holds two degrees from UC Berkeley (Go Bears!) and has spent over two decades in public education. When she isn't writing books she consults with school districts about creating environments for students that are more equitable, culturally responsive, and socially just.

Audrey lives in the San Francisco Bay Area with her husband, son, and Maltipoo, Luna.

When not working, Audrey is compulsively organizing something, cheering for her son at a dance competition, max betting on a slot machine, or watching the Golden State Warriors with a dirty martini in hand.

If you enjoyed
Audrey Lee's *The Mechanics of Memory*,
please consider leaving us a review
to help our authors.

And check out Mia Dalia's *Haven*.

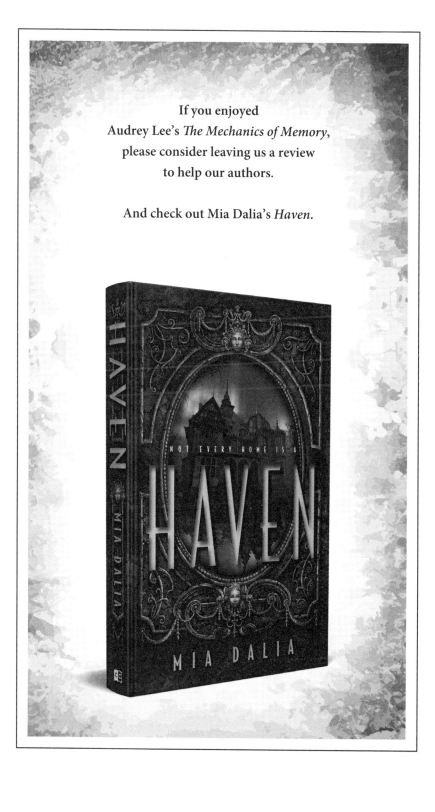

PROLOGUE

Once upon a time...

But no, of course not. Too many stories have begun that way, and this was no fairy tale, even though it might have been easier to think of it as one. A fairy tale with ogres and princesses. How lovely.

How wrong.

A life so meticulously structured around the present can become easily overwhelmed by the past rushing in. All it takes is one careless glance back. Those are dangerous. Just ask Orpheus.

All this free time can be dangerous too, making one nostalgic, retrospective. Looking back, looking forward, the pages of the book of time turn.

JEFF

DRIVE, DRIVE, DRIVE until the road is done with you. Until it spits out the final destination at you like some kind of begrudging reward. Until you're through. That's the deal.

The summer morning is unseasonably autumnal, as crisp as a freshly starched shirt. The leaves are looking festive, though it is much too early for them to change colors. Maybe they are gearing up for the months to come, putting on a dress rehearsal. In theory, at least, the leaves are meant to make up for the miserable New England winter that inevitably follows their departure.

Jeff tries to enjoy nature, and when that fails, he focuses on the road itself—the way it disappears beneath the wheels of their five-year-old forest-green Subaru. It's soothing in a way, the certainty of the motion, the steady progress forward. North.

There used to be a time when Jeff loved driving; a time that by now is but a vague, faded memory. His first car was a beat-up '87 Mustang, produced decades after that pony was at its prime, and the two of them were inseparable. The AC never worked, so the windows were rolled down for as long as the weather permitted, the wind blowing through his hair like freedom, like youth itself.

It seems that ever since then his vehicle selections have been increasingly less exciting, more sedate, staid. Practical. Now here he is, behind the wheel of a car that positively announced to the world that a liberal-minded, environmentally conscious family was inside it. A cliché if there ever was one.

Jeff knows that it suits the man he is today: a husband, a father, someone with a stalled but reasonably lucrative middle-management job; a man with a softening gut and receding hairline, wading knee-deep into the still, murky waters of middle age.

He sighs, adjusts the rearview mirror, and tries valiantly to ignore the kicking at the back of his seat. When that doesn't work, he snaps, abruptly and frustratedly.

"JJ, how many times have I told you not to do that?"

Jeff can feel his son's insolent shrug without turning around to see it. It's one of JJ's signature moves—the kid is the personification of a sullen, surly teen. Although they share a name and Jeff loves the kid, he recognizes nothing of himself in Jeff Junior.

His son is lazy, aimless, slovenly in a way that physically upsets fastidious Jeff. What's worse is that the kid doesn't seem to be clever or interesting or even funny. He gets by in school with barely passing grades, participates in no sports or extracurriculars, and spends most of his free time glued to one screen or another. The video games he plays seem too violent to Jeff, but he can't figure out a way to ban them outright, because (a) he doesn't want to be that dad, and (b) he doesn't necessarily believe in the connection between on-screen and real-life violence. After all, violence has been around long before video games were even invented.

Still, it's difficult to think of a bigger waste of time than these stupid games. At least the kid wears headphones to play them. The constant rat-tat-tat of guns in the background would have driven Jeff crazy by now.

Jessie is sitting next to her brother, occupying, it seems, only half of her seat. Wherein her brother's girth is forever expanding, Jessie appears to be shrinking. It makes her brittle, Jeff thinks, in appearance and temperament. So much like her mother.

The two kids are only a couple of years apart, but you'd never guess they were related. Never guess they came from the same house, the same people. There is a lot of nature vs. nurture baggage that Jeff doesn't care to unpack.

His daughter is unfathomable to him; the way she talks in text-message abbreviations, the eager manner in which she subscribes to the latest trends without ever taking a moment to examine them for herself, how appearance conscious she is.

This isn't a great time to be a kid. There's a steady bombardment of social media disseminating shallow values, unchecked materialism, and flat-out lies.

He doesn't even know what wave of feminism everyone's supposed to be riding now. Jenna might, but he is loath to ask. She wouldn't just answer: there'd be a lecture. Jeff despises being lectured and tends to avoid long-winded debates. He likes simple things: short, clear-cut explanations, yes-or-no answers whenever applicable.

Jenna is doing her nails next to him; *screech-screech* goes the thin emery board—a sound Jeff can feel in his vertebrae. He hates it, hates the way he has to just sit next to her and inhale the dead nail particles she's sending into the air, but asking her to stop would be as futile as expecting JJ to stop kicking the freaking seat.

Jeff likes to think of himself as a man who picks his battles. And there have been some. Over the years, that number has dwindled. Lately, he doesn't know if it's just something he tells himself to cover the fact that he has, slowly and inexorably, become a pushover.

Jenna is thin like their daughter, all gym-tight muscles and yoga-flexible tendons. She has been dyeing her hair the same shade of blond for so long that sometimes Jeff is surprised to see her natural light-brown color in the old photos. She looks good, younger than her years, certainly younger than Jeff.

If he doesn't tell her that enough, it's only because they don't talk that much anymore in general. Or maybe it's because her undeniable physical attractiveness appears to have lost the sunny warmth, easy charm, and shy sexiness of the Jenna he fell in love with so long ago. It's almost like his wife has Stepforded herself, trading in all the delightful aspects of her character, all of her fun quirky self for a perfect surface appeal.

Is that what two decades of marriage do? Or living in a society obsessed with youth and beauty? Or being a mother? Or—a more somberly horrifying thought—is that what living with Jeff for twenty years does?

Jeff wants to hit the rewind button and watch their lives again, in slow motion, noting every salient plot point, every crucial twist and turn, to understand how they got here. But it doesn't work that way, does it?

From one of his more interesting but ultimately useless college courses, Jeff remembers a quote: "Life can only be understood backwards, but it must be lived forwards." It's one of those sayings that sounds smart unless you really think about it, because once you do, you'll see that the former part of it is ultimately useless, while the latter is simply unavoidable.

Jeff had a good time in college. He did well in high school too: just smart enough, just fun enough, just inoffensive enough to ensure certain easy popularity that enabled smooth sailing amid the various social cliques and characters. After graduating, out in the real world, his stock began to slowly but definitively tank. He could never quite figure out why—perhaps something about the absence of predetermined social structure or increased expectations.

Either way, by the time Jenna came along, he grabbed on to her like she was a life preserver and had held on steadily and faithfully ever since. He had never done well on his own when he was young, found solitude oppressive. Depressing, even. Now, of course, he'd kill for some, but it is much too late. Even his man cave occupies only a corner of the basement at home—sharing the rest of the space with

Mia Dalia

laundry and storage and the moody boiler—and thus is perpetually loud and nowhere near private.

He likely isn't going to get much peace and quiet for the next month either, but he agreed to go anyway. After all, one simply doesn't say no to a free vacation. And sure, as he pointed out to Jenna while they were making plans, it isn't entirely free: there is the cost of gas, tolls, food, etc.; but the main expense, the house, is taken care of and so here they are now, driving, driving north.

"Are we there yet?" JJ pipes up from the backseat, too loudly because of the headphones he rarely takes off.

It was funny the first few times—no, not really—but now it grates on Jeff. He forces a smile. "Almost," he replies with false cheer.

The truth is, everything around here looks exactly the same to him: the same tall trees, the same tiny weather-beaten towns, the same road signs. If not for the chatty GPS, he would be hopelessly lost. He wants to thank his digital navigator every time she points out a turn amid a number of interchangeable ones; she seems to be the only helpful person around. Though, of course, she isn't even a person.

Jenna is listening to an audiobook. Without even asking, Jeff knows it's one of those domestic thrillers she loves that really ought to be shelved under "women's fiction." Something about scrappy heroines untangling their husbands' dark secrets. He tried a couple out of curiosity some time ago at Jenna's prompting and found them unoriginal, uninteresting, and blandly indistinguishable from one another. When Jenna asked for his honest opinion, he gave it to her, like a fool. They never spoke of books again. He shouldn't have said anything; he certainly shouldn't have added that it was still a step up from her normal self-help fare.

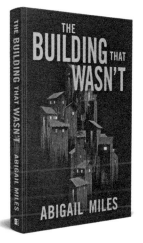
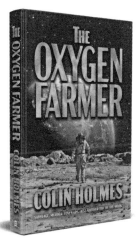
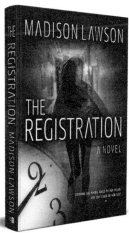

CamCat
Books

VISIT US ONLINE FOR MORE BOOKS TO LIVE IN:
CAMCATBOOKS.COM

SIGN UP FOR CAMCAT'S FICTION NEWSLETTER FOR
COVER REVEALS, EBOOK DEALS, AND MORE EXCLUSIVE CONTENT.

CamCatBooks   @CamCatBooks   @CamCat_Books   @CamCatBooks